The Pirate's Wake

Martin Blackshaw

Flintlock Publishing Ltd

Flintlock Publications Ltd
First Published in Great Britain in 2025

The moral rights of Martin Blackshaw to be identified as the author of this work has been asserted by him in accordance with the Copyright, Designs and Patents Act 1988

This novel is entirely a work of fiction. The names, characters and incidents portrayed in it while at times based on historical figures are the work of the author's imagination.

All rights reserved. No part of this publication may be reproduced, stored in a retrieval system or transmitted in any form or by any means, without the prior permission in writing of the publisher, nor to be otherwise circulated in any form of binding or cover other than that in which it is published without a similar condition, including this condition, being imposed on the subsequent purchaser

ISBN 978-1-0682913-0-2

For my wife, Emma.
The real captain of our ship.

This novel, while a work of fiction, is inspired by real events. Some characters, elements, and chronologies have been altered or invented for narrative purposes.

However, while no definitive account exists, some historians believe the final events unfolded much as they are portrayed here.

One

Jacob washed onto the beach like driftwood. Land. He hadn't felt dry land since the shores of England. The grains of sand clung to his cut and callused fingers like tiny gemstones–his reward for his courage. Or was it cowardice? He spluttered, crumpling into the wet sand. As the spume receded, his lead filled arms dragged his lifeless legs past the tide line. A turtle had more grace.

He supped shallow breaths so as not to reawaken the burning in his lungs. Straining his neck, he viewed the lush, dense forest edging the unspoiled beach. He risked another breath before flopping onto his back. Stifling a coughing fit, he lifted himself to his elbows, looking out to sea.

The musket balls had ceased chasing him. He was too far from the battle that roared on a thousand yards away. The Dutch had dispatched no barges in pursuit. He was just one enemy sailor fleeing the carnage. The English Navy would never find him again, he promised. The Caribbean would hide him. This was not how he expected his day to end, but he accepted it happily. His war was over.

"I must get home." He vowed under his breath for the hundredth time.

Feeling exposed on the beach, he knew it was time to move. Every muscle ached. He turned back to the forest, seeing its beauty. He slumped into the sand, the summer sun forcing his eyes to close. He would rest them, but for just a moment. He had won the battle with death–now replaced by the agony of life.

That morning Jacob's knees burned from salt and sand as he holystoned the quarterdeck of *HMS Kestrel*. His fingers cramped and his skin hardened from months of arduous labour. He hated *Kestrel*–her slippery boards that cultivated algae. The brush tearing at his fingers and the sand assisting the brush. The lieutenants who interrupted the hypnotic agony thrusting messages into his wounded hands, barking orders to charge fore or aft. "Make haste, boy." He heard those words in his sleep. Everything had to be done at double time, as if a second wasted would lose them the war.

Except for the captain's cabin, he had scampered over, up and through every inch of the one-hundred-and-thirty-foot frigate. In the day it was hot, at night it was cold, it was always damp and for many of the hours it was dark. He had chosen none of this. He hated it all.

Jacob had been a prisoner of *Kestrel* since New Year's Day 1667. Snatched from his hometown of Falmouth, he'd woken to find himself shackled to three–equally confused–hungover men. Shivering in a winter gale, his party was the interest of an officer, looming over them.

"You have two choices, gentlemen. Join this fine crew or swim ashore."

The four souls viewed the panoramic ocean horizon, concluding they didn't have two choices at all.

For six months Jacob scrubbed the decks, helped the cook, pulled this rope and that, and repaired rigging. All under the watchful eye of seasoned hands, while dodging kicks and punches. To be press-ganged was more akin to kidnapping and slavery. All for the spiteful navy of King Charles II.

His new skills might all become useful in later life—if he survived long enough to make use of them—but he'd made up his mind. He would abscond from this naval world at the first opportunity and make for home. Changing his name and stowing away on a merchant ship sailing back to England. He had a life back in Cornwall. A simple life, a hard life, but a happy life.

His mother must be worried. And the last thing she needed was more worry. He would have no doubt lost his fishing boat, Jane. Once belonging to his father and named after his mother, he'd left it moored in the harbour. The fishing community would have heard about young Jacob running away to join the navy and taken his boat, knowing his mother would have no use for it. Damn Mr Arundell and his trickery. And what of Lydia? She would feel abandoned. Not even a goodbye. Would she wait for him, or would her father already be seeking out suiters?

Jacob plunged his brush into the bucket, leaving his hands in the piss water to allow the blood to swirl from his knuckles. The urine stung his cuts.

"No slacking." A lieutenant called from the rail. "The sweepers are at your heels."

Jacob snatched his hands free, continuing his scrubbing. He glanced to the sky. The sun was a quarter high. Not long before his watch would end. For the first half an hour, he would hide in a quiet corner, loosening and massaging his fingers. Then the real misery would begin.

Bullying was rife in the English Navy, and *Kestrel* was no exception. The longer serving sailors shared their rituals with the younger, nervous, fresh bait. One sailor was particularly foul. *Kestrel* had its own William "Pitbull"–An Irish gunner, Malachy Doyle. When not on watch, he would drink his rum rations and sneak off to play liar's dice. When he lost—which was most often—he would skulk the boards, looking for some poor soul to bear the brunt of his foul mood. The sadistic giant had found an instant joy in Jacob. Vindictiveness flowed from him whenever the mood and opportunity crossed.

Within the first week aboard his prison, Jacob found solace, cowering in the hold. Doyle, being wise to this tactic, ferreted him out, cornering him in the sail room. A grizzly sailor held him down, laughing, wrapping wadding between Jacob's toes.

"Dance, pilchard boy," Doyle had slurred, standing over him. "Or ye feet'll be ablaze."

Jacob had lain paralysed with fear, staring at the murderous-rogue taller than the shadows.

"Whatcha, Doyle." This was Jacob's first meeting with Seth. A boy not much older than him. He leaned against the door frame, his arms folded. "Craywick's on the sniff for ya. Trying to catch you gamblin' again?"

"That snivellin' washbag. You ain't been gobbin' off, have ye?"

"Nah, Doyle. Just saw 'im on the orlop. Heading this way. Head up and over, you'll beat him back to mess, no bother."

Doyle had pushed Jacob onto the canvases. "See to ye later, pilchard boy." He'd thumped up the ladder followed by the grizzly.

Jacob peeled the wadding free, watching his new opponent.

Seth gave his name and offered Jacob a hand to shake.

"Jacob." He said, scampering to his feet and heading for the door.

"What's your rush?"
"Craywick's coming?"
"Ha. He ain't heading here. He'll still be dining in the officer's mess. You need to keep your wits primed. It ain't my job to save your skin."

Jacob offered Seth a thankful grin before they turned out of the store, scampering in the opposite direction to that which Doyle had gone.

Doyle had found Jacob a week later. Alone, huddled into a corner of the hold like a terrified puppy upon hearing the latch of the back door at two am on a Sunday morning, fearing his drunken owner. With ease, the big man dragged the scrawny pup into the bilge.

"Next time I say dance, ye'll dance, pilchard boy." Doyle had held Jacob under the filthy water until he passed into unconsciousness. That January evening Jacob thought he would die as the cold gnawed at his marrow, and in truth, he'd never truly thawed since.

He lived a dismal existence on *Kestrel*. Fear suffocated him like a wet blanket. It governed his senses, counselling his every decision. It lurked in every shadow, creeping up on him as he worked. The crew was a constant source of dread–but the officers could also deliver a ferocious bite. Their rigid codes and brutal punishments left no room for mercy. The mere thought of a flogging paralyzed Jacob; having already twice tasted the sting of the cane–once for forgetting to say *"sir,"* and once, out of spite, for not forgetting.

In a crew of two hundred and eighty, other than Seth, Jacob only considered one other not to be a threat–Mr Petigrew. The cheerful helmsman had taken a shine to young Jacob. Occasionally, he'd trusted him at his side while he manned the tiller. Never allowed to handle the tiller himself, Jacob would stand proud surveying his horizon, soaking up titbits of knowledge. Unfortunately, Jacob and

Mr Petigrew shared their watch with the short, balding, moody Navigator-Master Harvey. Always found with his pipe in the corner of his mouth, hovering over his charts, scowling at the horizon, while issuing clipped, sharp instructions to Mr Petigrew and the riggers.

Mr Petigrew stood at the tiller and caught Jacob's eye, offering a friendly nod. Jacob paused the brush to wipe his brow. The relentless summer sun beat down upon his weathered neck. Sweat trickling down his back. He raised a smile to Mr Petigrew before cocking a glance at Master Harvey. The disposition he's opted for in this moment was scowling–no chance to play captain today.

From above, the lookout's cry sliced across the deck with the shout of sails on the horizon. Moments later, Captain Tardebigge and First Lieutenant Matthews appeared on deck. They bustled Jacob aside like that dog as they huddled the rail. With the sun still low in the sky, it was unclear what had been espied as they squinted through their spyglasses.

"Ahoy aloft." Tardebigge gargled. "What do you see?"

"Unsure, sir. Quite large, though."

The captain paused, scratching his scalp through his greasy hair. "Mr Petigrew. Come about. Let's see who we're dealing with. All hands about ship."

"Aye, sir." Mr Petigrew replied.

Master Harvey snapped into action, sending clipped instructions to the riggers.

"This is Tardebigge's first commission as captain." Seth had remarked one evening at supper. "But we ain't likely to leave these waters any time soon. No trust from the admiral, you see. We'll be circling this stretch 'til the war's over–or by some miracle the cap'n can prove his worth. Not likely, I say, the man's tenpence to the shilling."

Kestrel had been sent to the Caribbean to patrol English waters and help protect the merchant shipping routes around Nevis that filled the coffers of the king during this second war with the Dutch. Seth had told how Tardebigge's father, an ex-Lord Commissioner, had stepped in and forced patronage after the embarrassment of witnessing his only son being passed over, several times, by lesser officers.

"God knows how many palms daddy had to grease to get his son even this shit pile," said Thackett, the gunner's mate, who shared Jacob's mess. "Didn't help him. Not even the crimps could sell the notion of service aboard *Kestrel*." Thackett turned to face Jacob, grinning with a mouth full of porridge. "No volunteers. That's why we have to press the likes of you scullies."

Seth ignored Thackett's jibe and continued his barrage of the captain's inadequacies, puffing out his chest, and cupping his hands in front of his belly. He bobbed around the mess table, jiggling his arms as he went. "My son needs to be taught the hard lessons of life." Seth barbled, causing the seven other messmates to chuckle into wooden porridge mugs. "My reputation in London will not suffer. He will return from the navy with rumgumption or not at all. I care not which." Seth slapped the table, attracting the attention of Lieutenant Craywick. The shine from his coat buttons dancing as he turned. The men quietened and Seth sat down sharpish, giggling.

This unknown vessel would be the perfect opportunity the rotund captain might seize to prove his worth, Jacob thought, peeping between Captain Tardebigge and Lieutenant Matthews.

"Maybe we should maintain our current course, sir?" Lieutenant Matthews interjected. "I fear we've strayed into Dutch waters."

"I know very well we're in Dutch waters, Lieutenant. Do you not think I'm not aware we're in Dutch waters? What the bloody hell do you think we've been doing for the last three days? We are exactly where I intended us to be. We are a ship of the line in the English Navy. Our job is to seek out and destroy enemy vessels obstructing our trading routes. And there you have it," he pointed south to the ship on the horizon. "An enemy vessel. What would you have me do, Lieutenant?"

"Well, sir..."

"Well, Matthews?" The captain shrieked. "Exactly. We must attack."

Lieutenant Matthew's morbid expression told more than Jacob's novice eyes could ascertain from his brief sighting of the distant ship–they were in trouble.

"Find your lieutenant, boy," Matthews growled, twisting Jacob's ear towards the steps. "Clear for action." He cried to the main deck. "Pray to the lord." He said, only to himself.

Two

Jacob unhook a mess table from its cradle, clumsily lowering it to the deck. Seth jumped the last step, swivelled on a stanchion post, and jogged over to help. He'd been pressed into service a year earlier than Jacob. At sixteen, he was a few months older—but suffered the same indignities. A bystander would not guess him to be the older boy. Jacob topped out almost a foot taller and much broader. Since that fateful rescue in the hold, they had become inseparable. Through strategic manoeuvrings and favours, they had wrangled themselves into neighbouring messes.

They carried the cumbersome table down the steps and into the hold. Seth was the one crew member Jacob trusted—always full of gossip and possessing more knowledge about the officers than anyone else aboard.

"Captain's ego's gunna' get us sent to the bottom." Seth whispered as they climbed the steps to collect another table.

Jacob nodded.

"He's a bloody fool." Seth continued, taking the weight of the next table with Jacob. "More pride than Henry bloody Hudson."

Men in earshot grunted caution, but their expressions denoted secret agreement. Not one crew member hadn't—at one time—grumbled about their inept captain.

Admiral Sir John Harman had assembled a squadron and headed south to intercept de La Barre's fleet. He'd issued standing orders for *Kestrel* to stay behind and patrol the waters around Nevis. A useless assignment, Tardebigge had openly expressed–as no serious enemy vessel would venture that far north when their real threat lay near Martinique. It did not matter to Tardebigge if he strayed a bit too close to the imminent battle and a little too far away from his duties. Once amongst his peers back in London, he and his father would spin the story any way fitting, so long as the outcome favoured the Tardebigge reputation. These rumbustious Dutch would be no match for the English–and Admiral Sir John Harman would soon take note of his name.

After weeks of traversing in unexciting circles - encountering nothing but fishermen–Tardebigge had ordered *Kestrel* to travel south to widen the patrol area. When this also proved futile, he again ordered the ship to head still further south, and then further south again. He refused to be left behind, determined to prevent others from stealing his glory. His reputation could not suffer.

As they ascended the steps back to the gun deck, Jacob heard the call repeated aft to fore.

"Beat to Quarters." Lieutenant Craywick's voice bleached the air, raising his cane as he harried his men into action.

"Good luck, powder monkey." Seth said, offering a despondent grin and his hand to shake.

"Good luck, Seth."

News had reached the gun deck that the enemy ship was a Second Charter of at least one hundred and eighty feet. It must have had seventy guns—and dwarfed their twenty-four-gun frigate. The chance to retreat had lapsed. To cut and run would relinquish the miniscule hope of victory and close the door, for Theodore Tardebigge, to every gentleman's club in London. He would rather die. And today he might. But not before every soul in his crew had been sacrificed. Honour and status came first.

Jacob's list slippers fell from his feet. Being too small, his toes lost grip of the soft inner sole, turning his walk into a shuffle. For fifteen, he was larger than many of the men and had much bigger feet than any previous powder monkey. He pushed back the wet canvas covering the magazine and was met by the orange glow of the lone lanthorn. Its dim light filtered through the glass of the light room—reflecting off the copper walls. Before his eyes had time to adjust, he'd be turned around and sent back up the zig zagged staircase to be met by the blinding pools of daylight flooding through the gun ports and curtained light shafts from the deck above.

His arms hung low when empty and burned with fatigue when he carried yet another clutch of cartridges filled with black powder. He placed each bag into the cartridge box between the brass monkey and the gun. The captain of the gun growled to make haste. Each pass was becoming slower as the pre-prepared bags had run out. The powder monkeys had to wait each time—in the unbearable heat of the ship's bowels—for fresh bags to be filled. He cursed Tardebigge again as he wiped his brow. The fat captain was too arrogant and stupid to care that today they would die.

At last, the cartridge box was sufficiently stocked. The captain of the gun was silent. Jacob rested. Sneaking a deep breath of fresh air through the gun port. His eyes widened as he glimpsed the hulk bearing down on them. Even to his unseasoned eyes, she seemed formidable.

"Get out of there, kid!" screamed the captain of the gun.

Jacob scuttled away, narrowly avoiding the carriage as the gunners tugged on the breech ropes rolling the gun forward, so the muzzle nestled up to the gun port. This routine wasn't new to Jacob. He'd endured hours of training while sailing from England to the West Indies. For safety, bags of sand had replaced actual gunpowder. The gun crews had only dummy primed and loaded while Jacob had raced up and down the stairs with the same bag until he could keep up the pace without being sick. Once they had reached Nevis, actual powder replaced the sand, and the guns fired for real.

But this was no drill. The gun crews were serious. Their actions more sombre–more deliberate. This was not to beat their previous best in the hope of an extra tot of rum for a job well done. This was war, and imprecision meant death.

Jacob felt the knot creeping back into his stomach. His hands were shaking. Was it fear or fatigue? Probably both. He clenched his fists to gain some composure. The battle hadn't started yet, and he already felt exhausted. This would be his ultimate moment of peace until *Kestrel* had miraculously won the battle, or he'd been captured or killed.

The gun deck rocked eerily quiet. The sound of the hull creaking and shouts from the officers to the riggers offered the only muffled sounds. Everyone poised–awaiting the order.

Jacob breathed deeply. Any moment the ship would be overcome by cannon fire. The timbers would rumble beneath his feet as each gun exploded into life. Smoke would choke his lungs and burn his eyes. The captains of the guns would scream orders to reload, but he would not hear them over the ringing in his ears. He would spring into action to retrieve more cartridges from the magazine. Into the darkness, then back into the smoke before heading back into the darkness. The never-ending horrific monotony of bringing six-pound bags of powder from the calm and gloom of the magazine back to the carnage and death of the gun deck. All the time avoiding the gunners in action, the recoil of the guns—and the inevitable splintering of wood as enemy shots blew chunks out of the hull. But in this moment, there was calm. It was almost peaceful.

He tasted salt as sweat dripped into his mouth. He avoided using his powder-stained hands to wipe his lips, daring to use his tongue instead. It was a poor decision. He spat onto the timbers. The water bucket sat between two cannons—but to sup from the ladle would break the silence.

His mind drifted to home. When he woke that first morning under the gaze of the lieutenant, he vowed he would make it back. His mother needed him. She was all alone, fending for herself with Mr Arundell's demands for her tithe. Without his labour, how would she pay? Would Lydia wait for him, not knowing where he was or if he would ever return? That vow now seemed impossible, standing in the gloom, waiting for the obliteration to begin.

He looked fore where Seth rested a hand on his cartridge box. The older powder monkey wiped his own brow. He looked tired. They both might die today—his only friend in the world, three thousand miles from their homes, fighting a war they knew little about. Only existing on maps, or in stories told by the old seadogs at the dock. Protecting goods, they would never experience, purchased by the rich, overfed, titled pigs who had no care for their meagre existence.

His fear boiled over. Now, standing still in the silence, the heat overtook him. He doubled forward. Lurching for the water bucket. The silence was broken by the splash. The gun crew groaned as they witnessed their drinking water polluted with this morning's porridge.

For five hours, they engaged the enemy. Jacob's body slumped heavy with fatigue. His face black with smoke, his throat rasped like he'd eaten lit embers. He'd made the journey into the magazine countless times, finding it easier to walk without his list slippers and the need to clench his toes. Wreckage cluttered the gun deck and on more than one occasion carpenters had to be called to clear away broken timbers and fix the steps leading to the lower deck. On his last pass, he'd returned late to the gun deck, expecting a scolding from the captain of the gun. Instead, he found his gun crew dead and the gun nowhere to be seen. What remained was a hole in the hull–large enough for a frightened powder monkey to crouch and consider his fate.

His final thought before he jumped was that he was proud of his friend. Seth was dragging the injured Thackett to the main mast to join the other wounded and dead. A glistening trail of blood followed the gunner's mate and, through the haze, Jacob recoiled as he noticed Thackett had lost his arm. Delirious with shock, Thackett screamed for Seth to fetch it from under the carriage of the one-and-a-half-tonne gun. Before Seth had the chance to refuse, a lieutenant seized the powder monkey by the collar and thrust him back to his gun crew, who were tugging on the breach ropes–realigning the gun. There was a sternness to Seth's face Jacob hadn't seen before. In the nightmare, he came alive, and looked proud of his temporary promotion–eager to fire his first shot.

Jacob called to his friend, but his voice was small over the violence. He turned instead to the water only eight feet below. There was plenty of debris floating beneath him, but also pools of open water. Jacob looked back at Thackett. The alternative was certain death. His fear had hardened into hatred, and it fuelled his resolution to return home. Tardebigge's arrogance had given him the chance to escape. He'd have been a fool to not have seized it. He jumped.

This was not the first time Jacob had found himself overboard of a vessel, but still he had to fight the urge to panic. He could do nothing but stare as the mizzenmast thundered into the ocean. The wave it caused sent a hefty splinter of hull hurtling towards his head. He inhaled deeply before being barrelled under the water.

Allowing his body to go limp, he steadied his mind. He thought of his father's survival lessons from when he was a boy. Through the hazy water, he could hear the muffled sound of desperate men yelling above him. He breathed out. Just a little, and watched the bubbles rise. He looked to the surface, but the bright midday sun was now a murky grey. He kicked upwards. As suspected, he found a barrier silking through his fingers.

He aimed his hands at his ankles and kicked in the opposite direction. Down. One of the mizzenmast sails had been dragged into the water. He needed to swim. Fast.

When he was sure he was out of the sail's reach, he strained his neck to see the surface. A glimpse of sunlight escaped the silky edge of the sail. He kicked towards it.

As a boy, his father had insisted he learn how to swim. The waters around Cornwall, where he had grown up, could turn tempestuous in an instant. Too many young men had died along the coast, not giving the capricious English weather the respect it deserves.

He had not risen more than a few feet when something clasped his ankle. Folding at the waist, he saw a hand flailing beneath him through the milky swirls. He gripped a wrist tightly–urging the sailor to gain some composure, trying to pull him upward–but they were sinking faster. The pressure in Jacob's ears and sinuses built like a drumbeat. With a wrench of guilt, he wriggled free. He kicked hard again–desperate now–toward the sunlight above. He'd tried to help, but the panic would have drowned them both.

He burst through the surface like the seals around St Clement's Isle, gulping in air and water. Almost choking while trying to regain some composure. He'd emerged between *Kestrel* and the enemy goliath–now less than one-hundred yards apart. A barrage from the great guns erupted from both ships. The enemy most definitely commanded the advantage.

He'd surfaced from under the rumpled sail facing the coast of a small island and not the open water. The island lay as a distant marker. It would be a long and tiring swim, but he had made his choice back on *Kestrel*, and there was no going back now.

A musket ball struck a gun port lid, floating next to him with a thwack. He squinted through the sun's glare, finding marine soldaats at their bow firing into the water. Another thwack. Jacob needed no more encouragement. He gulped again into his burning lungs–-and disappeared below.

When he next surfaced, he was a further thirty yards from the battle, but still a musket ball splashed nearby. There must have been at least one marine soldaat assigned with the task of shooting the escaping ship's boy. Another deep breath–and under he went again. He resurfaced, feeling confident he was out of range.

He turned to face the carnage. What he found petrified him. The dense hemp fibres of the mizzen topsail were becoming waterlogged. As the men became entangled, they were being swallowed whole. A screaming sailor leapt from the *Kestrel's* poop deck, smoke trailing from his breeches. He landed on the sail and disappeared as if through quicksand, dragging another sailor with him.

Lucky survivors, hoping for a miracle, cowered behind and under floating wreckage. The unlucky ones, thrashing in the open water, were picked off by soldaats. Jacob could see little distinction between dead crew and dead wood. He hoped Seth was not among them. However, where would be safe for his friend? Jacob could not imagine.

He raised one arm after the other. The effort needed already felt excruciating, but he had no choice. The cannon fire faded into the distance, and Jacob found solace in the meditative motion of each stroke.

He'd spent hours with his father on their tiny fishing boat around the south coast of England. While rowing back to the harbour, his father would insist Jacob swam the last one hundred yards. If Jacob tried to resist, he would be thrown overboard. *"You must respect the water."* His father would repeat. Jacob was grateful at this moment for his father's insistence on swimming lessons. He would never know it–but he had saved his son's life years after he'd lost his own.

Three

Jacob jolted awake. A hand smothered his mouth.

"Stay quiet, you feckless dog."

He blinked twice, adjusting his focus through the dappled morning sunlight. He could feel the rheum in the corner of his eyes–remanence from the previous day's battle. Filling his vision was Doyle with a grubby finger to his own lips, shushing Jacob. Jacob offered a steady gaze, giving Doyle the confidence to tiptoe away.

"What's going on? Jacob whispered, realising it was not only his eyes affected by yesterday's battle but also his hearing and his throat. He remembered clambering the fifty yards into the tree line before curling up from exhaustion. He must have slept all night.

"Shhh," Doyle replied. "We've got company."

Jacob eased himself up. His aching arms would not allow more haste. Doyle crept to the shoulders of two other crewmen peering out towards the beach. With their backs to him, Jacob didn't recognise them. Getting to his knees, he crawled towards the other survivors. Doyle snapped his hand behind his back, an explicit instruction to stay still. When Doyle's arm lowered, Jacob adjusted his body to glimpse between the strangers.

The thinner man glanced his way. Jacob sighed. Lieutenant Craywick. He now noticed the officer's jacket with the not so shiny buttons. He had lost his respected crimped bicorn hat and his hateful cane. The muck and grime on his uniform had beaten him to the appearance of a common sailor. Jacob hated Lieutenant Craywick as much as he hated Doyle. In fact, there was no fondness between any of the three. His first caning had been at the hand of the lieutenant. If Lieutenant Craywick held only disdain for the common crew, a ship's boy was beneath his contempt. He came from money. One of the elite and on a fast track to captaincy. Seth said the lieutenant's father was cosy with the king. He'd purchased his son's commission to the West Indies to season the young man to the ways of the world. At least he outranked Doyle. There would be a buffer of authority between himself and the maniacal gunner.

Between the lieutenant and Doyle, Jacob noticed movement on the beach. Bedraggled men were setting up a makeshift camp. Tarps obstructed his view, shielding some of their mysteriousness. They were not his own crew. But who else? They didn't look Dutch either. Not that Jacob had ever seen any Dutch sailors up close. These men weren't wearing much of a uniform to be naval. From behind a tarp, a stranger sauntered towards the trees, untying his waist cord as he approached. Whatever his nationality, this man needed a piss. And he was heading straight for them. The three survivors turned in unison and crept back into the jungle.

"With me, boy," Lieutenant Craywick whispered as he passed. "Keep low and be quiet." He stopped short of adding. "*Or there will be a flogging.*" But the tone implied the threat.

Jacob followed their lead, placing his feet in their tracks. One hundred paces further along the coast, the lieutenant lead the party back to the tree line, continuing the investigation. Jacob peered around the shoulder of the third crewmate. His identity was now clear. A potato-sized insect crawled over his bare foot, causing him to gasp. He resisted his instinct to kick out, instead crouched still, not making a sound. The cockroaches aboard *Kestrel* were big, but not as big as that. The insect disappeared. When the leaf litter ceased shuffling, Jacob returned his attention back to the beach.

The lieutenant was craning his neck to see a little further around the bay. "That ship anchored there was not the one we engaged yesterday." He pointed out to sea where a brigantine was anchored. "I'm pretty sure the Dutch scoundrels left these waters at first light. These are a new crew." He remained silent for a while. "Ah, see there. There are men on board *Kestrel*. They're throwing our valuables overboard onto the beach. They're looting the ship." The lieutenant's voice pitched an octave higher. "The bludgers!"

Jacob watched as more men carried an assortment of items to the water's edge. A low riding barge laden with barrels had recently cast off.

"They've stumbled on our wreckage and stripping her for plunder." The lieutenant slapped the ground. "Ragamuffins!"

From the main camp, four men broke from the group and started towards their position. A broad-shouldered black man led the way, carrying an axe.

"Time to go." The lieutenant whispered to his new section.

They backed away. Jacob stayed to the rear behind the third survivor, confident of his identity but still not seeing his face.

After five minutes of stealth, Doyle straightened his shoulders and widened his stride. "I ain't creepin' no more. We must be out of earshot by now."

The others followed his example and eased their stature. With each step into the bush, Jacob became fascinated by the array of flora they passed. Closer to the beach, he'd noticed tall trees with long finger shaped leaves. Palm trees. He'd heard mention of these trees around the mess table. Each tree had many green, brown balls hanging from beneath the foliage called coconuts. Deeper inland, the plants became denser with a variety of species. Some looked similar to those back home, but with larger leaves. Some Jacob would never have imagined possible. Such bright flowers or spiky leaves–if leaves were in fact what they were.

He dawdled, touching the plants and gawping into the canopy at the exotic birds perched overhead. Once he thought he heard rustling in the bushes, which encouraged him into a trot to catch the others. He imagined the scavengers following them. When the rustling stopped, Jacob's attention returned to the foliage. So mesmerised by the wonders, he almost thumped into Doyle as his three shipmates stalled finding themselves in a small clearing.

Many of the bushes encircling the clearing had long stripy leaves edged with pink. The sunlight bounced off their tips, creating a magical glade. It reminded Jacob of the woods near his home. If not for the imminent danger, Jacob could have curled up in the sunshine with his mother's pippin tart and a mint cordial. They crept to the opposite side, rustling inwards among the vegetation, keeping a clear line-of-sight back from where they'd walked.

Jacob was not the tallest of the survivors. Doyle stood well over six feet and rippled with muscles. Craywick was a slender man in his mid-twenties and now Jacob had the courage to scrutinise him, found that even under the muck he still leached that pompous air of aristocracy. The third man, shortest of the four, squat in stature with wide shoulders and muscular forearms was who Jacob had suspected. The navigator of *Kestrel*. Master Harvey. Why could it not have been Mr Petigrew who'd survived? He looked over his new comrades. Although he would not have handpicked them, he found a modicum of comfort in not being alone.

"What's your name, boy?" Craywick asked.

"Jacob, Sir." He'd told the lieutenant his name many times. The lieutenant showed no recollection of knowing him. He cursed at not having the instinct to conjure up a new name. "Jacob Penjerrick." He added. With only a split second, he tried his luck with at least a new surname and summoned to mind the home village of his mother. He tensed as he watched the lieutenant's reaction.

"Well, Jacob, you probably know me. I'm Lieutenant Craywick. This is Master Harvey." The short squat navigator grunted as he cleaned out his briar pipe that had somehow made it to the island unscathed. "And this is Doyle."

"Ah, old friends, are we now, ye little gombeen?" Doyle gave Jacob a punch on the arm, just the wrong side of friendly.

"Who were those men, sir?" Jacob asked, ignoring the sly look in Doyle's eye.

"Scavengers, boy. Here to pick the bones after our skirmish. Scum."

"They sounded French, sir," Jacob said.

"Like I said, scum," Craywick spat. "The Dutch have cleared off and our ship is half sunk, smashing itself to driftwood against the rocks. I suspect we're the only survivors."

"What's the plan, sir?" Jacob asked. "Do you have a plan? Is there a way off this island? Is it an island?" He closed his mouth and waited. The three older men gawped at each other. Jacob slumped his shoulders when no answer was forth coming.

He flopped to the ground, crossed his legs, and placed his chin on his fists, staring at the soil. Tiny ants crawled under his raised knees, all working together carrying leaves ten times their size. He envied the simplicity of their miniature world.

"It's an island." Master Harvey finally offered, having spent the last few moments grumbling as he rummaged through his damp tobacco pouch. "It ain't on any of the charts, so it ain't big."

"Without food or water, we'll be dead within days," lieutenant Craywick said. "We can't just hide here and hope for rescue."

"How about the coconuts? Can we eat them?" Jacob asked.

"They're edible," lieutenant Craywick answered, "but they take a long time to open even if we had our swords or knives. And they offer no sustenance. And they taste foul."

Jacob puffed.

The three men whispered a while, trying to conjure a plan. There was talk of hiding until the French had left, but that drew the obvious question. What about food or water? They had debated building a raft to row their way to safety, but most of the timber of any use was being collected by the scavengers. Rowing to safety also had the same problem as hiding out. No food or water.

Master Harvey turned out to have extensive knowledge of the West Indies. This seemed promising–until he told them their location was three days away, on a raft, from meaningful land. And that was French. Jacob sighed. The ants had gone.

Doyle proposed stealing a barge from the French, but even he admitted they were obviously outnumbered and fatigued from lack of water and so despite all his bravado, the idea would most likely end badly. The only tangible option: to die where they lay. Last man alive gets to eat the others. Doyle perked up at the mention of cannibalism. The lieutenant wasn't sure if it was a joke, but Doyle *was* smiling. By the end of the discussion and an hour later, all four had wilted in the heat–forlorn of ideas.

For ten minutes, Jacob had tried to ignore both the hunger in his stomach and a notion germinating in his head. Before he could stop himself, he stood, announcing his thoughts.

"I have a plan." He winced, wishing he'd stayed on the ground. "It ain't much. More the seeds of an idea for the start of a plan." He held his breath. At least this would break the silence. "I can speak French," he blurted. "I can speak to the men on the beach."

"And say what ye eejit?" Doyle said. "I should bleed ye for such blindness,"

"I dunno. It's only an idea," Jacob said. "I could ask if they wouldn't mind dropping us off at the next port." Jacob blushed. "They might be friendly?"

"Friendly? Stop acting the maggot, gombeen." Doyle stood towering over Jacob, who slumped back to the ground. Doyle's fists clenched and his eyes bored into Jacob's skull.

"That's quite enough, Mr Doyle." Lieutenant Craywick said. "We're all tired and thirsty but no need to resort to violence."

Master Harvey relinquished his tobacco pouch and eased to his feet. He placed a hand on Doyle's shoulder. Lieutenant Craywick did not move, allowing Master Harvey to half hide him. Doyle spoke between his gritted teeth.

"My feelin's they're pirates, gombeen. And pirates aren't known for being friendly. They're rogues, they're vicious, and cruel and cunning. They'd take one look at ye and strike ye through before they could think of a reason not to."

Jacob raised his hands in front of his face, waiting for a blow from the giant. Master Harvey eased the snarling Doyle a step away, calming him slightly.

"They might not be pirates." Jacob said. "Have you ever met a pirate?"

Doyle paused, thinking for a moment. "Ah, no. But we've all heard the stories." His shoulders eased further. "Crew so fed up with their officers, they mutiny, take the ship and turn to piracy to make their fortune." He glanced at the lieutenant. "They kill anyone who tries to stop 'em and head for the nearest pirate friendly port where they drink themselves into a stupor and find cheap whores for entertainment, before heading back to sea to find more plunder so they can return for more of the same."

Jacob suppressed a smile. "Well. Ain't that better than dying here waiting to be eaten by you lot. If they're pirates, we just need to convince them we're not here to judge their piracy. We just need safe passage."

Lieutenant Craywick stepped forward. "We're not asking pirates for help, boy. They're stealing our possessions. If anything, we should be turning them in to Governor Stapleton."

Jacob looked down at his lonely patch of ground.

"We don't have any better plans, sir," Master Harvey said, popping his pipe into his breast pocket. "And if they're not navy, it might not matter if they're French. Nationality don't mean the same thing in these parts. Let's give the boy's plan a run-through. What would you say to them, lad?"

Four

The scavengers were only yards away. Through the thin veil of shrubbery. Jacob took a deep breath before pushing through onto the beach.

"He, vous la, garcon." Jacob had expected the encounter–but it still shocked him. He stopped. The leaf curtain closed behind him. He glanced over his shoulder. No sign of his crewmates. They'd done as planned and retreated out of sight. Harvey had reassured him they would stay within earshot.

He stuttered a shallow breath before answering in his best French. "Hello, needs help. I am lost boys." He finished with a grin.

The surprised Frenchman turned to a fellow beachcomber, shrugging his shoulders. He took a step closer to Jacob with open arms, judging him quizzically. He had a cutlass at his side and a pistol hung from a cord around his neck, tucked into his sash. Jacob didn't move.

"What are you doing here, pup? Our captain will kill you, rip out your heart, and add it to Helario's stew. Where've you come from?"

Jacob furrowed his brow at hearing the true native French tongue. "I was a ships boys on the boat." He pointed towards *Kestrel*, where the French crew still appropriated timber, rope and anything else of use from the wreckage. "I was flew overboard during the ... fight with the Dutch boat and ended ... here. Me join you?"

"You want to join *our* crew?" Three other men joined the first with folded arms, listening with bemused expressions. "We're buccaneers lad? Why do you think we would let you join us? We are just as likely to kill you."

Jacob's throat tightened. "Buccaneers?" He said, nodding. At least they weren't pirates. He continued with a forced smile and over exuberant hand gestures to help convey his message. "Six months before now I was a ... fisherman in England, then forced to join English Navy."

"They kidnapped you?" The first buccaneer said. "You might have a slither of a chance with the captain."

Jacob nodded; not confident he'd understood the Frenchman's words. "I have loyalty not to them. Before fight with Dutch boat, I was looking for escape and... become free. When I saw you on the beach, I thought it... good and I should speak to you."

The buccaneers listened with puzzled amusement. The first buccaneer seemed to be the leader, so Jacob directed his conversation to him.

"You look like honest man who would use heart to help a young boys become free." Jacob pressed his palms together, staring at the smiles on the buccaneers' faces.

The first buccaneer stroked his droopy moustache above his bare chin. He wore a long, dark yellow stocking cap. His dirty white and blue striped shirt, half open revealing a dark tanned chest to match the colour of his face. A dirty blue sash banded around his dark wide legged breeches–emphasising his thick waist. Every item he wore, sun bleached and smudged through many months at sea. He had sad eyes.

"Carry on with the barrels lads, cap'n will be waiting."

The curious buccaneers resumed their task of loading water barrels at the edge of the beach, awaiting the barge's next approach. The pause gave Jacob a small reprieve, allowing his nose to pick up the aroma of cooking meat. He peeled his eyes away from the landing party to find a timber-framed structure over a fire further along the beach. The four men that had headed into the bush earlier stood around the flames with three dead wild boars at their feet. A fourth boar had recently been butchered. Strips of meat roasted above the wooden rack–tended to by an older man. Jacob's eyes widened at the sight.

The buccaneer turned back to Jacob, lowering his eyebrows–offering him a sinister smile. "Let's have a little chat with our new friend here." He said to himself. "What's your name, lad?"

Jacob swallowed, remembering Master Harvey's parting advice. "If they ask you your name, you might have a chance. It'll be harder for them to kill you if they know your name."

The grimacing expression was disconcerting, but Jacob answered with a smile. "My name is Jacob. What is yours?"

The Frenchman coughed a smile. "Moise Vauquelin" He replied. "You English?"

Jacob nodded.

Moise furrowed his brow. "You alone?"

Jacob glanced into the bush. Moise clasped a hand on his cutlass and called out over his shoulder.

"Isaac. Over here. We might have trouble,"

Over Moise's shoulder, a tall blonde sailor placed a barrel down next to the others and jogged over to his superior. "What's the problem, Moise?"

"I think we have more of your kind in the bushes." Moise had not diverted his eyes from Jacob and pushed for an answer. "How many, boy?"

Jacob took a small intake of breath. "Three. There's three mans in trees." Jacob pointed to where he'd left his small party. "Please, I was to tell you. I'm the only man who speak French. We don't want to ... frightens you."

Moise rubbed his forehead. "Tell them to come out. Slowly. You, come here." Jacob didn't move. He flashed glances between Moise and Isaac. "Come here, boy." Moise fixed a grin. "We won't hurt you. Step towards Isaac here." Jacob inched towards Isaac's outstretched arms. Before Jacob could resist, Isaac had snatched him close. A powerful arm wrapped across Jacob's chest–and a dagger chilled his collar bone.

"Stay still." Isaac whispered in English.

Moise pulled the cutlass from his sash and pointed it towards the trees. "Call your friends or Isaac will slit your throat."

He could feel the blade move to his Adam's apple. Isaac held it flat, encouraging Jacob to take only shallow breaths. He dared not swallow. "Lieutenant Craywick, Doyle, Master Harvey. It's time to come out." With his head tilted back, Jacob focused on the trees. Isaac stood at a similar height but held a solid physique. Jacob shifted his weight, and the thick arms tightened.

"I won't hurt you." Isaac whispered. "Just stay still."

Moise looked at Jacob and clenched his jaw tight. "Call them again."

"Lieutenant Craywick, Doyle ..." The bush rustled a few yards to the right–not where he'd left them. Moise, Isaac and Jacob twitched in unison to witness the three castaways emerge. Only Doyle stood tall, glancing at Isaac before holding the gaze of Moise. Jacob tensed as Moise widened his stance and locked eyes with the big man.

"This all of you?" Moise asked.

The lieutenant nodded to Moise, but offered no reply. Moise turned to Jacob, who translated.

"He is asking if there are any more of us," Jacob side-eyed Moise–still distracted by the dagger. "I promise, this is everyone."

Not taking any chances, Moise called over to the buccaneers near the fire. "Bakari, we might have trouble. Go search the bush for any more survivors."

The four buccaneers crashed into the bush, leaving the hogs to the older cook.

"So, what would four English seamen want from my band of buccaneers?" Moise relaxed an ounce, showing confidence as he contemplated the forlorn souls. His tone had a hint of joviality. His eyes, however, did not stray from Doyle.

The big Irishman had become distracted by the food thirty yards away–salivating as he eyed the flames hissing at the strips of pork.

Lieutenant Craywick pointed to his mouth. "Water. Aqua."

Moise ignored the lieutenant–instead, turning his head, alerted to a sound behind him.

In the time it took Jacob to introduce his three companions and explain they would join the crew for passage off the island; a fresh wave of fully armed buccaneers had joined the gathering. Moise waited for the leader to sidle beside him. Jacob inched his head as far as his bravery would allow. A newcomer stood, scratching his chin. His forefinger rubbed a scar travelling from the underside of his left eye to the corner of his mouth. His scar gave him a fixed grimace.

"Captain's inquiring what the problem is." The newcomer asked, narrowing his eyes. "He spied you prattling. Who are they? What do they want?"

"We've come across these English castaways." Moise explained. "They want to join our crew rather than stay here with the hogs."

The newcomer cast his eye over the English ragtags and chuckled. "They're crew of that ship there?" He pointed to *Kestrel*.

"Aye,"

"Best bring them on board then, Moise. We don't want to be hanging around any longer than needs be. Captain's only just calmed himself. We don't want to provoke him before we get home." "Jacob, tell your men to get in the barge with Mr Le Picard here. He'll take you to our ship. The captain will want to have a... little chat. You best hope the captain's still in a fine mood, otherwise..." Moise drew his thumb across his neck.

Jacob, Lieutenant Craywick and Master Harvey followed Le Picard submissively. Doyle, more reluctant to avert his eyes from the succulent hog meat, needed encouraging with a cutlass.

Jacob sat still—flanked by Le Picard and Isaac—as the barge rowed closer to the Brigantine. He wished he had never confessed to learning French. He pined for his simple life as a fisherman. Fishermen live happy lives, with their fisher wives and have fisher children. Stupid French speaking ships boys die young in the middle of nowhere. He sat fighting back tears, staring at the foreign ship as it loomed closer. A ship with a captain that the hard faced Le Picard was not keen to provoke.

Five

The brigantine was smaller than *Kestrel*–and in desperate need of repair. Jacob noticed it lacked a bowsprit, ratlines severed, and many shrouds secured by stoppers. He was still learning his ropes but standing on the main deck, Jacob struggled to find a rope not tethered to another incorrectly.

Stacked along the gunwale lay *Kestrel's* reclaimed rope and timber. Carpenters and riggers were busy putting the salvaged materials to good use. Two large sails hung from the rigging–drying in the sun. Beneath the sails–taking advantage of the shade–a scruffy white and brown mongrel terrier lay eyeing the surrounding commotion. He sat up with a start as another sea chest dropped on the deck near his front paw. Four great guns lay on the deck and would be used to bolster the ship's defences or at the very least add to the ballast weight. The buccaneers had been busy.

The four navy seamen lined up facing the stern. Jacob watched as water barrels were hauled over the bulwark. With a cackle, Le Picard once more refused the lieutenant's demands for water. As they awaited judgement under clear skies and the midday sun, all four prisoners began swaying. Only now–in this moment of suppression–did Jacob heed his throbbing head, as dehydration took effect. He realised why this crew might not waste water on four castaways. They were most likely destined to die.

Moise clambered from the ship's ladder, followed by Isaac. The beach leader passed the prisoners with little recognition, disappearing into the officer's sleeping quarters. Isaac offered Jacob a vacant expression with no hint of what to expect. Le Picard had ordered six crewmen in scruffy attire to stand guard with pistols at the ready and cutlasses tucked into their sashes. Bakari, the huge black axe wielder, was one of them. His wry smile encouraged Jacob's eyes to the floor.

Jacob stood at the end of the row next to Doyle–and, for the first time–happy to be so close to the Irishman. Master Harvey stood next to Doyle. Straight-backed, eyes front. The lieutenant stood at the other end of the line, dusting off his jacket and buffing his buttons.

The cabin door clattered open and out stepped Moise. He strode past them again, ignoring Lieutenant Craywick's pleas for water. He disappeared to the bow along with the cook from the beach. The smell of roasted pork wafted across the deck. Doyle tracked the cook, hoping to find the source of the delicious smell.

Jacob's eyes remained on the open cabin in front of them. The shadows shifted and from out of its darkness stepped a majestic, well-dressed captain. He sauntered towards his visitors with such confidence even Doyle turned and straightened his shoulders.

The captain paraded in front of his guests for many seconds, contemplating each one. Concluding in front of Jacob, musing a few seconds longer. Helpless, Jacob could only stare back at this magnificent man.

He must have been in his mid-thirties but commanded himself like a man many years his senior. His hair, straight and shoulder length, parted in the centre and exceptionally clean. Jacob had never seen hair this well-kept—not even in England, on dry land, with fresh water in abundance. He wore a thin moustache under his long thin nose and a goatee on his chin under his thin pursed lips. His clothing was immaculate. Each garment looked expensive. His jacket was a deep purple, finishing at his knees with gold buttons and gold edge trims. He wore a gold sash around his waist. A length of gold silk cord was tied around the handles of two ornate-handled flintlock pistols. The cord hung around his neck while the pistols were tucked into the sash. He fingered a gold-hilted cutlass at his left hip.

In his right hand, his most coveted item—a silver cup adorned with small green gemstones. The gemstones or the silver were not what captured the attention. It was the cool, fresh, crisp water. Presumably welled from the island, beading over the lip that all four sets of eyes rested upon.

"Monsieur's. Welcome aboard my ship. The Marquis de Villars." The captain spoke in French. "You are having a day you will never forget. I have been told by my quartermaster, Mr Vauquelin, who you met on the beach, that you wish to join my crew. Is this correct?" He looked at each of the four ending with Jacob.

"Oui, we have become stranded after we were attacked by a Dutch man of war. We feared we would be marooned on the island. We were relieved when your crew came ashore and hoped you would show mercy. We rejoiced when we discovered you were French, as we are allies. We would be grateful for safe passage back to a neutral port."

Dumbstruck faces turned to the lieutenant—as he had been the one to have answered. In French. Fluently.

Jacob's fingers rolled into a white-knuckled fist. Even Moise paused his overseeing of the hogs to check his ears had not deceived him. The captain cocked his head and suppressed a pleasurable yet quizzical smirk. He side stepped away from Jacob to the opposite end of the row. This time, he spoke in English.

"I am Captain Francois L'Olonnais, at your service." The captain gave a little bow. "You must be the young man who demonstrated bravery equal to any captain, in any navy, this side of France when you announced yourself from hiding to my Mr Vauquelin. Even though you must have been very frightened. Knowing you could have been executed where you stood for merely being English, you nobly stepped forward in an attempt to save your comrades' lives. Placing your final ounce of faith in the compassion of rough, weathered sea dogs. Hoping they would transport you to a safe port and free from months of marooning. How brave, how very brave." The captain held out a hand for the lieutenant to shake. "Jacob, it is a pleasure to welcome you aboard my ship. Bravo."

The lieutenant grasped the captain's hand with both of his. "Thank you, Sir. We are very gracious. My name is Lieutenant Craywick of *HMS Kestrel*. May I introduce my subordinates?"

"Please do, lieutenant,"

"This is Master Harvey. He is our ship's navigator. Very knowledgeable of all the waters around the Caribbean."

L'Olonnais raised an eyebrow and gave Master Harvey a sideways nod.

"This is Mr Doyle. He is one of our gunners. As you can see, very strong."

The captain looked up at Doyle, who glared back with a twisted smile.

"And this is Jacob. A ... ships boy."

"Ah, this is Jacob?" The captain took a sidestep back towards Jacob and placed a theatrical thumb and forefinger to his goatee.

"Erm, yes, Jacob. He's just the ship's boy."

"Very tall for the ship's boy? Erm, Lieutenant Craywick, was it?"

"Yes sir."

"I am a little confused." The captain turned back to face the lieutenant. "Mr Vauquelin told me it was the young man here who first introduced himself on the beach. The only one of you who spoke French. Not very well, I was told." He glanced at Jacob, shrugging his shoulders. Jacob blushed. "Not like you, Lieutenant Craywick. You speak French exquisitely. Where did you learn to speak La belle langue?"

"At Oxford Sir. I also speak Spanish and Latin." The Lieutenant puffed out his chest like a young naval officer receiving yet another commendation from the admiral of the fleet–prematurely assuming to be his equal.

"Bravo. I too am bilingual. Excuse me one moment." L'Olonnais stepped over to stand in front of Jacob and reached forward and, with a knowing nod, offered him his cup of water. Jacob hesitated. The captain nodded again, and so Jacob accepted the cool cup and drank. "Yes, I too am bilingual, Lieutenant." He turned back to face the lieutenant. "I also speak a little Spanish and a little English. Although I did not have my training at an elite school such as Oxford. Although, I must admit I have not heard of this school. Do forgive my ignorance. I assume it is a school of high reserve?"

"It is, Sir. The best England has to offer."

The captain stood in front of the lieutenant again, listening. "So, you are one of the best Englishmen England has to offer?" Lieutenant Craywick stood even straighter, staying silent, allowing the captain to continue. "I too was sent to school by my parents. A mere boy. No older than young Jacob here. I was shipped off from France to these waters to work on a sugar plantation owned by my Spanish employers. Many years I worked but for not a coin in payment. Some might say no better than a slave. Digging and planting and harvesting for hours every day in the excruciating heat.

The boiling house was the worst place on earth, and I would not wish it on my worst enemy." A smile pecked his cheek. "Well, I would. I'd happily pour the hot molasses into the eye sockets of any of my Spanish captors. Shush, I say." The captain turned to Jacob. "Don't be shy. Drink up, my friend." He turned back to Lieutenant Craywick. "I learned to speak their tongue so I could escape their wrath." He turned and interrupted Isaac, walking past, carrying timber to the growing pile at the gunwale. "Mr Dargate? Please bring up water for our guests."

"Oui, monsieur." Isaac strolled off to intercept a barrel and came back moments later with three fresh cups overflowing with the same cool water. The remaining thirsty Englishmen did not take their eyes from the cups.

"Day after day. Blister after blister. Lash after lash. These days were torturous, but they made me the man I am today. An education I suspect is far less privileged to that of your own, Lieutenant."

The Englishmen all stood statue still in front of this enigmatic man as he told his story. This was not the first time he had recited his upbringing. Every nuance timed to inflict maximum impact.

"Please, gentlemen" L'Olonnais gestured to Doyle and Harvey to take a cup. Which they did and drank eagerly, leaving Isaac with one cup in his hand. Lieutenant Craywick licked his lips. "Young man. What is your full name?" L'Olonnais asked.

"Jacob Penjerrick, sir."

"Mr Penjerrick. Would you like another cup?"

Jacob shot a surprised look at the captain and then over at his lieutenant. He tipped back his head, gulping the remaining pool of water from the bejewelled cup before switching with Isaac for a crisp new full one.

"Thank you, Sir." Jacob said.

"Thank you, captain," Harvey and Doyle replied, prompted by Jacob's politeness.

"You're very welcome, gentlemen. Where was I? Yes, the tough days made me the man I am today. English, I learned later as I traded with the rich merchants in Port Royal and Antigua. But my education did not finish there. I've learned many more English and Spanish words over the years." The captain fixed eyes on the lieutenant. "It's amazing the words that escape a man's mouth moments before you slice off another limb or crush his skull through woolding. Have you ever seen a man's eyes pop from their sockets, Lieutenant?"

Jacob lowered his cup. The sun's glare softened as it passed behind a cloud—the air cooled. The lieutenant had stiffened. What had caused a change to his mood Jacob thought?

"No, sir," the lieutenant said.

"Come, come, Lieutenant, you must have dealt out your fair share of floggings at least. I hear you English run a very disciplined ship."

Doyle took a sharp intake of breath and side glanced the lieutenant over the head of Harvey before returning his gaze back to his cup. Captain L'Olonnais flashed a look down the line.

"You have received a flogging, Mr Doyle?"

"Aye, sir."

"Has Lieutenant Craywick ever instructed for you to be flogged?"

Doyle paused, but only for a second. "Aye, sir."

Lieutenant Craywick glared at Doyle. "Of your own making, Mr Doyle."

"Why did Mr Doyle deserve a flogging?"

The lieutenant glowered at Doyle. Doyle glowered back, nostrils flaring, and then back to the captain. The captain feigned exacerbation and looked back at the angry gunner.

"Mr Doyle? Why did you receive a flogging from Lieutenant Craywick?"

Doyle answered, staring at his lieutenant. "Drunk, sir."

"Drunk?"

"Aye, sir,"

"Did you cause concern to any of the crew?"

"No, sir" Jacob raised a single eyebrow at Doyle's answer.

"Were you unfit for duty?"

"No, sir, we lay docked in Nevis, awaiting orders."

Jacob remembered lining up with the crew on the main deck to witness Doyle receive his ten lashes. A mixture of injustice–and satisfaction–had shared his thoughts as he stood watching his persecutor suffer on that blustery February morning.

The captain twisted the end of his goatee. "So just drunk?"

"Aye, sir,"

"Is this true, Lieutenant Craywick? Did you order Mr Doyle flogged for being drunk?"

"I'll have you in irons, Doyle, when we return home."

"Lieutenant Craywick? Have you ever received a flogging?" The captain asked.

The lieutenant stayed silent. Jacob could see his lips fluttering. Was he praying?

"Lieutenant Craywick?"

"No, sir. Officers are not flogged." The Lieutenant's eyes darted around the deck. High and low. He turned to Harvey. The navigator stared forward, a sailor on parade. Doyle was no use. He glared back at him, nostrils still flaring. Jacob dared a fleeting glance at the lieutenant. His heart beating fast.

"So only common sailors are worthy of the lash? What rules do the English navy consider deserving of a good old-fashioned flogging?" The captain drummed his fingers on the hilt of his cutlass.

"I ... I don't know, sir,"

The captain chuckled. "You must know. You're a learned lieutenant in the English Navy. Look at those buttons. Someday you aspire to be a captain. You must have served for many years and seen many floggings. You can't remember a single reason why a member of your crew would be in need of some discipline?" A wide smile materialised upon the captain's face, but the lieutenant did not answer. "On this vessel, Lieutenant, I do not flog crew members for being drunk while off duty. I do not use flogging as a punishment at all for any of the crew."

At these last words, the desperate lieutenant let out a hopeful sigh.

Jacob breathed easy—but something caught his attention. Deathly serious eyes accompanied the captain's smile.

"But, Lieutenant Craywick, you are not a member of this crew ... are you? You are a high born, Oxford educated pomp who speaks three languages and deals out floggings for his own gratification. You are craven, who coerced a boy to introduce himself to cutthroat killers on a beach, with only his wits as weapons, when it should have been you who stepped forward to negotiate parlay. No, on this vessel we do not flog crew members for being drunk." The captain placed a hand on the lieutenant's shoulder. "But we do flog foreign lieutenants for being cowardly. Your only saving attribute, Lieutenant Craywick, is that you are not Spanish."

The Lieutenant looked for an escape—but the five cutlass wielding buccaneers and the axe had crept in around him.

Jacob looked at Harvey and Doyle. Harvey; soldier straight. Doyle had clearly defected. Jacob could not help but align his feelings with the Irishman. It had become the low born against the high born. Lieutenant Craywick was alone among the scourge of the sea. A line had been drawn. He was no longer a lieutenant in the English Navy. He was a wealthy, educated aristocrat–and justice would be served. His only hope was for the captain to be merciful. But what stood in front of them was the devil himself. Larboard, starboard, bow or stern. Rigging or hull, there was no escape. The lieutenant was defenceless to the whims of this crazed captain.

"Your jacket, Lieutenant Craywick, if you please." The captain held out a hand as if the butler to a master returning home from a long evening at a laborious dinner party.

"This is preposterous," the Lieutenant blustered, finding his voice. He continued with more of a whimper than with any real command. "We have committed no crime. We are simply causalities of the battle. A battle not with you, or even your countrymen. We came to you for compassion and this is our reward. To be flogged like common sailors."

"Your jacket, Lieutenant Craywick." L'Olonnais bellowed, loud enough that every man aboard stopped their task to view the spectacle. Jacob and Harvey stood rigid. Doyle's face showed no fear. Only hatred for Lieutenant Craywick, and a feverish pleasure from the event unfolding in front of him.

"I beg you, sir. We deserve no punishment. This is unlawful." Lieutenant Craywick pleaded. "My father is very rich. He can pay you."

"Your jacket, Lieutenant Craywick," the captain said. A sinister undertone clear to hear. This was the last time he would ask.

Lieutenant Craywick removed his jacket and handed it to the captain, who passed it to Isaac who hung it upon the cabin door–as if on display.

"This way, Lieutenant Craywick." The captain beckoned the lieutenant to follow him to an upstanding grating where Le Picard waited with rope intended to bind Craywick's hands and thus secure his fate. "Bring out the bag."

Moise disappeared through the door to the officer's quarters. Moments later, he returned with a twelve-inch, square canvas bag. Tied at the top by a slim cord.

Le Picard tethered Craywick's wrists to the grating. Wide apart above his head.

"He's left his shirt on." Harvey whispered.

Doyle grinned.

"Mr Le Picard. Could you make sure Dr Venette is busy elsewhere for the time being?"

Craywick waited for the inevitable first whip. The few seconds felt like hours as the cat was taken out of the bag. Craywick flinched, hearing the nine tails as Moise flicked his wrist in practise. Craywick sobbed. The captain was calm now. He stood to the side of the grating for maximum view of the lieutenant's face, revelling in the humiliation.

"How many lashes did you receive from your lieutenant, Mr Doyle?"

Doyle smiled. "Thirty Sir."

"Thirty?" Craywick cried.

"Do you admit you are craven, Mr Craywick?"

Craywick lowered his gaze to the boards. "Yes sir."

"Very good. Thirty lashes, Mr Vauquelin. Count them out, Mr Craywick. And be grateful it is only thirty. Mr Doyle will come to find that cowardliness is a much darker crime on this ship than drunkenness."

For a lifetime, nobody moved. The ship swayed. The timbers creaked. The wind caressed the furled sails. Moise, the captain's whipping boy, lifted his arm... Crack.

"One." Lieutenant Craywick whimpered.

Jacob could see no blood–but the knots had done their worst. Moise had not held back. The shirt was already in ribbons. Lieutenant Craywick would forever own the scars of a common seaman.

"Aargh, two." Craywick's spirit had already broken. Jacob could not see how the Lieutenant could take all thirty strokes without passing out.

"Three." Blood trickled through the open cuts of the shirt. Craywick's legs almost buckled beneath him.

"Four."

Harvey flinched. His first reaction throughout the whole ordeal. As if noticing his slight lapse, he re-fixed his eyes to the middle distance–making every effort to not flinch again.

"Five." Craywick arched his torso. The pain must have been excruciating.

"Six."

Doyle smiled as he sipped from his cup–as blood sprayed from the whip's backlash across the main deck.

"Seven." Craywick was barely audible now.

The captain, seemingly bored with the whole affair, walked back past the bound captive towards his cabin. Craywick looked up hopeful, trying to regain some composure. He straightened his shoulders, but every inch of his body trembled. Tears streaked his cheek. His expression hinted at relief. Thankful the ordeal was over. He breathed a tremendous sigh.

The captain flicked a wicked smile. "Carry on, Mr Vauquelin. I will be in my cabin."

Craywick's eyes widened. "No. Please. I have taken my punishment. I deserved it. I have learned my lesson. Please no more."

Jacob's eyes followed the captain to his cabin. His stomach tight–but he stood rigid in an attempt to remain composed. The captain smiled at Jacob before striding back through the door and into the darkness.

"Eight."

Six

The sun's residual hue lingered, casting long shadows from the stern—hiding Jacob as he huddled next to the forward broadside gun. Alone. His head resting on his knees, leaning against the muzzle. The events of the day fussing in his mind.

"Wine?"

Jacob looked up and shook his head, still apprehensive about speaking to the man who had only that afternoon held a knife to his neck. Isaac, refusing to relinquish the moment, lingered—much like a concerned farmer would trying to coax an injured calf from a ditch. He leaned on the gunwale sipping from one of two cups.

"Where's your navigator and that Irish giant?"

Jacob shrugged.

"You were lucky we found you. You'd have been marooned on that island for months."

Jacob fixed his eyes on the bower cable coiled in front of him.

"You found the captain in a good mood. I think he likes you. He's happy to've stumbled on your Mr Harvey." Isaac sipped more wine. He offered Jacob a second chance to accept the other cup.

Jacob shook his head.

"It's a good crew, when you get to know 'em. All sorts. French mainly, but there's a couple of Dutchies, and the cook's Portuguese.

Odd fella. You will have noticed a few natives and a few blacks. As you can tell, I'm English. All welcome here my friend. You forget who you're supposed to be fighting. Captain will be fair with you–so long as you pull your weight and know your place." He took another sip. "No Spanish though. The captain hates Spanish. He would run a man through if he suspected his nanny once visited Madrid. Except Melchor. He's a Spaniard, but he's our Spaniard."

A cold gust whipped over the deck, encouraging Jacob to bury his head into his knees. He just wanted to be left alone. He didn't trust any of this new crew, especially someone who had held a knife to his neck.

"Sorry about this morning." Isaac's voice sounded closer. "I tried not to hurt you. And I wouldn't have liked it if I'd had to kill you."

Jacob crept his eyes over his knees to find Isaac in a crouched position with a friendly expression staring back. He couldn't contain the smirk that blushed at the corner of his mouth. He accepted the cup still offered by Isaac and took a sip.

"Come with me, lad. It's getting cold. I'll introduce you to Bastien. You can bunk with him in the hold. He'll show you what's what."

Jacob peered around the main deck. Sailors huddled into their favourite sleeping nooks. He'd already been threatened with a belaying pin once tonight for curling up where he shouldn't. It wouldn't be long before this particular spot would be claimed by somebody more foreboding than Isaac's offer. He accepted his compatriot's outstretched hand and followed him below.

"Isaac. Why me?" Bastien groaned when introduced to Jacob.

"Captain said to see him set up. He's a good kid."

Bastien was two years older than Jacob. He looked nimble. His official role on board was rigger, but everyone mucked in with whatever was needed.

"I ain't protecting him from Bakari and his mob. He'll have to fend for himself." Isaac just stared at Bastien. "You can set yourself next to that barrel." Bastien pointed to where the hull sloped. "I sleep here. And Henri next to me here."

The deck was dark. A few lanterns swung from the ceiling, lighting eerie corners. Men sat in secretive huddles. As Jacob scanned his surroundings, he caught the eye of a sailor–who held his gaze. He returned his attention back to Bastien.

"You got a blanket?" Bastien asked.

Jacob shook his head.

Bastien glared at Isaac. "Here, have mine. I'll find another one."

"Thanks, Bastien." Isaac said, leaving Jacob to settle in.

"You owe me one, English."

"You still owe me your life," Isaac retorted.

It was a safe recess between the water barrels in the hold. The air was thick and dank, but as quiet a place could be on a ship. He would be less likely to be knifed in the night. Bastien sat–eyeing him suspiciously.

"What's your story then?"

Jacob shrugged. "Just need to get to a safe port. Away from the navy."

"You a deserter then? You craven?"

"No."

"'Spose not. Talk is you strode up to Moise without a care in the world. You joining the crew?"

Jacob eyed Bastien–unsure if he should lie. "Where you going?"

"Home. Well, Tortuga. I suppose it's home for now. Spend our hard-earned coin."

Jacob offered a vacant stare.

"Tortuga? You'll like it. No navy there. You'll be free to do whatever you like."

Jacob lay a hand on the deck. Was better to use the blanket to buffer the damp boards or wrap it over himself to keep out the cold?

"How far's Tortuga?"

Bastien sat next to him. "About five days away. Once we've plundered your ship. You met Henri yet?"

"I don't think so." Jacob felt the floor for any sign of a dry spot.

"He's my brother. Not my real brother. Better. You'll see. Not sure if he'll like you."

Jacob closed his eyes, trying to ignore Bastien's wittering about *Marquise's* day-to-day politics. Most of which meant nothing to him. When Bastien shushed Jacob receded into his own thoughts. Would this Tortuga have a merchant ship heading for England? Five days wasn't so long to stay out of trouble. He dared another look at the men he shared his sleeping quarters with. The anxieties he thought he'd tamed back on *Kestrel* flooded back. At least on *Kestrel* he had Seth.

The last lantern flickered–then was extinguished. The low chatter faded into silence. Jacob's eyes adjusted. There was a faint light creeping through from the deck above. He turned toward the spot where Bastien had made his bed, and was sure there were eyes faintly reflecting back at him in the darkness?

Rebelliousness tickled Jacob's spirit as he helped collect valuable cargo from his ex-gaoler. Le Picard had instructed him and Doyle to follow Isaac onto the island to help strip *Kestrel* of the last items of worth. Isaac had spared the ex-navy men the distress of seeing their dead ex-crewmates by setting them the task of loading the barges with goods already renounced and set upon the beach.

"Distress, is it?" Doyle scoffed. "Ah sure, I'd take it as a pleasure to be up on those decks. There's a few officers I'd gladly see handed over to the devil himself, and no mistake."

Jacob nodded–not wishing to stir Doyle's temper.

"Think that little gobshite o' yours might be one of them?"

Jacob gritted his teeth and fought back his tears. Doyle grinned as he lifted a huge hogshead into the barge. Jacob turned away, hiding his sorrow. He scanned the assortment of furniture, considered useful, opting to fetch the furthest item. The navigator's table. Relatively unscathed from the battle. The drawers looked intact, and all four legs seems sturdy. Within each draw were implements he didn't recognise–or logbooks, half full. In a lower draw he pulled out a small leather-bound book tied with a length of leather cord. He unwrapped the cord. The pages were empty of words, but in the centre–forcing the spine–was tucked a simple quill. Both items looked unassuming, but Jacob found a comfort in their touch. He closed the book, wrapped the cord and stuffed it into the waistband of his breeches.

"Stop feckin' loafin', Pilchard boy," Doyle called from the shore.

Once the work was done, the scavengers abandoned the ship, and returned to the brigantine, leaving the rocks and waves to play their game with *Kestrel*. The island provided fresh water and twenty hogs—more than enough to feed the crew of eighty until they reached Tortuga. Ten were penned on the lower deck; the other ten had been slaughtered and cured.

That evening, *Marquise's* new recruits were rewarded for their hard work. Succulent meat. And rum. Doyle needed no encouragement when Jacob refused his rum rations. Swiping it from his hand and draining it in one. Jacob retreated as Doyle's confidence rose with each glug. He and Harvey did not share Doyle's assuredness. A keen eye could see most of the crew were not as welcoming as their captain. The new recruits expressed their gratitude at being spared the same treatment as their lieutenant. Nevertheless, side glances and sneers were the offered expressions.

The evening before *Marquise* was scheduled to sail, Le Picard thrust a bottle of rum and some bandages into Jacob's hands.

"Go sort your man then. He's your responsibility now, pup. Isaac! Show him the bowels."

Jacob descended into the shadows behind Isaac–past glinting eyes and glistening knives.

"In there, kid," Isaac said, unlocking and opening a heavy wooden door.

The light shaft through the crack in the door illuminated the lieutenant shackled to the hull wall. He sat slumped, facing away in a naked hump on the cold timber floor. Isaac patted Jacob's shoulder. With a creak and a clack, the door closed, leaving Jacob in the dim glow of his lamp. He almost dropped the bottle as the smell soaked over him. Foul, rancid, thick. Even the hogs had been given a light shaft, affording them some fresh air.

He heard the moans first. The silent stirrings of hiding. Small fidget scrapes on the boards. Tiny clinks of metal on metal. Eerie shuffles. He had met only one slave in his life. A young black man called William who worked on Lydia's father's estate. He and Lydia took pity on him–secreting scraps of food from her pantry and leaving them for him in a shared hiding place. Jacob hadn't thought of William since waking up aboard *Kestrel*, but now wondered if Lydia still risked a scolding to help the poor man. These must have been the conditions he endured before life on the estate.

Jacob retched from deep within his throat. Short intakes of breath followed by long gagging. His eyes watered and his nostrils burned with the flavour in the air. He stood, dry heaving, wiping the tears from his cheeks. Jacob raised the lamp while using the bandages to cover his mouth and nostrils. The low light cast over the first rows of dark faces who dared not look up. Even this dim light–too bright for their sensitive eyes. He must have looked like the angel of death as they raised their hands to cover their faces with a clank of their chains.

One man in the front row dared a peek and caught Jacob's gaze. There must have been at least thirty men and women in this small, confined prison. Jacob looked away–ashamed. It was not his place to have opinions on such matters and so lowered his courage with his lamp in the lieutenant's direction. Poor William.

Tending to the lieutenant's wounds, Jacob learned the malicious reason for leaving the shirt on a victim's back. He spent two hours in the dim light, carefully removing fragments of blood-soaked cotton from the open flesh wounds. All the time apologising for the further pain he caused.

Beads of sweat trickled down the lieutenant's body as he shivered feverishly. Between whimpers and intakes of breath, he said nothing magnanimous about his predicament. Blaming everyone but himself.

"If only you hadn't declared you could speak French, boy." He snapped after Jacob extracted a particularly long piece of fabric. "We could have lived for many weeks on that island."

Craywick was reminiscent of an egotistical young lord back in Falmouth. Nathaniel Ashcombe had knocked Jacob from the street as he rode his horse–without a care for a fourteen-year-old boy pushing his barrow laden with pilchards up the high street. A whole day's catch had been toppled to the cobbles and half trampled by the mare. The lord, who was only three years older than Jacob had had the gall to accuse him of bucking his horse. Jacob had escaped punishment by scuttling down a tight side alley–hiding in a tinker's cart. His father had laughed when he found out, but soon after offered a word of warning. *"Keep yer head down when ye come across these nobles. 'Tis easy for them to inconvenience us folk on a whim."*

"It's not an officer's responsibility to place himself in danger." Craywick spat. "That's what you commoners are for. Fodder. The negotiations always happen once the messenger has delivered the intention of a parley."

Jacob extracted the next fragment–with less care.

"I never administered more than ten lashes upon that Irish bastard. Thirty lashes was far too great a punishment for my crime. For there was no crime." He slapped the boards in pain.

The closest slave lurched backwards upon hearing the thwack–causing a wave of clinking. A rancid stench rippled back to Jacob's nose.

"And from a man who transports in such a manner." Craywick gestures to the slaves almost invisible in the darkness. "I bet he has no papers for such a valuable cargo. The admiral would reward handsomely for this knowledge." He turned to face Jacob, pausing his pain. "It doesn't matter now. The captain's setting us free. He sent word an hour ago. He said we can go back to the island."

Jacob continued his reconstruction of a deep hang of flesh creeping up the lieutenant's neck.

Craywick winced. "Did you hear, boy? We'll be free. Tell Doyle and Harvey there's no need to be seduced by the Articles. They're good men, really. No need for them to put their necks in a noose."

Jacob used the last of the bandages and placed the lid back on the bottle.

Craywick shuffled to face the lantern. "There'll be reward enough for a smart boy that helps save the skin of a respected lieutenant. I'll see you for a few coins."

Jacob stood, leaving his ex-lieutenant shivering in the dark. "I'll tell them your thoughts, sir."

The lieutenant snatched the bottle–huddling it tight. Jacob sighed and trudged to the door, leaving the lieutenant alone with the moans of his bunkmates and his own turmoil for company.

The wind had grown in strength as Jacob, Harvey, and Doyle stood on the main deck. Not a hint of hunger or dehydration amongst them. The island had been cleaned and now carpenters picked through the neat piles of wood and rope. Most of the crew were preoccupied with their duties or showed no interest in the new recruits. Isaac stood amongst a small group who had assembled to witness their numbers bolstered and gave Jacob a friendly smile. Grumbles could be heard as the English Navy seamen stood at ease. One in particular vocalised his displeasure–Bakari, the barrel-chested axe wielder. Jacob flashed a surreptitious glance between him and Doyle. He was shorter than the Irishman, but an even weight.

In front of the recruits, from the companionway, Craywick was dragged up to the main deck. Naked. Scowling with outrage. The captain exited his cabin to stand in front of his audience.

"We still have much work to be done before we weigh anchor, so I will keep this brief." He turned to the three English Navy seamen. "Do you wish to join our humble crew aboard *Marquise de Villars*? Or stay loyal to your lieutenant?"

The man radiated authority–proud and captivating in his purple coat. A contrast to the feeble lieutenant at his side.

Before Doyle could answer, the captain continued. "You may stay aboard and continue to Tortuga. There you are free to stay or leave as you see fit. Or you may join your lieutenant on the barge and serve under his governance on his remote island."

Doyle could not hold his tongue. "Ah, I'll stay sir. Keep me in rum and fed on that juicy meat and I will stay wi' pleasure."

"You'll hang when I catch you, Irish." Craywick spat through his lank, blood-stained hair.

Doyle strode towards the small table set up at the foot of the quarterdeck steps–making a show to nudge the lieutenant as he passed.

"Welcome aboard, Mr Doyle," Captain L'Olonnais said with a smile.

Jacob looked at Harvey, but the navigator did not move. Jacob stepped forward and picked up the quill. He signed his name under Doyle's–noting how Doyle had signed his full name and not just placed a mark. He shuffled back, raising his eyebrows at Harvey.

"Swine." Hissed Craywick.

The captain looked up from the parchment. "Very good Mr Penjerrick. Fine handwriting, young man. How about you, Mr Harvey? Will you be joining our modest crew?"

Harvey looked at Jacob, then at the captain and finally Craywick, who pleaded back with desperate eyes. Harvey took a deep breath and stepped forward to the table. Murmurs of acceptance were heard from the gathered crew. The captain clapped his hands together before snatching up the scroll and shaking Harvey's hand.

"Wise choice, Master Harvey. Very Good. God has placed you on this ship and I shall be very glad to accept you. You shall be rewarded handsomely. As shall you all."

To celebrate his three new recruits, Captain L'Olonnais ordered three larboard guns to be fired in salute. Jacob felt a surge of pride standing on the main deck—the crescendo marking his escape from the English navy and a new beginning as a free man. Albeit onto the ship of hardened sea rovers.

"I shall see you all hanged for desertion." Craywick coughed.

Jacob lowered his head and fidgeted with his shirt hem. He looked at Doyle, who had no such shame. He instead glowered at the lieutenant.

The lieutenant didn't know how lucky he was to be leaving *Marquise* with his life. The day after the flogging, while loading rope onto the main deck, Jacob had overheard the captain ordering Le Picard to bring up the prisoner. "Let's see if that sack of entrails floats in the salty sea."

Jacob had caught the captain's eye and, in a moment of amusement, had been asked for his opinion on the lieutenant's fate.

"He's a pig, sir," Jacob had answered.

The captain stroked his goatee. "And?"

"You should abandon him with the hogs on the island?"

"You think he'll survive, Mr Penjerrick."

Jacob shrugged. "I don't know, sir. He's pretty cut up."

"Weak. Only good enough for shark bait."

"It's unlikely he'll survive, sir," Harvey had interjected. "But if his only crime is to be born into privilege, maybe it's more fitting for him to finish his days no better than a hog."

"I should cut the cowardly lieutenant into a thousand pieces and drink his blood as if he were Spanish."

"We shall join willingly until Tortuga, if you spare him." Harvey said, patting a hand on Jacob's shoulder. The captain looked at Le Picard. "And upon hearing your plans," Harvey continued, "maybe serve under you proper."

Thus, Jacob was given a bottle of rum and tasked with tending to the lieutenant's wounds. With that promise still lingering in the air, ex-lieutenant Craywick of *HMS Kestrel* was lowered into a barge. Five buccaneers escorted him to his own private island–with little chance of survival.

"Welcome to the crew." Captain L'Olonnais said to the newest members of *Marquise de Villars*. "I'll make use of you before this journey's through."

Seven

"Captain wants to see you," Isaac said.

Jacob heard the words, but his mind made little sense of them. He'd spent the last two hours, stripped to his waist, knee deep in bilge water. Armed with only a wide faced wooden scraper, he'd filled countless buckets with slimy filth. The latest were lined up on planks traversing the arch of the hull.

Bakari had snatched him from his sleep and marched him to the lowest depth of the ship. Jacob had learned that Bakari was an escaped slave–with no intention of returning to the shackles. Part of a trio that included a Spaniard called Melchor, and a native called Klaude. They appeared to have free rein aboard *Marquise*. Bakari and Melchor were large men and so would throw their weight around. They had not been welcoming to Jacob. Ironically, if not for his association with Doyle, he might have suffered more indignities. If only they knew, they need only ask, and Doyle would willingly offer him up for sport.

After depositing Jacob in the bilge, Bakari had disappeared back up the companionway, presumably to the main deck to operate the chain pump, continuously sucking bilge water.

"What?" Jacob said, stretching his back with his arms wide open. Filthy water and grime dripped from his fingers. The thickness of the stench and the monotonous clanging of the chain pump had made him deaf.

"Captain wants to see you." Isaac pursed his lips, suppressing a smirk.

Jacob pulled himself out of the ooze. Standing on a plank, he palmed globules of scum from his bare legs and forearms. "Why me?"

"Just wants a word. Saw Doyle coming out of his cabin earlier."

Isaac was from Kent. One of the friendlier crew members, offering no grunts or sly remarks, unlike many of the others. Harvey suspected it was the familiarity of speaking his mother tongue–but Jacob thought there was something genuine fostering.

Jacob dropped the scraper into an empty bucket and shuffled to the ladder.

"You'll need to clean yourself." Isaac said.

Jacob ignored the comment, picked up his shirt draped over a damaged chicken crate, and ascended the ladder.

"Cap'n's waitin'" Melchor grunted as Jacob stepped into the officers' quarters. "You stink."

Jacob squeezed past the smallest margin Melchor had allowed him and stood at the captain's door. He knocked and waited, fearing Melchor's breath on his neck.

"Entrer," came the muffled answer.

Jacob eased open the door and tiptoed over the threshold. This was the first time he'd set foot inside a captain's cabin. Captain Tardebigge had never invited him in. Even with urgent messages, he would hand them over to a lieutenant who would take them the final few yards, before showing him the outside of the door.

The cabin sat central to the stern. Seven yards wide and four yards deep. The captain sat facing him at a simple desk under the stern windows. He looked up from his papers, taking a moment to sniff the air.

"Mr Penjerrick. Take a seat."

Jacob brushed past a hammock hanging from the ceiling, taking up most of the larboard depth. He closed the door, ignoring Melchor glowering at him. On the back of the door hung the captain's purple coat. Up close, it looked even more splendid. Each button must have been worth ten times that of Jacob's fishing boat. Above the coat hung a purple tricorn hat with a huge feather bowing from one side. He stopped gawping and nervously pulled the chair back and sat down. He sat upright with his hands on his knees, immediately wishing he had positioned the chair closer to the desk as shafts of sunlight from the high stern windows cut across his vision, making him blink every time the ship rose in the swell. Through the window, Jacob could hear the rhythmic sound of the ocean. He found the motion calming–even now, in the presence of such an imposing captain.

Two great guns secured with breech ropes sat at either side of the desk, flanking the captain. Their muzzles protruding through the port holes with half ports, sealing them into position. The ornate decorative wall panelling continued past the simple temporary bulkheads, suggesting this had once been a much larger, luxurious cabin.

"Isaac said you wanted to see me, sir?" Jacob had spoken in English. He sat with a timid smile, waiting for the captain to respond.

The captain chuckled. "Yes, Mr Penjerrick, I do." He replied in English with a friendly tone. "You have been with us now for over a week and I haven't personally welcomed you to the crew. For this, I hope you forgive me." He held his hand up, symbolising his apology. "The perils of being captain. There is always someone who needs your attention."

Jacob nodded.

The captain shuffled his papers before leaning back in his chair. "How is it you speak French?"

"My Grandmother was teaching me, sir. I'm not very good yet. I'm trying to learn. Bastien and his friend Henri are teaching me."

"Ah, Mr Trivette and Mr Bodine. Fine young men." The captain leaned forward, placing his forefingers together under his chin. "Your Grandmother speaks French? How so?"

"She is French, sir."

"You have French blood in your veins. Marvellous."

Jacob smiled. "She thought it might be useful, sir, in case King Louis made a claim to the throne of England."

"Ha, an intelligent woman."

A knock at the door interrupted the conversation. "Entrer," the captain gave Jacob a playful raised eyebrow.

Le Picard entered and strode over to the captain holding a note. "Tell Master Harvey to hold his course. I will be out shortly."

Le Picard gave Jacob a suspicious glance as he left the cabin.

"It seems your Master Harvey is a very accomplished navigator."

Jacob grunted a response.

"You are not keen on Master Harvey."

Jacob shrugged. "He seems a little looser since leaving *Kestrel*, sir."

"Well, he is certainly proving his worth. He has already saved us from making land in a Spanish port this week. The maps he is creating are the most up to date I have ever seen. They will no doubt be out of date, however, this next year." The captain smirked. "So much change in these waters. It seems our nations cannot sit politically still. Take your English King. Charlie. He has only been on the throne for seven years and has already ended one war with Spain, only to wage war again with the Dutch."

Jacob nodded blankly.

"You do not follow international news?"

"In Falmouth, I only cared about the weather, sir."

"Oh, how I pine for the simple life."

International news took an age to reach Jacob's young ears in Falmouth. When it did, it was little use to him–or he didn't understand the nuances. Since joining *Kestrel*, he had learned they were at war with the Dutch. Why, he didn't know. And he didn't care. Like most Englishmen, it was not the Dutch he hated–it was the Spanish. His whole family hated the Spanish. They hated the Spanish because they killed his grandfather when he was a merchant sailor during the war with Spain in sixteen fifty-nine. Jacob, only seven at the time, didn't understand. As he'd gotten older, he watched his grandmother grow bitter with grief. Many times, he'd witnessed her spit on the ground at the mention of Spain. While not in earshot of his mother, she had given Jacob strict instructions to kill any Spanish soldier he ever crossed. *"Jacob,"* she would say, *"revenge must be served, or your grandfather will not rest peacefully in heaven."*

The captain smiled, raising his arms. "I decided many years ago to be bound by my own decrees. The rest of the world be damned." Jacob watched the captain's arms dance theatrically over his desk. "We must carve out our own path in life. Do you agree?"

Jacob nodded nervously.

"Here in the new world is the perfect place. Do you know why, Mr Penjerrick?"

Jacob shook his head.

"Gold and silver. Mr Penjerrick. Gold and silver. It is everywhere. The kings of Europe know it. They fight their wars in Europe under their banners. Protestants fight Catholics. Catholics fight other Catholics. What do you think funds these wars?" Jacob opened his mouth, but before he could answer, the captain continued. "Gold and silver. The Spanish have known it for a hundred years. They thought they could keep it all to themselves. They draw up their maps, dividing the new world and all its riches. What entitlement does one nation have over another to say who can reap from this world because they have drawn a line on a map?"

The captain took a deep breath and eased back into his chair. "Mr Penjerrick. I asked to talk to you to get to know you a little better. For me, getting to know my crew is of the utmost importance."

Jacob smiled.

"I spoke briefly to Mr Doyle this morning. He's a strange fellow, I feel, but I would guess very useful in a fight. He seems very brave–or foolhardy? I have not yet decided." Jacob nodded with a wry smile of agreement. "I've spoken with Master Harvey on numerous occasions. As I mentioned, he's very skilled. He will be a much-welcomed member of the crew. I am hoping he will be tempted to remain aboard for our next voyage after we have rested at Tortuga."

Jacob sensed it was his turn to speak, but he wasn't sure what the captain wanted to hear.

"When we stumbled upon your island, it was only our intention to take on fresh water for our journey back to Tortuga. Picking up fresh crew was not part of the plan. Imagine our surprise when we rounded the bay to see two ships engaging in battle." The captain feigned a shocked expression and chuckled. "We laid off, obviously. That Dutch man-of-war was too heavily manned for us. We may have had a chance with your frigate. We would have been out gunned and out manned, but I surmised your captain to be no tactician. Was it a surprise attack?"

Jacob shrugged. "We had enough warning to escape. The captain refused to retreat."

"He must have been a fool."

Jacob hoped Captain Tardebigge had died in the battle. It was only what he deserved. His mind flitted to Seth.

The captain smiled. "I hope you didn't have friends among the crew. I think the Dutch made a clean show of killing everyone on board. They left in a hurry, though. Lucky for both of us. Did the others rescue you?"

Jacob swallowed. "No sir. My gun crew were killed, and I found myself in the water. I had no choice but to swim for the shore. The others must have done the same. They found me on the beach."

"I'm very glad you made it out alive. I suspect you'll become a valuable member of our crew." The captain leaned forward. "I would like to explain my actions regarding your Lieutenant Craywick." His eyes narrowed. "The revenge I sort was not for myself, Mr Penjerrick. It was for you."

Jacob blushed and shifted in his seat.

"What I saw standing in front of me on the deck of my ship were four desperate souls asking for help from potentially dangerous men. You did not know our intentions and yet you showed the bravery to approach Mr Vauquelin on the beach. I understood immediately your Mr Craywick had no place in our crew. As the commanding officer, he should have summoned more valour to negotiate a parley. Yet he left such an important undertaking to a fifteen-year-old boy."

Jacob sighed at the reference to him as a mere boy.

"He was lucky to escape with merely a flogging." The captain continued. "In different circumstances, I would have cut out his heart."

Jacob's eyes widened.

"I jest. There's much bluster aboard *Marquise*. All bluster, I assure you. Besides, there would have been no time to teach the retch any lessons. Your passionate pleas convinced me to simply maroon the poor man. Do you feel my actions to be unfair?" The captain leaned back, fingering his goatee.

Jacob sat for a short while, deliberating his response. "He got what he deserved, sir," Jacob said. "If the roles were reversed, he wouldn't have given you or your crew safe passage. He would have welcomed you aboard before shackling your wrists in irons. He would have had you hanged in London and promoted his own career in doing so, sir." Jacob blushed.

The captain laughed, raising his hands in the air before thumping them onto his desk. Jacob flinched, watching papers scatter, littering the floor. The captain looked down at the mess regaining some composer before roaring with laughter once more.

"You are so right, Mr Penjerrick. I have an instinct for these things. He was a man I knew I could not trust. I have no patience for people I cannot trust."

Jacob smiled.

"You are a fine young man, Mr Penjerrick. When Mr Vauquelin informed me of your bravery, I wanted to meet this young cockerel with nerves as strong as a galleon is large."

Jacob felt hot as the morning sun gleamed through the stern windows. The rocking of the boat comforted him and, although the captain commanded an obvious dominance, Jacob felt at ease in his presence. "Thank you, sir."

"You are young, Mr Penjerrick, with many years ahead of you and much to learn. You can command any future you desire in these new lands. Have anything. What is it in this world you desire most?"

Jacob knew what he desired most and before he could control his tongue, the words leaped from his mouth. "To go home. To marry Lydia."

"Ahh. All problems in the world lead back to love. Or money. Although the money is often to buy love." The captain sat for a long moment, smiling at Jacob. "So, who is Lydia?"

Jacob told the captain of the beautiful girl he had left back in Cornwall. The daughter of his mother's landlord, Mr Arundell. He was desperate to get back to her. Back to his life as a young fisherman and one day soon ask her to marry him.

"And will the beautiful Lydia marry you?"

Jacob sat contemplating the answer.

"Do you think her father will let her marry a fisherman?"

"I don't know." Jacob said.

"Every father wants the best for his daughter. Someone with prospects, and money."

Jacob's shoulders slumped.

"And I suppose Lydia would someday want land and fine clothes and expensive jewellery. She deserves it all." The captain rose to his feet, breaking the mournful atmosphere. He out-stretched his arms, as if concluding the final act of a theatrical performance Jacob had heard about in London but never seen.

"My rare lad," he said. "I foresee you are a fellow of right mettle. I fear your days of fishing are over."

Jacob furrowed his brow.

"Your country has abandoned you, as my country abandoned me. We are kindred spirits free to pursue new allegiances. We are master of our own destinies. Do not accept the loss of your Lydia. You could not live with yourself."

Jacob nodded as he listened.

"You will see when we anchor in Tortuga the coin that can be had for a few months at sea. In the bowels of this very ship, not twenty feet below you, are riches that would make your Lydia's heart sing. And we carry only a fraction."

Jacob watched the captain with raw enthusiasm.

"I have a notion to bring to being a fleet to challenge all that has come before in the Caribbean and that ever will come. I need bold men such as yourself and Master Harvey. Our names will be etched into history by the scribes. You see a small crew, but in Tortuga there are many men awaiting our return. You're wasted as a mere swabbie. I see a glorious future for you, if you wish to take it? I see how the men consider you. But they will grow to respect you. If you join, I'll assign you to assisting Master Harvey. And Mr Le Picard will teach you all there is to know. The adventures will be wild, the work will be fierce, but you will be stout and case-hardened by its end, and the rewards will be unmeasurable beyond your wildest fantasies. I can teach you how to be ruthless and feared by men. I will make a fine buccaneer of you. Teach you how to take all you desire from this world. I will make a rich man of your young bones, Mr Penjerrick."

"But, what about fishing?" Jacob asked.

The captain chuckled. "You'll be able to offer your Lydia all the fineries of life. You'll have no more need for fishing. Servants will fetch your fish. This is the moment you will remember when your life changed forever."

"But I enjoy fishing."

"Then fish. Buy the best boats Cornwall has to offer and spend your days with the best nets and lines. If that's what Lydia would want." The captain stepped from behind his desk, raising Jacob to his feet. "From Tortuga, we set out once more. An adventure so great it will be engraved into the history books. When we return, rich men, I promise a ship to take you back to England where you'll rescue your Lydia. You will return a hero with more gold and silver than any man in Cornwall. You shall live like a prince. What do you say to joining my crew proper, under the tutelage of Master Harvey?"

Jacob allowed the captain's words to filter into his mind. "I will not lose Lydia." Jacob said. "She deserves to be rich." Jacob stood listening to the stern wash through the window. "I will join your next adventure, Captain."

The captain raised his arms. "Fantastic, Mr Penjerrick. Fantastic. I knew you were a young man I could trust. I have an instinct for such things." They stood in the moment before the captain wrapped an arm around Jacob's shoulders and walked him to the door. "Now, do you think Master Harvey is a man we can trust?"

Jacob nodded.

"Do you think you can help me convince him to join our next expedition?"

Eight

"So, you're to be my new apprentice?"

Jacob grinned as he loitered by Harvey's navigator's table. "What are these?" He asked, opening a pair of pins that pivoted at their ends.

"Put those down." Harvey barked. "They're dividers. They were set to twenty miles."

Jacob placed them back on the charts and clasped his hands behind his back. "Sorry."

"Step away. I don't need you messing." Harvey puffed the last remnants of tobacco–knocked the bowl into his palm–before pocketing his pipe. "Let's begin with the tiller. I can make use of you over here." Harvey nodded to Klaude.

"Master Harvey, sir," Klaude said before striding off to find a use elsewhere.

Jacob took the tiller head from Harvey, feeling the smoothness of the wood after hours of use. He gripped harder as the tension surprised him. Mr Petigrew's slender frame made the action seem effortless.

"Keep her true. Like this," Harvey said, clasping a calloused hand around Jacob's, bracing it tight. With his other hand, he forced Jacob's elbow to a bend. "Open your stance." They stood for a moment, swaying with the swell. "You feel her?" Harvey released his grip.

Jacob could feel Harvey judging him. He anchored his feet, concentrating on the torque. He glanced at Harvey and nodded.

"Good." Harvey pointed to the horizon. "North, northwest."

Jacob followed Harvey's finger, but seeing no distinguishing features other than the ocean, he concentrated on not moving a muscle. Harvey looked his apprentice over and returned to his table. He opened his sailor's rudder and continued with his notes.

Jacob stood rigid for ten minutes. It felt like an hour as he maintained his focus. Confidence filled him a little, and he risked a glance to find Harvey chuntering, scribbling onto his hand-drawn maps. "Have you spoke to the captain?"

Harvey grunted towards the horizon.

"Did he ask you to join the crew?"

Harvey hunched closer to the maps–furrowing fresh deep marks.

"He asked me," Jacob offered.

Harvey placed a large table weight at the centre of the maps and stood from his table. "And what did you tell him?"

Jacob shrugged. Then remembered the tiller and tensed his body. "You gonna join?"

Harvey pulled out his tobacco pouch and refilled the bowl. He took a step closer to Jacob and corrected his grip. "I think once we reach Tortuga, I'll keep my eyes open for a ship heading back to an English port. Unlike a lot of the crew, I signed up for the navy and wish to re-join it." A large wave threw spray across the foredeck, causing a commotion at the bow.

"What about the coin he's promising? The navy ain't paying much, even when they do get round to handing it out."

"I'm not in a mind to be turning pirate anytime soon."

"Pirate?" Jacob gasped. "I thought they were buccaneers."

"Buccaneers are pirates, lad. Long gone are the days of selling cured meat to passing merchants."

Jacob let go of the tiller and turned to face Harvey.

"Mind your grip, lad. If you're gonna be a helmsman, you'll have to learn to rattle and steer at the same time."

Jacob re-gripped the tiller head and stared at the horizon. "Is it just Spanish he steals from?"

"I don't know, lad. I don't wish to find out."

"You ain't tempted by a little extra coin?"

"Look, lad." Harvey lowered his voice and checked on Moise and Le Picard, who conversed out of earshot. "Coin or no, the captain's only got a mind for himself. He'll tell you what he thinks you want to hear and then sell you short when the time suits."

"You saying there ain't no treasures?"

"There might be treasures, lad, but the Spanish aren't just gonna hand them over. This corner of the world's gripped by the shiny stuff. Everyone imagines they'll be living like kings. The proper kings have it right. We go off searching for riches and, one way or another, it all ends up in their coffers. But mark my words, there'll be too many murdered before we all come to our senses. Once greed's got a grip, it never let's go. Just a bit more and then I'll be happy, you'll say. Just a bit more."

Jacob clenched his jaw.

"Look, lad. If you want my advice. Get yourself back to Cornwall. A content fisherman is better than a dead adventurer."

Jacob's shoulders slumped. Pride would not let him release the tiller, but the task no longer interested him.

"North, northwest." Harvey said, pointing to the compass binnacle in front of them.

For the next hour, Harvey schooled his young student, introducing the feel of the ocean. The subtleties in vibrations through the tiller. Explaining the differences between the waves. Jacob could only see water, but he nodded and smiled. The man might be a grump, but it had to be said he held a great respect for the ocean. And for a fleeting moment, Jacob was sure he witnessed a grin creep into the corner of his teacher's weather-beaten mouth.

"Voile, voile" came the shout.

Jacob cocked his head from the seat of easement at the bow of the ship. He retrieved the swab hanging in the ocean, wiped–and without waiting for his arse to dry–pulled up his breeches and scurried back to Harvey at the tiller.

Squinting through the mid-morning sun, he followed Bastien's voice through the rigging to find Henri in the crow's nest. Some fifty feet higher, Henri–in the nid de pie–as the French called it, was pointing past the bow. Jacob could see nothing unusual.

Le Picard produced his spyglass from an inside jacket pocket and trained it on the horizon. The lieutenant looked in his mid-forties. The scar made the left side of his face look older–as though time had gripped it with a tighter hand–the flesh drawn thin and weathered. His expression permanently twisted into a sneer. No beard grew along that side–leaving the scar exposed.

"What do you see aloft?" La Picard shouted.

Both the lieutenant and Henri spoke in French. Jacob realised he still had much of the language to learn–so listened carefully before translating to Harvey.

"Topsails, on the horizon, straight ahead, to the north." Henri shouted back, "The sea's glare is limiting my vision. Six or seven leagues. Heading East."

"Make sail. All hands to stations." Le Picard shouted to the boatswain, Denis, who turned to the crew with the same order, picking out individuals for specific tasks. "Henri," Le Picard called back. "I'll send up lunettes." He turned to find Jacob staring back at him.

"What you staring at, lad? Take this spyglass aloft and train your young eyes on something useful. Stay with Henri until you're sure what we chase."

"Yes, sir," Jacob said, lowering his gaze. He tucked the spyglass into his belt, tightening the cord. Sad to leave his new role as Harvey's shadow, but with no choice, he swivelled out onto the ratlines.

"Be careful lad," Harvey called. "You only have to fall once."

"Ah, don't be fallin' now, pup," Came Doyle's Irish taunts from the main deck. "We wouldn't want that pretty face o' yours gettin' mangled, now would we?"

Jacob ignored the jibe and concentrated on the rope ladder. Only six months earlier, the equivalent climb terrified him. He was used to the ocean–having worked with his father–but the fishing boats did not require traversing to heights where the wind engulfed a person and magnified the degree of angle so greatly. *"If you don't show willing in the rigging, you'll be a landsman forever."* Seth had encouraged him back on *Kestrel*. *"Like it or not, you're stuck with this life. Best scrape out what you can."* He'd conditioned himself to conduct such climbs–and pure stubbornness had helped him suppress his fear of heights.

Jacob pushed on, one hand over the other, looking only at the ropes and shrouds. Not even ten feet from the gunwale, the captain emerged from his cabin with his own spyglass directing it at the distant ship.

"Lookout, do you see her colours?"

"The distance is too great yet, sir." Henri made a show of pointing to Jacob. "Maybe his young eyes will be keener than mine."

"Very good." The captain followed the ratlines to see Jacob making haste some twenty feet lower. "Mr Penjerrick."

The captain interrupted Jacob's rhythm as he climbed hand over fist–keeping an even pace. He gripped the ropes, trying to hear the captain over the wind. "Yes, sir."

"Be keen with your eye. A true telling will earn a reward."

"Thank you, sir," Jacob answered with a puzzled smile.

"Maybe he'll get a good buggering and be grateful. Won't you pup?"

The captain flashed a glance onto the main deck and then turned his attention to his lieutenant. "Mr Le Picard? We'll make chase. But do not take them for fools. No trickery. The day is long. Keep it simple. Let's see who we're dealing with."

Pierre Le Picard rallied the crew. On hearing the captain's comments, Jacob caught his eye once more. He grinned with a nod–adding more pace to his ascent.

"All hands. Clear the deck." The captain concluded before returning to his cabin.

For the next hour, chests, hammocks, hog–and anything else not needed–were sent down and secured in the hold.

Jacob's young eyes were proving useful. In the two hours in the crow's nest, he had described many details of the ship to Henri.

Jacob had insisted Henri speak French so he could further learn the language. Henri had agreed and conversed patiently. Once Jacob's descriptions had been deduced, their meanings were shouted down to Moise, Le Picard, or the captain who were discussing tactics on the quarterdeck.

"So how you finding life on *Marquise*?" Henri asked during a lull.

"Anything's better than the navy."

Henri nodded and shuffled closer so they could talk over the muffling wind. Henri had tiny black scars peppering his right cheek. His fingernails grubby through hard work. Although smaller than Jacob, he stood tall and strong within his own stature. From the moment Bastien had introduced him, Jacob had liked his easy way. They hadn't spoken much, but unlike most of the buccaneers, Henri didn't treat him like a child.

"More rum and less floggings, I bet?" Henri said.

Jacob nodded. "Is it true you're pirates?"

Henri laughed. "Course we are, mate. What did you think we were doing? Kraken spotting."

"I thought you were buccaneers. Selling hides and meat. I saw the slaves and guessed you weren't totally legal, but figured you'd taken them from a Spanish ship."

"Boucanie? If you like. Corsair if we get an agreeable governor or Forban if not. Sometimes it depends who's wake we cross."

"What about these?" Jacob nodded at the distant ship.

"We'll see. If she's Spanish, then God help them." Henri smiled, showing his biscuit brown teeth.

By mid-morning, *Marquise* had closed the distance. Jacob lowered the lunettes with a grin.

"She has a Dutch flag."

"Are you sure?"

"Yes. Top of the mainmast. Orange, white and blue."

Henri shouted the news to the quarterdeck.

"She's changing course." Jacob said, slapping Henri's shoulder to regain his attention.

Henri glanced away towards the sun–then back to the Dutch vessel. "We've been hidden until now. She's testing us. A ship of force would turn and face us."

"Testing us?" Jacob raised the spyglass, looking for more clues.

"Yeah. If we follow, she'll know we mean to engage."

"But they're Dutch, not Spanish."

"So?"

"I thought you only attacked Spanish."

"No. We definitely attack Spanish. All others. We'll see."

"France isn't at war with the Dutch, is it?"

"It's a merchant ship, mate. She'll be full of valuable goods."

Jacob stared at the Dutch vessel as *Marquise* was ordered to change course. The chase was on.

On the quarterdeck, the captain conversed with Moise, Le Picard, and Harvey. The prey was trying to outlast until the darkness swallowed her. They were closing in, but the hour was getting late, and the sun was fast disappearing. Henri thought the captain had been too cautious, and this outcome was inevitable.

As dusk turned to night and with only a half-moon, Le Picard's spyglass proved near useless. Both *Marquise* and the Dutch ship had extinguished all lights, leaving Jacob and Henri in almost total blackness. Sitting under the stars, Henri educated Jacob in the Dutch ship's options.

"She'll most likely change course now, even a few degrees, and we'll be miles apart by morning. She may strike a hull and just sit in silence as we sail straight past her in the darkness—never knowing how close we came. I'm not sure if they'll risk it with half a moon. Half a chance we stumble on 'em."

"What happens if we lose them?" Jacob asked. "Would we continue to Tortuga?"

"Probably. We've got enough loot. No need chasing one Dutchie around when we could be knee deep in wenches."

As the hours passed, Jacob toiled on his task. Occasionally, he thought he saw sails on the horizon, only to be unsure if it was even the horizon or just the peak of a closer wave. His eyes drooped, and he feared he would fall asleep. He nudged Henri—waking him from his slumber.

"It's your watch," he said.

"Any news?"

"Just black waves under black sky."

The ship's bell had been silenced, and it felt unsettling without the thirty-minute punctuation. Only the sounds of the waves and the creaking of the rigging could be heard. Jacob settled into his corner, but his mind had awoken with the change of position. He sat for a while watching the blackness through the ropes, but the nagging thought of piracy sat foremost in his mind.

"Where have you come from?" He asked Henri.

"How d'you mean?"

"*Marquise*. Where was the latest voyage?"

Whether it was the lateness of the evening, Henri's tiredness, or the isolation—swaying together in the crow's nest—but Henri talked freely for the next hour about their recent escapades.

Marquise de Villars was the flagship of a fleet of eight ships. They'd sacked Maracaibo and Gibraltar, having spent two months in Lake Maracaibo, taking a vast amount of plunder. They'd also taken a large amount of wealth from a Spanish treasure ship. Most of the loot was on *La Cordeliere*, captained by another Frenchman, Michel le Basque. Le Basque was heading to a place called Cow Island to divide the plunder before heading to Jamaica to sell a captured Spanish treasure ship, before rendezvousing in Tortuga.

Marquise was delayed putting to sea, having lost her navigator to fever. Under duress, the governor of Maracaibo had offered up a Spaniard promising to know the waters. He had proved half-witted and sailed astray. Not capturing favourable winds, they'd headed east instead of north. The half-wit had been tossed overboard.

The lack of a qualified navigator had proved favourable for Jacob and his small band of navy castaways—as L'Olonnais had, on the morning of the half-wit's demise prayed for a sign to deliver them to safety. The next day, they'd stumbled on *Kestrel* and Harvey.

Jacob sat, engrossed by the tale. "Why does L'Olonnais trust Le Basque to share the plunder equally?"

"What was that, mate?" Henri shouted over a particularly loud gust of wind.

"I said, why does L'Olonnais trust Le Basque to share the plunder equally?"

"Le Basque wouldn't dare cross L'Olonnais. There's not a man in the Caribbean who would. He knows how to get the most out of a voyage, but he can be vicious. If you see him in one of his moods—you'd best give him a wide berth."

Jacob only caught every other word, so he stood to hear better over the blustery wind. "How did you come to join the captain?"

"Me and Bastien joined the crew last year back in Tortuga. The captain was already famous after he'd escaped certain death." Henri chuckled. "He says he can't be killed."

"Really?"

"He's come close. He was shipwrecked near Campeche. Everyone survived the wreck, but Spanish soldiers attacked, killing everyone except L'Olonnais. He lay wounded but not dead. Do you know what he did to survive?"

Jacob shrugged.

Henri sidestepped, so they rubbed shoulder to shoulder. "He hid amongst the dead. Smeared blood and sand over his face and clothing and lay under his crewmates for seven hours. Can you believe it? Until all the Spanish were gone. Image laying still for seven hours under your dead shipmates while Spaniards stripped you of your possessions. All the time flies and mosquitos crawling over you, feeding on your wounds."

Jacob questioned his own capacity for bravery.

"Nobody believed it when he came back to Tortuga. The famous François L'Olonnais. The man the Spanish could not kill. He'd even rescued one of their slaves. Klaude. Have you seen Klaude?"

Jacob nodded.

"L'Olonnais freed him in Campeche. He repaid the favour by helping him escape back to Tortuga. It didn't take much to convince Klaude to join the crew. You see, Spanish soldiers raped and killed his daughter, and he's been reaping revenge with the captain ever since. If you watch him closely, after he's killed a soldier he curses their bodies. So they can't pass into heaven."

"Really. Do you believe in such things?"

Henri shrugged. "Klaude does. I don't want to be the one to test his beliefs."

Jacob and Henri stood silent for a while, hypnotised by the black waves.

"When the captain stumbled on me and Bastien," Henri continued. "We were living wild in the hills near the fort, having just lost our captain. The fool was found dead owing too much to his lender. We joined L'Olonnais and his promise of riches. He ain't disappointed yet. We ain't returned to Tortuga without our purse overflowing."

"What do you do with all the money?"

"Spend it, brainless." Henri laughed. "With this latest fill, we'll live like princes for weeks."

"Nobody thinks to save any? What about the captain?"

"I dunno. He cares about the loot, but I think it's the fame he craves. He's desperate to be remembered as the famous François L'Olonnais–the man the Spanish cannot kill. His latest byname is The Bane of Spain." Henri chuckled. "So long as he keeps filling my purse, he can call himself what he likes." Henri slapped Jacob's shoulder. "Your watch." Henri retreated to the timber planks of the nest.

Darkness shrouded Jacob and after what felt like the entire night but was only two hours, he twitched awake from a hypnotic trance. He knew every inch of moonlight that danced over the black sea, under the black sky, but now he was sure he could see a distant flickering glow. He focused for a full five minutes. It was definitely getting brighter. He strained to see if Henri was awake. He pressed his face deeper into the darkness. He pressed too far, and his forehead touched Henri's nose.

"Shit."

"Is it my watch?" Henri yawned.

Jacob straightened himself back to the rail.

"Jacob? My watch?"

"Erm? Yeah."

"What's that?" Henri said as he stood.

"I saw that light. Could it be the ship?"

"Go wake Le Picard." Henri said, leaning into the night.

Jacob groaned.

Ten minutes later, Jacob returned with Le Picard. The lieutenant climbed over the rail, leaving no room for Jacob, who clung to the rigging below. The lieutenant stared intently.

"Has there been sight of a light before now?" Le Picard asked.

"No, sir. Jacob's turn on lookout, but there was no sign on my watch,"

Le Picard craned his neck to face Jacob below. Unaware their faces almost touched, Jacob reached his neck to face the lieutenant. "Had you seen any light before, lad?" He whispered directly up Jacob's nose.

Jacob could smell the rum on his breath. He eased back before he spoke. "No, sir. I'm sure of it. Although it's hard to be certain with such a dim moon."

All three studied the light for a full fifteen minutes until Jacob spoke again.

"Doesn't seem right, sir."

"Speak up, lad."

"I've been watching this ship for over a day now, sir, and I swear this is the swiftest we've been catching it?"

Le Picard stayed quiet for a moment, rubbing his scar, eyeing the light. "I think you're right, lad. I think they mean to trick us."

Jacob looked blankly. He then realised the lieutenant could hardly see his face so would not know his confusion. "I don't understand, sir."

"A false fire, lad." Jacob still looked confused, but Le Picard must have pre-empted his lack of tactics and continued to explain. "They have set a small fire in a barrel or boat and hope we follow that light while they make their escape on another course.

"What do we do now, sir?"

"Go wake your Mr Harvey. Tell him to meet me in the officers' quarters. There's a good chance we won't see the fluyt again. Henri, don't let that tub out of your sight."

Jacob inched down the rigging, eager to deliver his findings to his tutor. Maybe the ship had given them the slip–and they could continue to Tortuga, unimpeded?

Nine

Jacob awoke to an overly enthusiastic kick in the arse from Bastien. He scampered to his feet—confused. He'd missed the bell for the forenoon watch. Glancing at the horizon and judging by the mood of the crew—he guessed the Dutch ship was lost. Another lookout had replaced Henri in the crow's nest. Jacob didn't recognise him. Moise accepted his requested to ascend the quarterdeck steps with a friendly flick of the head. Jacob strode to Harvey, who again manned the tiller.

"Did we lose her?"

Harvey grunted with a nod. "We bundled the barrel in after you'd gone to bed. No clues on it about the ship. Captain's given me strict instruction to find her." Harvey pointed north—at nothing in particular. Jacob followed his finger. "Last night I set her last heading by compass. We've set all the sheets she can carry." He moved his finger to the rigging, showing Jacob that both masts were full. "She'll pop up. I bet my pipe. Before the sun strikes its height, she'll be on the horizon. But if I'm right, she'll be windward to us, and it'll be a long chase." Harvey's face was stalwart as usual. "The captain trusts me to steer by my command. If she appears, suppose I'll have to catch her."

Jacob caught a hint of excitement in Harvey's voice. He remained with his tutor, discussing the geography of the Caribbean and learning more about Tortuga. He was enjoying his time with Harvey and felt he might have misjudged the navigator he knew from *Kestrel*. As the information became more complex, he made notes in his newly found notebook. Harvey placed a flat palm on the book-obviously recognising it as one of his own.

"You can keep it, lad. Next time, ask-or at least be more discreet."

Jacob grinned sheepishly.

Within the hour, Harvey became preoccupied by the thought of the chase.

"Nothing more for you here, lad," Harvey said. "Go find Le Picard. He'll give you something more useful to do."

Disheartened, Jacob slumped off in search of the lieutenant.

The cook preferred to work wearing only slacks and a waistcoat. A rotund man, but firm and held his weight proportionately well. He must have been the oldest member of the crew. Hanging at his right hip, tied around his thick waist, sat an open sack. At each tasting, he would remove premixed herbs, sprinkling them mindfully into the broth. His name was Helario and originally from Portugal-but he now called Jamaica home. That was the only information Jacob had gleaned in an hour. The man would talk of nothing but food.

"You stir like this," Helario said, taking the wooden spoon from Jacob. "You hold like this." He offered the spoon back.

Jacob held the spoon as instructed-like he would a quill.

"You stir clockwise." Helario rotated his wrists with an imaginary spoon. "Up and down. Slowly."

Jacob did as instructed.

"Very good, Jovem."

"What's Jovem?" Jacob asked.

The cook laughed. "It means youngster. You are young. Fresh meat."

Jacob sighed—at yet another comment about his age.

The cook chuckled. "You don't want to be young? You want to be old like me?"

Jacob smiled. Despite the monotony, he could not help but enjoy Helario's company. He seemed to find pleasure in the dullest of environments.

"Voile, voile."

The shout from the crow's nest roused all hands, once more, into excitement.

"Dinner will have to wait," Helario said. "Help me move the pot off the flame."

"What's happening?" Jacob asked.

Moise'll call a meeting. We must vote to decide if we attack the ship or leave it be.

"I thought the captain wanted to capture it."

"That may be. But he's got one vote like you and me. Gets no special privileges. Only in battle does he take command. He'll be itching to be back as top dog."

Jacob waited for Helario to tie the pot to the fiddle rail, then skipped over Tomihlo, the terrier, who sat guarding the kitchen. Helario lead Jacob up the steps—just as Moise began.

"As you know," Moise spoke from the quarterdeck. "We've been tracking an unknown vessel for over a day's space."

The crew listened keen eared to their quartermaster. "You lot have a decision to make. Thanks to young Jacob's keen eyes and Henri's patience, it would seem we've stumbled across a merchant fluyt with Dutch colours. She's riding low, but we can only guess her cargo. I'd say logwood or slaves."

Murmurs rose as neighbours exchanged their own thoughts. The captain stood at the bottom of the steps–eyeing the men for any signs of how they might cast their votes.

"We are well equipped to engage and have made sufficient repairs thanks to *Kestrel's* bounty."

Many faces grinned at Jacob or Doyle or Harvey, giving ironic nods of thanks. Jacob grinned back. Doyle and Harvey looked at Jacob, not fully understanding what had been said–as Moise had spoken in French. Jacob had taken every opportunity to embrace the language, and his confidence was growing. He nodded to Harvey. Their code for *'everything was fine, I'll explain later'*. The two non-French speakers returned their attention to Moise, listening to the odd word they might understand.

"Our intent when we left Maracaibo was to head directly to Tortuga, collect our plunder and spend our well-earned coin on rum and women."

Instant cheering erupted at the mention of debauchery. Moise shushed the crew. "This can still be our mission if that's the majority vote. Unfriendly winds and an incompetent navigator have cast us further east than we'd have hoped.

Harvey shot a glance at Jacob upon hearing the familiar word–Navigator. One of a few he'd pick up since joining the crew. Jacob grinned back, mouthing the words. "Not you."

"We are behind the season," Moise continued, "but maybe we've been guided well by the lord. He has delivered us three new able crew, refitted our ship and maybe now he's offering a chance for more spoils. Master Harvey is confident there's no land of note the chase can make before we catch her. My guess is she'll be worth the trouble. The usual shares will be divided with the inclusion of our three new members."

"Captains pup will get a bonus I bet," came a hidden remark.

Jacob retreated behind Helario–who scanned the crowd for the culprit.

Moise pressed on. "So, my brothers, we must vote. Shall we engage and hope for more booty or break off and continue onwards, as planned, to Tortuga?"

The first responder was quick to cast his vote. It was not from Bakari or Melchor, who seemed to be the loudest of the crew–but Lieutenant Le Picard. "I say we leave them be." He said. "As you say, Moise, we're already behind the season. Our hull's already full. We don't need to take more risk. Let's head back to Tortuga and spend our coin."

There were some nods of approval from the crew–as they looked to each other for affirmation.

"What do you say, Mr Touppin?" The captain asked, silencing the murmurs. "You're a sensible fellow."

The boatswain reacted with a start–a little shocked to be asked. Denis was a quiet man who went about his duties diligently. A man happy with nothing more than hot food in his belly and a cup of rum at the end of his watch. He eyed his captain for a long moment. L'Olonnais grinned back at him, nodding subtly.

"Well, captain. I think that we should maybe keep up the chase."

The captain nodded more obviously–encouraging Denis to continue.

"We're pirates and she looks to be a healthy prize."

Bakari reacted quickly, raising his axe and rallying the crew, encouraging hands to be raised. Shouts of "easy pickings" and "pirates' life" and "cowards beware" sprang from their mouths. Before long, a wave of enthusiasm had washed over them.

Jacob noticed Le Picard shake his head–distance himself from the ruckus. Jacob's heart sank. The quick, quiet passage to Tortuga would be violently interrupted by yet another clash of fire at sea.

On hearing the chorus from the men, the captain elevated himself onto the quarterdeck, where he encouraged the rabble. They were his rabble now. With the vote cast, he officiated his role as sole commander during battle.

He faced his crew–standing with his arms raised–pausing a moment before teasing out his orders.

"Right then, you worthless sea dogs. If my ears do not deceive me, I think the vote is clear. We delay our rest at Tortuga by a few days more." He cast his eye to Moise, who retreated one step–signalling the captain had command. A cheer from the crew signified the vote was official. "We've much work to do before we are in possession of that juicy prize. Everyone, make yourselves busy, you know your roles. Mr Touppin, get these soggy rascals ready for engagement."

"Aye, sir." Denis said.

"Mr du Boc, prepare the guns."

"Very good sir," Replied Alphonse, the master gunner.

"Mr Dargate, fetch the muskets, three per topman." Isaac turned and headed to the armoury.

"Master Harvey," the captain spoke in English. "Hunt them down. Get me within hail."

"Sir."

"Mr Orta, get that broth served. These black-hearted devils need food in their bellies before they can scramble to the enemy's deck." The captain paused for dramatic effect. "Oh, and Mr Orta. Ready that potvaliancy."

"Aye sir," Helario called with a wide smile, catching the eye of many of the men.

A second cheer erupted as the crew anticipated their rum punch before battle. The captain turned on his heels and headed back to his cabin with Moise and Le Picard close behind.

Jacob followed Helario down into the galley, still gripping the large wooden spoon used to stir the broth.

"Do you think the merchant will surrender quickly?"

"Who knows, Jovem? Whatever happens, keep your green shoots away from danger."

"Yeah, who's the new navigator gonna bugger if he gets himself killed?"

Jacob looked up to see Bakari pushing to the front of the queue, forming for the potvaliancy.

"Ignore him, lad. You did well yesterday spotting that fire tub." It was Piero, stepping to Jacob's defence. "Bakari's just hoping the captain don't swap his role back to chief scrubber."

"You taken a fancy to the cabin boy, Piero? He's a big lad. You sure you can handle him?" Bakari said, dunking his cup deep into the rum punch being prepared by Helario. He stomped to the companionway, laughing.

"Ignore him." Piero shouted after Bakari. "He's only brave on a ship. Too scared to set foot in a port in case he's recaptured."

"Save that talk for the enemy." Helario interjected. "Pass me your tankard."

"Thank you." Jacob nodded to Piero.

"You just keep your head down when the fighting starts." Piero said, brushing away Jacob's thanks. "Word is you've got to stay alive to save some grisette back in England. You don't want to be wasting your life hanging with the likes of us."

Life at sea was an entirely different experience from Jacob's quiet life in Falmouth. But this coordinated pandemonium very much reminded him of the early morning encounters at the dock when the fishing boats landed. The feral crowds would gather, eager to seize the best of the catch.

The men were fed, and the potvaliancy had lifted their courage. The stove had been extinguished–there would be no more hot food until the battle was won. Helario no longer needed Jacob's services. He stood amongst the organised chaos, seeking Le Picard for his orders.

Standing for a moment on the main deck, it became clear no individual action was an accident. A lively rhythm hummed, yet there was a deliberateness to each man's preparations. They worked meticulously within their team–and each team was an integral component to another.

A sailor called Rolant bowed his fiddle. Not officially the musician–*Marquise* lacked that position–but he felt inclined to raise morale when the occasion arose. There was never a more worthy occasion than the moments before battle. He nodded to the captain as he strode amongst the men, raising a vicious tune across the waves. Isaac heaved the last chest of muskets onto the main deck, shaking a smile at Rolant as he sauntered by.

"Make us a sea song English." Rolant called.

"Aye. Someut with grit." Moise shouted down from the quarterdeck.

Isaac laughed aloud–raising a musket in his fist–encouraging others to follow along.

Gather 'round, me hearties, let me hear you roar,
The cannons, they'll be rumblin', strike their sails once more.
With courage in our steel and a cutlass by our side,
We'll cross the stormy water, with Harvey as our guide.

Harvey embodied the ocean, currents and winds. He'd correctly anticipated where his prey would appear and by crowding the sails–almost to the point of dangerous–*Marquise* was reeling her in. Even at this healthy distance, he was careful not to ride her wake or be eaten out of the wind.

Denis, the boatswain, called orders to stow the hammocks and secure the last of the chests in the hold. The riggers climbed and trimmed the sails to Harvey's instructions, finding the necessary wind as he adjusted course accordingly–aiming to keep the prey leeward.

Heave ho, me lads, raise the sails high,
Into the fray we go, beneath the raging sky.
With a bottle in our hands, remembering our past,
For glory and for treasure, this fight won't be our last.

The gun crews became enlivened as they prepped their guns with grape shot as of the captain's orders. They checked the charges, ensuring they were dry. The axles silently oiled. The handspikes, powder horns, rammers and sponges brought up from the armoury were checked for any stress or damage. Isaac dealt out muskets and pistols as he sang–majority were old matchlocks with some newer flintlocks. Each checked and oiled by their new owners. Cartouche boxes examined. The powder carefully poured onto cloth to ensure moisture had not caused lumps which could clog the barrel. Smoke grenades brought up from the magazine were hoisted to the fighting tops.

Our fighting tops are loaded, let their cannons blast,
For the thrill of the fight, we'll make our stand fast.
The enemy's there yonder, their colours flying bold,
The captain will strike with fury. His heart is never cold.

Melchor sat loading a huge blunderbuss with shot. Jacob lost count after he'd rammed home twelve musket balls. God help the man who found that muzzle facing him.

A continuous hum of stone on steel could be heard as the armourer sharpened cutlasses on the whetstone. Deadeyes tightened, and knots double checked. Marlinspikes were placed in easy reach–ready to repair any broken rigging. A slack rope or misfired pistol could be the difference between success or failure. A blunt cutlass could mean life or death for he who brandished it. This band of cutthroat bandits had become organised and fastidious at hardly any instruction. Each knowing his responsibility with military precision.

Heave ho, me lads, raise the sails high,
Into the fray we go, beneath the raging sky.
With a bottle in our hands, remembering our past,
For glory and for treasure, this fight won't be our last.

On the fighting tops, sharp shooters would fire at the officers and helmsman on the main decks. And at gun ports, clearing them of crew. The intent was to inflict confusion long enough to allow Harvey to come alongside.

"Powder monkey, Mr Penjerrick." Le Picard ordered–with a smirk–upon finding the young man admiring the chaos. "Guns one and two."

"Aye, sir," Jacob replied with slumped shoulders.

"See Denis for some list slippers."

"Aye, sir." Jacob had no intention of finding Denis. He would opt for bare feet. That was one lesson he would be heeding.

> *The powder monkey's ready, with cartridges in tow,*
> *To aid the fiercesome gunners, their eyes all aglow.*
> *With a roar and a volley, we'll send them to the sea,*
> *For the love of the ocean, we'll fight to be free.*

Jacob returned with his first cartridge to find Doyle among the crew of number two gun. He placed his package into the cartridge box, turning his back to Doyle.

"Not in the box, eejit. Not 'til we have three by the gun."

Jacob turned and placed the cartridge next to the gun and retreated to the stairs.

"Best not keep us waiting, gombeen. Don't want your slouching costing us this battle."

Jacob returned with more powder to find the remaining gun crew in a finer mood and less belligerent than Doyle. Even sharing friendly banter with their young monkey.

"Nice peepin' last night, kid," Marin said–the gunner of number two gun. Jacob had seen the gunner on deck but never considered him approachable. From the reactions of the rest of the crew, he was not considered the most intelligent. Today Jacob thought him to be a likeable fellow.

"We wouldn't have this opportunity without your keen eyes, lad," Marin continued.

Doyle removed his arm from the gun's muzzle and stood towering over the other gun crew. Jacob smiled, not waiting for any comment from Doyle.

Being a smaller ship than *Kestrel*, *Marquise* had shorter gangways with fewer steps down into the darkness. This minor victory alone aided Jacob's vivacity.

With less crew, many of the men contributed to multiple tasks. Bastien, being another of the junior members, accompanied Jacob and two other seamen in supplying gunpowder cartridges to the gun deck. He'd boasted he would join Henri as a loader on the fighting tops once the battle began. Jacob wasn't sure what his role would be once they caught the prey. He'd hoped to keep his head down and slip through the entire encounter with little incident, but it was becoming clear there would be no hiding if the fluyt did not surrender quietly.

Marin caught his eye. Seduced by his encouragement, Jacob raised a fist and joined in with the sea song before skipping off to the magazine. Every man would play his part–and he was no exception.

> *Heave ho, me lads, raise the sails so high,*
> *Into the fray we go, beneath the raging sky.*
> *With a bottle in our hands, remembering our past,*
> *For glory and for treasure, this fight won't be our last.*

Ten

Harvey had outmanoeuvred and outfoxed her beautifully. The ocean and the winds had been his tools. *Marquise* lay broadside within half a nautical mile–and drawing closer. Only now, when almost within hail, did Harvey's eyes betray a hint of emotional conflict. There would be no bearing away. He was now but a pawn–no option but to execute his tactics to his best ability.

On the quarterdeck, the captain paced in small circles–a guard dog tied to a gatepost, desperate to taste blood. With each yard gained, he gripped the hilt of his sword tighter, surveying his crew, muttering expletives.

Thirty boarders now stood anchored fast to the deck, swaying to the motion of the waves. They fiddled with cutlasses or pistol locks–willing the prize closer. Le Picard stood as their leader. Each man side eyed his comrade–grinning as if proof of his bravery. His comrade would, in turn, impart his own grin until each man brimmed with overconfidence.

Isaac stood among the boarders, equipped with a loaded pistol and a cutlass. A red scarf tied around each man's arm or waist. It would be all too easy to shoot a comrade in the back once amid the confusion of battle. Jacob would remain with the gun crew but eagerly accepted a sash tying it around his waist, stretching it as wide as possible. In a squint, he had the look of a buccaneer.

The captain gazed at the merchantman, watching his victim inch closer—a fluyt, low in the water and indeed flying a Dutch flag from her mainmast. Gun ports flanked her hull, but no sign of any guns.

The captain stepped forward and raised his arms. The potvaliancy still encouraged the crew as they turned, eyeing their captain. Jacob faced the quarterdeck, relishing the flamboyant exaggerations from the man in charge.

"It's time to show your mettle, you black-hearted rogues." The captain roared. "God rewards the brave."

The crew erupted, waving cutlasses and pistols.

"Within your grasp is plunder a plenty. Our new Master Harvey has delivered it to you on a platter." He half turned, offering a head bow to his new navigator.

The crew cheered once more. Harvey did not stir, fixing his gaze on the enemy vessel.

"This is your time, you devils, to honour your new helmsman's efforts and bring home the bounty. The weather has been kind, and *Marquise* has enslaved the sea. God is truly with us on this glorious day." The captain raised his head to the skies, and the crew whooped and yelled to the heavens.

Jacob was stunned by the show of fire and rage mixed with raw excitement. The crew, previously content and light-hearted about their return to Tortuga, were now brimming with anticipation. The musketeers on the fighting-tops yelped with animalistic vigour. Aiming their blood-thirsty anger at the enemy vessel. A bare-chested Doyle, swab in hand, screamed an incoherent war cry—full of murderous rage—at the ever-closer fluyt.

The captain lowered his tone and his arms to inject an air of majesty into his words. "We are hopeful we find her captain poor-spirited and lukewarm from the chase, willing to give up his bounty freely and with little quarrel." He raised his fists and his voice to deliver impact to his audience. "But, like us, he is of the sea and most likely a stubborn beast. So, we do not expect such a man to offer a fair weathered encounter. We are men of spirit. Always prepared for a fearsome fight. I suspect it will be the job of you murderous cutthroats to convince him to part with his bounty with force rather than cunning." He took a breath and pointed towards their prize. The crew screamed louder across the ocean – truly incited now.

"After this short distraction, we will continue on to Tortuga and spend even more wealth on women and rum." The captain raised his fist again and turned to face the enemy. "We shall be kings once more."

The crew erupted. Rolant once again screeched his bow across the strings, encouraging more ferocity. Jacob faced the ship, looming larger. He felt the knot tighten in his stomach. He could now see figures in the merchant rigging and movement on its decks. It had been his actions the previous evening that had led to this outcome.

Marin slapped his shoulder, screaming indecipherable words into his ear. The slap had stung his arm. Mid rub Marin scooped up Jacob, inciting him to join the contagion. The pair screamed and roared at the ocean, untangling the knot a little in his stomach.

The hysteria grew. Cutlasses thrust forward. Rolant played, dancing between the men. Le Picard growled at the enemy vessel. Success or failure would be measured by their fierceness. Any hesitation would be seized upon by the enemy and the momentum could be lost.

The merchant ship was within one hundred yards. Jacob caught his breath, distracted by Moise climbing the steps to the quarterdeck. He offered the captain the talking trumpet. Marin eased his grip, but left his arm draped over Jacob's shoulder. The rabble shushed.

"Shall we hail them, captain?" Moise called over the waves.

Captain L'Olonnais raised the trumpet to his crowd. "Let's see what they have to say for themselves. Raise the colours. Let's show our intent."

The crew cheered again as Moise retreated down the steps to relay the order to raise the Fleur-de-lis. Although, their enemy must have known they were in for a torrid affair–after such a long and fraught chase–and the noise from their pursuer.

Jacob suppressed his trembling. He stood sweat smeared with Marin. Doyle was the last to quieten calling insults over the gunwale. Jacob had one eye on the captain, the other on the men in the enemy rigging. He hoped they were lookouts and not armed, as his own crewmates were. Every man on board *Marquise* hushed, waiting.

Using the trumpet, the captain hailed across the water. He spoke in French. "Whence came ye?" He waited for the reply. A minute passed with no response, either in words or action. The captain spoke again, this time in English. And waited.

"From Campeche." Came the response in English, barely audible over the crashing waves.

"Where are you bound?" Captain L'Olonnais raised his arms flamboyantly for dramatic effect.

"Amsterdam. Where came ye?"

The captain turned to his crew mischievously before returning his answer. "Out of the sea, you dogs. You face Captain L'Olonnais. Strike amain and we'll spare your lives." The captain lowered his trumpet. "Get ready lads."

Collectively, the crew held their breath. High above, the sharp shooters aimed their muskets. With linstocks held, the gun captains eagerly awaited the moment to lower them to the touchholes.

Jacob caught Doyle's menacing eye, who grinned back with his swab gripped in his fist. "Refuse, ye pigs." Doyle rasped.

A few minutes felt like an eternity as Jacob watched the topmost rigger flaunt with the Prince's flag. Moise and the captain stared through their own spyglasses. The enemy first mate turned and shouted an inaudible instruction down to their main deck, igniting an eruption of movement. Jacob sighed as the Prince's flag did not lower. Instead, the gun ports opened, and two guns rolled through. *Marquise's* crew, upon seeing the act of aggression, exploded into a cacophony of noise and action.

There would be no quiet surrender–*Marquise* would have to fight for its bounty.

On the enemy deck, the opposite crew awoke, screaming insults back across the sea–raising their swords and pikes in defiance.

Marquise's guns were loaded. Every gunner's eye waiting for the signal.

Captain L'Olonnais gave the order to the Master Gunner, Alphonse. "Exercise the guns."

"Tampions out. Guns loose." Alphonse bellowed.

The captains of the guns peeled free the oakum, sealing the vents.

"Run her out" Alphonse called.

The four-man gun crews heaved the already loaded guns through the port and stepped back.

"Prime the guns."

Jacob watched as the captain of number two gun pierced the cartridge with the priming wire. He opened the pan, filled it with powder from his horn and shut it firm.

"Point the gun." Number three gunner took up the hand spike and iron crow, raising the rear of the gun until the gun captain was satisfied.

"Make ready the lint stock." Number four gunner lowered the lint stock four inches from the base ring.

"Fire," shouted the captain of number one gun to Jacob's left as he touched the linstock match to the powder. And a few seconds later, Jacob's left ear caught the torrent of the explosion.

"Fire," shouted the captain of number two gun on the next roll of the ocean. Jacob's world exploded into one of smoke and thunder. The force shook the boards. The gun recoiled back until it reached the tension of the breech rope–causing Jacob to flinch. He steadied himself and caught sight of the enemy ship as the grape shot ripped through the rigging and masts. An enemy rigger fell as the rope he clung to was snatched from his grasp.

"Fire" Number three gun fired to Jacob's right. His ears were muffled by the first explosions. Number two gun was steadied by its crew. Doyle, with his wet swab, quickly mopped out the barrel before reversing the sponge ready with the rammer. The loader took a cartridge from Jacob's pile. Shoved it in the muzzle as far as his arm would allow. The moment his arm exited; Doyle rammed home. The shot next, followed by oakum wadding, and Doyle rammed home again. Jacob was impressed by Doyle's professional approach to his task. Halfway down the steps, Jacob's world erupted once more–sending him on his heels. His stomach tightened as he descended into the dark.

This battle was a different beast than the one Jacob had suffered on *Kestrel*. This was not boxers, toe to toe, exchanging thunderous blows, crippling their opponent's hulls. This was fox and hound. The fluyt proved a wily opponent, often outmanoeuvring *Marquise*. Harvey would not be deterred. The fluyt would twist and *Marquise* would counter. Harvey would show confidence by heaving to just long enough for Alphonse to order a barrage of cannon fire—only for the fluyt to slip out of the firing line. Neither ship had suffered a huge amount of damage.

The only injury was suffered by Piero , the slim landsman. He gingerly made his way down the ratrun, having been struck in the arm by a rare bullet from the fluyt's musketeers. Jacob recognised him. When not on watch, he could be found playing cards with anyone willing to take his bet. He disappeared down the companionway–seeking the barber surgeon, who had commandeered the orlop cockpit as the makeshift hospital.

A strained grunt alerted Jacob on a pass to the magazine. The surgeon clanked the musket ball into the metal trough, having dug it out of Piero's arm. Piero snatched the medicinal rum from the instruments' table and guzzled half the bottle before Dr Venette could pry it from his mouth.

"Out my way, pup." Bakari thumped his way down the steps with no regard for Jacob carrying his latest cartridge. "Get it out." He demanded as he rummaged through the medical equipment for a scalpel before thrusting it into Dr Venette's hand.

Jacob continued up the steps, concerned it might be the doctor soon in need of medical assistance. On his return, he was shocked to see the barrel-chested ex-slave shrug off the doctor and refuse even a bandage for his open wound. After a good glug of rum, he pushed past Jacob yet again to raise his fists in defiance at the enemy.

The battle had found a rhythm. The fluyt had yet again outmanoeuvred her pursuer. Jacob's cartridge stockpile was almost sufficient. Once more into the magazine and he could rest. As he descended the steps, he heard Dr Venette's call.

"Boy. Here, boy. We need you."

Jacob tiptoed towards the operating table. Piero's sweaty hair obscured his face as he wrestled his entire body weight in the shadows. Jacob's eyes adjusted, trying to understand the scene.

"Hold his leg." Dr Venette ordered. Jacob hesitated. "Hold his leg, boy."

Jacob shuffled around the table to where the doctor pointed.

"Just above the knee, pull the skin towards his groin and hold it tight."

Jacob clasped his hands around the left leg, turning his sights on the face attached to the body that he and Piero now wrestled together. He would remember those eyes in his sleep–desperately pleading as they locked with Jacob's. Terrified.

The right leg kicked out, clearly still holding all its strength. Jacob lowered his upper body, using his weight to suppress it. He readjusted his grip on the left leg. The broken tibia protruded through the flesh just below the knee, causing the leg to hang at an awkward angle. Jacob focused his attention on the thigh, pulling the skin towards the groin as instructed.

"You ready, Piero?" Dr Venette asked, picking the amputation knife from the instruments table."

"You sure it needs to come off, doctor?" Piero asked, probably not for the first time.

"Of course, I'm sure. Do I question you when you're loading your musket?"

"This is a man's life."

"A pirate's life."

Piero shook his head. "Sorry my friend." He placed a wooden chock in the victim's mouth. "Bite on this."

"Pomeroy. This is going to hurt." Dr Venette said. "Hold tight lad. He'll want to fight."

Jacob clasped the left leg, forcing his body onto both thighs, lifting his own legs from the ground to add maximum weight. He dared a peek as the doctor drew the hooked machete style blade across the thigh just above the knee–tearing the muscle as much as cutting it. Pomeroy thrashed and screamed. Then became still.

"He's out, Doctor," Piero said, relaxing his grip a little.

Jacob wiped tears from his cheeks that had leaked from him out of sheer exertion. "Is he dead?"

"No, lad," Dr Venette said, "but he'll soon wish he was. Hold tight."

The doctor placed the blood covered amputation knife back on the table and picked up the bone saw. Jacob winced at the thought of the damage this implement could cause–big enough to cut down a small tree. And maybe it's last use, judging by the rust speckles on the blade.

"Hold him tight, lads. He's not going to like this."

Jacob resumed his position, making sure his fingers were clear of the dozens of teeth. He risked looking. The doctor drew the blade from tip to toe. Pomeroy didn't flinch. It didn't seem real–like sawing wine-stained white wood. It took seconds to cut through the thigh bone, but then the doctor continued through the flesh on the underside of the leg. Pomeroy awoke. Catching Jacob off guard. He forced his body down hard, pushing his elbow into Pomeroy's groin.

"Damn you, you bastard. You butcher, I'll kill you." Pomeroy passed out once more.

The lower leg fell unceremoniously to the floor. The doctor threw the bone saw onto the table, fumbling for two pairs of forceps. Blood pooled over the operating table–dripping upon the lost appendage. The doctor pulled arteries from the leg stump and clamped the forceps tight. Jacob turned away as the smell of burnt meat filled the air.

"Don't look, lad." Piero locked his gaze on Jacob. Jacob followed Piero's lead and retreated into his own mind.

"Let go, lad. I need the skin." The doctor placed a hand on Jacob's shoulder, forcing him to stand.

Jacob couldn't help taking a peek as the doctor continued the operation. The doctor dropped his button cautery–used to sear the tissue–into a nearby water bucket. It hissed as it lost its heat. Pulling the thigh skin tight over the leg stump, the doctor stitched the flesh together. The bleeding had stopped, but the pool still cascaded onto the floor.

"Toss it the bucket, lad," Dr Venettes said, nodding to the leg under the table.

Jacob grimaced as he scooped up the broken flesh and bone. It was surprisingly heavy, and he had to pull it to his chest just to support the weight. He dumped it into an empty bucket in the corner. He held his hands as far away as possible–searching for something to rid him of the blood and mucus.

"Use the water." Piero nodded to the bucket with the button cautery protruding over the lip. He was now standing, panting, holding his own injured arm.

"Is it over?" Jacob asked. "Can I go?"

Piero flicked his head to the stairs. "Best get back. You did well, kid."

Jacob let out a huge sigh, relieved the ordeal was over. Guns erupted on the deck above, reminding him of his duties.

Eleven

"Are we ready, Master Harvey?" Captain L'Olonnais asked, stifling his impatience.

Harvey stood, steadfast at the tiller, coaxing *Marquise* closer to the enemy's starboard flank. His prey tamed. "Almost Cap'n. I have a niggle I can't shake."

"What is it, Master Harvey?"

"It's a talented crew, sir."

"Aye."

"Difficult to catch." Harvey glanced at the sails of the fluyt–looking for a clue.

"Aye."

"We clearly out gun her, sir, but I feel she's making it too easy to come alongside. She must have more fight."

"She knows she's beaten. Now is the time to attack." Harvey did not answer. "Master Harvey?"

"Moise? Take the tiller." Harvey retreated to his navigation table, pulling his rudder from his haversack and fingered through his hand scribed maps. Before the captain could join Harvey at his side, the rudder disappeared back into the haversack. Harvey strained his sight to the middle distance.

"Captain. I need men on the lee anchor."

"The lee anchor? We need more speed, not less. What's the problem, Master Harvey?"

"Have you ever sternhauled, captain?"

The captain's brows knitted. "I've never had the need, Master Harvey."

"Well, sir, we have the need now." The captain began his protests, but Harvey cut him short. "Do you trust me, captain?"

"Master Harvey, I have no need to trust any man."

"How badly do you want that ship, sir?"

The captain examined the fluyt, so temptingly close. "She's a fine ship."

"If we stay on her course, we might be beached, sir. Or possibly sunk."

"Sunk. We're in the middle of the ocean. How can we become sunk?"

"Time is not our friend, sir. If you want that ship, you're going to have to trust me?"

The captain glanced at the fluyt and then back to Harvey. "Master Harvey, she is there. We only need take her."

"In a moment she will not be there, sir, and we will be sunk unless we take decisive action."

The captain didn't answer but just stared at the fluyt.

"Sir, no decision is still a decision. I will be forced to change tack."

"Do what you need to do? But if you sink my ship, Master Harvey, I'll make sure you follow her to the bottom."

Harvey eyed his prey, taking a deep breath, before calling out to Denis. "Mr Touppin, I need men on the lee anchor. Range the cable for forty yards. Bring a hawser through the aftermost gunport and send it outside. Make it fast to the anchor ring."

Denis did not move. He just stared at Harvey. "You mean to haul the stern?"

"Aye."

"Why? That's madness."

The captain bustled forward. "No time to explain, Mr Touppin. Just do as Master Harvey bids."

"Yes, sir." Denis turned to the rail and sent orders down to the men.

Harvey scoured the main deck until he found his target. "Denis. Position Bakari and his axe, ready to cut the line. Tell him to wait for my order. And tell the men to hold tight."

Puzzled glances roamed the quarterdeck. Moise found the captain's eye. Both bewildered.

"Master Harvey, you best know your business." The captain said as Harvey retook the tiller from Moise.

Word travelled of Harvey's supplemental request and the crew strapped themselves to anything fixed or heavy. Jacob and his crew, as did every other gun crew on Alphonse's order, closed their gun ports and roped their equipment securely, extinguished the match and hid away the cartridges under tarps.

The fluyt's crew bawled insults to *Marquise*. Harvey's eyes flicked from the riggers manning the merchantman's main sails and then to their captain.

A musket ball whistled past Harvey's ear and lodged itself into the floor of the quarterdeck, breaking the helmsman's concentration.

Harvey glared at the enemy rigging, seeing a lone musketeer training his sights on him. "Will someone shoot that bastard?"

The sun was three-quarters through its arch. He eased the tiller, pressing *Marquise* closer. The two ships raced within forty yards. Harvey fixed his gaze on their captain—a tall, slim man with a full beard and a seaman's linen cap. The captain raised an arm. Harvey grinned with satisfaction.

Crack. From Jacob's crouched position, he witnessed Henri exchanging an empty musket with Bastien for a newly loaded one. Henri had missed. A few seconds later. Crack. Jacob glanced over his shoulder, confirming he had not missed a second time. A foreign musketeer lay unmoving on the fighting top.

"Main sails only." Harvey cried to his riggers. For the last day, they had dutifully obeyed Harvey's every order, and their actions had been rewarded. They dared not disobey him now.

Captain L'Olonnais locked eyes with his new helmsman, took one step forward, then stepped back. *Marquise* began losing ground. Harvey, eagle eyed, his prey as the fluyt tacked leeward–leaving *Marquise* floundering in its wake.

"Release the anchor." Harvey cried. "Let the stopper take the strain."

Those of the crew with no immediate job stood dumb silent. They heard the cable dragging on the orlop deck as the anchor descended into the ocean. Across the main deck, Jacob watched the hawser disappear through the furthest gunport until it snapped tight to the belaying pins. Bakari stepped forward with his axe fixed tight in his hands. Waiting.

"Full sail." Harvey called. "Crowd as much as possible."

The riggers shimmied to unfurl every sail. The headsails were thrown aback first and the rear of the ship began to coast towards the wind. Slow at first and then with every inch of movement, the speed increased.

As the ship leaned at fifteen degrees, the musketeers clung to the fighting tops. Men slipped from their feet. If they could not find purchase from handrails, rope, or rigging, they slid into the gunwales. Jacob clung to the breeching rope with his left hand while his right arm linked with Marin's, who gripped the breeching rope with his fists. Gun number two twisted worryingly closer to Jacob's face. He could feel the residual heat from the muzzle.

The ship lurched to a halt and righted itself with equal force. The crew momentarily slipping and grasping in the opposite direction. Timber and rope screamed under the tension. The ship fell even with a sharp jerk. A moment of calm. The crew composed themselves, checking for injuries.

Jacob unhooked his arm from Marin's and stood looking out to the open ocean. His mind filled with relief. Whatever had happened had resulted in losing the fluyt. He spun around. Other crew members concluded the same.

"She's starboard." Came a call. "She's escaping."

Jacob fixed his gaze starboard to see the fluyt's stern racing into the distance.

Harvey righted himself at the tiller and strode to the stern rail to confirm his suspicions. The captain regained his composure and followed. Harvey pointed into the ocean fifty yards aft. A dark line stretched from north to south, as far as the eye could see. The water beyond looked shallower. Frothy white foam crested along its edge, swirling where the currents met.

"The ridge of barracudas." Harvey said–unveiling the Dutch captain's trap. "All sorts of shallow reefs and turbulent currents."

The captain clasped a hand to Harvey's shoulder as he saw with his own eyes foam frothing the shallow waters *Marquise* had avoided.

"You are a unique man, Master Harvey. How many times have you performed such a manoeuvre?"

"Haul of all." Harvey called as he and the captain returned to the tiller. "First time, sir."

Bakari severed the hawser with a mighty thwack of his axe. From the orlop, the anchor cable slopped into the ocean. The afteryards were swung and, as they filled, *Marquise* began to make way. She was free. The chase continued.

The fluyt had made little headway. Their captain would be surprised to see his adversary still pursuing and not smashed to pieces by the lowly submerged volcanic rock.

Harvey grinned. He sent orders for the sails to be trimmed. He now owned the wind.

Upon their approach, many of *Marquise's* crew gawked over the gunwale to witness the submerged plateau. It lay parallel to them. Between *Marquise* and the plateau, the fluyt was in a desperate battle to avoid the coral reefs that snaked beneath her starboard side, in places, lying only ten feet below the surface. *Marquise* had ridden the fluyt's wake and now steered her towards her own trap.

"Do we have them, Master Harvey?"

Harvey nodded. He could not hide his delight. His irrevocable act of precision seamanship was to lay *Marquise* on a full broadside.

"Grappling hooks over, you rogues, and heave to!" L'Olonnais shouted when the merchantman was within range.

All four irons found a purchase. Three men on each line strained every muscle, hauling the two ships together. They collided with a thump, straining the main wales.

The fluyt's railings stood higher than *Marquise's*, encouraging the crew to stand on the gunwale rail. With no need for orders, the iron's cables were knotted. More rope was summoned and with each wrap, the ships were lashed tighter.

"Right, you butchery devils," Le Picard bellowed, "time to earn those kingly rewards. Over we go."

The boarders screamed murderous war cries as they climbed the gunwales with cutlasses glinting. Le Picard paused only for a moment as he judged the motion of the ships, then leaped to the enemy's main deck.

Jacob's role as a powder monkey was over. He stepped back to the mainmast and breathed in the surroundings. He caught sight of the captain, who stood majestic.

The musketeers in the rigging rained down smoke grenades that exploded between the two tribes on the fluyt's main deck. The boarders now had enough cover to gain their footing in sufficient numbers to attack.

Henri, positioned on the mainmast fighting top, took aim at a lieutenant who was mustering a small group of men. He squeezed the trigger. A second later, the lieutenant lay on the deck, blood seeping from his shoulder into the greedy caulking. Henri smiled, satisfied. The lieutenants' men, now leaderless, but not without courage, stepped towards their enemy.

The first buccaneers over the rails plucked their pistols from their sashes and steadied themselves to face a dozen enemy. Some brandishing muskets and cutlasses of their own, some with long pikes.

The defenders retreated to the main mast and formed a ragged semi-circle. Musket shots fired from *Marquise's* rigging peppered the defenders, packing them tighter towards the mast.

The wounded lieutenant was dragged to the centre for protection and given a pistol. He barked orders to his men. The attackers had the advantage now and were quick to profit. Isaac's boots landed second on the enemy deck, but he was the first to take aim at the men in the huddle.

"Surrender." He ordered. "You do not need to die."

A crew mate to his left fell to a musket ball through the eye socket, causing him to seize on the deck before resigning his soul to God. A second shot hit home into the kneecap of a buccaneer who had ventured beyond the smoke. His leg buckled, and he lay calling out in pain.

Isaac fired his pistol, striking a seaman in the shoulder, sending him back into the defenders. Le Picard followed Isaac with his shot, striking another seaman in the arm. The other buccaneers followed their lead, with a dozen pistols firing in quick succession. Shots finding homes in chests, arms and legs.

Many of the defenders stumbled to the deck, calling out in pain. Those who still had shot aimed their own muskets and pistols at the rabid devils–vengeful for the harassment they had endured over the past two days.

Two buccaneers crumpled in pain as the enemy musketeers rained down shot from the fighting tops.

The remaining boarders roared through the smoke like banshees out of a forest mist. The defenders braced themselves, anchoring their pikes into the deck and raising cutlasses, expecting the imminent wave of attack. The buccaneers met their expectations, clattering into their mass like a tidal wave of metal and men. The pikes and cutlasses tore through flesh and bone, but they did not inflict enough damage to deter the attackers. Cutlasses struck home into skulls and limbs. All thought of compassion lost.

Both sets of musketeers ceased firing into the melee for fear of hitting their own crew. Both turned their attentions to their opposites. Henri received a loaded matchlock from Bastien. He blew on the wick before aiming at a blonde enemy marksman only fifteen yards away. He paused, only for a second to account for the swell of the ocean, allowing him to shoot at his higher positioned counterpart. He squeezed the trigger, turning the blonde hair red.

"Got him," Henri smiled. Under the momentum of the ocean swell, the dead man's musket slid from the fighting top–startling the company of defenders around the main mast below.

The next wave of boarders crashed their heels onto the enemy deck. Bakari, with his blood-stained chest, was among them carry his boarding axe, followed by Melchor carrying the blunderbuss at his hip. With a looping arch, Bakari turned his attention to the cabin door of the officers' quarters. Melchor turned his back on his comrade, offering the blunderbusses gaping mouth as protection.

Jacob watched the terror being unleased only yards away. As the ocean swell raised and lowered, he caught glimpses of skirmishes across the entire enemy deck. The two ships now lashed together creaked in unison. The rope party had done their job. Four of that group, which included Klaude, boarded the fluyt and climbed the quarterdeck steps, advancing on the foreign captain. His personal guard of three rallied, offering protection. They fired a musket volley.

The first buccaneer grunted as he fell forward, obstructing the top step. Klaude leaped over his fallen comrade and charged at the personal guard and the captain, forcing them back against the stern rail. It was three against four, but the Dutch had little time to relinquish their muskets and arm themselves with their blades.

Within minutes, the cabin door cracked and buckled. Bakari's final blows crashed through the two-inch timber. Hooking his axe to the backside of the door, he ripped the hinges from their fixings.

Melchor teased the blunderbuss through the opening. "Do you surrender?"

A pistol shot whistled past his ear, answering his call. Melchor's blunderbuss exploded into life. The power being so great the average man might be blown overboard, but Melchor merely stepped backwards a pace. Bakari tossed a grenade into the darkness and seconds later, it exploded. Smoke coughed out and moans followed, signifying the surrender.

From *Marquise's* quarterdeck Captain L'Olonnais squeezed the rail. He stretched taller on tip toes, bellowing down for volunteers from the gun crews to bolster the attack.

"A l'abordage!" He shouted.

Doyle twitched. Guessing the French command and encouraged by the captain's gesture. He picked up a fallen boarding axe, laughing as he bumped past Jacob.

"You ain't scared are you pup?" He taunted, jumping the foredeck steps two at a time.

Jacob's stomach lurched. A fog clouded his judgement as he watched Doyle leap to the fluyt's foredeck without breaking stride. Sensing all eyes of the crew and his captain upon him, he shuffled to the rack and with trembling hands collected a cutlass. His heart pounded. He stood on the gunwale, his free hand grasping a backstay. He viewed the confusion, another world away. The ringing of steel. The moans. The cries. He breathed the acrid smoke. Pushing off from the gunwale, he jumped the rolling gap to the enemy main deck. His world slowed as he floated down with a crash.

His feet slipped on blood oozing between his toes. Fear gripped him. The grenade smoke wrapped around him, hiding him from the worst of it. He could hear grunts and groans only yards away. What had he done? Why had he jumped? The captain would see his bravery. He stepped forward through the smoke. An enemy sailor fell down the forecastle steps. He scrambled to his feet and fled past Jacob. To Jacob's right, Doyle had become a frantic tornado of ferocity, thumping merchant crew who were stupid enough to attack him.

Through the smoke, Jacob found Isaac's blonde hair. The main buccaneer force was pushing the remaining defenders back towards the opposite gunwale. With his cutlass outstretched flickering a tremble, Jacob inched towards his countryman. From a distant world behind him, he thought he heard his name, but he was almost within touching distance. From out of the melee, a pike escaped the mass of bodies, narrowly missing Le Picard and stopping only an inch short of Jacob. He froze. He had never felt fear so intensely in all his life. The pike retracted, and the fight continued.

"Isaac." Jacob wasn't sure he'd even spoken his compatriot's name aloud. He touched Isaac's shoulder, feeling his sweat sodden shirt.

Isaac spun, almost elbowing Jacob in the neck. "What you doing, kid?"

Jacob thought he might cry. He raised his cutlass, trying to control his shaking. Isaac turned from the imminent victory, gripping Jacob's wrist in one motion. Raw strength mauled Jacob back to the fluyt's tethered gunwale.

"Captain?" Isaac growled over to L'Olonnais.

Jacob snatched his arm free from Isaac's grip but conceded to the open hand of the captain.

"It's not your turn, my brave lad. Maybe next time." L'Olonnais helped Jacob over the gunwale and back onto *Marquise's* quarterdeck, "Good lad. Brave lad. But not today." L'Olonnais gave a hefty pat on Jacob's back. "Get yourself over to the tiller and collect yourself."

Upon being released from his stupor, Jacob allowed Harvey to collect him like a lost lamb. He stood trembling, finding the sober eyes of the remaining gun crews. He could not hold their gaze and lowered his head, thrusting the cutlass to the floor.

"Pick it up, lad," Harvey said. "We'll be out of this life soon enough. Until then, don't show them signs of weakness."

Jacob blushed and heeded the wiser man's words.

"You're a brave lad but a foolish one. There are more battle hardier men that didn't heed the captain's call. Train your peeps and learn where the wise decisions lay."

Jacob found the eye of Marin next to his gun. He could not hold his gaze. He turned instead to the fluyt.

The fluyt's captain still staunchly defended himself along with three of his personal guard. He broke free of the morass of biting, punching, and kicking. He seized the opportunity to scream an order to his remaining musketeers on the fighting tops to aim their latest shot at the marauders surrounding his guard. His musketeers took heed and aimed at the small melee. In an effort to avoid their captain, they shot wide and inflicted no damage.

At the starboard gunwale, Isaac returned in time to help encourage the defeated merchant crew to lower their weapons. They stood panting, exhausted, their pleading eyes locked on their attackers.

A bare-chested Doyle had cleaned the forecastle and now prowled his domain, ready to rain down butchery on anyone who might have second thoughts about surrendering.

The ferocious merchant captain fought on, his linen cap lost, revealing his long ash brown hair as he sliced and kicked. But all too soon, he knew he was beaten. He raised his hands in submission and shouted to the stragglers fighting smaller skirmishes to do the same.

Captain L'Olonnais strolled to the taffrail, elevating his arms. "Victory is ours." He shouted, raising his hat to the heavens, congratulating his courageous crew on a fierce fight.

He offered an ostentatious bow to his opposite captain. The merchant captain found his own cap and raised it in submission. He slumped over in despair. The skirmishes ceased and the crew of *Marquise* cheered. Exhausted. Their cries faded to a ringing silence. They had taken victory, but it had not been easy. The cost would be reckoned, and the spoils divided, but first they must tend to their wounds.

Moise strode past Jacob into the officers' quarters. On his return, with his ledger in hand, he boarded the captured ship to account for every piece of plunder before it slipped away into the crew's pilfering purses.

Jacob retreated down the quarterdeck steps, distancing himself from the bloody sights on the defeated ship. He had survived. But he'd been a fool. Moisture swelled in his cheeks. He clenched his jaw and surreptitiously edged to the larboard rail. His stomach lurched and Helario's stew disappeared over the side. Now food for the oceans fish.

Twelve

"Naked?" Jacob asked.

"Not naked." Henri answered. "But Moise'll demand they give up anything fine and valuable."

Jacob and Henri stood watching the last of the officers of the fluyt disappeared below to be met by Moise, where he would log all their valuable possessions in the plunder book.

"The same will happen with the main crew. They sharn't be seeing their finer garbs again."

"What happens to the clothes?" Jacob asked.

"You looking to get your hands on some new fittings?"

Jacob fidgeted and turned his attention back to the hammocks they'd been ordered to retrieve from the hold.

"The captain's name is Jan Lucas." Bastien said accosting Jacob and Henri as they climbed the steps. "The captain seems to like him. They were bound for Europe with a hull full of logwood. Also hides, tobacco and some sarsparilla. Not much else, though." Bastien tutted at Jacob, snatching the hammock. He unrolled it and restarted the bundling process, before stowing it in the netting. "The ship's called *Stad Gouda*. The captain's happy with it." Bastien continued talking to Henri. "Hoping this Lucas will join us on the next voyage."

Jacob stopped rolling his latest hammock. "This Lucas would join L'Olonnais?"

"Why not? Seems down on his luck. Well, he is now. He'd no sponsorship so funded the voyage himself. He couldn't pay for too many men, so kept the crew light. They only had ten soldiers among them. Mean fighters, though." Bastien laughed. "Isaac and the lads killed one of 'em and another two of the seamen. Venette has two more on his table. I don't give 'em much of a chance. The survivors ain't happy, but they'll get over it."

"But we just attacked them and stole their cargo."

"These are tough waters, Jacob." Henri said. "Besides, the captain has shown them quarter. It could have been worse. We gave them a chance to surrender, and we didn't kill hardly any of them. Besides, what option do they have? Marooned on the next deserted island? If they've any sense, they'll join."

The following morning, Jacob and Harvey bent over Harvey's navigation table. Jacob, extracting what his mentor knew of Tortuga. Their conversation tailed off as they strained to hear the two captains strutting the boards harmonising over their hatred of the Spanish and discussing *Stad Gouda* joining the fleet.

The Dutchman had long hair to the nape of his neck tied in a ponytail–revealing an earring in his left ear. He wore a dusty green thigh length coat in need of some repair. The temporary confiscation of his sword and pistol left him with an unassuming appearance.

"If you hadn't given over your name." Lucas said. "We may have conceded willingly. When my crew heard they faced Captain

L'Olonnais, they proclaimed they would rather fight to the death than risk being tortured."

L'Olonnais turned to find his lieutenant. "Did you hear that Mr Le Picard?" The captain laughed. "My reputation precedes me."

Le Picard doffed his wide-brimmed hat with a blasé air before turning back to the main deck.

"So will you join, Mr Lucas?" L'Olonnais asked, placing a hand on his shoulder.

"If you are so confident you can deliver on that promise you made, I can see no reason why not. I have but one condition. My crew are to determine their own fate. Any not wishing to join can instead continue an honest life once we dock at Tortuga."

"Agreed." The captain spat into his palm and held it forward. Jan Lucas did the same, clasping L'Olonnais' hand–sealing the agreement.

"Although." The captain continued. "Honest is a strong word. I suspect you have more dogs amongst your crew than you'd like to admit. I'll convince two score to join me before the journeys end."

A faction of *Marquise's* crew, captained by Moise, were dispatched to *Stad Gouda* to pilot her to Tortuga. Jan Lucas accompanied them to relay the message he would be joining the fleet. He would welcome any man wishing to join him in his new endeavour. Otherwise, they were free to leave his employ in Tortuga. The crew of *Stad Gouda* had been surprised when the fierce François L'Olonnais had not lived up to his reputation as a butcher and a lunatic. The promise of riches swayed twenty-five of them to join–leaving eighteen of the surviving crew wishing to remain honest.

More than half of the new recruits were English. Almost all ex-navy. They had been abandoned after the first Anglo-Dutch War or had escaped their impressment and been forced into a life

"Very good lad," Andrieszoon said. "I shall keep an eye on you."

"Indeed Michiel. You owe me your allowance of rum."

Michiel Andrieszoon smiled, turning back to his conversation with Le Picard.

Jan released Jacob from his grip. "Well young Jacob, I shall be wary of playing you at ombre any time soon. You have a keen eye and a keen nose that can sniff out a deception at twenty leagues." He held out a hand to his new adversary and shook it firmly. A little too firmly. "Well done, young man."

"Thank you, sir." Jacob blushed. The captain turned back to Harvey, continuing his barrage of compliments.

"How did you know to cast the anchor, you swine?" Jan asked.

Harvey smirked. He unrolled a chart and glided his finger along a freshly redrawn line north-east of their current anchorage. Jan followed his finger and roared with laughter.

"You are indeed a fine navigator. The best I have come across. I dare say there isn't another man this side of the Atlantic who would have known of that plateau."

"You did." Harvey grinned. "You almost had me fooled."

"And how you avoided it. I have never seen the like. What would you call such a manoeuvre?"

Harvey shrugged. "Don't know if it has a name. Sternhauling, maybe?"

Jan and Harvey chatted for many moments, discussing the repercussions of Jan's plan if it had worked. Captain L'Olonnais skipped up the steps and glided over to the tiller. He wrapped a lazy arm around Jacob's shoulder.

"Captain Lucas. Have you met the youngest member of my crew?" Jacob fidgeted at the captain's smothering's.

"I have, captain. I was congratulating him on his part in our capture. One to keep an eye on."

flaunting the edges of legality. For some, joining *Marquise* was the obvious progression, enticing them across the hazy honesty line in pursuit of riches that civil employ did not offer.

The eighteen honest seamen were transported over to *Marquise*, where they were held under guard in the hold. L'Olonnais opined they could not be trusted to roam freely upon either ship for fear of treachery. Many of the men grumbled but for the duration of the voyage they were treated humanely–unlike their clinking neighbours.

Once back aboard *Marquise*, Jan Lucas climbed the quarterdeck steps with his first mate. A cloth sling supported the first mate's injured left arm. Jacob remembered him as the fallen officer who Henri had shot during the battle. He hung back, engaging in conversation with Le Picard while Lucas stalked the quarterdeck. Harvey professed not to see the slim Dutch captain as he edged closer.

"You sir, owe me a ship." Jan said, raising a finger at the shorter man.

Harvey feigned an inordinate amount of interest in his map as the shadow cast a confrontational greyness across the navigation table. Jacob tensed as Harvey had no choice but to raise his head and address the shadow's owner. Jan Lucas scrutinised Harvey's eyes for several rolls of the ocean. Jacob edged closer to Harvey protectively. Jan shot a glance to Jacob, allowing a small smirk to flicker at the corner of his mouth. He winked. His face broke into a wide smile, and he spoke sincerely.

"I jest sir. You owe me nothing. I wish to congratulate you on your skills as a navigator." The captain laughed at his little prank.

Harvey's sober expression turned to one of embarrassment upon hearing the tribute. He muttered something about just doing his job. He patted Jacob's shoulder, releasing him from his duties bodyguard.

"Nonsense, my friend. You are a fine helmsman. You bested fair and square. Where did you learn your trade?"

Harvey shrugged. "The English Navy."

"Your foresight encumbered my every stratagem and handicapped our escape. A neutral would have wagered many doubloons on my evading capture. Your doggedness wore away at my lead, leaving me fewer and fewer options." He held out his hand. "My name is Captain Jan Lucas. At your service."

Harvey accepted Jan Lucas' hand. "It was a close-run thing, sir. I thought you'd given us the slip that first night." He glanced to Jacob. "If it were not for young Jacob here, with his keen eyesight, we may never have espied you again." Harvey turned to present Jacob.

Jacob blushed, shifting his feet, aware he bore the focus of many eyes. He raised his head and rolled back his shoulders, taking in a deep breath. The Dutch captain scrutinised the young man. His puzzled expression betraying his thoughts.

"So, I have you to thank for my encounter with your fine crew. How did it come about that you unveiled our ruse, young pup?"

Jacob looked the captain directly in his eyes. "Your fire was too obvious."

"Ha." Captain Lucas laughed, throwing his head back. "How many times have you witnessed a chase set a false fire?"

"Yours was my first. But the speed we caught the barrel was swift. I'd watched your ship for over a day, and we'd never gain much so quickly."

Captain Lucas turned to his first mate. "Mr Andrieszoon, you hear that? Your false fire was our downfall. Ha. The youth here saw through our ruse like a child's game." Jan wrapped arm around Jacob, presenting him to the first mate.

L'Olonnais, they proclaimed they would rather fight to the death than risk being tortured."

L'Olonnais turned to find his lieutenant. "Did you hear that Mr Le Picard?" The captain laughed. "My reputation precedes me."

Le Picard doffed his wide-brimmed hat with a blasé air before turning back to the main deck.

"So will you join, Mr Lucas?" L'Olonnais asked, placing a hand on his shoulder.

"If you are so confident you can deliver on that promise you made, I can see no reason why not. I have but one condition. My crew are to determine their own fate. Any not wishing to join can instead continue an honest life once we dock at Tortuga."

"Agreed." The captain spat into his palm and held it forward. Jan Lucas did the same, clasping L'Olonnais' hand—sealing the agreement.

"Although." The captain continued. "Honest is a strong word. I suspect you have more dogs amongst your crew than you'd like to admit. I'll convince two score to join me before the journeys end."

A faction of *Marquise's* crew, captained by Moise, were dispatched to *Stad Gouda* to pilot her to Tortuga. Jan Lucas accompanied them to relay the message he would be joining the fleet. He would welcome any man wishing to join him in his new endeavour. Otherwise, they were free to leave his employ in Tortuga. The crew of *Stad Gouda* had been surprised when the fierce François L'Olonnais had not lived up to his reputation as a butcher and a lunatic. The promise of riches swayed twenty-five of them to join—leaving eighteen of the surviving crew wishing to remain honest.

More than half of the new recruits were English. Almost all ex-navy. They had been abandoned after the first Anglo-Dutch War or had escaped their impressment and been forced into a life flaunting the edges of legality. For some, joining *Marquise* was the obvious progression, enticing them across the hazy honesty line in pursuit of riches that civil employ did not offer.

The eighteen honest seamen were transported over to *Marquise*, where they were held under guard in the hold. L'Olonnais opined they could not be trusted to roam freely upon either ship for fear of treachery. Many of the men grumbled but for the duration of the voyage they were treated humanely–unlike their clinking neighbours.

Once back aboard *Marquise*, Jan Lucas climbed the quarterdeck steps with his first mate. A cloth sling supported the first mate's injured left arm. Jacob remembered him as the fallen officer who Henri had shot during the battle. He hung back, engaging in conversation with Le Picard while Lucas stalked the quarterdeck. Harvey professed not to see the slim Dutch captain as he edged closer.

"You sir, owe me a ship." Jan said, raising a finger at the shorter man.

Harvey feigned an inordinate amount of interest in his map as the shadow cast a confrontational greyness across the navigation table. Jacob tensed as Harvey had no choice but to raise his head and address the shadow's owner. Jan Lucas scrutinised Harvey's eyes for several rolls of the ocean. Jacob edged closer to Harvey protectively. Jan shot a glance to Jacob, allowing a small smirk to flicker at the corner of his mouth. He winked. His face broke into a wide smile, and he spoke sincerely.

"I jest sir. You owe me nothing. I wish to congratulate you on your skills as a navigator." The captain laughed at his little prank.

Harvey's sober expression turned to one of embarrassment upon hearing the tribute. He muttered something about just doing his job. He patted Jacob's shoulder, releasing him from his duties as his bodyguard.

"Nonsense, my friend. You are a fine helmsman. You bested me fair and square. Where did you learn your trade?"

Harvey shrugged. "The English Navy."

"Your foresight encumbered my every stratagem and handicapped our escape. A neutral would have wagered many doubloons on my evading capture. Your doggedness wore away at my lead, leaving me fewer and fewer options." He held out his hand. "My name is Captain Jan Lucas. At your service."

Harvey accepted Jan Lucas' hand. "It was a close-run thing, sir. I thought you'd given us the slip that first night." He glanced to Jacob. "If it were not for young Jacob here, with his keen eyesight, we may never have espied you again." Harvey turned to present Jacob.

Jacob blushed, shifting his feet, aware he bore the focus of many eyes. He raised his head and rolled back his shoulders, taking in a deep breath. The Dutch captain scrutinised the young man. His puzzled expression betraying his thoughts.

"So, I have you to thank for my encounter with your fine crew? How did it come about that you unveiled our ruse, young pup?"

Jacob looked the captain directly in his eyes. "Your fire was too obvious."

"Ha." Captain Lucas laughed, throwing his head back. "How many times have you witnessed a chase set a false fire?"

"Yours was my first. But the speed we caught the barrel was too swift. I'd watched your ship for over a day, and we'd never gained so much so quickly."

Captain Lucas turned to his first mate. "Mr Andrieszoon. Did you hear that? Your false fire was our downfall. Ha. The young pup here saw through our ruse like a child's game." Jan wrapped a long arm around Jacob, presenting him to the first mate.

"Very good lad," Andrieszoon said. "I shall keep an eye on you."

"Indeed Michiel. You owe me your allowance of rum."

Michiel Andrieszoon smiled, turning back to his conversation with Le Picard.

Jan released Jacob from his grip. "Well young Jacob, I shall be wary of playing you at ombre any time soon. You have a keen eye and a keen nose that can sniff out a deception at twenty leagues." He held out a hand to his new adversary and shook it firmly. A little too firmly. "Well done, young man."

"Thank you, sir." Jacob blushed. The captain turned back to Harvey, continuing his barrage of compliments.

"How did you know to cast the anchor, you swine?" Jan asked.

Harvey smirked. He unrolled a chart and glided his finger along a freshly redrawn line north-east of their current anchorage. Jan followed his finger and roared with laughter.

"You are indeed a fine navigator. The best I have come across. I dare say there isn't another man this side of the Atlantic who would have known of that plateau."

"You did." Harvey grinned. "You almost had me fooled."

"And how you avoided it. I have never seen the like. What would you call such a manoeuvre?"

Harvey shrugged. "Don't know if it has a name. Sternhauling, maybe?"

Jan and Harvey chatted for many moments, discussing the repercussions of Jan's plan if it had worked. Captain L'Olonnais skipped up the steps and glided over to the tiller. He wrapped a lazy arm around Jacob's shoulder.

"Captain Lucas. Have you met the youngest member of my crew?" Jacob fidgeted at the captain's smothering's.

"I have, captain. I was congratulating him on his part in our capture. One to keep an eye on."

"Indeed." The captain winked at Jacob. "He'll be a fine pirate one day. I sense a natural talent. And I see you've met Master Harvey?" He unwrapped his arm and ruffled Jacob's hair before striding over to Harvey, slapping him on the back. "Have you ever witnessed a manoeuvre such as that before?"

"We were just discussing it. Sternhauling Master Harvey calls it."

"Indeed." The captain shook his head at Harvey. "He is the best navigator in the West Indies. I have no intention of letting him go."

Harvey breathed a deep sigh, lowering his brows over his eyes.

"I suspect you're right." Jan Lucas said. "There might not be a better navigator in the western hemisphere."

Harvey coughed, rolled up his maps, tucking them away in his leather haversack before scuttling back to the tiller. "Very good, Sir."

Captain L'Olonnais chuckled. "Yes, I must not lose such a man."

"Indeed." Jan replied with a smile before sauntering over to his first mate.

The captain strutted to the quarterdeck rail observing the main deck busy with bodies old and new. "I see you are all becoming acquainted. But while you scruffy sea snots get matey, we have rewards to present." The crew paused their chatter and looked to the mischievous captain. "We have Mr Bodine and Mr Penjerrick to thank for their observations in the nest."

Jacob jerked his head from the tiller. All eyes had found him or Henri, who was standing amongst the crowd on the main deck.

"As many of you scoundrels know who've sailed with me for many years, it's my custom to reward the owner of the eyes who spot a prey with a prize from the loot." Some scoffs were heard from the newest members. "Apologies, my new friends." The captain held up his hands. "On this occasion, Mr Bodine outright espied the merchantman. But with the help of young Mr Penjerrick, we were able to track and capture her. As Mr Penjerrick is one of the newest members of the crew and also the youngest, I feel it is only fair he receive an honest share of the prize."

There was a mixture of groans and cheers from the other sailors. Jacob blushed and fiddled with the hem of his shirt.

"For his keen eye, I reward Mr Bodine with a new musket. A flintlock non the less. A much-needed upgrade from our old matchlocks. Hopefully, from now on, Mr Bodine, your aim will be true and more befitting of that keen sight of yours."

A short cheer broke out as the captain raised the flintlock above his head before leaning it against the Quarterdeck rail.

"Young Mr Penjerrick." The captain continued. "When choosing your prize, Mr Le Picard and I had much debate. You are in need of so much garb." Chuckles leaked from the crowd below. "Should we present you with new shoes, or maybe a fresh shirt? A hat or new breeches."

Jacob gave a bashful smile. Since arriving on *Marquise*, he had made do with his navy clothes. His breeches looked shabby and torn and his shirt was in tatters. He was barefoot. And he hadn't worn shoes since the ill-fitting list slippers on *Kestrel*.

"We decided all these, although practical, were not as sagacious as what we finally agreed upon."

Le Picard stepped forward with a wide grin and revealed a cutlass he'd been secreting behind his leg. Jacob noticed, the first mate of *Stad Gouda* Michiel Andrieszoon stiffened at the sight of the sword confiscated the previous day.

"This weapon will stand you well for many years to come." The captain continued. "It's a fine blade that we thought fitting for our youngest member of the crew."

Quick as a cat, the captain raised the cutlass above his head and zig zagged it back to his side, cutting the air playfully. He picked up the musket and grinned at Jacob and then to Henri, gesturing for them to step forward and claim their prizes.

"Well done, Mr Bodine." He said, presenting the musket as he climbed the steps.

"Congratulations, my new brethren." The captain bowed to Jacob, offering him the hilt of the new cutlass. "You are now equipped and a full pirate at arms."

Henri gripped Jacob's free hand, raising it aloft. The crew cheered. Jacob blushed, nodded a thanks to the captain and returned with almost a skip to Harvey at the tiller.

The twenty-five-inch blade shone brightly. It looked newly sharpened. It had a deer antler grip and pommel shaped like a fish with a seashell guard. Jacob held his new weapon in both hands, presenting it to Harvey for inspection. Harvey offered back an ambivalent smile and raised eyebrows.

Jan Lucas bustled Michiel Andrieszoon to the taffrail, distancing themselves from the presentation.

Jacob sheathed the blade back into its scabbard, of dark leather stretched tight over a wooden core, and tied the leather belt around his waist. Once the congratulatory murmurs had settled, the captain recaptured the attention of his flock.

"Very good. We have about seven sleeps before we land in Tortuga. I imagine you'll all be best buddies by then. But now, we have much work to do. Mr Le Picard, can you find roles for the new brethren? Mr Touppin, let's get this ship bound for Tortuga."

Pierre and Denis barked orders to their respective crews, and the deck sprang to life.

"Make sail." The captain continued. "We've got booty to sell, rum to drink and women to harass." The crew, new and old, erupted in unison at the prospect of weeks of debauchery among the taverns and brothels in a town most respectable people would see as the arse end of nowhere.

"Mr Le Picard, send word to Mr Vauquelin. We set sail at twelve of the clock."

"Aye, aye sir."

The captain stood for a time, savouring the moment before turning on his heels. Upon passing Jacob, he stopped and inspected the new cutlass. "You look ferocious, lad–a fine-looking pirate."

Thirteen

Jacob caught his first sight of the plunder that almost three months at sea had yielded. He was among a steady snake of men carrying assorted items from the barges to Monsieur Garnier's warehouse, only yards from the dock at Port de Tortuga. They had waited until dusk to unload. Once inside the warehouse, tarps were used to cover the treasure trove–and guarded heavily.

The slaves were too emaciated to help. They were transported to a different warehouse further around the coast and sold to an out-of-town trader. Jacob hoped they would be treated fairly, but knew they faced a lifetime of backbreaking labour on the sugar plantations becoming prevalent throughout the Caribbean.

Isaac had enlisted Jacob to help him carry a heavy chest and chatted freely about the plunder.

"This is only a fraction." He said. "Le Basque divided the rest at Cow Island. He left our share with the governor." He chuckled. "This made up over a third of our hold. We'd ransomed five hundred head of cattle back in Gibraltar. *Marquise* should have carried one-hundred-and-fifty, but we had to leave seventy behind. And many barrels of water." He shook his head. "Your life might have been very different if our thick heads had given over more room for beef and water."

"How much is there?" Jacob asked as they thumped the chest down with the others.

"It ain't all been sold yet. Moise ain't tallied his ledger, but there must be over two hundred thousand pieces, what with the Spanish dollars as well as gems, silk, silver plate and them slaves."

Jacob's eyes widened at hearing the numbers. "Is this normal?" He asked in awe, pointing at the canvas mounds.

"He's an excellent captain." Isaac continued as they walked back to the barge. "This is pretty big. But it's what we're growing used to."

After unloading the ship, the crew mingled in the warehouse. The mood was turning boisterous as they awaited word of the value of their plunder. Jacob slipped outside. Standing on a wooden gangway to the rear of the warehouse, he surveyed what he could see of the island of Tortuga. From his position, he could see how some might say it resembled a turtle—the island rose to large hills in the centre, which he supposed represented the turtle's shell. The rugged stone fort dominated the western side of the island, overlooking the coast. As *Marquise* had anchored, Harvey had educated him to its name. Fort de Rocher, meaning fort of the rock—which was apt as it stood imposing upon the rocky hills.

Jacob's eyes lowered below the fort's foundations to the bustle of the town. It sprawled from the port, thinning out as it reached the foot of the hills—a combination of larger timber structures and shacks. Some were no better than tents. Timber walkways nearer the port made way to gravel paths and eventually mud tracks the further a traveller ventured out of town. Oil lamps were being lit outside taverns and shops, casting light onto the streets, alive with sea-faring men and traders. Jacob was surprised to see many women going about their business. What that business was, he couldn't tell.

Jacob's collar was tugged. He turned to find Henri beckoning him back inside.

"Jacob. The captain's back from the governor."

The captain was in a foul mood after his meeting with Governor d'Ogeron. He exploded into the warehouse. His usual theatrical manner stirred the crowd with anticipation. His hands raising and falling as he raged Tortuga was not the island it used to be. Lamenting how the governor had grown miserly with his usual generous rewards.

The crew patiently endured the pacing and beard scratching until Moise stepped forward, suppressing the captain. He read aloud the rewards for the sacking of Maracaibo and Gibraltar, along with the raid on the Spanish treasure ship. The costs for the voyage and the rates for the wounded and dead had been deducted. The crew hung on every word.

A great cheer erupted upon the verdict as each man imagined how they would spend their one hundred and twenty pieces of eight. A supplemental cheer followed as each member of *Marquise*–including Doyle, Harvey and young Jacob–were awarded an extra ten pieces of eight for their part in the taking of *Stad Gouda*. Moise explained how logwood was in an abundance, so its price had diminished somewhat. Surprisingly, the sarsparilla had helped bolster the final amount.

When Jacob and Harvey reached the front of the line, the captain was waiting to greet them.

"Here, Master Harvey." He pushed an extra pouch into Harvey's hand. "An extra share for a fine job at the helm. I will be expecting you back manning my tiller when we next raise the anchor."

Harvey mumbled a "thank you, sir," before turning out of the warehouse.

The captain pushed an extra coin into Jacob's hand as he shook it. "There'll be plenty more of this in your future, Mr Penjerrick."

"Thank you, sir," Jacob replied with a skip in his voice.

"You best encourage your friend to continue his teachings ready for our next voyage."

Jacob followed Harvey onto the wooden deck, but hung back when Doyle approached the navigator. His Irish temper had risen upon receiving his scant share–and was in the mind for trouble.

"Only six weeks ago we were stranded on a beach facing what we thought to be certain death." Harvey said. "These buccaneers have welcomed us into their union. They didn't have to share their spoils."

Doyle was glowering back into the warehouse, only half listening.

"The bulk of the plunder came from Maracaibo." Harvey said. "We had no part in that. If you manage this coin well, you might make it stretch until you set sail again. Then you'll have a chance for real riches."

Doyle looked back at Harvey, then down at his fist. "Ah, sure now, ye've the right of it. I'll mind me coin, I will. I'll have this pouch burstin' before long—just need to find a game of liar's dice. Ye're not so stiff-necked as ye pretend, eh?" He thumped off towards the town. Jacob side stepped his huge shoulder as he passed.

Jacob shook his head and walked with Harvey in the same direction. "You coming round to the idea of these riches, then Harvey?"

"Not me, lad. Here." He reached into his second pouch and gave Jacob five pieces of eight.

"What's this for?"

"You got us off that island."

Jacob blushed.

"You're a brave lad. I figure there's a ship in this flea pit going to an English port. I mean, to find it and get myself back to the navy. You with me?"

Jacob answered without hesitation. "I ain't going back to the navy, Harv. You can leave me here if that's your offer." He pushed back Harvey's coins.

"It ain't safe here, lad," Harvey said, refusing the coins. "Keep 'em."

"I ain't saying I wanna stay here. I want to get back home. But the navy ain't goin' to get me any closer. And it ain't going to get me any wealth to take back with me."

Harvey shook his head. "You're a good lad. But not the smartest sometimes. I'll set about looking for a ship. Stay out of trouble."

"Henri and Bastien will look out for me."

"Henri and Bastien will get you and themselves killed."

"Damn it." Jacob gripped the barrel of the musket, compressing his frustration into his fist and forearm.

"You're getting better matey." Henri said. "That one nearly hit."

"Not bad for a fisherman." Bastien chuckled, sitting on a nearby rock, honing his cutlass.

Jacob glared at Bastien.

"Try again." Henri said, taking a sidestep–breaking Jacob's eyeline to Bastien." Just concentrate on your breathing."

For the last two weeks, Henri and Bastien had taken Jacob to the foot of the hills in Tortuga, east of Fort de Rocher. They were teaching him the fundamentals of the musket and the cutlass. Jacob had become quite adept with the wooden training swords made by

Joseph the head carpenter aboard *Marquise*. He hoped today Henri would let him try out his new gifted cutlass. Henri had commented that with his size and strength; he could be quite formidable with a sword. The musket, however, he was finding arduous.

"I ain't got a problem with the breathing." Jacob snapped. "It's the aiming I'm struggling with." He thrust the musket butt into the ground. "This heat ain't helping. The powder's clagging. Now I've got him poking fun at me. Imagine the stress when a platoon of Spaniards are charging at us."

Henri placed a hand on Jacob's shoulder. "Calm down. The powder's fine. Just take your time. The trick is patience. Nothing matters but you and the musket. You're lucky we've now got some flintlocks. You'd be no use with the matchlocks we've had to put up with."

"Probably burn his eyeball before he sparked the pan," Bastien said.

"Can we practise with the swords again?" Jacob pleaded.

"Not yet. For someone with a good eye, you ain't hit the target once today. We don't want a wild shot from you hitting one of us when you're shooting something for real."

Bastien sniggered from his rock.

Henri shot him a look. "Ignore him, Jacob. He ain't much better."

"Hey, I'm as good as you, Hen. Uncle Gefrei used to say I could be one of the best hunters in the new world with some practice."

"Well, practice then. Maybe someone could load for you on the next voyage. You ready Jacob? Steady, breath. Fire."

Jacob breathed out slowly, aimed and squeezed the trigger. Bang. He remained still. "Did I hit it?"

Henri squinted at the target. "I think you did. You just grazed the top left."

"I'm having that."

"It's your best shot today." Henri grinned at Jacob, who responded with a pleading look. "Sword training?"

Jacob shot to his feet. He hitched his musket next to Bastien. "Who's Uncle Gefrei? I thought you weren't related?"

"No, not by blood." Henri said. "We've known each other for fifteen years. Uncle Gefrei found him when he was a nip living in the woods in Hispaniola. His parents had been killed by the Spanish." He spat on the ground.

Jacob sat down near Bastien on the sandy grass.

"The clever kid would catch pigeons and roast them." Henri said, taking a piece of pork out of his knapsack. "We all escaped to Monte Criste. My whole village settled there. I was only six. My father and older brother were killed the year before, and I only had my mother left."

Bastien shuffled to the ground, accepting a piece of pork from Henri. Jacob accepted a portion, and all three sat together in a line, leaning against the rocks.

"The Spanish pushed further west and raided again three months later, killing my mother. Uncle Gefrei got us on a boat along the coast to Bayaha. We lived there for years. Hundreds of us from all over Hispaniola. Uncle Gefrei taught us how to hunt and cook. He taught us how to fight. We thought we were safe, but the Spanish came again. We gave it back double, and they left us alone, but Uncle Gefrei took a shot in the belly. It took him three days to die." Jacob noticed Bastien wiping his eye. "We're all we've got. The village looked out for us, but when we were old enough, we set out for this place. We wanted revenge and there were rumours of riches, so we went looking for a ship. After a couple of desperate voyages with some scuts and yellow dogs, we came across L'Olonnais."

Jacob contemplated the two scrappy orphans. "Do you ever just want a normal life?"

"What's normal?" Bastien scoffed. "Growing patate douce or raising cattle. Not likely. You ain't going to get rich working your hands raw 'til you die."

"My father was a fisherman. Said there was nothing more noble than working the land or the sea."

"Where is he now?"

"Dead."

"Did he leave any money or land behind?"

Jacob didn't answer, just pushed another piece of meat into his mouth.

"I wouldn't mind raising cattle." Henri said. "A little métairie down the coast with Jasmin."

"When did you fancy yourself as a farmer?" Bastien said.

"We can't keep this life up forever. The noose is bound to find our neck sooner or later."

"Hopefully sooner if I find myself with a herd of cows to feed."

"When I've earned enough to free Jasmin, I mean to buy some land around the coast and build a little house."

"Be quiet lubber." Bastien scoffed. "No time for dreaming. We steal from the Spanish. And if they try to stop us, we kill 'em."

"That bit, we agree on." Henri grinned.

"I think my grandmother would have liked you two," Jacob said.

Henri and Bastien stood and readied themselves for sword training. Jacob bounced to his feet to join them.

After an hour of swordplay, the tired trio stood panting and laughing in the evening sun.

Bastien threw his broken wooden sword to the ground. "You'll have to ask Joseph for another one, Jacob. You broke it."

Jacob raised his own sword to the sky victoriously–before slumping with the other two back into the sandy grass.

"Got you a gift." Henri said, handing a knapsack to Jacob.

"Happy name day."

"That was in June. I was born in August. Either way, you're late." Bastien laughed. "We'll have it back then."

"Sixteen, aye?" Henri said.

Jacob opened the knapsack. "Thanks." He pulled out a pair of slacks and looked back at Bastien and Henri. "What's this?"

"New clothes matey." Henri said. "Don't thank us. It's pure selfishness. We can't ramble around with the local mendicant any longer. You're starting to stink."

Jacob smelt his shirt and looked back at his friends for confirmation.

"There's more in the bag." Bastien nodded.

Jacob looked inside and pulled out an off-white shirt, a pair of socks and a pair of latchet shoes. "Where did you get these?" He said, holding the shoes up for inspection. "These are a bit gentlemanly for the likes of us."

"Don't know how they came to be here, but they're strong and solid." Henri said. "Well, try them on then."

Jacob whipped off his grey navy shirt and slacks and pulled on his new gifts.

"They ain't new, but they're a hell of a lot better than that English garb you've been wearing."

Jacob shuffled himself inside his fresh clothes, feeling the newness against his skin. The slacks fell short against his long legs, but he didn't mind. It had been a long time since he had worn clean clothes. He'd noticed Henri and Bastien wearing new fittings but hadn't wanted to comment. He'd only seen one shop selling clothes on Tortuga. Nothing resembling high fashion, but when Jacob had stopped by, he had so little money he couldn't even afford an old waistcoat from the slop's chest. He'd left dejected.

"The new clothes come at a cost." Henri said.

Jacob eyed him suspiciously.

Henri bundled up Jacob's old clothes. "You have to burn these flea ridden rags. You ain't in the navy no more. You're free now matey. Burning these shows you ain't never going back. You're one of us."

Jacob pretended to think it over. "Deal."

"Here, you can have this too," Henri stood, offering him his old coat. "I got myself a new one." Gesturing to a tanned leather coat overlaying a rock. "It's warm." Henri continued. "You'll be grateful for it in a month. It can get cold at night in the jungle."

"Thanks." He said, nestling his arms into the sleeves. The mid brown wool felt tight. It fell to his thigh. A darker, worn leather covered the collar, hem, and cuffs. He twiddled one of the ten buttons that looked to have been recently refitted. The linen lining was in good order. He caressed the seams, noticing the tautness of the stitch even considering its age. It would certainly keep him warm. He admired his new garb, tightened the cord at his waist, then buckled on his leather belt and letting the scabbard hang at his hip.

"What with the new clothes and the cutlass, you look like one of us now, Jacob." Bastien grinned. "Someone might shoot ya for being a filibuster."

Jacob picked up the knapsack and offered it back to Bastien, who raised his hand in acceptance. Before he could grasp the bag, Henri pushed it back to Jacob.

"Keep it. You'll need that too."

Jacob took off the jacket. The last of the summer heat made it too warm to wear. He sat back on the grass, smiling.

"Oh, look here." Henri took back the coat. "It's got a secret pocket inside the real inside pocket. You pull down the flap and there it is, inside the lining."

Jacob checked it out, feigning puzzlement. "It's empty."

"You've just had free clothes. What more do you want?"

Jacob looked at his hands. "A bath."

Fourteen

Henri had gifted Jacob money so he could clean himself ready for his new clothes. The parlour behind the tavern had a tin bath and, for a price, would warm the water. Henri had fed the fire beneath the bath with Jacob's old navy clothes–ceremoniously cleansing him of his old life and baptising him into his new. As the last daylight disappeared between the maze of buildings, Jacob and Henri fell into Bar de L'Entracte, laughing.

Being the furthest tavern a sailor might stumble upon when making his way from the dock, it was a marginally quieter haunt. Like many buildings in Tortuga, its structure was timber built. Henri remarked how it bore no resemblance to its namesake in Paris–where he'd heard famous French writers frequented to find their inspiration.

"You'll fit right in with your quill and parchment." Bastien had mocked.

Unlike the shiny tiled floor in Paris, here a patron walked on bare earth, which had soaked up every spill and bodily expulsion over the years. No amount of hay and sawdust could suppress the pungent tang–slowing every punter who entered, obligating them to hold their breath until brave enough to bite into the rancid air. Regardless of the smell, Henri professed it to be his favoured drinking house due to the cheapness of the ale. They had noted, however, the prices steadily rising.

Tonight was typical; alive with seaman, lowlifes and wenches. Ale, rum and wine flowed–and business giggled upstairs in the bordels.

Harvey and Isaac occupied a quiet corner next to the open fire.

"Nice toggery," Harvey said, using his pipe stem to point at Jacob. "You certainly look like a buccaneer now." He leaned forward, sniffing. "And you don't smell no more neither."

Jacob smiled, opening his coat for inspection. "You might think about a change of clothes too, Harvey."

"I'm fine as I am," Harvey retorted, sitting back in his navy garb. Jacob sat next to him.

Isaac rose to go for a piss while Henri disappeared to find the bar keep.

"I thought I had a good lead yesterday." Harvey said in a huddle. "But it was dead in the water. Most of the ships are here to join the fleet. Haven't found one yet, that's heading to an English port."

Jacob looked up from admiring his new clothes.

"I'll make sure there's room for you, lad. The navy will take you back. They need good lads like you. I'll vouch for you. Not our fault. Any of this."

Pierre Le Picard disturbed them as he slumped down, sloshing his flagon of ale. "Have you seen the captain?" He asked with a slight slur.

"I haven't." Harvey replied, sitting up straight.

"We'll miss the season. We've been here three weeks already, and we were late getting back, what with your frigate and then *Stad Gouda*. The hurricanes'll be in full force."

"He's in Le Canard Rouge." Isaac said, having returned from the outhouse. "Just seen Piero at the privy. Said he's in muster with some new folk."

"You're not so bad," Le Picard said, using Isaac's shoulder to support himself as he rose. "Thanks lad."

"Prick." Isaac said, watching the lieutenant amble past the window back towards town.

Henri pushed a flagon of ale into Jacob's hand, who'd become distracted by the ladies working the room. It hadn't taken him long to discover the business the women had in Tortuga–very differently to those back in Cornwall. Here, they would partake in all sorts for a price. The rates had risen to two pesos for any man wishing to make use of a room on the upper floor with the exotic Anemone. If a man's purse was not so endowed, there was always Daphné who would meet you in the tents out back to massage your ego.

No sooner had *Marquise* and *Stad Gouda* docked the tavern wench whisperers had passed word of L'Olonnais' return. Three weeks earlier, the port simmered with activity following the arrival of the first seven ships of the fleet. Upon seeing the flamboyant captain gliding up the key in his favoured purple coat and purple rimmed feather plumed tricorn hat, the excitement resurfaced. All the ladies had washed and combed and jostled in the windows and doorways, beckoning their favourite punters.

On their first evening, Henri had taken up residence with Jasmin, who resided in Le Canard Rouge. Bastien raised an eyebrow when he told Jacob she was the only one he ever visited. Bastien was not so particular. Bragging about a different woman each evening. Jacob glanced past his tankard at Harvey, side-eyeing the ladies. The prudent navigator had dismissed any accusation of spending an evening with a doxy. But Jacob was sure he'd spied him in the shadows, leaving the back tent behind the Les Gars de la Marine adjusting his breeches.

It had become the hour Jacob usually made his excuses and disappeared to his room at La Petite Tortue, which he shared with Bastien and now Henri, who'd decamped from Jasmin's bed. Tonight, the warmth of the fire had seduced him. His thoughts had wondered too deeply nursing his ale. A peckish kiss on his forehead drew his mind back to the present–and before he could resist, she delicately pressed herself onto his lap. In previous evenings, he'd strategically positioned himself with his back to a wall. Tonight, he'd dropped his guard and sat with his back to the room–in the danger seat. She shuffled a little, making them both comfortable, before releasing Jacob's grip of his tankard. She sipped his ale whilst ruffling his hair. He tried hard not to look at her exposed breasts.

"You're a new one, ain't you lad? Straight from the tit. How old are ya?"

"Sixteen?" He asked. His mind fogged by her beauty. She may have had long brown hair, and she definitely had large, wide, flirtatious eyes. Jacob sat mesmerised. She smiled. Took another sip of his ale. He watched her rouge lips, being careful not to glance any lower.

"It's fine." She whispered. "You can look." She bit her lower lip, giggling–caressing her right breast with her left hand.

"Thank you." Jacob peeked before turning his gaze to his companions, hoping they might ease his tension. No such luck. Henri and Isaac spat out their drinks, sitting back in their chairs chuckling drunkenly from the front row, enjoying the new performance that had found itself at their table. Even Harvey grinned. Jacob gazed stupidly into the eyes of his new friend.

"It's free to look, my sweet." She said. "But I should be careful not to touch. You have to pay for the blossom."

Jacob tentatively placed his hands on the table-being careful not to touch her half naked thigh. Isaac roared with laughter, slapping Henri on the shoulder, almost sending him into the fire. Harvey steadied Henri's fall and couldn't help laughing himself.

"What's the matter, little master? Don't ya find me pleasing?"

Even though she spoke French, Jacob could hear an English accent.

"Yes mam. Very."

"What is it then?" She asked coyly.

"I just ... don't have any coin to spare for ... you know?" Jacob felt his cheeks flush. He could feel the heat in his ears.

"My name's Agnes, my sweet. There's no need to rush. You seem like a fine, honest lad. What's your name?"

"Jacob mam." Agnes smelt like Cornish lavender-a heavy contrast to the tavern air. After months at sea with sweat soiled men, she smelt like heaven.

"Well, Jakey, why don't we sit somewhere quiet, and you can buy me a drink?"

"Erm..." Jacob had so far been frugal with his coin, but he had still spent ten of his sixteen pieces on lodgings, food and drink. He would soon become very short of funds. He hadn't accounted for heading upstairs with doxies. No matter how enticing he found her ... eyes. He searched for the words that wouldn't cause offence, to aid his escape. His brain felt like it was upside down. He'd forgotten how to breathe. Henri composed himself and leaned forward-interrupting the negotiations.

"I think what my young mate here's trying to say, Agnes, is that he's new to our crew and ain't yet built up a kitty to afford such a treat as yourself."

Agnes turned with a snap to face Henri. Her expression melted as she noticed the three pieces of eight in Henri's outstretched palm.

"Maybe you could buy my friend a drink instead. Treat him to some of your delights?" Agnes slid the coins from Henri's palm and turned back to face Jacob with a wide, rogue smile.

"What do'ya say, Jakey? Shall we disappear to the boudoir for a drink?" Agnes shot to her feet–snatching Jacob to his.

"But ... but Lydia." Jacob spluttered. "What about Lydia?" Jacob's eyes pleaded with Henri.

"Jacob, listen. You're three thousand miles away from Lydia. Soon you'll be off on another expedition that'll make you a fortune. After that you can head for home. But what's the point of returning a mere boy? Lydia doesn't want to marry a boy; she wants to marry a man. A man who knows how to treat a lady. She doesn't want someone who fumbles around." He nodded to Agnes. "Let the beautiful Agnes help you."

"Why, thank you Henri." Agnes gave a half curtsy.

Jacob stared at Henri, trying to make sense of his words. Then to Harvey sitting back with his arms folded, offering no judgement either way. Finally, he turned–enticed by Agnes' lavender scent. This was all the pause she needed. She squeezed his hand and gently kissed his lips. He stood with his eyes closed, feeling her touch and tasting her. Before he had a chance to steady his mind, Agnes pulled his arm almost from its socket and hurried him away towards the stairs. Henri, Isaac, and even Harvey roared with laughter at the sight of the desperate boy being dragged up and out of sight to the boudoirs.

"Money well spent." Henri gasped in between fits of laughter. "Poor Jakey. He needs to raise his sail by the way of a woman. We might be away for months, and we need no more pining after his Lydia every night. At the very least, we might get to hear a change of name."

"Poor lad's homesick." Harvey replied, being the first to compose himself.

"Well, if anyone can make a man forget 'bout home, it's Agnes."

Twenty minutes later, Jacob returned to the fireplace–suppressing an enormous grin. Harvey was absent, but Isaac and Henri sat chatting with Bastien, who had joined them fresh from Le Canard Rouge. The conversation melted away with the arrival of the newest member of the manhood gang.

"So, Jakey?" Henri laughed. "How's Agnes? Did you get my three pieces worth? You seem less tense."

Jacob grinned, easing his shoulders back into the chair. He gulped ale from his refilled tankard, smiling at the red rim stain left by Agnes. A memory to when he was a mere boy. "She said to say thank you. And to say she has some change."

Henri chuckled. "Did she now? Well, I'll be sure to collect that before we leave the island." He checked his tone. "Not a word to Jasmin."

Jacob smiled, shrugging off the adulterous feelings his friend felt towards a prostitute who–at this very moment, was probably arousing the member of another crew.

"Where's Harvey?" Jacob asked, changing the subject.

"He didn't say. Just sloped off, saying something about trying to find someone. He's a bit solitary, your friend. One of the best navigators any of us have ever seen, but very strange." Henri took a sip of ale. "Anyway, Bastien was telling a tale. Carry on mate."

Jacob leaned back, folding his arms, and huffed as Bastien stole the limelight.

"It ain't a tale. I saw them. Over in the Le Canard Rouge Me, Doyle, Piero, and Marin were chatting with this Dutch fellow called Montbars. Daniel, I think he said."

Jacob half listened for a while, but his thoughts still lingered in the bedroom. He wished his body was still there–wrapped in her arms. Relaxed at her chest. He sighed. He sat up as Agnes glided down the stairs and caught his eye. She flashed him a smile before disappearing to the far side of the room and out of sight. Jacob sipped his ale, hoping to glimpse her again, but she didn't return his way. He sat for a while with his memory and a stupid smile.

Bastien was still chattering about some fellow from Brazil, but Jacob had lost the thread and couldn't keep up. The warmth of the fire wrapped itself into his new coat–nuzzling his sleepy mind back to his beloved Cornwall. He had plotted many routes home, but all seemed to be dead ends. He would not give himself back to slavery in the navy. A merchant ship back to England seemed the most logical, but they were proving scarce. And he wouldn't return home any richer. But to follow L'Olonnais would take a dangerous path. And in the wrong direction. But he couldn't deny his time on *Marquise* wasn't exhilarating.

Was there a safe option? Life in the Caribbean was proving dangerous. He'd endured two sea battles and been lucky to escape with his life on both occasions. The risks back in England might be no less. The plague had returned, creeping through the country–and the threat of starvation was always present. Only last year he heard his mother whispering of the return of the pirate moors, snatching fishermen off the coast of Looe, to be enslaved in Africa. Not long before he'd been pressed, he'd had heard of a fire in London. Death never felt far away. Was his only option merely to survive? Maybe the navy *was* the best he could hope for?

Agnes had shown him there was more to life-one he couldn't find serving in the navy. A night like tonight, but with Lydia. A life that would not require three pieces of eight. He could have this night, every night. For free.

"You ain't seen all them in that one room. How many mad dogs you had?" Henri scoffed.

Jacob sat up straight and grinned at the table. He sipped his ale, realising his tankard was empty.

"I'm telling ya. It's happening." Bastien protested. "The big one. We'll all be rich."

The four messmates sat for a while listening to the crackle of the fire-three of them turning over the curls of the night's news, while Jacob sat oblivious to Bastien's tale.

"Well, I say there's nothing we can sway sitting here with half empty mugs." Bastien stood, palms on the table. "Let's ditch the ale. Do you think they have any hangman's left in this flea pit?" Isaac and Henri raised their hands in protest.

"No, no, no thanks." Isaac protested the loudest. "I'll stick with the ale."

"Yep, me too." Henri said. "I've a view to remember my time with Agnes later. I don't want to wake up next to Fat Marion with my purse lifted."

Bastien grinned at Jacob. "Jake will stay on the ale, too. It's his birthday into manhood. Let him remember it and not wake up in the morning wondering if it was all a dream."

Bastien stood with a playful dejection, raising his arms like a scolded child. "I suppose I'll get in an overpriced flagon then." He skipped off in the direction of the bar keep. Isaac and Henri watched him leave, shaking their heads.

"Do'ya think it's happening?" Isaac asked.

"I suppose we'll know soon enough." Henri turned his attention to Jacob with a wide smile. "So, Jakey." Henri chortled. "How was Agnes?"

For the next hour, Jacob sweated under the inquisition of his messmates–until he had given up all his secrets of his twenty minutes with the prettiest women this side of the Atlantic. When he'd finished, and the flagon empty, the four drunken comrades purchased a jar of wine to take back to La Petite Tortue.

"It's coming." Bastien said, almost falling through the tavern door. "I tell ya. The big one's coming."

Fifteen

Jacob stood in awe–and a little overwhelmed–by the enthusiasm sparked with very little effort. The captain had returned with a great reputation and now stood upon a rock protruding a little further and a little higher than its surroundings. It elevated him like Jesus delivering his sermon on the mount. The bright buttons on his purple coat shone in the midday sun, making him look majestic. Every soul who had made the journey to the cove whooped and cheered for the captain's proclamations. He could propose certain death and dishonour, and these buccaneers would still staunchly follow.

If the captain was to be believed, every man would be rich beyond their wildest dreams–able to retire in luxury anywhere in the Caribbean. It was difficult to not be swept along with the showmanship. He gave no details but spoke of attacking the Spanish main. Contagious greed embodied each man as they imagined how they would spend their riches.

"He won't tell us where he intends to attack yet," Isaac said, standing with Jacob, Henri, and Bastien. "There's too many spies among us."

"Spaniards?" Jacob said.

"Maybe. But there's spies in all nations, selling information for a price. Just 'cus you know where a man's from doesn't mean shit out here. National loyalty disappears as soon as you've suffered genuine hunger and desperation—there's no trust beyond the line."

Jacob scoured the crowd. "You mean all these men will blindly follow, not knowing where the captain will strike?"

"They'll follow, but they won't sign up proper 'til they know more. When we're closer and preparations made every man still has a choice to turn away. Some will. Folk are funny. We all have our reasons to do something, or not to do it."

Amongst the crowd, four captains represented some six hundred men. At least four hundred had pulled themselves from the alehouses and brothels and trudged the two miles to listen to the captain's promises. They would meet up with at least the same number in the coming weeks. Messengers had been sent to Port Royal, Petite Goave and St. Dominique—rousing all sea rovers to join a brethren unmatched so far in the Caribbean.

The congregation imagined the locations twelve hundred men could attack. Some sizeable towns or cities were bandied about. Some of the more educated men calculated the haul would have to be huge to feed such a party. They soon began speculating on potential targets. Campeche, Vera Cruz, Cartagena, Panama were all feasible, but even twelve hundred would surely struggle to raid these heavily fortified strongholds. "El Dorado." Someone shouted—followed by a tremendous roar of laughter from the crowd.

The crew of *Stad Gouda* mingled with *Marquise*. Jacob caught sight of *Stad Gouda's* first mate, Michiel Andrieszoon, eyeing his hip. The gifted cutlass from L'Olonnais must have belonged to him. The Dutchman no longer wore his sling. Jacob noticed he had a new blade at his side. It was not as ornate as the one Jacob now possessed. Jacob wrapped his coat around the hilt—feigning a search of the crowd. He found Doyle behind Jan Lucas, infected by the captain's words, whooping louder than anyone. Since making land in Tortuga, Jacob had seen little of Doyle. He had taken his measly amount of coin and disappeared. The Irishman had not a care in the world, finding kinship with his new comrades–even if most were English, the usual foes of his people.

Jacob turned his attention back to the captain as he finished with a flourish. The consensus was overwhelming. The infection had spread–every buccaneer would follow.

Jacob explored the dispersing crowd for any sign of Harvey. They'd not arranged to meet at the gathering, but it was surprising he'd not turned up–if only to keep up his pretence. When the meeting was announced, Harvey sought out Jacob, laying out his plan to get them back to the navy.

"Might be we have to hide in the hills until the fleet's departed." He'd said. "More likely to find passage with the merchants once the port's quieter."

He'd concluded he couldn't slip away unnoticed, now he was L'Olonnais' favoured navigator. It had been made clear the odds of success of this next voyage would be greatly improved with him at the helm.

"He hasn't given me up, I'll bet. I've heard of men taken into the life and held against their will. Sometimes, their families are held hostage to keep them from escaping."

Jacob had almost given up his search when he spied Harvey with his back to the crowd, standing only yards away from the captain and Moise. He was certainly keeping up the pretence. Had he abandoned his plan and been drawn in by the captain's captivating speech?

Into the early evening, many senior men huddled in smaller meetings until eventually the cove became quite tired of talking business. Preparations were made for rum and wine to be brought from the town. Multiple buccans were set up like beacons along the beach, slowly curing fish and strips of wild boar. Old friends and new sat talking and jesting around fires. Crewmates reunited and sat reminiscing about raids gone by.

Jacob sat with Henri and Bastien close to the crew of *Marquise*.

"That's Michel le Basque." Bastien said, nodding to the far side of the camp. L'Olonnais raised a cup to his compatriot, saluting their achievements in Maracaibo. "He don't seem very warm to the captain."

"Bit odd." Henri said. "They were as thick as thieves during the voyage."

Jacob remembered Henri's mention of the captain trusting Le Basque with the bulk of the plunder.

"That's that Montbars." Bastien said, pointing out a scruffy looking fellow speaking with Jan. "Told ya I'd seen them all in La Canard. "He's that one that claims to be a captain, thinks he's a gentleman, even though he ain't got a ship. Out for revenge for the killing of his uncle."

"That's the guy who says he's killed a hundred Spaniard and gives away most the loot?"

"That's him."

Henri looked past the so-called captain to his small crew. "They don't look like they could take a galleon." Henri laughed. "There's du Puis. I told you he'd be back."

Bastien pursed his lips. "That surprises me. I thought he'd be long gone once he got his own ship."

Henri turned to Jacob to explain. "Anthony du Puis was our first lieutenant. When the captain captured *Marquise*, he gave his ship *Tigre* to du Puis as reward. Bastien was sure he'd be off. He didn't like some of the captain's tactic."

"Phillipe Bequel." Bastien said, slapping Henri to gain his attention. "Over there with Moise. Told ya I'd seen them in the back room. All secret like."

"Who's Bequel?" Jacob asked.

"I told you the other night. You need to wax out your ears."

"He weren't listening the other night." Henri chuckled. "Too busy dreaming about Agnes's tits. How do you know that's Bequel? You ain't never seen him."

"I have. We saw him when we first crossed the strait. Before we signed on with that Russian, Razin."

Henri stroked his chin, thinking.

"And Piero told me," Bastien added. "He'd served under him a few years back."

Bastien turned back to Jacob. "Bequel's a veteran. He sails out of Jamaica, but he roves anywhere. Mad Krack says he now calls Santo Domingo home. If I'm honest, until the other night I thought him dead. But there he is, strolling around, very much alive, like he's on a secret mission." Bastien continued scouring the masses. "That's Roche." He whispered, lowering his gaze, nodding towards a small beady eyed pirate.

Jacob nodded, not wanting to admit he hadn't heard mention of anyone called Roche.

"Roche Braziliano." Bastien shook his head. "He's a vicious Dutch sailor. Absolute villain of a man. There's all sorts of stories about him. None of 'em good. My favourite's where he set fire to a couple of farmers because they wouldn't give him one of their pigs." Bastien chuckled. "And never refuse a drink from him."

"Why?"

"If he's drinking, everyone's drinking. He thinks he's being friendly. But if you refuse, he gets angry. I've seen him cut a man's nose off for declining some rum. His mind don't work like most people. No pig? I'll roast you alive. Don't drink my rum, I'll slice off your nose. He's a mad man."

"Doesn't look like much." Jacob sniffed.

"You wouldn't say that to his face. The man's full of cruelty when his minds full with liquor."

"You weren't lying. They're all here." Henri said. "If they're here, they must trust the captain's plan."

"Told ya. Something big's brewing,"

Jacob followed Roche Braziliano as he stepped from his crew, thrusting a skin of wine into Moise's hand. He boomed, conjecture that the quartermaster to be the smartest man among them. Moise laughed, taking a swig before embracing the Dutchman. A small man but with a solid physique. His rodent eyes darting for a victim to swing an insult—or maybe a cutlass.

Roche circled *Marquise's* crew, berating anyone who met his sinister eye. Jacob retreated away from the fire into the shadows. He noticed Henri and Bastien were also quiet. The atmosphere amongst the closest camps had turned to one of restless apprehension. Jacob eased himself to the ground with his back to the cliff face.

"Take a drink, lad?" Harvey said, sitting down, offering him a skin of wine.

"No thanks, Harv. I've had my fill today. I'm hoping to keep a clear head." He watched Roche circle back to his own fire.

"Good lad. Take the skin and pretend to drink then—I have news." He shook the skin under Jacob's nose and winked a friendly wink. Jacob offered the wine to his lips, letting a few drops wet his tongue, waiting for Harvey to start his piece.

"I've found a ship." Harvey hushed, careful to lower his head, scratching his thinning scalp.

Jacob glanced up, unable to suppress his smile. He could smell Harvey's tobacco breath as he spoke.

"Last night I was swapping tide depths for our rudders with this fella in the Marine. He's the navigator of *Griffin*. He's a fine Hampshire fellow called Richards. Said they were heading to Bermuda."

"When does it leave?" Jacob interrupted.

"Two days, hopefully. They're just waiting for the last of the supplies–which is proving difficult with so many ships at anchor. After Bermuda it's heading direct to England, and Richards said they're happy to accept hard-working crew."

"That's before *Marquise* leaves. When will you board? Tomorrow?"

"No, it's too risky. Some of his men know the captain. He ain't their favourite fella, but someone still might let slip." Harvey lifted his head, risking a smile, looking at his young friend for the first time since offering him the wine. "We bide our time tomorrow. Get up late, meet up with the gang. We'll act the part to join L'Olonnais. Then, in the early hours before *Griffin* is set to leave, we make our way to Le Bâtard cove, up the coast and hide out until morning. Richards will meet us with a barge. When *Griffin's* about to leave, we'll be the last to board. His captain will be expecting us."

Jacob sifted sand through his fingers watching the tiny grains form small piles.

"You are coming, aren't you, lad?"

Jacob brushed the sand flat. "It's great news Harv." He watched the captain, who had claimed a large smooth boulder as a seat elevating him slightly above the crew. He was holding court through the flames, laughing and bellowing jibes. "He raises spirits right enough."

"He does, lad," Harvey replied, glancing at the captain. "But he's single-minded and sure to sacrifice us all to see himself in the history books."

"You ain't tempted by the riches?"

Harvey shook his head. "Even if we survived. What you going to do with riches? Lock yourself away so nobody can get to them. Wrap yourself in fancy clothes you're too afraid to fray. Eat rich foods 'til your belly bursts and you're no use at the tiller. No lad. Enough food and the open waves is all any man needs."

They both paused, listening to the laughter around the fires. Bastien was teasing Piero about his wounded arm.

Jacob nodded. "Tomorrow night we'll meet this Richards." He wiped a tear from his face with his sleeve, letting out a tremble sigh.

Harvey put an arm around Jacob. "You're going home, son. You'll see you mother again and your Lydia." He squeezed his shoulder and removed his arm. "Keep your head down tonight. Get yourself back to town sharpish. I'm going to slip off soon. Everyone's used to me getting an early night."

"You gunna ask Doyle?"

Harvey furrowed his brow. "Not sure yet. Richards said there would be room for three." Harvey shrugged. "Leave it with me. In the meantime, don't say anything to anyone. Not even Henry or Bastien. Just because they bought you some new garb and dressed you up like a pirate don't mean you owe them your life. Until we firm our plans, let the world see what it sees. We're excited to be joining the crew. Wherever they might go."

Jacob nodded and took a swig from the skin before offering it back to Harvey. He considered the misfits littering the beach. He leaned back against the rock–his shoulders relaxed for the first time since he could remember.

Harvey took a swig of wine and strolled back to the fire sitting in the circle. Piero embraced him. Jacob sat alone for a while in the shadows, watching the fire scenes. He poured cool sandy gems through his fingers. The sun set and the temperature fell. Jacob sat in the shadows, grateful for his newly gifted clothes. Wrapped in his warm guilt–he watched Roche Braziliano as he crept in the shadows.

Sixteen

Roche Braziliano's erratic behaviour could not be ignored. Complimenting one fellow–forcing quarrel upon the next. Jacob had sat for an hour watching the Dutchman prowl the cove. Henry and Bastien had joined Jacob, nuzzling themselves into his rocky inlet. They were only yards from their captain. A position offering no obvious route past unless a person wished to leap through the fire. It spared them from Roche's spiteful humiliation.

Many of the seaman slumped, keeping their eyes fixed on their drinks. The sour flavour in the atmosphere was making Jacob nervous. Harvey had disappeared. Jacob yearned to follow–itching for his room above Le Petite Tortue. He nudged Henri, who'd nodded off beside him.

"Shall we get a stride on?" Henri said with a yawned stretch.

He elbowed Bastien in the ribs, who had fallen asleep with his head awkwardly resting upon a rock. He woke with a start and reached for his rum, knocking it from its perch by his knee.

"Shit." Bastien tried to rescue the remenance of the cup, but it was too late. "What you do that for, Hen? Has that prick Roche gone yet?"

"Nope." Jacob whispered–elbowing Bastien. "Lower your voice. I've lost him in the crowd, but I think he's floating over by Jan's crew. There might be trouble. I saw Doyle eyeing up his skin."

Bastien sat up, cricking his neck. His eyes scanned the darkness. "That'll be a fine match up if Le Roche tries to upset The Giant."

"As fascinating as that sounds." Henri said. "I'm reasoning we head back to L'Entracte for some afters. It'll be quiet tonight and I'm reckoning they'll be reasonable prices on offer. What 'ya say?"

Jacob needed no encouragement. Standing before Bastien had time to answer. Bastien held out a hand, fumbling as he stood. Jacob steadied his friend before he fell into the rocks and, in doing so, took a backwards step out of the shadow. The firelight danced off his new clean shirt, visible under his new coat.

"What say you? You will drink my wine?"

Jacob turned into the firelight to see Roche Braziliano practically striding through the flames with his wine skin outstretched.

"You been hiding, nipper? Drink my wine and be merry."

Jacob stood petrified–staring down into the Dutchman's rodent eyes. He opened his mouth and stuttered the first words that fell out.

"If you don't mind, sir, I'm happy to decline. We're heading back to town now and have had quite enough for tonight." Jacob blushed, trying to hide back in the shadows. Suppressed chortles could be heard around the fire.

"If you don't mind? You've had quite enough?" Roche snarled, thrusting the skin into Jacob's chest. Jacob had no choice but to grasp the wine–otherwise, risking it falling to the ground. "What's your name, pup?"

Jacob stared at the wine skin. "Jacob, Sir."

"Well, Jacob. I'll say when you've had enough." Roche stepped back, relieving his neck as he looked up at his victim. "You're a big lad, ain't ya? I think you could drink that skin whole and still be thirsty." Roche stood firm, moving his hand to Jacob's elbow, forcing the wine to his mouth. His other hand on the hilt of his cutlass as he nodded his head with a menacing grin.

"Jake, have a sip mate, don't be shy," Henri stepped from the shadows, "but pass it over here when you're done. I could have a tip more." Jacob took a pull on the spout and waved the wine skin over to Henri.

"Hang on, lads. The whelp didn't get his portion. Pass it back, and let him taste the bottom of the bag."

"It's fine, Roche," Henri chirped. "He's only a young'un. Nobody wants to see him spew. I'll be happy to take his challenge." Henri eased the bag from Jacob and poured the wine into his gullet. Before he could take his second swallow, the small captain suckered Henri in his stomach–causing him to splutter the contents of his mouth down his chin. The sack dropped to the sand, sloshing over Roche's soft leather shoes. The seated crowd stirred, sucking sharp intakes of breath.

Roche danced away from the liquid and unsheathed his cutlass. "Now you've spilled my wine. There's nothing I hate more than wasted liquor." He glared at his feet. "And you've coloured my ribbons."

Jacob caught a flash of the cutlass and retrieved the sack–pulsating wine onto the beach. "It's ok Mr Braziliano I'll drink it. I've acquired a taste after that last mouthful." Jacob shakily raised the bag to his lips and, ignoring the sand, congealed around the rim, committed to drink the remaining contents.

The bystanders winced, watching the poor lad finish the entire sack, before handing the empty bag back to Roche. He stood quiet and very still. He could feel the heat rising from his feet–through his legs–and into his cheeks.

"Fank you, shir. I nee'ed tha'. Fanks."

Henri stood up with the help of Bastien, having spent the last thirty seconds doubled over coughing. He placed an arm around his drunken buddy.

"You right, pal?" He wheezed. "Well done. You're a real man now. Thanks Roche. He needed some pluck. You're quite right. Poor lads fresh from England and hasn't been rightly christened yet." He turned, directing his soon to be dead weight companion away from the crowd – and hopefully out of the mind of the gassy captain.

"I don't think he's had enough." A mischievous grin adorned Roches face. "That skin was only half full after your antics. I say he's big enough to take another half. These English think they can drink. Let's see how much he can stomach." Roche turned to the crowd. "Who's got a sack to spare? It don't need to be wine. Any grog'll do." Roche paused and thought for a second. "Anyone got any rum." He scowled at the figures sitting in the firelight until he spotted a bottle of kill devil cradled in the hand of a half-drunk seaman. "You, dog, fetch that rum."

Piero looked at his captain. He stood, making a deliberate show around the fire to the unprotected bottle. Before the rum made it back in Roche's hand, L'Olonnais raised his head from beneath the shadow of his hat, directing his gaze through the fire at his opposing captain.

"Leave it be Roche. The lads had enough. He's proven his worth. He's sodden already. No need to poison the pup." The flames danced in front of his face, creating a menacing vision, causing the veteran pirate to pause. But only for a second.

"We're just having some fun, François. These kids need teaching. Otherwise, they'll never be men. I say he can handle a cup more."

L'Olonnais stood from his stone seat with such speed his movement caused the flames to dance, sending embers into the night sky. "He's had enough, Roche. Leave him be."

Roche turned to face the fire full on, offering his back to Henri, Bastien, and Jacob.

"I'll say when he's had enough, François. You may think you're the cock around here, but we all know it's the fox that rules the roust. These pups need to know who's boss and I don't see you teaching 'em anything useful. Taking their liqueur should be every new sea snot's first lesson. We ain't even begun to teach 'em how to take a beating yet. Don't want them yelping at the first sign of danger, do we?"

Many of the drunk crew shifted, trying to tip themselves back to the side of sober. Worried eyes found each other and hands fingered daggers and pistols.

Moise, who hadn't long returned with Le Picard from conversation with Le Basque stepped forward. "Captains. I think we're all halfway to a good time. There's no need to trespass into an ugly evening. It's bedtime for these pups, leaving us elders to enjoy the spoils and discuss the important matters. Roche, my old friend, let the whelp to his bed and sit down and recount the tail of your shipwreck off the coast of Campechy. You were thought to be dead. Only to return with two captured ships armed with nothing but thirty men and a canoe."

Roche eyed Moise. He smiled. Relaxed his shoulders and lifted his hand from his cutlass. Moise patted L'Olonnais on the shoulder, easing him back to his seat.

"Piero?" Moise said. "Pass Roche the Rum. Let's hear his brave tail. Sit up lads. If you haven't heard this, you're in for a treat."

Roche snatched the rum.

Piero eyed him for a second before sitting back in the circle.

"I'll retell my story, Moise." A smirk appeared in the corners of Roche's mouth. "It's a good fable. But like you say, there's folk here who ain't heard it but once. I'm betting Jacob here's one of 'em." He turned to find Jacob and his two pals just about to ascend the stone cut steps leading back up to the coastal path. "Jacob my lad. Come back here and sit awhile and listen to the greatest turnaround these waters have ever witnessed. What you say, lad?"

Jacob turned to face the flame lit faces. His own face warmed by the fire–causing him to retreat. His cheeks filled with moisture. He found his captain.

L'Olonnais eyed Jacob for a second, stroking his chin. "Come, Mr Penjerrick. Mr Galle, move up some. Let the boy sit. Nobody can spin a yarn like Roche here."

Jacob shuffled into the circle and flopped down next to Piero, who wrapped a protective arm around his shoulder–steading his balance. Jacob clenched his teeth, fighting the gurgle brewing in his throat. Bastien and Henri sat close by at the edge of the circle, keeping one keen eye on their young friend and a suspicious eye on Roche. Roche shouldered a drunken seaman from his stone perch, sending him sprawling onto the beach. He sat himself down, legs wide, leaning forward, ready to tell his tale. As if a great secret was about to unfurl. He eyed Jacob sitting close to L'Olonnais and smirked.

Isaac, who had been keeping quiet, sitting a little out of the circle, now moved closer to the fire–positioning himself between his young crewmate and the fabulist. Roche huffed in Isaac's direction and poured himself a cup of rum. He offered the bottle back to the circle, encouraging it to be passed on.

"This is no yarn, François." He sat for a short while–teasing his audience–and then began his story and his new game. "Well." He began whipping his cup upwards, spilling some of its contents into the fire with a hiss. "The journey had started so promisingly, as so many of my journeys do. We'd captured six Spanish ships carrying much plunder. Plate and sugar, for the most part, each time converting the bellies of the merchantmen into a great deal of coin. All with the help of D'Oyley of Jamaica."

Generous nods of acknowledgement from the audience as they recognised the liberal governor's name.

"We were following our usual route back to the Spanish main, where we had word of a galleon heavy with cocoa and slaves. A tasty booty, if we'd 'av found 'er. We sailed off the coast of Campechy when a dismal tempest surprised us. You never have seen such a storm. It would have ripped a lesser ship in two, but my *Groningen* was holding tight. We thought we 'ad 'er. Me and Yellahs had to man the tiller as one. Tied one to the other like twins we were." Roche laughed. "Each not daring to leave the other." Roche stood from his rock and played out the storm with his arms. Simulating gripping the tiller with both hands. "I'd given the order to hoist the canvas. All the way to the gallants we were, and still the temptress held tight. The beast grew too great and with a mighty coming together as big as a kraken, the main mast finally gave itself to the sea. By some miracle, the last barge was still tethered and with some fight we made our way to the shore, which if you can believe it was only half a league away.

"Knowing the waters we'd be waking up in, we had enough sense to rescue what muskets we could, with a few bullets and powder. *Groningen* was sunk on the bar in front of our eyes. She was a good ship but a fair trade when you hear what's to offer from this fine adventure."

Roche stepped forward towards the fire, snatching the stuttering bottle three shy of young Jacob. He took a slug before passing it back–one man along–encouraging the rum to continue its journey around the circle. "A wise man I am and knowing where we sat, I marched us up the coast to find Golpho Triste. Have you been to Golpho Triste, my man?"

Isaac looked up, now the owner of the rum. "Aye, sir. I frightful place. Not a beauty to be found in any the whore houses."

Roche laughed, rolling his head back. "You ain't wrong, my lad. But to Golpho Triste, we headed. Safer than the land we sat at. There be thirty of us made it to the sand, all full of thirst and hunger. But before we came within three leagues, we were hounded by one hundred mounted Spanish bastards." The audience cheered and booed at the introduction of the enemy.

"One hundred, I say, against thirty, tired, thirsty and hungry marooned men. We were doomed. No place to retreat. 'twas as if we were sunken with *Groningen*. We sat with the ocean at our backs and Spanish dogs sniffing our scent. Well up I stood." Roche raised his arms and danced his feet in the sand, "and proclaimed these Spaniards were no match for our superior marksmanship. A few sound volleys, I say, and they would turn and run. Together me and Yellahs, we rallied the men. We made our way to the tree line and fanned ourselves along more than fifty feet. There we waited. Quietly."

He placed a drunken finger to his lips and grinned. "The horsemen came at a canter along the beach." He whispered. "All clean and tidy in nice, neat rows. They could see we'd disturbed the sand, but then vanished. They trotted deeper into our trap, all the time wondering where we be at. The furthest of our men fired, exposing our position. Now, no horse wants to run into trees, so the Spanish pigs were at a quandary. Seeing a few of the men, they took aim and fired." He danced with excitement. "The bush was too thick, so no harm done." He stopped for effect and lowered his voice again. "But then, seeing the horses had ventured north of the beach, our rear guard stepped forward out of the tree line and we opened fire. We may have been hungry and thirsty, but our training had not waned. Bang, Bang," He roared. Shock and laughter erupted from his audience. "Each shot striking at least horse or rider. It was a marvellous sight." He stood straight, gazing into the middle distance. "We retreated back into the tree line only for the next group of loaded muskets to step forward and pick up where we left off. Bang, bang." Roche fired his imaginary musket towards Jacob, who was fighting his own battle with the pressure building in his throat. More Laughter. "Six rounds I let fly and each found a target. It did not take long before it was the Spanish who were outnumbered and desperate. We had the advantage. Those Spanish cuttlefish soon fled back south to whence they came, and we feasted on horse meat that night. Have you eaten horse meat, Jacob?" Roche snatched the rum from Piero's fist and took another slug before thrusting the bottle into Jacob's hand. Waiting for the young man's reply.

"No shir." Jacob stared at the bottle. "Nefer needed to. Captain only ever offeshed fine hog on *Marquise*."

L'Olonnais nodded a wink at Jacob.

"When the ambush was complete, we made sure no Spaniard lived." Roche unsheathed his cutlass and playfully stabbed the embers of the fire with its tip. "There was enough water in the dead Spanish packs to see us through a few more days. One poor soul's knapsack even offered rum that was most welcome." Roche paused again and–with the tip of his cutlass–he gently encouraged Jacob's hand to raise, lifting the bottle to his mouth. "We feasted that night on bloody horse flesh and rum. Tasty rum." At the thought of blood and the smell of the rum, Jacob's cheeks welled with saliva. To his right he sensed Isaac shift uneasily and over his shoulder Henri inhaled. He knew all eyes were fixed on the bottle and his mouth. Would he drink, or would he spew? No-one dared breath. A dark silence crept over the neighbouring campfires–until the entire cove hushed. Roche stood statuesque; the tip of his sword poised under the base of the bottle, subjecting it to the slightest pressure. The smell of the rum so close to his nose conjured a memory of its taste making Jacob's head swim. He sucked his lips to the bottle and sipped.

"Leave him be Gerrit."

Roche eyed L'Olonnais with contempt at the sound of a name years lost.

L'Olonnais stood fanning the fire, breaking the spell. "He's a pup. We don't need him ruined at such a tender age. Mr Penjerrick, my lad, pass the rum on, and off back to the town if you feel you can. Mr Bodine, Mr Trivette. See him right."

Jacob allowed the sailor to his left to take the rum. He stood up quickly, too quickly, stumbling backwards and gratefully into the arms of Henri and Bastien, who lifted him out of the circle and half carried him back towards the stone steps.

"Who are you, Jean-David, to ruin the camp's fun?" Roche bellowed.

As the trio made their way up the stone steps and out of harm's way, the commotion followed them on the wind. Their captain berating the drunken raconteur while Roche moved the topic to a ship he purchased from the Frenchman a month previous calling for recompense.

Jacob clung to his friends for support. "I'll miss you." He said before his head flopped backwards.

"Don't worry. We won't let him find you. Let's get you away, my friend."

"What happened in Golpho Triste?" Bastien asked.

"Not now, Bastien. Let's just get him away to bed." Henri halted at the summit of the steps to take a breath–listening to the outcome below. "This'll disrupt the voyage if there's enough memory of it in the morning. If I were you, Jake, I would keep my head down 'til we leave. Roche might be seeking revenge."

Seventeen

Jacob was back in Falmouth with Lydia—only it wasn't Lydia. It was Agnes. His gut told him it was Falmouth, but it looked more like Tortuga. A brightness enhanced the sounds and sights. The ocean twinkled a vibrant blue, and golden sand replaced the seaweed-stained beach. Pigeons were parrots. Dogs were wild boar. Lydia was angry. *"You smell like fish,"* she was saying. *"Where is my Spanish gold you promised?"*

He was falling. His mind swirled, but his bed was still. Too still. He'd grown used to the sway of his hammock, and now, as he drifted from the fever dream, he became aware of the rigid, unfamiliar surface beneath him. He outstretched his hands, gripping the edge of the bed. His world was spinning. Too late—he rolled over and vomited into a chamber pot conveniently positioned on the floor.

"You're awake. Good. I thought you might drown in your own gerber." Henri sat on the chair in the corner of the room sharpening his folding knife on a whetstone, with a mug of coffee on a table next to him.

"Where am I?" Jacob croaked. His lips, so dry, he had to force his mouth open. He'd spoken in English. Henri responded in Jacob's native tongue—with a hint of resentment.

"You're in the La Petite Tortue. Where do you think you are? How's your loaf?"

Jacob rolled onto his back and felt the wet vomit stain on the bed.

"I've been sick on your bed."

"You have. I had to sleep on the floor last night."

"Sorry Hen. What happened?" Jacob sat up, leaning against the wall. He felt more vomit on his chest. A cool breeze from the open window caressed his body–a contrast to his hot and sweaty skin. His stomach cramped as he bent forward. He fought the impulse to be sick again. He looked up at Henri with a sullen expression, waiting for an answer. His breath smelt of stale wine. He checked his pouch around his neck.

"Don't worry. It's all there. Not that you ever had much." Henri eyed him under furrowed brows. "So, you want to know what happened?"

Jacob nodded–then pressed his hands to his forehead.

"Well, my grey-faced friend. You somehow got into a tangle with one of the most madcap pirates in the Caribbean. And then dragged L'Olonnais–your captain–to your defence. I thought François would fillet Roche at one point." Henri stopped sharpening his knife and took a sip of coffee. "What's the last thing you remember?"

Jacob thought for a few seconds, keeping a keen eye on Henri's knife. "Harvey. I was talking to Harvey."

"Right, then what?"

Jacob stared at the back of his eyelids. "Nothing. A sea breeze. Sand. Leaning on the rocks. Then... nothing."

"Well, the grog has washed your memory, my friend. In between having a chat with Harvey and spewing in my bed, you managed to jeopardise the entire voyage." Henri folded his knife and secreted it away in his inside pocket. "It's now hanging on frayed rope.

Braziliano and Le Basque are refusing to join the voyage unless L'Olonnais apologises. And guess what?"

"What?"

"What?" Henri snapped. "L'Olonnais has told them both to be damned. Said he would rather sail with Spaniards than with those cowardly catfish," Henri leaned forward. "That's four hundred men the fleet lost last night. And not one Spaniard had to fire a single shot."

Jacob sat, holding his stomach. Henri laughed–a deep belly aching laugh slapping the side of his chair. "Your headrot is the least of your worries. You're in deep shit, my friend. I wouldn't want to bump into Roche or Le Basque any time soon. I've no idea what L'Olonnais' thinking. You're fucked." Henri composed himself. "And so are me and Bastien."

"What did you do?"

"Nothing. We just rescued you."

Jacob thought for a moment. "What did I do?"

"If I'm honest, you didn't do anything. I think Roche and L'Olonnais have been looking for a reason to cross swords for a while. Roche certainly showed his hackles last night. I think you just gave them an excuse."

Jacob slumped to one side, recoiling from the damp patch. His body seized the opportunity to swing his legs out of bed. He stood. The room started spinning, causing his ears to buzz. The breeze caught his attention, and he noticed he was naked. "Where are my clothes?"

"There, over by the window." Henri Chuckled. "You took them off before bed, pleading for us to find Agnes."

Jacob winced and scratched his cock, feeling for signs of nocturnal activity. He walked to the window and retrieved his breeches. "You didn't get her, did you?"

"Not a chance. You've already had one free shag from me and the prices have doubled since then. You ain't even got enough coin to cover a wasted fumble with Fat Marion."

Jacob sighed, "Thank God." He walked over to a bowl next to the window and swilled his face and chest with the warm water. He ran his wet fingers through his hair. He stared at the bowl for a long moment, taking in deep breaths. "Can I drink this?"

"I wouldn't." Henri said. "Here, have this." He picked up a second mug sitting on the floor next to his chair. "Jasmin makes it. Some sort of ginger tea."

"What's our plan?" Jacob said, accepting the mug and draining its contents in one gulp.

"Well, it's put us in a fix, that's for sure. Bastien's out feeling the temperature. I don't think Roche will make too much of an effort to hunt you down, but you don't want to chance bumping into him."

"Do you think he'll hurt me?" Jacob said, fighting on his shirt.

"Last night, after we'd got you out of there, Isaac told us he butchered one of Jan's crew's ear clean off for not finishing that bottle of rum. The poor gamecock knew nothing about it. Face down in the sand before he'd got halfway down the bottle."

Jacob stood rigid at Henri's words, with one shoe on a foot and the other in his hand.

Henri couldn't help allowing himself a brief smirk. "God knows what he'll do to the young pup who scuppered his chance to join the biggest fleet the Caribbean has ever mustered."

Just then, the door to the bedroom burst open. Jacob threw his shoe at the intruder and turn headfirst into the opposite wall, sending him sideways into the wash bowl, knocking its contents over the floor, through the floorboards to the room below.

"Aw. What'ya do that for?" Bastien shouted, throwing the shoe back at Jacob, missing him just above his falling head.

"Any news?" Henri chuckled.

Bastien closed the door behind him. "There's a lot of talk about last night. Jan's not happy about his man's ear. Roche hasn't said he's looking for you, Jake, but the view is you shouldn't stumble across him while you're fresh in his memory."

Jacob sat on the floor, fumbling with his second shoe. "I need to hide. I could head for the hills for a few days until we leave."

"You could." Bastien said. "But I've spoken to Le Picard. You can head back to *Marquise* and help load up for the journey. He said L'Olonnais will hide you."

"He's not angry with me?"

"No." Bastien eyed Henri. "He doesn't hold you to account. Got you pegged as some sort of good luck charm. Said it's a blessing. Braziliano would lead them all to perdition—whatever that means. He's glad he's gone."

Henri raised an eyebrow. "Well Jake, not sure why the captain likes you so much, but let's get you back on the ship. You fit for moving?"

Jacob scanned the room—looking for his belongings. Realising he was wearing almost everything he owned. He snatched up his cutlass and knapsack. He paused, scratching his head, before rubbing his palms into his eye sockets. "Ready."

The trio left the sick stained room and locked the door.

"Where's Harvey?" Jacob asked as they crept down the stairs. "Did you see him while you were out?"

"Nope." Bastien said. "He's not in his room and I popped over to la Marine, but he wasn't there. The Molly said she hadn't seen him this morning,"

"Come on, Jake." Henri said. "Gather yourself. Let's get you back onboard before the dock wakes up and finds a gibbering lost boy with a hex on his head. I'll head back to town once you're safe and get news to Harvey."

The three young seamen skulked out of the tavern's back door, keeping to the back alleys heading towards the dock. The gravel tracks evoked a memory of Falmouth only five years previous. But those were happier times for Jacob when he would secretly follow his father through the town pretending to be a spy. These streets, however, stopped his heart at every turn. He expected to see a crowd of buccaneers with cutlasses raised, jeering his name. But it was still early – and most still slept on the beach. He just needed to get back to the ship. God knows why, but the captain would protect him.

Jacob slumped on the main deck, huddling the shade cast by the quarterdeck. His journal lay on his knapsack with his quill and an ink pot next to him. His descriptions of the Caribbean had turned more into a diary of events. And with everything that had happened, Jacob was compelled to commit his thoughts to paper.

His hangover had taken the whole of the previous day to release its grip. The worse of which he suffered in Monsieur Gardier's warehouse, where Henri had hidden him while Bastien casually hunted for their captain. Moise had returned an hour later to transport the terrified Jacob back to *Marquise*.

"The Cap'n will hide you youngun'." Moise had said on the brief journey in the barge. "No doubt want a word when he sees you next. Between you and me, he's never liked Roche. Causes too much unrest with the crew. There should only ever be one bullock in the paddock. It's a shame about the men, though. Two full ships is a lot to replace. Best keep your head down. Not everyone will be as merciful as the captain."

A skeleton crew manned *Marquise*. Moise had returned as quartermaster, having relinquished his temporary captaincy of *Stad Gouda*. Joseph and three carpenters were refitting the ship. Inner walls had been removed, creating larger quarters to accommodate the additional men. Helario stored and prepared food for the journey while Piero, who had lost all his money gambling, was content with at least one hot meal every day.

Moise had given Jacob instructions to help whoever might need him until it was time to depart. He had spent most of the previous day in between bouts of nausea helping Helario stack grain into the store. Joseph and his small team had enlisted him this morning to help with the cleaning of an area of the hold. The same area Jacob had encountered the slaves. He shuddered, remembering their scared faces. Now with lantern light swaying from fixing points in the ceiling, he and a fellow swabber, Gaetan, slopped the floor free of the slaves' bodily wastes.

Having light did not make the job any more pleasant. The smell Jacob remembered from his last visit had multiplied.

"How did you get lumbered with this job?" Jacob asked Gaetan when they had stepped up to the main deck to get some much needed fresh air.

"Joseph said clean the hold, so I clean the hold."

"Is he your boss?"

"He saved my life. I would clean a thousand dirty holds for Joseph."

"What happened?"

"Another time. Now we clean and dust with lime."

When the hold was dusted Joseph had told them to rest. They could do little else until more timber was purchased to construct new mess tables and benches.

So now Jacob sat in the fresh air, avoiding the scorching sun, trying to piece together the missing hours of the beach meeting. Moise jolted him back to his senses, striding from the cabin and over to the gunwale. The quartermaster leaned over the rail to view the harbour.

"Make yourselves lively, lads. Capt'n's approaching." Jacob scampered to his feet and continued the scrubbing he'd started over an hour ago. Five minutes later, the captain raced up the Jacob's ladder and vaulted over the rail. Jacob halted his scrubbing and stood tall and straight.

"Mr Penjerrick. How's that head of yours?"

"Much better, sir."

"Good to hear it. Keep up the good work." The captain strode up the quarterdeck steps to meet Moise, where they spoke for a while.

Jacob continued his scrubbing, but eased closer, trying to hear his superiors' conversation. The captain would surely have more to say after the escapade on the beach. The talk was about food stocks for the journey and materials needed for the refit. After a few minutes, their voices quietened, and they turned, taking a few paces aft. Jacob kept his head down, feigning focus on the boards beneath him. He trained his ears, but the flapping of the sails, the ropes creaking in tackles and blocks–and the hum of the harbour in the distance–suppressed their voices.

He glanced up from his work to stretch his back and momentarily caught the captain's sideways stare. He reverted his gaze back to the boards. The brief eye contact was enough to encourage a brisk pace from Jacob's bones. He gripped the brush tight and turned to face the steps, looking for a secluded area to scrub.

From Jacob's left, Isaac's head popped up from the gunwale. Jacob smiled. Isaac looked to the quarterdeck and found his captain talking to Moise. He stuttered long enough for Jacob to seize the opportunity to shout across to him.

"Morning, Isaac."

"Jacob." Isaac said, striding closer. "How's your head?"

"Good. Have you seen Harvey today?"

"Sorry, pal. There's talk he's disappeared. Did he say anything to you last time you spoke?"

"He didn't. Maybe he's with Marguerite?" Jacob smiled as he realised this might be the first time Harvey's antics with his secret prostitute may have been spoken aloud.

Isaac chuckled. "I don't think so. Le Picard checked with her. The captain's sent out the feelers with Braziliano and Le Basque in case they've kidnapped him for their own." Jacob looked shocked. "Don't worry. They haven't. He's just vanished."

Jacob diverted his eyes to the quarterdeck. As if encouraged by their conversation, the captain danced down the steps two at a time and announced himself between his two juniors.

"Keeping yourself busy, I see? How are we this fine morning?"

Jacob nodded.

"Good, good. The Devil hunts for idle hands."

"We were just discussing Harvey," Isaac interjected.

Jacob shot his countryman a glance.

"Ah, yes. Your Mr Harvey. We've lost him." The captain fingered his goatee and smiled, lingering eye contact with Jacob. "Have you any idea where he might be, my honest fellow?"

"Erm." Jacob fidgeted with the brush stave. "No, sir. I haven't seen him since the meeting in the cove."

"Are you sure, my friend?" L'Olonnais inched closer to Jacob, narrowing his eyes. "I see you chatting together at the tiller, all quiet. Or by the fire in a snug huddle. He never let slip of a plan to disappear? Hmm? No talk of his blessed English Navy?"

Jacob took a half step backwards and swished the brush. "No, sir. I don't think so. He seemed thrilled to be joining the next voyage. I think the allure of manning the helm won him over."

"Did it now?" L'Olonnais locked eyes with Jacob. He feigned a smile.

"Did you want me to head back to town, sir? I could try to find him? I could ask Henri or Bastien if they have any news."

"No, my smart lad. You best be staying here. You don't want to be bumping into Monsieur's Braziliano or Le Basque. They ain't happy with the outcome of the meeting the other night. Monsieur Braziliano is blaming you for being ousted. Saying a pup should drink his medicine and shut up while he's at it. If I'm honest, lad, there's many a man not happy with you right now." He rubbed his goatee and leaned in. "Rumours around you challenged Monsieur Braziliano causing him to lose face. Men are saying you're the reason the fleet's only half manned."

Isaac opened his mouth to speak but said nothing when the captain peeped him with a side glance. The captain placed two comforting hands on Jacob's shoulders.

"I know it ain't true. You only defended your honour. And I think his actions were aimed at me more than you. But I would keep myself fixed here and wait for it all to blow over. As soon as we set sail, all thought of killing will be forgotten." Jacob's eyes widened. "Wait 'til you see the fleet we have waiting for us in Matamana. The lads'll soon forget about Monsieur's Braziliano or Le Basque. And we'll protect you, won't we, Mr Dargate?"

"We will Jacob. Don't you worry. You've probably already been forgotten at the bottom of last night's jar of wine. Roche was looking for an exit anyway. Everyone knows it. He's already left... "

"He's already left the fleet." The captain interjected. "So no more harm can come once we set sail. Ain't that right, Mr Dargate?"

"Yeah, that's right," Isaac replied. "Not your fault, mate."

"Well, so says maybe. But you must be thinking it's best to keep your head below the waterline 'til we leave." The captain left a healthy pause, encouraging Jacob to answer his rhetorical statement. Jacob nodded.

"I'm sure you'll be seeing your Mr Harvey again. He'll turn up. They always do. In the meantime, best keep busy. You can start by helping Mr Dargate unload the latest goods from the barge. There's a good lad." L'Olonnais strode off towards his cabin.

Jacob smiled and nodded a goodbye. "Thank you, sir." The cabin door shut with a thud—leaving Jacob in Isaac's charge.

"Go fetch Joseph." Isaac said. "Tell him I have the first of that timber he's been needing."

"Do you think Harvey will turn up?"

Isaac smiled. "The captain will find him."

Eighteen

Jacob peeked up from behind his barrel on hearing the hatch door open. Henri and Bastien descended the steps, striding between the new mess tables. Their arms wide and their grins wider. Tomilho, the terrier, sat up from his slumber and ran to meet them, wagging his tail.

"Jake, my tankard-mate." Henri said, fussing Tomilho as he jumped up. "Glad to see you're alive. I thought you might have skipped back to port for our last few days. What you been doing?"

Jacob embraced his friend, eyeing his empty hands as they released. "The captain told me to stay on board. Said Roche was out for blood and there would be trouble from the crew if they eyed me too soon in the journey."

In the time Jacob had been hiding in the hold, with only Tomilho for company and Helario coaxing him up to the galley for food, he had become suspicious of everyone.

Henri took a step back, his head tilted. "You mean you've been here since we smuggled you from the port? That was four days ago."

"But Roche."

"Roche sailed two days ago. Had his own plans all along. Word is he had no intention of joining the fleet. Only came down to the meet to poke holes in his old toads' plans."

"He wasn't after my skin? I thought he blamed me for L'Olonnais kicking him out of the fleet."

"That's what we thought. Captain told Moise to tell Bastien here it was best to set you to hiding. While you rubbed the wine from your head, Roche was loading his sloop. He probably didn't give you a second's thought–just some pup he almost made spew."

"We thought you knew, Jake," Bastien jested as he hoisted himself onto a mess table.

Jacob fingering the hilt of his cutlass secured tightly at his side.

"You mean I've been twitching down here for the last three days? I haven't had a wink of sleep. Every rat that scuttled by I've thought was a turncoat sneaking up with a dagger for my belly?" He inhaled a deep lungful of stale air. He crashed his fists down onto the mess table, causing Bastien to jump and shuffle back towards Henri.

Henri held out his hands, a worried countenance marring his expression.

"Why didn't the captain tell me?" Jacob's hand flickered to his cutlass, then to his head. "Roche isn't out for me?"

Henri risked a chuckle. "No, my friend. He was in fine form when we last saw him in L'Entracte. Even tried to persuade Le Picard to join his crew."

Jacob lowered his arms and allowed a grin to surface to his lips.

"You're free from this stale air." Henri placed both hands on his friend's shoulders, easing him from his torment. Jacob exhaled and hugged Henri.

"He'll be asking for matelotage next." Bastien quipped.

Jacob pushed Henri away and laughed. "Where are we?"

"Still in the harbour. About to cast off for Bayaha."

"What's in Bayaha?"

"We'll resupply."

"The captain revealed where we'll attack yet?"

"Not yet," Bastien said. "Got more ships to collect, then we'll be on our way."

"Where's Harvey? Did you find him?"

"Yeah, he's at the tiller." Henri said. "He turned up this morning. Said he went off to explore the island. He's in a foul mood now. Not speaking to anyone. We're guessing Marguerite upset him."

"He's here? On *Marquise*?"

"He's stitched himself to the tiller."

Jacob pushed past Henri and Bastien and skipped to the stairs. A few seconds later, he stood on the main deck, squinting through the late morning sunlight. He found his old confidante on the quarterdeck stooped over his maps. Harvey seemed to have glanced his way, but there was no hint of recognition. Jacob stood exposed on the main deck amongst the crew.

"Aye up, Jacob. Good to see you're still with us. Where you been hiding?" It was Marin who asked as he climbed over the gunwale, fresh from the latest barge.

"Hey, Marin. Just been helping with the refit." There seemed to be no animosity in Marin's tone. The crew looked in high spirits, collecting their orders, happy to be back out on the rolling waves.

The fresh air and the familiar sound of the sail canvas dancing with the wind sang to Jacob for a few seconds more. These familiar sounds had been mere muffles down below. He felt uplifted to be up top and out of the ship's dank, dark belly. He glanced back to the Quarterdeck finding Moise observing the men coming aboard. Catching his eye, Jacob nodded towards Harvey. Moise raised an eyebrow and flicked his head in response.

Jacob strode up the steps and sidled up to his sombre older friend.

"Jacob." Harvey did not look up from his navigator's table. His palms flat on the corners of a map.

"Harvey. I was worried about you. Where have you been?"

"I think it's best if you keep your distance, kid. There's been a change of plans. I'm not going to be able to teach you no more."

Jacob lowered his voice and bowed to whisper into Harvey's ear. "You were looking for a ship. What happened?"

"No need to worry about that no more, kid. We'll be having another turn with the captain."

"What's going on? What ain't you telling me?"

"Nothing to tell, kid. Just don't need you cluttering up the quarterdeck no more."

Harvey eased himself up straight, releasing the map edges, causing it to roll shut on the table until it resembled long field glasses. He shooed Jacob backwards away from his table.

"Harvey. What you doing? What's changed?"

"Away with you, kid. Find Le Picard for new orders."

Confused. Jacob peered over his shoulder to see everyone in ear shot on the main deck, pausing their tasks and staring up at the commotion. He shuffled towards the steps, looking back at Harvey, holding back a tear.

Harvey re-rolled his map before taking his usual stance at the tiller. He looked Jacob directly in the eye. "Stay out of trouble, lad."

Six ships lay in anchorage at the small port of Bayaha. Three ships had accompanied *Marquise de Villars* from Tortuga. *Leopard*; a sloop-of-war of eight guns, captained by Philippe Bequel and carrying one hundred men. *Tigre*, the eight-gun sloop, captained by Anthony du Puis. *Stad Gouda* was the third ship. Jan Lucas had been reinstated as its captain and had taken Daniel Montbars as his quartermaster.

The remaining two ships were a four-gun schooner of one hundred and twenty men and a ketch with no guns, only two swivel guns, with eighty men. All six captains had disappeared into the officers' quarters of *Marquise*, to the excitement of the crew. With a chatter of enthusiasm, the five other captains exited onto the main deck.

As the last excited head dipped below the gunwale and into the awaiting barges, Moise set up a table before heading up to the quarterdeck.

"Right then, brothers. Gather round. The time has come to reveal the plan." Moise offered the stage to the captain.

Captain L'Olonnais sauntered onto the quarterdeck and raised his arms. "We're now six fully stocked ships and over seven hundred men."

"That's a lot of mouths." Helario whispered into Jacob's ear.

"Our fellow captains are full of excitement for our latest campaign. As we speak, they return to their crews to share the glorious news. They have declared me to be the Admiral of the fleet. Which I have humbly accepted." The crowd shuffled. Some looking overboard to the barges below. The captain snatched the rail and leaned forward. "The plan is simple. There'll be no fortified strongholds. No armies in defence. These are ports that have seldom been attacked before. They won't be expecting us."

The crowd remained still in quiet anticipation.

"We strike for Gracias a Dios at the tip of Honduras. And we head south for Blauvelt in Nicaragua."

Confused muffles escaped lips. Before concerns could grow, the captain raised his arms.

"And we strike every Spanish town and port in between. We estimate there's a dozen rich targets, each with an abundance of gold, silver, plate, cotton, sugar and slaves. Not one will expect our attack. We'll take no prisoners, and by the time they realise what has befallen them, we'll be on to the next until we're safe in Blauvelt. There we'll divide the rich plunder."

There came a pause as each man ruminated over the announcement. A slow ripple of acceptance and understanding nodded through the crew until they erupted with the allure of wealth. A simple plan, no grand attack, but they made sense of it. Quick and easy. They imagined the luxuries that these emerging ports would offer. This would be the easiest of expeditions. There would be minimal casualties. Only wealth. As much wealth as twelve towns could hold, and six ships could carry. They looked to their neighbour and allowed their excitement to grow.

"If you greedy lot are all in agreement." L'Olonnais continued. "I encourage you to see Mr Vauquelin at the articles."

Moise returned to the table at the foot of the steps beckoning each man to take the oath upon the bible and sign the ledger. L'Olonnais slapped Harvey on the back as he made his way to the table, signed his name, and returned to the tiller.

As the queue formed, Jacob shuffled into line with Henri and Bastien. His shoulders slumped as low as his frown.

"Jake. What's with your face?" Henri said.

"He's still pining." Bastien answered.

"You need to stop the fretting." Henri said, "You'll be home soon enough. What's your hurry?"

Jacob shrugged and shuffled forward.

Henri sighed and grasped Jacob's wrist, pulling him to the gunwale. "Give us a minute, Bastien. Jacob needs his eyes opening."

Bastien shook his head and fell back into the queue.

"I know you miss your mother and that Lydia pepee." Henri said. "But what's with all the moping?"

Jacob sighed. "I didn't ask for any of this. I was happy with my fishing boat."

"You'll be fishing again. But you've got to face facts. You're miles away with no way back." Henri fingered the pouch around Jacob's neck. "Even if you found this magical ship heading to England, you've got no coin to pay for passage. You can't trust the navy. They'll have you signed up before you get chance to spit out your first weevil." Jacob huffed at the floor. "Look, you can either mope around pining or you can sign up and get something out of it. There's no point going home empty-handed, is there? And this cruise sounds as easy as getting a virgin laid in a whorehouse." Not even a smirk from Jacob.

Henri tugged at his forelock in his clenched fist. He raised an eyebrow and grasped Jacob's shoulders, shaking him, demanding his attention. "Have you heard of Audebert Queval?"

Jacob shook his head.

"Audebert Queval?" Henri repeated. "Uncle Gefrei knew him before the raids. One of the first buccaneers to try his hand at piracy. He had a small crew, maybe six men. They raided Spanish merchants in canal de la tortue. The water between Hispaniola and Tortuga."

Jacob looked down and puffed out his cheeks, kicking an invisible piece of debris with his foot.

"On only his third or fourth raid, he came across this Spanish merchant. Queval hailed the captain under the guise of a trader offering turtle meat for the journey back to Europe. The captain, being the suspicious type, was reluctant but with a bit of persuasion and the lure of the exotic meat Queval and his crew made it aboard. Queval and his men turned a couple of turtles on their backs and while the amused captain became distracted, they overthrew the crew, taking the ship by surprise."

Jacob looked up, feigning interest.

"Now, Queval expected to find logwood or tobacco, maybe sugar, take his tax and let the merchant on his way."

Henri paused, waiting for Jacob's interest to peek. Nothing. "But instead, he found something else."

"What?" Jacob asked. Finally playing along.

"While his men kept the crew on guard on the main deck, Queval took the captain to the hold and ordered him to show him his cargo. Behind the usual barrels of water and grain and provisions for the journey, Queval found a dozen chests. Heavy chests. So heavy, Queval needed the help of another of his men to move one. When they opened them, they found each one full of Spanish silver or gold. Full. To the brim."

Jacob eyed Henri suspiciously.

"It turned out this merchant ship had been separated from the treasure fleet. One tenth of King Felipe's personal shipment destined for Spain was in front of Queval. It gets better. The captain was not really the captain. He had overthrown the real captain and chucked him and his loyal crew overboard." Henri laughed. "He'd stole the dinero for himself."

"How much was there?" Jacob asked, leaning into Henri.

"In total. Twenty-five thousand doubloons. Doubloons." Henri replied with a whistle. "Each chest held pesos, escudos, reales. All divided nice and neat."

"What did Queval do?"

"What do you think he did? He ordered the Spanish into his barge and took the ship and its loot for himself. He gave one chest to the Spanish captain. A parting gift, from one thief to another. Last we heard, Queval changed his name and was a lord in the lowlands of Germany with more money than he knows what to do with."

Jacob crumpled his nose and frowned. "Did that really happen?"

Henri slapped Jacob's shoulders and laughed. "It did. And it could happen to us." Henri turned back to the queue. "Bastien. What happened to Queval?

"The Count of some German province,"

"Piero? You heard of Queval?"

"Yeah, pilfered twenty-five thousand doubloons from King Felipe."

"You see. What would your Lydia say when she finds out you made it all the way to the Spanish main, the sworn enemy of England, and didn't return with Spanish treasure?" Henri paused, but Jacob didn't reply. "She'll be furious."

Jacob pursed his lips and nodded.

"If you came back empty-handed, she would demand that if you really loved her, you'd jump back on a ship and pick up where you left off. I ain't saying we'll stumble on a pot as rich as what Queval did, but this voyage could set you up for life back in England. A year ago, you had no idea the likes of us could have such riches. We're so close. How many fish would you have to catch to see such a fortune? How many days doffing a cap to nobility as they brush you aside in the street? This is our chance, Jake. Our time to make something of our lives. I don't know about you, but I ain't letting this opportunity slip through me fingers. The last time L'Olonnais set off, we only had two ships and look how much loot we brought back." Henri turned Jacob to face the quarterdeck, leaving his arm wrapped around his shoulder. "Look." He pointed to the tiller. "Harvey's signed. He don't strike me as your piratical type, but even he knows a sure thing when he sees one."

"But ain't it dangerous?"

"Look about. There's three hundred men on this ship and another four hundred on the others. Ain't no danger when seven hundred men run at a town. The Spanish cowards will just raise their hands and point to the gold."

Jacob huffed, unconvinced.

Henri lowered his voice. "Just stick in the middle of the pack and shout and scream. You're not bad with a cutlass, and I've taught you to load a musket. There'll be a musketeer that'll be grateful for your new skill. The trick is, don't try and be a hero. There's braver men than you. Let them do all the grunting. We all get the same share. Three or four months from now, you'll be a rich Cornish man." He let go of his friend's shoulders and beckoned him back to the queue. "You sticking with us a little longer, shipmate?"

Jacob's eyes stayed on the quarterdeck, contemplating Harvey. To Harvey's left, L'Olonnais stared down at them. The newly appointed admiral nodded to Henri, then grinned when Jacob caught his eye. Jacob returned to the queue.

"You're right Henri." Jacob said, returning to the queue. "There's no point going home empty-handed. I'm so close. Lydia will be delighted she waited. Especially when she sees the riches I bring back."

Nineteen

The fleet set sail from Bayaha and, two days later, made landfall at the port of Matamana on Cuba's southern coast to gather their final supplies. Jacob, Henri, and Bastien looked on as twenty men from each ship loaded into barges and rowed towards the shore. The small army descended on the local fishing community, dispossessing them of their flat-bottomed canoes.

Bastien found it amusing when they tipped the boats, forcing the angry fishermen to swim ashore. At the beach, the wet inhabitants pelted the buccaneers with stones and coconuts.

Denis stood a few yards along the gunwale. He caught Jacob's concerned eyes. "They'll be back fishing in no time, lad. It only takes 'em a few days to hollow out a new canoe."

Jacob stared at the poor fishermen, unconvinced by Denis's words. These were simple folk just trying to scrape a living from the ocean. Just like his father had done and his father before him. How would they react if their livelihood was stolen, and they had to start over? His father had a dream. He'd hoped to one day have saved enough money to purchase a mid-sized lugger–the beginnings of his and his son's fishing empire. The dream had never begun. But maybe that dream could be resurrected using the riches he would bring home. Enough Spanish treasure to purchase many luggers.

Helario bustled in next to Jacob. "Have you ever had turtle meat, Jovem?" He pointing out the sea creatures being loaded into the captured canoes.

"No," Jacob replied. "Is it anything like crab?"

Helario chuckled. "Not really. You're in for a treat. If you thought my pork was tasty, wait 'til you try my turtle broth."

Jacob forced a smile, looking back to the beach. A scuffle had broken out between one of the raiding parties and a small group of locals defending their catch. One of the local women, wearing little more than a cloth skirt, pelted Bakari with fish, much to the amusement of his fellow crew.

She ran out of ammunition and darted to outlaying rocks. Bakari trudged into the shallow waters, cornering her. She feinted left and ran right. She was quick, but Bakari was too wise for her ruse. On a second attempt, he snatched her by the throat and, in a swift motion, threw her body to the sand, submerging her head under the shallow water. Her legs kicked frantically. Her hands grabbing at his eyes and nostrils in a desperate attempt for survival. At last, her arms slumped to the surf. Bakari grunted, raising himself from his knees. As he stomped back victoriously to his crew, her male companions crept forward, dragging her body out of the water.

Jacob watched with bated breath as one of the group–probably her husband–straddled her, shaking her vigorously, trying to remind her lungs of the need for air. Waves lapped at her lifeless ankles. The husband thrashed the ground before raising his hands to the sky, letting out a chilling shriek audible from *Marquise's* decks. Bakari didn't even turn upon hearing the scream.

Jacob white knuckled the rail, desperate for the native woman. Her death was meaningless. Perhaps she had been stupid, but Bakari had most definitely been cruel.

Her torso twitched. Convulsed. She spat water and gasped for air. Jacob almost cheered, stopping himself just short of a whimper as he remembered the company he kept. He turned to Henri and Bastien, who were equally engrossed. All three thinking they'd seen the woman take her final breath.

Henri let out a stunned guffaw. "I thought you were going to die in sympathy then, mate," Henri said.

Jacob could not hide his relief and chuckled along with the other spectators.

"Come, Jovem." Helario said. "We prepare for the turtle. Wait 'til you taste my calipach. Excelente."

The crew sloped away, but Jacob stayed watching the beach as the woman gingerly got to her feet. All fight now extinguished from the natives. They receded back into the trees leaving the raiders alone to pick amongst their belongings.

Jacob turned to the quarterdeck. For a fraction of a moment, he locked eyes with Harvey before the navigator lowered his head and returned to his maps.

As the fleet headed for the Spanish Main, Jacob pushed thoughts of returning home any time soon to the back of his mind. He let the excitement build as he imagined the treasures they might find, immersing himself in the daily life at sea. He'd volunteered for duty in the rigging, hoping to speak with Harvey—even if only in an official capacity. For three days, the navigator had avoided his eye, forcing Jacob to admit defeat and focus on the task at hand.

He'd been hauling a halyard through the blocks when the mainsail slumped against the mast, and for a moment, Jacob thought he'd let the line slip–or lost tension on a belaying pin. Looking around, he found his crewmates eyeing the sails with the same bewilderment. It took Harvey no time to realise their predicament. They'd been found by the dead weather.

They were at God's mercy–drifting north. The fleet was lost to the horizon. Their only hope was to wait it out. Some found humour in the event, as they saw an opportunity to rest and partake in extra rum. Piero instigated dice and card games to pass the time. Seasoned mariners gathered along the gunwales, eyeing the horizon for any hint of clouds, sniffing the air for clues or climbed the rigging, hunting for the topsail of one of the five other ships in their fleet. Others prayed for a sign from their god to deliver them from the doldrums.

Jacob's feet had fidgeted on every inch of *Marquise*. His bony bum had sat on every board and his back had rested on every rail. He had passed comment on every topic with every crew member bar one. Idleness, after nearly a week, felt far worse than honest work.

"Where's Rolant?" The admiral bellowed, striding from his cabin. "Strike up a lively tune! This cursed silence would drive a man to cast himself overboard!"

Jacob listened from the forecastle with Isaac, as Roland did his best to keep up morale. They sat cleaning pistols under an awning rigged up, offering shade from the late summer sun.

"You heard about Gaetan?" The question was from a newcomer, Reinhardt. Originally of *Stad Gouda*, he'd stayed with *Marquise*, having been seduced by Helario's cooking. He slumped down next to Isaac.

"No." Isaac replied.

"Found in the bilge drinking from the chain scoops. That black fellow, Bakari, had to clout him and lock him in the brig to calm him down."

Isaac chuckled. Jacob scrunched up his face as he weighed up the consequences of such madness. He hoped Gaetan would recover. Finding water was becoming more ludicrous. He'd witnessed sailors waking up before sunrise to climb the rigging. They would lick the morning dew from the sails before the heat evaporated it dry. The very awning he now sat under became a hive of activity at first light. Elbows out, as men palmed damp puddles into their mouths. He'd done it himself that very morning.

"Makes you wonder," Reinhardt chuckled. "Where's this voyage heading?" He leaned into Isaac. "L'Olonnais. How long you sailed with him?"

"A couple of years."

"You think he knows how to make a man rich?"

"He has so far."

"You ever have doubts?"

Isaac stayed silent.

"There's talk he has lost his touch; no?"

Isaac placed his pistol in his lap and looked Reinhardt directly in the eye. "He can't be held responsible for the doldrums."

"How long do you think it'll last?" Jacob asked, hoping to diffuse the conversion.

Isaac picked up his pistol. "I've heard tales of ships being becalmed for months."

"Months? I can't float about here for months." Jacob said.

"Don't worry, mate. That won't happen to us." Jacob looked up hopeful. "We'll be dead before then. Ain't enough water on board to last more than a week."

Jacob's shoulders slumped. He knew as much himself, having helped Helario in the store.

"Don't lose your screws." Reinhardt said, referring to two lockplate screws pivot rolling away from Jacob's reach.

"It's taking too long. It's been ten months since I was pressed." Jacob snatched the screws, dropping them into his cleaning cloth. "I need to get my riches and get back to Tortuga to find a ship."

"What's the hurry?" Reinhardt said.

"Lydia."

"Who's Lydia?"

Isaac rolled his eyes. "You must be the only one who ain't heard about Jacob's sweet lass back home."

Jacob ignored Isaac. "She'll be sixteen soon. Her father will be eyeing up suiters."

"Suiters?" Reinhardt scoffed. "Sounds noble."

Isaac chortled along with Reinhardt. "You still think she's waiting for you?"

Jacob shot Isaac a scathing glance. "She's waiting."

"If her father has suiters lined up, why do you think he'll let her marry you?" Reinhardt asked.

"I don't care what he thinks. He's the reason I'm in this mess."

"How so?" Reinhardt asked.

"It was him that got me pressed."

Reinhardt leaned in. "Tell me. I haven't anything better to do."

"He offered to meet. He said he wanted to talk about buying my fish for a big Epiphany feast he was having. Said he needed forty fresh pilchards."

"What a rotter." Reinhardt laughed.

"When I turned up at the tavern, he bought me a flagon and sat me up a corner while he chatted with some businessmen. Two hours I sat there waiting for him to finish listening to them chat about land taxes and how they would have to put up rents. He kept buying me ale. I said my mother don't like me drinking too much, but he kept insisting. So I sat, waiting for my turn."

"How is this a mess for you?" Reinhardt asked.

"When his cronies disappeared, we started chatting about the fish. He offered me a great deal. Almost double the usual rate. I was drunk now and had to keep checking the numbers. He told me he liked me and he might be able to do a deal with my mother to lower the rent since my father had died."

"Why don't you like this Rijkman?" Reinhardt asked. "Surprised he's not sent out a search party for you."

"It was all a trick. By the time we'd finished, I couldn't stand straight. I remember stumbling outside to use the privy. Next thing, I'm waking up with a sore head on *Kestrel*."

"You think he planned for you to be pressed?"

"I'm sure of it. I've run it through my head every way. We were in The Seven Stars. It's a place for gentlemen. Not like The Rusty Anchor in town. You never see the pressgang snooping around that part of the harbour. And he hated my father and never liked me calling on Lydia. So why offer me double for my fish and to help with the rent? It was all just bait. Get me drunk, then send me into the night when he'd arranged for the pressgang to be waiting. Job done. No more problem for his daughter."

Isaac puffed out his cheeks. "If he's gone to the trouble to get rid of you, it doesn't sound like he'd let you marry Lydia anyway, even if you made it back."

"I ain't a boy no more. I'll kill him." Jacob blushed. "Anyway, he'd have no say in it if I turned up with a chest full of silver. Me and Lydia could do what we want." Jacob wrapped a cloth patch around the cleaning rod and forcing it down and then back up the barrel.

Reinhardt shook his head with a smile. "We've all got our reasons, I suppose. Yours ain't no dafter than anyone else's, my friend. How sure are you that she'll marry you?"

"We're in love." Jacob snapped. "I just need to stop her father from marrying her off before I can get home."

Isaac wiped his lockplate before cajoling it back into the walnut stock. He admired its fit before inserting the screws. "But she'll only marry you with your pockets full of silver?"

Jacob huffed. He snatched up the cloth, spilling the screws back onto the deck. "She'll marry me."

When the last screw was inserted, they sat for a moment, admiring the pistols. Jacob mused over Isaac's final words.

"You don't feel the mutiny in the air?" Reinhardt said. "I've been hearing whispers."

"I've heard them." Isaac replied. "Best ignore them. It'll come to nothing. Just whispers. No point joining a mutiny when there's no way to sail. And once the wind finds us, all thought of mutiny will be forgotten."

"I don't know, my friend. It's not just the hands whispering. I heard a couple of officers are taking it seriously."

"You best watch who hears you." Isaac said. "If you've any sense, you'll let it die there–just talk, nothing more."

Jacob sat pouting for the next hour. From the forecastle, he watched Harvey sitting on the quarterdeck. The navigator eased himself to his feet. Shielding his eyes from the sun, he stood gazing at the sails.

"Wind." Harvey shouted hoarsely across the decks. "We have wind. Moise, Denis. We have wind."

The ship's bell rang out, awakening the crew from their delirium. All talk of mutiny dissipated in the wind. The hunt for treasure resurfaced in the minds of the greedy. But first, they must find water.

Within a turn of the sandglass, *Marquise* had set full sail. They mustered barely a knot, but to a crew who hadn't felt so much as a breeze in nearly three weeks, it might as well have been the fastest ship on the seas. They had drifted much farther north than planned and instead of Nicaragua, the charts told them the Westward drift had deposited them in the Gulf of Honduras. Moise called a meeting and offered their options.

"We can sail south back to Nicaragua as planned. San Juan ain't too far. Maybe we'll find the fleet." Helario pushed forward, but Moise anticipated his remarks. "I know, Helario. We have no more supplies. The other option is to make land and seek provisions where God has willed us."

The vote was unanimous. Honduras or Nicaragua? It made little difference to the crew. They would ransack any Spanish town or native camp. They had been on scrapings since the wind had returned–and there was not a scrap of food to be found in the stores. Once they had settled their debt with their belly's they would continue the hunt for the real treasures.

Many recognised the lands espied on the horizon. The river Xagua was around the headland. The captain was quick to boast of his cleverness to seize the canoes, perfect for navigating its shallow waters.

As the mouth of the river came into view, a cry rang out from the crow's nest. "Ships off the bow!"

The admiral strode from his cabin to take in the view. "Ah, not as planned, but God still favours me. Mr Vauquelin? Send an envoy to call a meeting on the beach."

Marquise was not the only vessel to have suffered in the doldrums. The entire fleet had been ensnared by the currents and deposited together.

Majority of the buccaneers made camp on the beach, dividing the dismal supplies from each ship according to need. The beach crawled with sloth like chaos as all six crews swapped stories of boredom and boredom. A foraging party was organised with men from each of the six vessels.

Jacob lost Henri in the crowd as they made their way to the estuary mouth. His frustration peaked as he pushed through a huddle from *Tigre*, before being spat out into an unlit fire pit owned by *Leopard*. "Watch it, kid," came the call as he was pushed into another melee. Being spun on his heels, he stumbled into the back of a crewman from *Stad Gouda*.

"Watch out." Came a familiar voice.

"Doyle!" The old nerves rushed through Jacob's body. He hadn't seen Doyle since Tortuga. *Stad Gouda* had welcomed the Irish giant, and Jacob had hoped he'd seen the last of him. He straightened his shoulders and stood tall. Still not as tall as Doyle, but he was sixteen now, a man, and he refused to be bullied.

"Howda, gombeen." Doyle said, clasping his hand to Jacob's shoulder, pulling him closer. He stooped to meet Jacob eye to eye. "Surprised to see you here. Thought you'd done a bunk. Scared of that Brazilian."

Jacob tried to pull away, but Doyle's huge hand held tight.

"Did they ever find Harvey? I heard he abandoned you. Fed up of showing you how to hold his tiller." Doyle laughed, allowing Jacob to wriggle free.

"He's on *Marquise*."

"So, the pious prig's turned pirate. This new world really is upside down."

Jacob locked eyes with Doyle, gripping the hilt of his cutlass. Doyle lowered his gaze. "Big man now, are ye?" He said stepping back with a grin, hands raised. "Ah, go on so–draw that shiny blade o' yours. I won't stop ye. Me da always gave me one swing before he offered the back o' his hand."

Jacob weighed up the odds. Doyle made no attempt for his own cutlass. His enormous fists like clubs hovering next to his thick head. A huge grin in the centre waiting for a mistake.

"Jake. What are you doing?" Henri stepped into the invisible combat zone, grabbing Jacob by the elbow. "Le Picard's waiting for us. Hey Doyle. How's life with the Dutchies?"

Before Doyle could respond, Henri dragged Jacob through the crowd. Jacob turned, but Doyle had not followed. He just stared through the mass of men–laughing.

Twenty

Jacob knelt in the fifth of the twelve stolen canoes. Each canoe held a crew of ten to twelve men. Half of the men rowed while the other half aimed their muskets into the jungle. Jacob was appointed as an oarsman, as he was not considered a marksman. His youthful arms ached as he paddled. Any exposed skin itched from mosquito bites. Occasionally, he eased his suffering by raising his oar from the water, allowing his free hand to scratch the puncture wounds. When spotted, Piero, who sat behind him, rewarded him with a kick in his ribs for slacking.

The rowing became monotonous, and his mind soon strayed to home. As a boy, he was fascinated by stories of coastal smugglers. His father would warn him of the dangers beheld by such a world, and he would nod dutifully, promising to stay law abiding. But his rebellious daydreams had always meandered to concoct a future full of treasures and the freedom of the ocean.

Before Jacob had stepped up to become the man of the house, he and Lydia would hide out in the cave at Maenporth beach, watching the boats on the horizon. They imagined themselves part of a crew rowing ashore in the dead of night–moonlight casting imposing shadows. A mimicked owl call would drift across the sand to signal the awaiting beach party. They would unload contraband from the

New World into hidden coves. Tunnels cut into the cliffs would secrete the stolen goods into underground cellars before horse and carts would disappear it across The Downs. Fine foods, spices, and silks from around the world would be bought for a fraction of their cost. They would trick the rich into buying back their own goods. The poor would rain accolades upon them. They would be heroes. Now he found himself thrust into the reality of one of his adventurous daydreams. Would he ever find his way back to Cornwall? One thing was certain. To come all this way and not return with his riches would be to squander a fine opportunity.

The tree canopy reached for the sky, thickening the air, suffocating his daydreams. The deeper inland they rowed, the closer the trees encroached the riverbank until their roots no longer needed the land but grew straight out of the water like spindly legs.

"Mangroves." Piero said. "Mind the crocs. Rip your arm off before you get a chance to wave it goodbye."

The boats funnelled into single file to avoid the roots. Jacob leaned over, watching the mangrove shadows. The men were suspicious of these lands, having heard rumours of untouched civilisations that ate human flesh. Some claimed they had witnessed such cannibalism with their own eyes only just escaping by the skin of their teeth. The musketeers kept eager eyes on the riverbanks. Their senses heightened by the stories as the oarsmen battled the current.

Henri sat in front of Jacob with his new musket, searching high and low. Jacob startled when the musket twitched at the growing shadows.

The fleet rounded a bend. A small village nestled into a clearing. Timber huts encircling a large fire pit. Two dugout canoes, smaller than their own, were moored at the shore. If not for the dugouts and smoke wisping from the embers, the settlement would have seemed disused. The men quietened as each canoe sighted the village. The silence amplified the monkey screeches and birdsong high in the treetops. As Jacob's canoe rounded the bend, a flock took flight some distance to the south, causing the men to jerk their heads upward in unison. The lead canoes paddled to the shore.

A dozen men crept onto the land. They edged up the steep bank into the village, being careful to stay away from its centre. Bakari led five men to the left, and Melchor did the same to the right. After a cautious five minutes of checking each hut's entrance, they met at the farthest end of the village. It had not long been abandoned.

The clearing could not berth all the canoes, but the river widened, and the slower current allowed many to float together in the middle. Mooring ropes were tied from each neighbour, creating a floating bridge until the last canoe nestled at the opposite bank.

L'Olonnais danced across the bridge and strode to the centre of the village. He prodded the pit with his cutlass.

"They haven't long left, lads." He gnarled. "These heathens are sure to have food. Go get 'em."

Thirty men, led by Anthony du Puis, Jan Lucas and Philippe Bequel, entered the village with less need for stealth, disappearing into the bush at various points of the compass. The largest party following the path towards the disturbed flock of birds.

Le Picard took charge of the village and ordered Jacob and a dozen others to pick a hut and search for any remanence of food or water. Jacob made for a hut closest to the river's edge. Rectangular, thirty feet long and half that in width. The ends of the hut were rounded, and the palm leaf roof fell so low he had to stoop to enter. Warmth from inside welcomed him. The floor raised under foot allowing him to brush his fingers against the low ceiling.

To his right, a fire pit with a clay pot sat upon three clay feet. The embers of a fire still smouldered, hazing the air. He lifted the pot's lid. Still hot to the touch, he dropped it back with a dull thud. He swore under his breath and looked around for something he could use. He found two wooden sticks within reach resting against the hut wall. They had been fashioned with hooks at their ends. Using the sticks, he lifted the lid by its ears, revealing a broth inside. He crept back to the door and peered out to the busy camp. Everyone was securing the canoes or otherwise searching huts.

Back at the pot he breathed in the aromas. The broth smelt appetising. Upon a small three-legged stool sat various bowls and from the roof hung a wicker basket containing wooden spoons. Using his newfound tools, Jacob took a sup. It tasted salty but rich. Grain and herbs mixed with chicken. A stray terrier on Falmouth dock would not have eaten faster. After his second delicious bowlful, Jacob wiped his mouth and replaced the lid, content having never tasted such a satisfying meal. He suppressed a burp and surveyed the rest of the hut.

Medium-sized animal furs lay together on the ground, which Jacob took to be beds. Three wooden stools hugged the right-hand wall, each with blade cuts on their seats. At the furthest end of the hut, a tree trunk leaned against a hole in the ceiling. A closer inspection revealed notches cut into the trunk serving as foot holes. He climbed the crude ladder and eased his head into the eaves. The attic was empty of people. This did not surprise him–but he was still relieved. Smoke wafted through the room, and Jacob had to wait for his eyes to adjust to the haze. He crawled out onto the floor on all fours, feeling the thick bamboo, rigid beneath him. When his eyesight had accustomed itself, he found the attic was sparse of furnishings with only animal fur beds on the floor. In the far corner, he spied two swollen bags.

The roof sat low, and Jacob more than once brushed his head against the underside as he crawled to investigate the bags. The palm leaves had been carefully woven; layer upon layer creating a thick roof so dense Jacob thought they must last any downpour. As tough as any thatch he'd seen back home. At the far end of the attic, he found the bags full of grain. Jacob remembered the broth below him and the taste like pearl barley. He hauled the bags to the opening and lay on the palm floor, resting a moment enveloped by its surprising comfort. The room felt warm and his belly full. Maybe he could sleep here until the buccaneers left. They wouldn't miss him. Harvey didn't seem to care. Henri and Bastien would come to find him. He sighed and sat up.

On the ground floor, he took another peek outside before taking up his position back at the fire pit for another delicious bowl of sustenance. Once satisfied, he headed back outside with his haul. Bastien had added his own finding to a growing pile. Jacob smiled, noticing a glistening moisture around his friend's mouth.

"What you find?" Jacob asked, wiping his chin.

"Just some bags of grain and a chicken." Bastien replied, putting a finger to the corner of his mouth. "There's a pot of something on a fire which I'll need your help to bring out and share with the crew." He noticed Jacob eyeing his chin and could not suppress a smirk. "How about you?"

"Pretty much the same," Jacob laughed.

Twenty minutes later, all the huts had been searched, and the haul laid out around the central fire. Ten slaughtered hens, a dozen bags of grain and six pots of stew.

"Hum." The admiral inspected the spoils. "That'll not keep us fed for more than an hour. Let's hope the others return with a rich bounty." He pointed to Henri and Bastien. "Get those chucks plucked and on the fire. They'll need a feed when they get back."

Before the meat had time to catch even a hint of heat, musket fire cracked far off to the south, arousing the village. A second search party hustled into the bush. Doyle, who had been loitering around the buccan, huffed when he was ordered to follow. L'Olonnais commanded a dozen men to stay behind to defend the village and keep the fire burning–hoping more food would return. Henri followed his comrades into the bush, while Bastien and Jacob stayed behind to tend to the chickens.

"Keep those birds turning. Nice and slow," Henri shouted before disappearing.

After an hour and a half, the chickens looked cooked. The hunting party's raucous voices could be heard ten minutes before they trickled back to their new camp. From the buccan, Jacob watched Bakari and Melchor push five dark-skinned native women, with bound wrists, into the clearing. L'Olonnais exited a hut, wiping his chin, and stood firm in the centre of his village, welcoming the rightful inhabitants.

Doyle strode over to the fire pit and threw two chickens at Jacob's feet. "Start cooking. It's all you're good for, wench." He snatched a chicken leg from the buccan and turned to his admiral. "There's plenty more coming, sir. The Indians had loads of 'em."

Michiel Andrieszoon stepped from the tree line with two more chickens hanging from his fist. He followed Doyle's example, throwing them at Jacob's feet. He stood. His stare lingering at the cutlass at Jacob's hip.

"Good job, lads," the admiral said. "Mr Penjerrick." He smiled at Jacob. "Get these chickens on the spit. There's a good lad. These hungry devils deserve a good feeding tonight."

"Yes, sir."

Michiel Andrieszoon backed away, swallowed by the growing crowd of returning buccaneers.

The men smiled, happy with a good day's work. After depositing their bounty by the buccan, they slumped in small groups around the fire and at the water's edge. Sacks of water had been discovered and the men who hadn't already refreshed themselves now took their turn.

Jacob picked up the closest chicken at his feet and tuned to Bastien for guidance. Together, they started plucking.

Henri was one of the last to emerge from the bush and saw his friends betraying his trade. "What you been up to? You'll have the meat part raw, and part burnt. Give it here." He picked through the pile of supposedly cooked chickens tutting to himself. "I thought you'd been watching Helario! You'll have us all bringing our guts up." He gazed over the camp, pausing at Doyle tucking into his chicken leg. He looked at Jacob and smiled. "I ain't wrestling it off him. I'm sure his belly can handle it." He turned his attentions back to cooking the chucks, showing Jacob how it should be done.

Henri and Bastien constructed a second crude buccan for the new batch of chucks while Jacob distributed the chickens they felt confident enough to share.

"So, Mr Vauquelin." L'Olonnais said to Moise, on the other side of the fire pit. "What did you find? Did we lose anyone?"

"No losses, Admiral. Some of the lads don't feel at their best, though. The mosquitos are taking their toll. The Indians fled when they saw us. Women and children mainly. They'd packed up what they could, but we rounded up those five before they got away." He took a chicken leg from Jacob. "Thanks, lad." Moise said. "Figured you'd want to ask them a few questions."

"Good work, Mr Vauquelin. Thank you, Mr Penjerrick." L'Olonnais said, taking a hunk of chicken. "Cooked to perfection." Jacob skipped to the next group of hungry hunters. "Mr Obasi? Set our guests over by that hut. No food or water. We want them eager for talk." Bakari, ever present with his boarding axe, gestured to the natives to sit with their backs to the hut. He positioned himself ten yards away with a full chicken leg in his fist, taunting his prisoners.

The light faded, and the meat was served. Jacob sat on a stone seat by the buccan. Henri joined him, offering his folding knife with a chunk of meat fixed to the end.

"Eat up mate. We're going to need our strength these next few days. News will travel before us, warning the other tribes we're here. This might be the last feast we have for a while."

Jacob accepted the knife and took a bite. He returned his attention to the five native women. They sat with their legs crossed and their bound hands in their laps. Not once did they try to communicate with their neighbour. Their expressions: emotionless, with their sights set on the middle distance. The camp offered nothing to rouse them from their stoic trance. He wondered if they felt humiliation like he would.

"What do you think they think of us?" Jacob asked.

"Who them?" Henri nodded. "They hate us. Given a chance, they would slit our throats and eat our flesh."

"You ain't one who believes in cannibals, are ya?"

"That's what I've heard. They eat their own babies."

Jacob turned to face Henri. "Don't be daft. Why would they eat their own babies?"

"It's just what I heard."

"Then why are we sitting here eating their chickens? Doesn't seem likely if they had chickens ready to eat, they would be eating their own babies. I think someone's trying to scare us. I bet they ain't no different to us, only they ain't got no use for money."

"Or a chemise" Henri laughed and took his knife back from Jacob, who had finished his meat and becoming too familiar with the blade.

"Helario told me they traded with the first white men that came their way, but as the years have gone on, they've grown to distrust us 'cus we keep killing 'em."

"Well, whatever the reasons," Henri replied. "I wouldn't want to meet their men if I were alone without my cutlass. I don't want to get eaten for something Melchor's granddaddy did forty years ago. I'm happy to leave them be and find Spanish gold."

Jacob's eyes drifted towards L'Olonnais and Moise as they walked over to Bakari. Moise pointed to the prisoners, causing Bakari to stomp to the closest, and drag her to her feet by her bound wrists. She trembled in the firelight. L'Olonnais strolled over and without a word, produced a dagger from his belt and slit the prisoner's throat. The body went limp and fell to the ground in a heap. Blood pulsed from her jugular. Jacob stood. Henri followed, almost choking on a chicken bone.

"Bloody hell." Henri spluttered. "He's got the taste again."

Twenty-One

A silence flooded the camp. Moise gestured to Bakari, who snatched up a second captive.

Jacob gawped at the sight through the flames. "Why did he kill her?" He whispered.

Henri shook his head. "The darkness has found him again." He said, keeping his voice low.

All eyes found L'Olonnais.

"The darkness?"

"He wants answers." Henri said. "I've seen him cut slices off Spanish prisoners before. Torturing them until they reveal where their treasure's hidden. He's burned them alive or used woodling 'til their eyeballs pop from their skull–he loves the rack. But I've never seen him murder natives."

Jacob squeezed the hilt of his cutlass.

"Klaude?" L'Olonnais shouted. "Where's Klaude?"

Klaude ducked from beside a hut.

"You mean he's done this before?" Jacob asked.

Henri nodded.

"You didn't mention any of this when you sold me the idea of being rich like that Queval guy?"

Klaude past the buccan hustling to his captain. His eyes fixed on those of the second prisoner.

"Weren't it obvious?" Henri said. "He's the Bane of Spain. How do you think he gets seven hundred men to follow him? You don't get rich on Spanish silver by asking nicely." Henri's eyes returned to the scene past the fire pit.

"Ask her where her men are," L'Olonnais said to Klaude. "And how far it is to the nearest Spanish town?" He raised his dagger as Klaude translated his questions. The prisoner stared at L'Olonnais, unfazed.

"What's the difference?" Henri said, not taking his eyes off the dagger. "You don't have to torture no one. We head to The Main, kill a few Spaniards, and come back to Tortuga rich men."

"What do you mean, kill a few Spaniards? You said stay in the pack. Do a bit of shouting and collect our share. They would just hand it over when they saw how many we were. I ain't stupid. I knew the risks, but I didn't think I was sailing with a madman."

Henri shot Jacob a sharp eye. "Shhh. You're right. We just keep our heads down and stay out of trouble. Let the admiral do his thing, then collect our money."

Admiral L'Olonnais placed his dagger to the prisoner's throat, offering her one last chance to save herself. With no response imminent, he eased the blade through her windpipe. He stepped forward. Their noses almost touching. He snatched the dagger back to his hip and a second body fell in a heap next to the first.

With no persuasion, Bakari picked up the third prisoner. Younger than the first two; slim and muscular. A hint of trepidation in her eyes. L'Olonnais stepped closer to the younger women stroking his blood-stained blade across her skin from her stomach to her neck. He hissed his question.

"Where are your men and how far to a Spanish town?"

"The man's a madman." Jacob said under his breath. Klaude translated. The young native stiffened, finding her bravery. A few seconds later, L'Olonnais retracted the dagger from her eye socket. She slumped to the ground.

"Admiral!" Jan stepped out from the crowd and teased over to the bloody scene. "Maybe a little compassion may be given. They are frightened and alone. May I question this next one?"

L'Olonnais turned to face the Dutchman and shot him a glare. Jan stopped his advance but did not retreat.

Bakari lifted the fourth, more elderly native, to her feet. Klaude pleaded the question again. This senior tribeswoman made it obvious she would not give up her knowledge. L'Olonnais' anger rose. He forced his blade so deeply into her throat that her head hung backwards, hinged on her spinal cord. He thrust the body into the lap of the final native, who still sat silently stoic.

Jacob turned to Henri, witnessing the same panicked eyes, unable to speak. He looked at Jan, who had no motivation to help the last native. He faced the camp to see not a soul moved. Daniel Montbars stood with Michiel Andrieszoon and Doyle, all absorbed with the bloody scene dancing in the firelight. Bakari pulled the fifth native to her feet. Both he and the tribeswomen glistened with blood. Neither seemed to notice.

The captain stepped forward and turned to face Klaude. "Tell her I will slice her open from her privates to her chest and cut out her innards and throw them in the fire while she is still awake if she does not answer my very simple questions."

Klaude turned to the final victim, wrapping his fingers around her bound hands, pleading into her apathetic eyes. Before Klaude could finish, the native craned her neck forward and whispered into his ear. He stumbled backwards, almost falling over Bakari. The native raised her hands to the heavens and screeched in an inaudible tongue. L'Olonnais raised his knife in defence and in a single swipe the native thrust her bound wrists through the blade, freeing her binds. She raised her arms wide to the heavens and chanted again.

"What is she saying, Klaude? What is she saying?" L'Olonnais asked.

Klaude stood frozen, unable to answer his admiral. Frightened shouts from around the camp punctuated the silence. "Kill her. Kill the bitch."

"Klaude? What is she saying?" L'Olonnais urged.

It was all over in seconds. The native lowered her hands, grasping the fist of Admiral L'Olonnais. She thrust the dagger into her own belly, pulling L'Olonnais close, forcing the blade up and into her heart. She dropped to the floor with her womenfolk. Dead.

L'Olonnais stood frozen to his spot. His hands an oozing mess of blood. He turned to Klaude and asked again. "What did she say?"

Klaude stood still for many moments. He composed himself long enough to turn to his long time brethren. "She has cursed you. She has summoned Papa Nahualli." Klaude turned away and sat at the fire opposite Jacob and Henri. His eyes staring into the flames.

L'Olonnais stood silent, staring at the pile of natives on the ground. "Nonsense." He scoffed.

"You will not survive the year," Klaude said, turning from the flames. "Once Papa Nahualli is summoned, he will never stop. Only revenge will satisfy the curse."

L'Olonnais stared at Klaude, seeing the seriousness in his eyes. He turned to the stunned crew. "Nonsense. It's hoccum. These Indians eat their own. They're mad. I defy this Papa Nahualli, whoever he is."

Jacob caught L'Olonnais' eyes. Wide and crazed.

"He will not kill me," L'Olonnais bellowed, throwing up his arms. "I cannot be killed. I will kill him. Bakari, throw the bodies into the water. Let their spirits trouble some other part of the river."

Bakari picked up the first body and cast it into the river. Jacob sat back on the ground, watching the corpse bob to the surface. Face down, arms wide. She drifted with the current around the bend. He wrapped his coat tight around his chest, protecting himself from the chill.

The camp remained silent for a long time. Only the cracking of firewood and the babbling of the river could be heard between Bakari's grunts and the five splashes. L'Olonnais snapped from his trance.

"Double the sentries. They'll be plenty of eyes on us and they won't be happy. Wits sharp lads." He walked over to the buccan and, using his bloody blade, sliced himself a chunk of meat from a charred chicken carcass. "Tomorrow, we continue south. Let's hope the next village can settle our stomachs."

There was no great cheer. No rapture of enthusiasm. L'Olonnais' words managed only to coax their minds back to reality. Eyes locked and false brave smiles flashed across worried faces.

"We're all going to die?" Jacob said slumping back to his stone seat.

Henri joined his friend on the ground.

Daniel Montbars spoke next, rallying the men. "Sharp eyes. Like the admiral said. No more thought of this witchcraft. Just desperate words from a dying woman. We have a job to do. Henri? Jacob? Carve that next batch. Let's get fed before the sun disappears. There's much to do before we're back at our ships. No time to waste."

Jacob and Henri trudged to the buccan, startling Bastien as they cut away the blood-stained meat disposing of it in the fire. An anxious focus gripped all three as they sliced the chicken carcasses before offering them to the crew. Hardly a word was spoken for the remainder of the evening as the camp ate, deep in thought.

"Who's Papa Nahualli?" someone asked.

At the earliest sign of daybreak, the men needed no encouragement to raise themselves and gather their belongings. Jacob was no exception. He hadn't slept at all, haunted through the night by the stoic faces of the natives as they accepted their fate. As he walked through the camp, the atmosphere felt skittish–but surprisingly not because of the killing of the innocent women, or even by the ensuing revenge of their kin, but by the curse of Papa Nahualli.

"I heard tales of this Nahualli in the Yucatan." Jan said as the crew packed the canoes. "It's a shadow that follows its victim, whispering evil thoughts into his ear. It'll drive you mad. You'll either kill yourself or someone will kill you. I've heard tales of men killing their matelots over a chicken only to swallow the chuck whole and choke on the bones. Only when you're dead does Papa Nahualli rest. Waiting to be awoken by the next call of the curse."

Other crewman had heard similar stories about the boogie man and had their own tales of needless murder. Back in Cornwall, Jacob had grown up with fables of spriggans. Pixie-like creatures who would protect their lands. Lost cattle would be attributed to the spriggans. If a traveller went missing, his father would claim the spriggans had tricked them to their death. But his father would always have a glint in his eye–a suggestion of jest. A cautionary tale for children who wandered off too far. This Papa Nahualli seemed no more credible than these over territorial sprites. He could not believe these grown men were taken in by such tales meant to scare children. Even so, he collected his belongings with as much haste as any of them.

L'Olonnais expressed no concern for the curse. Instead, taunting it, striding the camp, laughing at his imminent demise. The crew nodded and grinned as they loaded the canoes with food destined for the men back at the ships.

"He won't wash." Henri said into Jacob's ear as they sat waiting for the canoes to depart.

Jacob gave a sideward glance at L'Olonnais. His face and hair were still smeared with the blood from the native victims.

"He was of this mind in Maracaibo." Henri continued. "He went for weeks before he cleaned his hair. Not long before we picked you up. His eyes had a vacant look. Like they weren't quite his own."

As L'Olonnais ducked behind a hut, Jacob noticed him run his fingers through his bloody hair. He was sure he even witnessed him lick his fingertips clean.

They sat, waiting. Jacob's knees rested on the stolen animal fur, which he had been told were from ocelots or leopards. Each of the twelve canoes had, in some way, been lined with the soft skins. He felt uneasy leaving the natives with no beds, but he could not deny the blessed cushion the fur offered to his knees. The furs would be the least of the native's concerns. Jacob's eyes explored the decimated camp. Chicken carcasses and broken stools littered the ground. Huts left dishevelled. Even this would mean nothing compared to the loss of five of their womenfolk.

Le Picard ducked out of the furthest hut and strode over to the admiral with a pistol in his outstretched hand. "Admiral? One of the lads found this in that hut?"

L'Olonnais took the firearm and stared at it with furrowed brows.

"It's Spanish, sir. Figured the natives must be trading with them. Or at least stole it from them. We must be close to a Spanish port."

"I figure you might be right." L'Olonnais paused, thinking. "Change of plan. Tell the lads we won't push on up the river. We'll head back to the ships. If I'm right, there'll be a port not far and plenty of food and water to be had. Hopefully, plenty of plunder to boot."

Back at their ships, they unloaded the spoil, relieved to be back among their comrades. They told their tales of murder and curses—jettisoning much of their nerves.

The food from the native camp was divided between the ships, with strict instructions for quarter rations. Not enough had been foraged to risk the journey back to Tortuga, or even to Jamaica or Cuba—especially with the lingering threat of dead weather. Sailing west along the Honduran coast was their only choice, committed now to finding the Spanish port.

Jacob stood at the quarterdeck steps. Moise glanced over to Harvey, who looked up from his maps. He responded with a shake of the head.

"Sorry, lad. Master Harvey's got no time to be chatting. Go find Le Picard for your duties."

Jacob stood for a while pondering what had changed with his relationship with his onetime mentor.

"Ville, ville," came Henri's call from the crow's nest. A long spit of beach protruded into the ocean. Beyond which the trees had been felled and replaced with stone and wooden buildings. Small boats were moored along the coast, with one larger ship anchored off the shore.

"It's a big town, Admiral," Moise mused as he lowered his spyglass. "But it ain't fortified."

"That Brig ain't fully manned either." L'Olonnais replied, lowering his own spyglass. "I don't think the Indians have warned them of our being. We should act quickly. Send word to the other ships."

"Any man found lagging," L'Olonnais growled, "will be run through without question. We can ill afford to be discovered, and I do not trust any of you soggy dogs to not spill our plans before your guts. We attack at dawn, so we have no time for rest. If we make haste, we might get a few hours' sleep before the cock crows."

Three hundred men packed up their belongings and melded into the jungle. Fifty men remained guarding the barges, ready in case of a swift retreat. A small party of twenty men lead the way, carrying only a musket each. They fanned out and in short bursts, ran, stooped and covered their partner as he ran past and did the same. They repeated the manoeuvre until they disappeared from sight and sound.

"How many do you think we'll find?" Bastien asked, sidling between Henri and Jacob.

"Depends on that warehouse." Henri said. "If a mule train has arrived from the mines, then it should be heavily guarded."

"Do you think the natives tipped 'em off?" Jacob asked.

"Shouldn't think so. They ain't exactly happy with the Spanish. Most are put to work in the mines. No better than slaves. Just as likely to join the fight with us."

"Not after we killed their women?" Jacob asked.

"No 'spose not."

"Are they good fighters?"

"Some are. Some poison their spear tips. Don't matter who your enemy is if they drop to their knees before he can draw his cutlass."

Jacob felt for his own cutlass, then investigated the dense jungle all around. His pistol, issued to him by Denis, was in his knapsack, but it was unloaded. Like all the firearms carried by the crew, not one was loaded or primed for fear of a misfire, warning the enemy of their approach.

"How many do you think we'll find?" Bastien asked again.

Jacob looked to see Bastien bouncing in his stride.

"I don't know Bastien. Calm down," Henri said.

"What's up with Bastien?"

"He gets excited when we might be killing Spaniards. He was like this when we sacked Maracaibo. He'll get himself killed if he ain't careful."

Bastien stopped bouncing, but Jacob could sense his excitement hadn't abated. "You got the itch too, Hen. I can tell." Bastien said.

Jacob glimpsed a smile at the corner of Henri's mouth.

"Uncle Gefrei would be proud of us," Bastien pushed.

"Maybe. But killing ain't for fools. Calm your innards or you won't be avenging anyone."

"How many Spaniards have you killed?" Jacob asked.

"Nine." Bastien blurted.

"When have you killed nine Spaniards?" Henri interjected.

"Maracaibo and Gibraltar."

"I ain't seen you kill nine Spaniards. Three, maybe."

"Ain't true. I killed at least four when we raided the fort."

Henri shook his head. "If you say so."

"Doesn't it bother you that you've killed people?"

"They ain't people. It's more like killing a cockroach." Bastien quipped.

"But they have lives and families just like we do."

"Are you half Spaniard? They're like mosquitos." Bastien said. "The lowest insect on earth. Sucking gold like blood to feed their empire. When they've killed someone you love, you'll know."

Jacob opened his mouth but thought better of continuing the conversation. The trio walked in silence for the rest of the journey. The further they walked, the quieter the column became. Jacob noticed the route kept the convoy close to the coast. He could smell the salty air to his right, never more than one hundred yards away. After two hours, they reconnected with the scouts and rested. The sun had disappeared, leaving only a faint hue of light dappling through the trees. The weary troops sat, grateful to not have to strain their eyes any longer. Reinhardt pushed through the bush, relaying his findings to the admiral.

"They ain't seen us, sir," Reinhardt said. "There's only one guard house between us and the town."

L'Olonnais grunted under his breath, running his fingers through his hair. "Is this the only road in?"

"'Tis sir. Straight through to the port itself. The land narrows to no more than a thousand yards. Beach to the right. It's about a mile 'til the first houses. We've had a sneaky stroll, but no sign of life to that point."

"Very good. Mr de Jaager. Get some rest." L'Olonnais turned to Moise and Le Picard, who had made their way to the front of the column. "We rest for a few hours. No fires. And any man caught disappearing into the bush will see his innards on the end of my blade. If they need to piss, piss where they stand. We ready ourselves before dawn."

"Aye, sir" Le Picard and Moise turned and headed back to spread the orders to the platoon leaders.

Jacob huddled his knees to his chest and wrapped Henri's old coat around his shoulders like a cocoon. Grateful for its warmth. The shadows grew longer, blackening the world around him, leaving only the murmurs of the men. As the darkness fell, the silence spread, which heightened Jacob's thoughts. He'd grown to fear the silence. His head was a hum of confused thoughts he didn't much care to entertain. He tried to conjure to mind the riches he would take back to Cornwall, but the unknown dangers of the next morning's escapades would not let him get a moment's sleep.

Twenty-Two

High in the tree canopy sat the howler monkey. His brown tail wrapping the branch as he sat with his furry arms hugging his knees, contemplating the hundreds of unfamiliar humans intruding on his territory. His troop had retreated to the edge of the town, but he had remained, keeping a watchful eye–ready to sound the alarm. He'd locked eyes with a boy sat below an adjacent tree hugging his own knees.

Jacob could account for every second of the previous night. Every creak of a tall pine tree, every shuffle of an animal. The sentries calling back men who'd wandered too far from camp to take a shit. Jacob's only comfort came from the waves lapping the coast.

The first signs of daybreak had glinted through the southern trees, offering enough light for the buccaneers to see their neighbour for the first time in hours.

Jacob smiled at the monkey. They had formed a bond. Both intrigued by the other.

The admiral rustled past, finding his lieutenants, sending orders down the line to ready themselves. Jacob glanced back to the canopy. The monkey had gone.

Before the morning awoke, the three hundred men had tip-toed down the dusty track to the town many suspected to be Puerto Cavallo.

"Mr Penjerrick." L'Olonnais said. "Rear guard. Keep yourself out of trouble. Mr Bodine, Mr Trivette. Stay with him. Keep him safe."

"Sir." Bastien protested. "I ain't signed up to nurse a frightened pup."

"Do as I say, Mr Trivette." L'Olonnais marched back to his lieutenants.

A mist whispered from the ocean over the golden beach, blurring the only road into town. The only signs of life were a dog barking in the distance and a mangy cat who'd stopped in the clearing to lick its leg. Captain Lucas and Captain du Puis had been ordered to attack the anchored brig just before first light. The buccaneers stood in rows along the tree line waiting for the first shot of a great gun in the harbour basin.

Jacob eased his cutlass from its scabbard. In his other hand, he held his now primed and loaded pistol. For the first time, he felt the true weight of his new sword. He'd held it many times, practising with Henri, but now it felt real. A man's weapon. Death and protection in his hands. His breath felt shallow and erratic. Breathing through his mouth eased his anxiety. But he could still feel his heart pulsing through his chest. Henri and Bastien stepped to either side of him. Jacob looked to his left to see Henri grinning back. His black marks on his face giving him a menacing demeanour. To his right, Bastien scowled at him. Humiliated to be at the rear. His excitement was still visible as he swayed from foot to foot.

"Any minute now," Bastien said. "Come on du Puis, fire that gun."

"Don't be a hero." Henri said to Jacob.

Jacob nodded. His new shoes were tight around his ankles. His pistol felt awkward in his left hand. His throat felt tight with a fearful hunger. The taste of Helario's salted chicken lingered on his tongue from his morning mouthful. Silence. His nose itched. He dared not scratch.

From a distance, the great gun broke the anticipation. Three hundred buccaneers internally counted. Jacob stared at Le Picard, who stood yards away, keenly eyeing L'Olonnais forty yards to their right. L'Olonnais lowered his cutlass. Le Picard's arm fell along with three other company leaders along the line. They ran. Not a scream or a shout as they padded along the narrow spit of land. The open ocean was to their right and the large bay of water to their left.

In the distance the howler monkey howled, alerting a sleepy sentry who had only moments earlier awoken to the sound of the gun out at sea.

The sentry turned to face his post. Through the little guardhouse, he could have seen nothing but dust. Six hundred boots had churned the gravel path into a desert scene. As the first of the marauders approached, the sentry aimed his gun. It was futile, so he raised his barrel in surrender. At the last moment, he fired his musket into the air with a crack.

As the bulk of the column continued past the guardhouse, Le Picard halted and extended his arm to accept the enemy's firearm. He flashed a sympathetic smile. The Spaniard surrendered.

Jacob ran past in time to witness Le Picard accept the musket and presented his own to the prisoner's face. Jacob heard the crack. He glanced over his shoulder and through the dust, he saw the Spaniards' body fall to the ground. His head nowhere and everywhere to be seen.

The buccaneers separated as they crashed into the town like fresh water hitting a dry riverbed. Men diverted left and right or continued straight until the streets sent left or right deeper into the town.

Until this point, Jacob had followed L'Olonnais straight on. But his path now seemed to lead closer to the beach–away from the fighting. Henri tugged at his sleeve, and Jacob followed him and Bastien left onto a cobbled track. The admiral continued straight and out of sight. Henri pushed forward. Bastien followed.

When the buccaneers found the first of the town's folk, the screaming began. The three turned right in the direction of the port. Henri sidestepped as a half-dressed Spaniard tumbled out of a house with a sword held high. The Spaniard looked stunned as the horde of screaming teeth and metal cascaded toward him. He roared in defiance, but was met by Henri's cutlass as it sliced into his raised arm. The Spaniard spun sideways to be met by a cutlass blow from Bastien across the back of the skull.

Jacob hurdled the dying citizen. He eyed the surrounding horror. Children lay crying in open doorways. Women grasped their husbands, dying in their arms. A boy, maybe only four years younger than Jacob, fell through a door in front of the trio. Henri raised his cutlass, but seeing the frightened youth offered him the blunt hilt to the skull, knocking the boy to the ground.

Bastien stopped, crazed with revenge. He slashed at an old man who attacked with a broom, then struck an unarmed man in the thigh, causing him to crumple to the ground. Bastien crowed. As they ran together, Jacob noticed him glance at his unstained cutlass. They clearly no longer lingered in the rear guard. Bastien nudged Jacob into the next townsman, who stumbled into their path.

Jacob stopped, allowing a wash of mayhem to encircle himself and the middle-aged Spaniard. The man looked terrified. He was wearing a white apron. Maybe he was a baker. Jacob felt many eyes casting judgement. Would the English pup make his first kill, even if it was only a civilian? The Spaniard stood rooted. Wave after wave of death crashed around the pair, only half noticing in their private stand-off.

A fleeting image of his grandmother flickered in Jacob's mind. He twitched his sword, only an inch, enough for the Spaniard to strike. His right hand thrust from behind his back. Jacob saw the knife, and in an instant turned his body to evade the blade. Sneaky Spaniard. The blow missed Jacob's stomach, but his left forearm did not escape the four-inch blade.

He dropped the pistol and yelped. The Spaniards' momentum had taken him forward, and he snarled into Jacob's ear. He pulled the knife away and steadied himself for another thrust. Jacob's world slowed. He gazed at his open wound. The blade came again. With pure instinct, he slashed his cutlass into the man's left arm, lodging it fast. The Spaniard stumbled back, pulling Jacob forward. The cutlass freed itself. Jacob slashed again. He missed as the man fell to the ground.

Reinhardt thrust his sword into the Spaniards' belly, finishing the kill. He turned to Jacob and pointed forward. "Watch out, lad."

Jacob steadied himself in time to see a rapier followed by a soldier out for revenge. Death screaming through his teeth. He sidestepped behind a tussle between a landsman and two unarmed Spaniards. He ran in pursuit of Henri and Bastien. He looked over his shoulder to see Reinhardt fire his pistol into the mouth of the oncoming soldier. Dead.

Bastien and Henri disappeared down a side alley. Jacob jumped a young man thrown from a house, then parried a chair wielded by an elderly woman screaming obscenities at anyone in earshot. He took a left down the side alley and almost collided into the back of two Spanish soldiers. They ran forward, unaware, leaving him alone.

He rested his hands on his knees, panting. For a moment, it was peaceful. He caught his breath. His left arm throbbed. Blood trickled down his forearm, making his fist sticky. He dared not look too closely. There was no time to patch it up.

A side door opened. Jacob raised his cutlass and jolted upright. Immobile. She stood bare foot, haloed by the dim light from within the home. Wide eyed wearing a bright yellow dress, not entirely collected at her chest. Long brown hair hanging loose about her tanned nape. Jacob stared. He lowered his cutlass until the tip touched the cobbles. Blood pooling from its point. Her deep desperate brown eyes thanked him before she ran past, back the way he had come.

She paused a moment at the alley's opening before running across the main street, shouldering open a wooden door. Her yellow elegance reclaimed by the shadows. The bedlam faded to silence as he convinced himself it was all a dream. He'd almost killed a man. The man had almost killed him. And amongst it all, a beautiful woman disappeared–like an apparition–with a slam.

A musket crack from a foreign soldier ripped him back to his senses. He and the soldier ran. Neither chasing the other. They just ran. Away from the violence. They burst out of the alley, crashing into a stone building opposite.

Jacob turned right, making his way closer to the port; the destination Henri had told him they should aim for. The soldier turned left. Jacob heard a scream and from over his shoulder he saw Bakari wrestling the soldier to the ground. His thumbs disappearing into the soldier's eye sockets. Jacob grimaced. Up ahead, he saw a flash of Henri's tanned coat as he ran into a shop. Jacob approached, colliding with Henri and Bastien as they burst back into the street.

"Jake, this way," Henri said, grabbing his sleeve.

Bastien grinned at the sight of Jacob's cutlass. "Come on. Le Picard's rallying the troops."

The street opened to a town square. Shops encircled the perimeter, facing a central statue of a portly gentleman that meant nothing to the outsiders. To the left, desperate Spanish soldiers were being pinned back against a bakery by a flood of buccaneers. Le Picard stood in the centre of the melee, arms raised, leading the troops forward.

"Let's round up some Spanish bastards." Bastien said, heading for the bakery.

A rogue soldier shoved Bastien aside, looking for an escape. Henri wrestled him to the ground. "Grab his legs, Jake. Grab his legs."

The soldier had Henri pinned to the ground, both facing the sky. Henri clung on to his chest as the soldier tried to wriggle free. Jacob stood for a second, unsure what he should do.

"Grab his legs," Bastien shouted, turning back mid run. The soldier elbowed Henri in the ribs, causing him to loosen his grip. Jacob threw his sword at the foot of the statue and clasped his arms around the soldier's ankles, receiving a kick in the stomach as reward. A forgotten pain exploded from his forearm. He held on tight, the tension somehow suffocating the agony.

Henri scrambled to his feet, keeping hold of the soldier under his armpits while Jacob held the wriggling ankles. "This way," Henri said, carry their prisoner towards the buccaneers assembling at the other side of the square. They dumped the soldier into the centre, receiving a rapturous cheer. Jacob caught the gaze of the brown eyed Spaniard before he was punched and kicked unconscious.

"Well done, lads." Followed by pats on the back as more buccaneers surged in behind them.

Screams and roars turned to cheers as the buccaneers around the town sensed the victory. Women wailed and children cried at the realisation of the morning's nightmare. Husbands and fathers lay dead in the alleys and streets. The attack was over. Now the genuine horror would begin.

Jacob crouched, holding his arm as Spanish men and soldiers were rounded up and filed into the church occupying the entire northern side of the square. Disgruntled buccaneers guarded the doorways. The remaining buccaneers turned their attentions to the hunt. The treasure would find itself. Women and liquor were what they yearned for first. They had been without for long enough. Not an officer in the Caribbean could hold back their urges. Nor would any want to.

Henri clasped a hand around Jacob's shoulder, guiding him to join their spirited friend.

"Let's get some liquor and make ourselves rich." Bastien said, handing Jacob back his cutlass.

"How's that arm of yours, Jake?" Henri asked, noticing Jacob wince.

"It'll be fine." He said, snatching a cloth from an upturned bakery table.

"Let's see how the Dutch got on with that brig," Henri said.

The trio turned and walked the short distance towards the port. Spanish screams echoed on the wind as the buccaneers devoured ale and wine; wickedness filled the air.

At the port, Moise looked out to sea. The sun still kissed the ocean, illuminating the two ships. He lowered his spyglass. He raised his pistol, firing a shot, and waited. Thirty seconds later, a great gun replied, signalling the buccaneers had control of the brig.

"You made it then, Jake? I hoped you would."

Jacob turned, still blowing hard, to find Isaac with his arms outstretched. Jacob embraced his English compatriot, grimacing with pain.

"See you wetted your blade, Mr Penjerrick. I hope you kept him safe, Mr Bodine." The admiral continued past towards the dock to meet his quartermaster. Over his shoulder, he called back. "Mr Dargate? Make sure our youngest brethren gets rewarded tonight."

"Aye sir." Isaac grinned, slapping Jacob's good arm.

Jacob smiled, clutching his forearm.

"So, what's first on the list? Women or liquor?" Isaac asked.

"Liquor." Bastien answered.

"Who's hungry?" Isaac said. "Jacob? Are you alright?"

Jacob fell to the ground with a thump.

Twenty-Three

Out at sea, a storm threatened. Dark clouds tumbled over the horizon. A huge rain shaft sliced behind the closer clear skies. In the town square, Jacob sat in the afternoon sun, assessing the scene. His belly was full and his head no longer swooned. He sat with Henri, Bastien, and Isaac, who were chattering about the happenings of the morning–each painting their heroic version of events. Jacob only half listened as he turned over his own violent encounter. Would his actions have made his grandmother proud?

A cool ocean breeze tickled his neck. Through a side street to the left of the church, he could see the port. The rest of the fleet had joined *Tigre* and *Stad Gouda* in anchorage. Harvey would be at the tiller or pawing over his maps. They hadn't spoken since Tortuga. Jacob was sure they'd shared a bond–having spent hours at the tiller. What had made the navigator retreat to his cantankerous ways?

He took a sip of wine and fidgeted with the bandage around his left forearm. The adrenaline had dissipated, and the throbbing had begun. Isaac had assured him that although the cut looked deep, no major damage had been done.

"You'll survive lad," Isaac had said with a wink when Jacob had found his focus after collapsing in the square. His comrades had gathered chairs and a table outside the bakery and set Jacob down to rest. Isaac cleaned out the gash before surprising Jacob with rum into the wound. He'd tied a tourniquet tight to stem the bleeding.

"Don't let Venette get a peek," Isaac said, noticing Jacob rubbing his forearm. "He'll be quick about using his old saw. I don't think he knows of any other tools. If in doubt, hack it off. Never trust a surgeon who's been pressed."

"I think I'll take my chances. It ain't too bad." Jacob wiggled his fingers. "See."

"Open the bandage later to let out the bad humors." Isaac stood and faced the square. "Aye up. Moise is back. Let's see how much plunder was had then."

The others at the table looked up to see the quartermaster carrying his logbook towards the statue.

"You'll get an extra hundred pieces if you let the doctor cut your arm off, Jake," Bastien jested.

Jacob held his bandage tight, following the others into the growing crowd.

"The news ain't good, lads," Moise began. He shushed the groans. "I ain't one for lying, and these numbers can't help but speak the truth. We ain't yet even covered costs."

Some of the men headed back into town to join their comrades, who'd stayed in the alehouses and brothels, not wanting to leave their newly warmed beds. They didn't need Moise to elaborate on what they had already guessed. Rum and women tasted as good in Puerto Cavallo as they did in Tortuga–and today it was all free.

Moise continued to tell how there had been nothing of real value in the town. The two stone warehouses were both empty. No gold or silver from the mines. That ship must have sailed. Not even coffee or tobacco. Captain Lucas had reported back that the ship they'd taken was in itself a healthy prize. It had twenty-four guns and sixteen mortar pieces, which would add more firepower to the fleet. But its cargo was disappointing, as it only carried sugar and flour.

"Where's the loot?" Came a voice from the thinning crowd.

"We should have gone south. The admiral's lost his touch." Came another.

"The admiral has a plan, lads." Moise said. "Calm your voices. Tomorrow, we push on to find the real treasures,"

"Real treasures? The treasures have sailed. The storehouses are empty. We missed the season." Came a voice from the back.

Jacob caught sight of Le Picard as he raised his eyebrows in agreement. The crowd grew in confidence. Isaac, Henri, and Bastien stayed quiet and watched on.

"We need a new leader." Jacob noticed the crowd part around Reinhardt as he spoke. "We need to take a vo—"

Crack. A pistol shot silenced the crowd. Before their nerves had a chance to settle, L'Olonnais leaped onto the statue base and faced his audience.

"Be quiet, you lousy dogs."

The crowd quietened but still irritability filled the air.

"A week ago, we were drifting in the doldrums. Today we are all fed, and many loins have been relieved." Some nodded in agreement, but many needed more. "This is not our preferred destination, but needs must. We needed food. I found us food. We were low on fresh water, now we overflow. We have yet another ship which offers us flour and sugar."

"That's not enough, captain. We didn't come all this way for flour."

"I agree Mr de Jaager. But we haven't finished yet. We are back to full strength and now we push on and find the real treasure."

"Where to?" It seemed Reinhardt de Jaager had become the unofficial spokesman for the agitated crowd. He was well-liked, a natural leader who had already earned the respect of the original crew.

L'Olonnais lept from his stage and made his way into the centre of the crowd. He dragged with him a Spanish soldier whose hands were bound behind him. His walk no more than a shuffle. Bastien danced as he passed. Henri stood rigid to his right, taking in the vengeful moment. The admiral stopped when he reached Reinhardt, only a few feet from Jacob.

"Where, you ask? We shall find out where." L'Olonnais eased his knife from his sheath and raised it to the soldier's eye. "Where is the treasure, my Spanish friend?" He asked in French and then again in Spanish.

The Spaniard's eyes darted left then right, but found no mercy among the crowd. Only grins and sneers. L'Olonnais asked again, placing the tip of his blade so close to the Spaniards' eyeball any movement would be blinding. The Spaniard tried to pull away, but L'Olonnais placed a hand behind his head and held it so. The Spaniard blinked nervously, brushing his eyelashes against the knife tip.

"The treasure is gone. It sailed to Spain." More groans amongst the crowd causing the prisoner to tremble.

"When did it leave?" L'Olonnais asked with a soft growl.

The prisoner let out a whimper. A dampness formed in the man's trousers. Laughter rippled through the crowd.

"He's pissed his breeches," somebody cried.

"Two months ago." The Spaniard sobbed.

Jacob noticed Le Picard shake his head before striding out of the crowd.

L'Olonnais sighed. "Mr de Jaager?" He turned and found Reinhardt behind him. "Hold this." L'Olonnais stepped aside, not moving the blade, offering it to the vocal crewman. Reinhardt cautiously accepted the knife between his fingertips. In a swift motion, L'Olonnais nudged Reinhardt's elbow, causing him to stab the blade deep into the Spaniards' eyeball. "Mr de Jaager, my dear fellow. You are so clumsy."

The Spaniard fell to his knees, unable to raise his bound hands to his face. Jacob turned away. His fists clenched tight. The morning's events had left him twitchy and this malicious act by L'Olonnais pushed him closer to hysteria.

"Mr de Jaager," L'Olonnais continued. "You must put this poor soul out of his misery. Finish him."

The Spaniard's head raised, searching, having heard his captor's words, blood seeping from his wound. His good eye blurred with tears. Reinhardt looked to L'Olonnais for some sign of jest, but found only venom. An eerie silence rippled through the crowd. Some found excitement at the imminent Spanish murder. Some repulsed. A few of the more fearful who were towards the outskirts slipped away to the safety of the nearest ale house to spread the word that the admiral was at it again. Jacob wished he could slip away, but he was too close.

"Mr de Jaager. Finish him." L'Olonnais urged.

Reinhardt raised the knife to the Spaniards' throat and winced as he cut his gullet from ear to ear. The Spaniard spluttered before slumping to the floor, blood flooding the cobbles.

"The knife." L'Olonnais extended his hand. Reinhardt placed the blade back in L'Olonnais' grasp. "Don't ever question my judgement again." He hissed.

Reinhardt backed away, trying to hide himself in the crowd.

"Next Prisoner." L'Olonnais called back towards the statue.

Bakari, Melchor, and Klaude had already led three more Spanish soldiers into the melee. Bakari brought forward the most senior. At least the rank of captain. His left eye bruised so heavily the swelling had caused it to close. His right brown eye stared at Jacob accusingly as he passed. Jacob shied away.

"Please, señor. I will tell you what you want to know." The man spoke in Spanish, but those not understanding had no trouble interpreting his intent.

"Very good. Where is all the treasure?"

The Spaniard stood immobilised by the convulsing horror at his feet. L'Olonnais tutted and raised his knife to his belly.

"San Pedro, San Pedro" The Spaniard blurted. His attention fully with L'Olonnais. "There is treasure in San Pedro."

"How much treasure?"

"Lots, señor. The mule train comes with gold from the mine in Agalteca and a new mine in San Antonio de Yeguare. The warehouses will be filling fast."

L'Olonnais relaxed his posture, just a little. "Where is San Pedro?"

"I show you, I show you, señor."

"No. You will tell me. Where is it?"

The Spaniard paused. Glancing at the blood pooling around his feet. "It is south, señor. Ten leagues, maybe twelve"

"Is it a safe journey?"

The prisoner gulped. "No, señor."

"Why is it not safe?" L'Olonnais raised his knife again.

The Spaniard paused once more. "Ambuscades, Señor." L'Olonnais closed in on the Spaniards' good eye. "We sent two men south across the bay when we heard you attack. San Pedro has been warned."

"Ambuscades!" The crowd shuffled backwards as L'Olonnais erupted, turning away from his prisoner, pacing as he threw his hands into the air. "Ambuscades!" He turned to face his victim and quick marched back with his knife outstretched.

"No, sir." Jacob couldn't believe his own outburst. Without hesitation, L'Olonnais tacked left and aimed the knife at Jacob. With only an inch to spare, he caught himself and allowed his body to catch up with his outstretched hand. The knife–an inch from Jacob's left eye.

Jacob stood fast, fearing a warm wet patch at his own breeches. Fortunately, none came. The closest onlookers gasped, and those in the back must have wondered why there was no cheer for another dead Spaniard. L'Olonnais lowered his knife and snarled at his subordinate. Saliva gathered at the corners of his mouth as he stood contemplatively.

"No?" He said softer than Jacob expected.

Jacob gulped. "He is helping us, sir. He will help us avoid the ambush." Jacob could not feel his face.

"He is Spanish scum, is what he is." L'Olonnais' face turned purple. "He's sent word to San Pedro of our arrival. He has not helped us." L'Olonnais turned to face the captain of the guard and, on seeing his lousy expression, couldn't help stabbing him in the belly. Then again, in the chest. And again, in the cheek. The Spaniard dropped to the floor, wailing in pain. L'Olonnais crouched over the dying man and stabbed his full hatred into his body, over and over. "Next prisoner!" he roared.

Henri tugged on Jacob's sleeve and eased him away from the front row, hiding him behind frightened seamen.

Melchor led a third prisoner to meet the French devil. L'Olonnais stood in front of his victim, his chest and shirt covered in Spanish blood.

"Do you know of these ambushes?" He boomed at the frightened man.

"Si, señor. I will show you. I promise. Please do not kill me." He looked down to see his comrade twitching on the ground.

L'Olonnais ran his fingers through his hair and caught a hint of Jacob as he tried to hide. "Mr Penjerrick."

The crowd parted, revealing L'Olonnais to Jacob in all his horror. Blood stained from head to navel, smiling with a raised finger, beckoning Jacob forward. The sea breeze blew through the crowd, hardening Jacob's face. Laughter could be heard from the closest tavern. A scream from a bedroom. Silence from the crowd. Jacob held L'Olonnais' gaze, anger swelling inside him.

"Shall I kill this Spanish pig?" L'Olonnais teased. "Come, defend his pitiful life."

Jacob inched forward to stand in front of the sadistic admiral. L'Olonnais smiled, encouraging Jacob to speak.

Twenty-Four

Jacob stood in a mire of confusion. He stared at the dead Spaniard on the ground. The wrong answer and he knew he would end up in the mess at L'Olonnais' feet. His heart raced. What answer could he give that would save himself? "Kill him." He said meekly.

L'Olonnais stood, dumbfounded.

"Kill him." Jacob repeated, louder this time. "Kill them all." What choice did he have? He must play to L'Olonnais' ego. He clung to a memory of his grandmother spitting on the ground–trying to find strength in her hatred. "We do not care for the life of a Spaniard. We only care that his death helps you lead us to riches." Jacob turned, finding Bastien and Henri pleading for some encouragement. They whooped and cheered, encouraging others to join the chorus. Isaac followed their lead. Within seconds, a cacophony of screams filled the crowd.

"Kill him. Kill him. Kill him" Infectious chanting took hold. L'Olonnais gazed at Jacob, then to the crowd. He raised his arms to the sky, accepting the accolade.

The Spaniard met L'Olonnais' gaze, silently pleading with the beast behind his eyes.

L'Olonnais holstered his knife and unsheathed his cutlass. The crowd parted to make room, exposing the lone Spaniard who scuttled left and right like a crab.

L'Olonnais raised his cutlass above his head. He paused, basking in the reverence.

Jacob winced, feeling the fear in the eyes of the Spaniard–his grandmother's sworn enemy.

The buccaneers held their breath. Waiting. With a diagonal slice, the cutlass hacked into the Spaniards' left arm. A groan rippled through the crowd. L'Olonnais pulled the blade free, and with an opposite slice, hacked at the other arm. Nervous laughter infected the crowd. The Spaniard fell to his knees, both limbs useless, hanging by his side. The cutlass struck the top of his head with such ferocity the sound was surely heard in the nearest streets. Whoops erupted.

Blood splattered Jacob's face, causing him to freeze. He could not take his eyes from the bloody mess in front of him.

"Drink up, you sea snakes." L'Olonnais bellowed. "Tomorrow, we march to San Pedro. We will kill more Spanish pigs and become rich." The crowd cheered, pulsing a fever of enthusiasm.

"It looks like it ain't the Spanish I have to protect you from." Henri said, pulling Jacob through the crowd. "That ain't exactly keeping your head down, is it?"

Many near last night's incident were surprised the pup still lived. L'Olonnais would not usually suffer such pertness. The few with intellect understood that L'Olonnais could not kill the boy after such a show of loyalty. By denouncing the Spaniard, he had not only escaped punishment but also rescued Reinhardt by turning the tide on mutinous intentions.

Once Jacob had regained his composure the previous evening, the fear had overwhelmed him. To placate their young friend, Henri and Isaac had hidden him in an attic of a tavern with a jug of wine and large flat breads from the bakery. Bastien made enquires among the buccaneers, but it seemed L'Olonnais had no interest in Jacob that night.

Bastien did learn that a rack had been erected in the square to satisfy L'Olonnais' thirst for blood. Twenty-seven soldiers had been set upon it. Regardless of their answers, each one had met a vile yet novel death.

Every other man, woman and child not being used for pleasure was locked in the church where they contemplated their fate. Moise had been made governor with orders to hunt down every inhabitant and root out every last piece of gold, silver, and anything else of value. L'Olonnais made it known he expected the two empty storehouses to be full on his return.

Three hundred buccaneers trudged out of the town at first light. Almost half of the crew remained in Puerto Cavallo to compile provisions. When they readied themselves for departure, L'Olonnais casually approached Jacob and shepherded him to the vanguard. He wrapped an arm around Jacob's shoulder as they marched.

"I shall keep you close, my young brethren." He laughed. "In case I am in doubt as to whether I should kill our guides."

Jacob offered only a fleeting glance as he nodded. They walked a stride behind two Spanish soldiers who'd been snatched from the church and so spared the rack. Their wrists were bound and a length of rope tethered to two buccaneers flanking the column – reluctant blood hounds on the hunt for a Spanish gold in San Pedro.

"I see that bravery is still in you, young cockerel." L'Olonnais said. "Fancy yourself as a real villain, do you?"

Jacob kept his eyes on the ground as they walked.

"Did I frighten you when I directed my dagger in your direction?"

"Yes, sir."

"Good. Your bravery is encouraged. But you will never undermine me again. We all must learn to respect authority. Next time, it won't only be a Spaniard at the end of my blade."

"Yes, sir."

"Very good." L'Olonnais flashed a smile.

Jacob realised his demeanour must have projected one of fear. He mustered his own smile. It felt unconvincing.

L'Olonnais tilted his head. "Do you know why I hate the Spanish?"

Jacob nodded.

"You do?"

"They almost killed you in Campeche, sir."

L'Olonnais laughed. "They cannot kill me. I cannot die. They tried. They have not stopped trying. But they will never kill me. My hatred began many years before that uncomfortable day in Campeche. Years of backbreaking exploitation had prepared me for a few hours of laying still. The sugar plantation made this man you see before you. They may as well have planted a weak poor boy in their ground and harvested a vengeful killer."

Jacob took shallow breaths, trying to remain calm.

"I reaped my revenge. Did you know that?"

Jacob shook his head.

"Me and Klaude returned with fifty men. We strode through their fields. It was poetry. We left no Spaniard alive. I lied when I said my dream was to pour hot molasses into the eye sockets of my

Spanish captors. It's now but a pleasant memory. But it's fading. I struggle to see their faces. No matter how tightly I try. For years, I learned to avoid their eyes for fear of the whip, or worse. When I got my revenge, it was fleeting. Their faces were not what my mind remembered. All too quickly, their tyranny evaporated. They were weak. I find all men are weak in the end. But there are many more Spanish plantation bosses. Many more eye sockets... Shush." He turned to face Jacob and smiled. "If you do not wish to respect authority, Mr Penjerrick, you must eliminate it."

Jacob ceased breathing. He locked eyes with L'Olonnais.

"I shall take my own plantation soon enough and enslave as many Spanish pigs as I can find. My own procession from the fields to the boiling house. Can you imagine such a beautiful sight?"

He unwrapped his arm from Jacob's shoulder, raising his hands to the sky and projecting his voice so others around could hear. "But first we must become rich and powerful so that no man will dare take it away."

The closest men cheered, stirring a soft ripple through the ranks which evaporated with the heat. Jacob could only muster a whimper.

"But I haven't forgotten my promise to you, my brethren. I shall get you back to that lass in England. I will make you the prince of Cornwall. A thank you for your part in retaining the services of Master Harvey."

Jacob offered an uneasy nod before facing front with a confused expression. He traced the dusty footsteps of the Spanish soldiers ahead. He and the admiral walked in silence until a front runner returned and L'Olonnais stepped aside.

A pebble clipped Jacob's ear. He turned to see Henri and Bastien grinning back at him. He forced a smile as he slipped back to join them.

The army padded through the dense jungle, attempting to keep their sounds to a minimum—an impossible task for six hundred feet to be silent as they kicked, cracked and snapped every dry leaf and twig in their path. The guides tried to be good to their word, but only a fool would think three hundred marauders could sneak up to the front gates of a town forewarned of their approach.

They had travelled only three leagues when Reinhardt, who had been rewarded with front guard duty, returned in a panic reporting an ambush followed by the crack of musket fire in the distance.

L'Olonnais turned, instructing his lieutenants to send word to form into companies and fan out. Anthony du Puis and Philippe Bequel nodded their agreement before finding their subordinate company leaders. Anthony du Puis found Le Picard and Philippe Bequel found Jan Lucas.

The five companies took cover as each man loaded his musket and pistol. Jacob remained with L'Olonnais' company, forming the centre of the attack. Piero thrust one of two muskets into Jacob's hand and knelt beside him.

"It's loaded." He said. "You just keep passing me loaded muskets, kid, and you'll be fine with me. Henri says you can load?"

"He's been teaching me. Got it down to under a minute."

"That's good. Time to break that record of yours. I need your quick hands today, not your quick tongue. A weapon in my hand every thirty seconds. Got it?"

Jacob nodded, tilting his head, frowning at the musket. He looked to his left, finding Bastien loading for Henri. A huge grin on his face. The clicking and scratching of weaponry lessened, and the jungle returned itself to the birds and the insects. Jacob flicked a mosquito from his arm and rubbed the puncture wound. He watched as a droplet of blood ripened on his skin. He pulled at a large leaf tickling his ankles. Then another, clearing himself a small patch of land where he might load the muskets unhindered.

"No need for that, lad. We won't be here long."

Jacob scratched his leg and looked down to see green ants scurrying to find a new home.

More musket fire in the jungle ahead. The scouts were close. Shouts hurtled through the foliage, "Ami. Ami." The company ignored their friends as they ran past into formation beside them. They waited. The bushes rustled unnaturally fifty yards in front. Piero raised his musket to his shoulder while lowering his body until he resembled a ball of clothing with the barrel for a beak. Crack. Smoke enveloped Jacob as dozens of muskets fired into the bush. Piero lay his weapon at Jacob's feet and snatched the loaded firearm and aimed again.

Jacob summoned to mind the instructions given to him by Henri and went to work loading the musket. He fingered out a cartridge from his cartouche box hanging over his left shoulder. He bit off the end, forgetting to spit out the unneeded paper. He poured a small amount of powder into the firing pan, remembering to knock the pan with his palm to distribute the powder closer to the flint. Subconsciously, he counted. Ten seconds. He closed the frizzen and turned the musket upright. The musket stood four feet in height so Jacob couldn't crouch like Piero, so instead Henri had taught him to squat. He felt exposed as his head extended two feet higher than his partner. He teased the remaining powder down the barrel, followed by the cartridge paper containing the musket ball. Twenty seconds. He pulled the ramrod from its cradle, lifting his body onto the balls of his feet to gain a few extra inches until the rod escaped. He twirled the rod in his fingers, an action he had mastered quickly and particularly proud of. No time for pride. He inserted the rod into the barrel and, with a modicum of force, inched the cartridge down. He bounced the rod twice before removing it. He twirled again and reinserted the rod back into its cradle. Forty seconds. He pulled back the cock and held out the musket for Piero. The musketeer hadn't fired his second shot. Had anyone fired? He spat a paper ball into the long grass.

Another volley sounded as L'Olonnais' platoon spotted the brown jackets of Spanish soldiers exploding from the trees. The buccaneer's shots struck home, and screams were heard only yards away. Piero lowered his musket and took the loaded gun from Jacob's proudly outstretched hand. Piero raised from his squat and bobbed forward in a crouch. His legs gliding without raising his head more than a couple of inches. His musket out front, eager to find a target.

"Stay there, kid. Come find me when you're loaded.

Jacob didn't answer as he concentrated on every action. When he finished, he crawled the ten yards to Piero's side. Large leaves partially hid him from the invisible enemy. His left forearm throbbed after the short crawl, and he looked to see his tablecloth bandage had come loose. His wound had opened. He pulled the bandage tight just as Piero fired his third shot.

He passed over the musket, starting the loading process once more. His hands felt tense. He was holding his breath, but he was finding his rhythm. Smoke stung his eyes.

He wiped the sweat with the back of his hand, slowing his loading by a few seconds. Piero fired again and stretched out a hand. Jacob wasn't ready. Piero didn't turn his head. He waited to accept the musket, all the time watching the trees for his next target. The screams continued. Jacob pulled back the cock and offered the musket. He picked up the discarded firearm and fingered another shot from his pouch.

He finished loading his latest round. His mind surfaced back to his immediate surroundings. Spanish shouts were only yards away through the next veil of jungle. Much closer than he expected. His tear smudged eyes darted left and right, probing the bush for enemy soldiers. Any moment they would burst upon him.

Through the muffled chaos, L'Olonnais gave an order in French. In one motion, his company turned and ran. Jacob looked to Piero, desperate for information.

"Run kid. Follow me."

Piero ran back the way they had come, screaming, but his face showed no panic. Jacob stood snagging his cartouche box on a tree root, spilling half its contents into the leaf litter. As he stooped, a bullet whistled above his head, lodging in a tree trunk. He had no time to bless his luck as he ran after Piero.

Henri and Bastien bunched up to Jacob's side, both screaming, encouraging him to run faster. The company halted and Jacob almost careered into Piero as he stopped. The musketeer crouched and aimed his firearm once again. L'Olonnais laughed as he ran to Piero's right and aimed his own musket into the trees.

"Wait, lads," L'Olonnais ordered, flashing Jacob an encouraging, manic smile. "Let them come. Any second now."

Jacob eyed the bush, gulping in the acrid air. Smoke bit at his throat. He felt the tears trickle down his cheeks.

Spanish screams became louder, more like war cries, full of anger, as they tracked the retreating buccaneers. Jacob looked at Piero and then Henri and lastly L'Olonnais. All three aimed their weapons but did not fire.

L'Olonnais raised his hand and roared into the trees. "Fire, fire."

Jacob almost fell forward as the entire jungle erupted at once. His own company fired as one and from his left and right hundreds of muskets could be heard as du Puis, Bequel, Le Picard, and Lucas ordered their companies to fire from the flanks.

"Forward" L'Olonnais screamed.

Every man from every company stood and unsheathed their cutlass. Jacob followed Piero through the foliage with his own cutlass raised to witness the easy pickings. The Spanish had defended themselves bravely, but it had proved futile. Through the smoke and confusion, some had managed to escape, but most were cut off. The annihilation took only minutes. Those remaining stood shocked and confused among their dying comrades. A writhing mass of green leaves, brown uniforms and dirty red flesh. The jungle floor wriggled with death.

The moaning lessened as buccaneers meticulously stepped between the dying Spaniards, bringing comfort to those who tried to make peace with their god. The less lucky were stripped of their weapons, made to kneel, and forced to witness the aloof sentences delivered upon their compatriots.

"Don't kill them all, lads," L'Olonnais cackled. "We'll need some for new guides and for sport."

Jacob couldn't bear to witness any more of the casual massacre, so made his way to an unmolested patch of jungle to catch his breath. Away from the pleading, he stooped to address his bandage. He went unnoticed as he rested his arm on his thigh, accessing his wound. The flesh was beginning to knit together, and Jacob was having to resist the urge to scratch the itch. A short distance away, Reinhardt passed with L'Olonnais a step behind. They disappeared out of sight into the heavy vegetation. Jacob crouched into a huddle, but their faint conversation pricked his curiosity. He retied his bandage and crawled closer, pausing behind a large pine trunk skirted with ferns.

"You think I ain't noticed you contriving a mutiny?" L'Olonnais hissed. "While we sat in the doldrums wishing for a breath of wind, you sat conspiring to take my ship."

"It is not true, sir. Whoever says it, they are lying."

"I says it. You saying I'm a liar?"

"No, sir. But I'm no mutineer. There were rumours, but I was not the one who started them."

"Who started these mutinous mutterings if it wasn't you?"

There was a pause. Jacob strained to hear.

"Who you taking your lead from, Mr de Jaager? Tell me now or the ledger will have you among the dead before this skirmish is over."

Another pause. "I'll tell you, sir, put the dagger in your belt, and give me a head start. I'll tell you the ringleader."

"How about I put the dagger in your belly, and I give you a head start to hell?"

"No, no, I'll tell you."

Jacob inched forward, risking his head through the fern leaves.

"Le Picard was coveting the captaincy. He says you've lost your touch. Says we took too long getting back to Tortuga, and we stayed too long, and now we've missed the season. Chasing our sails, he says. We won't find treasure in these parts... Admiral, I told you the truth. Admiral, I ain't no mutineer. Admiral, wait..."

Jacob held his breath. Nothing, then a thud. He slithered back around the tree, nestling under the leaves. He pushed his eye sockets into his knees, hugging his legs.

"Le Picard, aye?" L'Olonnais said as he strode through the clearing, back to the victory celebrations.

Jacob waited a long time before creeping forward to find Reinhardt laying face up, staring expressionlessly at the jungle canopy. Flies already feasted on the blood congealing at his neck. Jacob raised his hand to his mouth, suppressing a small scream. He crouched and shook Reinhardt's shoulders, but his body felt lifeless. Reinhardt's eyes were already glazed. Soulless. A now familiar expression. Jacob's memory once only held one such vision. A dead dog he'd found in an alley behind the blacksmiths. Since being press-ganged, the dog had gained many companions.

"Rest in Peace, Reinhardt."

The captain was already butchering his second victim, to the equal delight and displeasure of his men, when Jacob slipped back into the looting ground. He almost tripped over Isaac, stripping a dead Spaniard of his weapons.

"Good work today, Jacob. You did well." Isaac looked up when he received no reply. "You feeling right lad?"

"Yeah. Just all the excitement." Jacob folded his arms tight gripping his elbows. "What you got there?"

"Get stuck in. There's plenty of weapons to be had. Anything of value, let du Puis know. He's the purser while Moise is away."

Jacob nodded and feigned interest in a dead Spaniard. A musket and cartouche box lay next to the body. He left the musket but pulled the cartouche box close, claiming its contents for his own. From inside the inner pocket of the Spaniard's jacket, Jacob slipped out a small pouch. A slight clink indicated it held coins. He glanced at Isaac, but he was busy patting down his own Spaniard. Jacob stuffed the pouch into the secret pocket of Henri's coat. As he stared into the dead Spaniards' eyes, he thought of poor Reinhardt only yards away. He closed the Spaniards' eyes and whispered a brief prayer.

An overly loud cheer snatched his attention. L'Olonnais had thrust his dagger into yet another Spanish eyeball demanding to be told another way to San Pedro. Jacob stood from his soldier and found himself drawn to the dramaturgy unfolding in the centre of the camp. L'Olonnais had become infested with a cool fever–calculated with malice. Around him, his usual coterie. Bakari stood by his side, with his boarding axe over his shoulder, belly laughing as the latest fatality fell to the ground. Melchor held the next victim by the back of the neck, guiding him towards L'Olonnais. Klaude and Montbars guarded two more weeping Spaniards. Many of the men circled the theatrics. Their focus shifting from the looting to the admiral's antics.

"Thought you'd got yourself killed." Henri said. He and Bastien had been drawn in by the commotion. "We even started searching the bodies. Where you been?"

Jacob shrugged and nodded towards L'Olonnais. "He's got the taste again?"

"Think so," Henri said. "I'm all for killing Spanish bastards, but I like a nice, fair fight. I ain't seen a Spaniard torture no-one. He can't help himself. Let's hope he calms down if he gets an answer he likes."

"It don't look likely." Bastien said, gesturing towards the loudest outcry so far.

All eyes were now fixed on the spectacle. Jacob had a clear view through the crowd as L'Olonnais teased his dagger into the chest of his latest sacrifice, sawing upwards through the breastplate. The soldier spluttered blood down his chin to meet the red river pulsating from his chest. Melchor wrapped his arms under the victim's armpits, forcing his torso open. Many men averted their eyes–some abandoned their front row seats. Piero doubled over to heave into the bushes before disappearing, wiping his mouth. Jacob's eyes widened. He felt intoxicated by François L'Olonnais.

The mad admiral took a step closer, snarling into the face of the dying man. With a treacherous smile, he reached inside the chest cavity. Jacob's mouth gaped open. To his disbelief, the man did not immediately die. The soldiers' last sight before his eyes rolled back and Melchor took his full weight was that of his enemy gnawing at his beatless heart. Jacob's stomach lurched as L'Olonnais tore through the muscle with his teeth. Melchor dropped the man to the ground, but L'Olonnais held tight. The arteries snapped as he fell, flicking blood droplets into the crowd–even those splattered did not make a sound. Possessed with menace and evil, L'Olonnais' blood-covered face turned to the next Spaniard held tight by Montbars.

"I will serve you all alike, if you show me not another way." Fragments of chewed heart dripped down his chin.

The new Spanish victim spluttered, but pure fear inhibited his speech. Montbars tightened his grip, anticipating the struggle. Before the Spaniard could even scream, L'Olonnais thrust the bloody heart into his open mouth, teased the dagger up through his jaw, skewering the heart before finally piercing the Spaniard's brain. Montbars released the man and laughed as he danced his final moments. He fell to the floor with a limp thud.

This was more horrific than any fable or folklore that had passed the lips of any sea dog who'd ever made port in Falmouth. If he ever made it home, the patrons of The Rusty Anchor would never believe he'd witnessed such a sight.

"Jake." Jacob was lost in the moment. "Jake." Henri took his friend by the shoulders, trying to break the spell. "Jacob. Let's go." Jacob shook himself free and looked at his friends with amazement. "There's nothing left to see, my friend. There's two Spaniards standing. If I know L'Olonnais, he'll tear himself free and spare their lives for a safer route to the town."

Jacob prised his eyes away and followed Henri and Bastien to a huddle of men cleaning and exchanging weapons around a small fire.

"I've seen L'Olonnais in these moods before, but I ain't seen nothing like that," Isaac said as they sat down.

"He ate a heart." Jacob forced the words from his mouth. "He cut the man's chest open and pulled out his beating heart."

A few of the men who had not witnessed the event looked up, shocked. Hushed murmurs flooded the circle as those who had seen the spectacle told those who had not. Jacob slumped to the ground, resting his back against a pine tree.

"You alright, Jake?" Bastien asked.

Jacob fumbled at his knapsack, pulling out a hunk of cooked Puerto Cavallo pork. He nibbled the fatty edge. It tasted bland compared to Helario's recipe. "Just another name for the ledger." He giggled.

"Jake. You feeling right?" Henri asked.

"Where's Le Picard?" Jacob asked, staring at the pork.

"He's around. Get some rest, my friend. It's been an exciting day."

"I need to warn Le Picard." Jacob said.

"All's well, mate. Get some rest."

Henri returned to the telling of the tales while Jacob drank water to settle his nerves. Blood–his fingers were smeared with blood. Was it Reinhardt's? The Spanish soldier's? His own? It didn't matter. He ripped leaves from a bush and scrubbed.

While talk of thieving and murder happened all around, Jacob half emptied the contents of his water flask scrubbing the blood stains from his hands.

Twenty-Five

For eight long hours, the guides led the buccaneers through the thick jungle; the silence broken only by the chop of cutlasses and the distant cries of unseen wildlife. Jacob would never have guessed such humid temperatures existed anywhere in the world. He longed for even the gentlest zephyr that often swept the Cornish coast.

"Cactus."

Jacob heard the word but did not understand its meaning.

"Cactus." Henri repeated.

"What's cactus?" Jacob asked. The men in front fanned out, allowing Jacob full view of what had halted their toil. Above his head, huge spikes protruded in every direction. Some were as big as daggers. He had seen the plants before on the outskirts of Tortuga, and passed many on their journey, but never as large as these. Or so plentiful.

Jacob giggled at their predicament. It was a giggle he'd tried to stifle since he'd awoken that morning when his senses confirmed what he'd hoped was only a dream. Death was everywhere. He walked to the closest thorn and raised a finger to testify to its sharpness. "Ouch."

L'Olonnais pushed his way to the front and stroked his goatee. "Find a way round. We ain't being halted by plants." He run his fingers through his hair. "Bring me the guides."

Jacob skulked away to the safety of his friends, sucking his finger.

The fuss lasted for two hours until scouts reported back that the cacti field spread for miles in all directions.

L'Olonnais' patience boiled over. "Mort Dieu, les Espagnols me le payeront," He spat.

The mood of the buccaneers ranged from sombre to rage, as it became obvious they would have to turn back.

"It was a trap." L'Olonnais snarled. "You knew this way did not lead to San Pedro."

Bakari had led the guides to the thorns and thrust them to their knees. "No, Señor. They are new."

L'Olonnais turned to face the cacti, some towering twelve feet tall. His features twisted, revealing a sinister grin. "New. This cactus is new? You mean to tell me it was not here yesterday?" He snatched the closest guide by his hair. Before the guide could get to his feet, L'Olonnais thrust his face into the thorns. His shriek muffled and as more force was added, his head and the plant's flesh became one. His legs violently scraped the earth bare of vegetation until they became limp in the dust.

Jacob sloped after Henri and Bastien, who were retreating into the pack to avoid any overflow from L'Olonnais' wrath. They didn't need to witness the demise of the second guide.

"They'll be at our rear," Henri said. "The Spaniards will have followed us. They've herded us into a parc à bétail."

It seemed the admiral knew as much himself.

"Right lads. We've no choice but to push on direct to San Pedro. The Spaniards will think they have us pinned in. They couldn't stop us last time and this time will be no different. We've had casualties, to be sure, but so have they. They will be no match for us. We'll need a replacement in the front guard for Mr de Jaager." The captain raised his hands to the treetops in remorse for their fallen comrades. Upon lowering his hands, he found Jacob's gaze, and pointed in his direction.

"Mr Bodine?" L'Olonnais grinned. "You wanting to make use of that new flintlock?"

"Aye, sir," Henri said sheepishly from behind Jacob. "She's ready and hungry for more Spanish blood."

"Very good. Join the scouts. No time for rest. We need to leave."

"See you in San Pedro. "Henri said to Bastien and Jacob. "Don't be a hero." He said, forcing a grin to Jacob.

"Right, you cruel hearted dogs." L'Olonnais said. "They know how many we are, and they think they have us trapped. So, this time we're going to keep it simple. Mr Penjerrick, hand these out."

Le Picard threw a canvas bag full of red sashes–the same used when boarding *Stad Gouda*.

"There will be no stealth or cunning this afternoon. Their last attack had a good number of civilians. This next will have even more. Use the sashes so we can tell friend from foe. The front guard will keep them busy and retreat our way. We'll march south and when we meet them the five platoons will form line. We'll be the centre platoon. Captain Bequel and Lucas will be on our left, and du Puis and Le Picard will be on our right."

As Jacob handed out the sashes, he listened, deducing his role would find him in the thick of the action. He handed a sash to Bastien, who was grinning as usual.

"I think you'll be using that cutlass good and proper today, Jake." Bastien said.

Isaac was Bastien's new musket partner. He winked as Jacob passed him a sash. "Good luck, kid."

A chest of grenades, lugged from Puerto Cavallo, bundled past Jacob and were set down at the front of the platoon.

L'Olonnais continued his speech. "We've no secret weapons. You're the secret weapons. You vile motherless rogues are what all Spanish pigs will fear most in the world when this battle's over. You are the scourge of the Caribbean and there's no men more fearsome than L'Olonnais' French buccaneers with a thirst for gold."

Murmurs of agreement leaked from the men. The other company leaders roused morale in much the same way.

"So, it's quiet as mice until we show our teeth." L'Olonnais looked down the column to see du Puis finishing with his platoon and signalled for him to follow.

"You with me again, kid?" Piero asked, kneeling down at Jacob's side.

"Guess so. Is it loaded?"

"Since this morning. Ain't no Spanish bastard getting the jump on me. I see you still got the other one."

Jacob nodded and loaded the musket he had kept from the last skirmish. When he'd finished, he crouched, gripping the barrel tight.

Make believe on the beaches in Cornwall had never seemed so far away.

The crack of muskets in the distance alerted the men. Jacob rechecked his loaded musket. Piero placed a hand on his shoulder.

"You're ready." He said with a confident nod.

As they crouched, Jacob looked to his left and found Bakari only three men over. Bastien had told Jacob how Bakari had been freed by L'Olonnais while taking the Spanish treasure ship near

Maracaibo. He'd been enslaved by the Spanish, but when the French attacked, he and another slave took up arms against their captors. He had killed four Spaniards in the attack. The other slave had been killed, but Bakari had survived and L'Olonnais had welcomed him as a free man. Bakari had pledged his allegiance ever since. Jacob took solace from knowing he was in tough company. He, oddly, missed Doyle. Now he was in real peril the Irish giant was one hundred yards away with his new platoon. This might be the perfect time for those huge fists of his to repay all those months of repression.

The skirmish ahead sounded closer. The musket cracks grew louder. Jacob nestled with Piero in the second row, waiting. Piero had tied his hair back in a queue using a sliver of lace. Jacob noticed his own hair hung at a length that would soon hinder his vison but not quite long enough to scrape back. He tucked the longer lengths behind his ears. He fingered the hilt of his cutlass, trying to control his breathing–where was Henri?

The sporadic crack of muskets still punctured the air, followed by the odd scream or shout. The voices sounded Spanish, but he couldn't be sure. He checked his cartouche box. He tucked it between his elbow and thigh and eyed his surroundings for any stray twigs or branches–nothing obvious. Everything he heard may only be through the next curtain of shrubbery. He concentrated on his breathing.

Crack of another musket. Only yards away. It must be one of their own men. Any second now. He looked to Piero. Musket raised to his chin. Brows drawn low across his eyes. His gaze fixed on the trees ahead, looking for the faintest movement signalling the beginning of the chaos. Jacob breathed in–found focus–breathed out.

"Attack, Attack" came the order from L'Olonnais as he sprang from his semi veiled position in the grass. Jacob startled upright.

Piero sprang to his feet like a spark in a flintlock. He'd travelled ten yards before Jacob reacted.

"Run Jake. Run" Bastien had caught him and screamed for him to follow.

Jacob stood and ran, forcing his bravery–or was it foolishness? No time to debate the difference. Bravery was the reward of the living. The dead would be the fools. He jumped a fallen log and inched through the foliage, finding Piero just as he discharged his first shot. The slim Frenchman looked around for his partner. Jacob obliged with an outstretched hand, taking the empty musket.

He knelt amongst the grasses loading the firearm. Adrenaline fuelling his fingers. That must have been his quickest yet–thirty-five seconds. He stood with an outstretched hand, but Piero hadn't fired his next shot.

A grenade exploded yards away. A blend of grass and earth, followed by a bloody shoe, rained through the undergrowth. He heard a muffled moan through the haze. Jacob guessed it belonged to a shoeless Spaniard. As he stood watching the skirmish through the smoke, he realised it was not the moan that was muffled but his own hearing. He hoped it would return before he found himself staring at a Spanish soldier with one less sense in his armoury.

He scanned what vision he had looking for Henri. Piero fired at a Spaniard who'd inched too far through the bush. The man stumbled before falling at their feet–dead. Jacob handed the loaded musket to Piero and relinquished him of the used one.

"No time to load it, jeune homme. It's time for steel." Piero ran through the bush, cutlass raised–out of sight.

Jacob's mind filled in the blanks his ears couldn't quite hear. His heart pounded. The battle was coming to him. It would not be fought at even the small distance of muskets hidden in the trees, but face to grimacing face. Death was coming, and it had Spanish eyes.

He giggled. The words of his father rattled in his mind. *"Steer away from the rogues. That's where death hides."* Not today. Today he was the rogue and the Spanish would not swindle him out of life. He had treasure to find. These new lands were not the sole ownership of Spanish pigs–he wanted his share.

Jacob drew his cutlass and stood hidden in the smoke. No time to stand and stare. He followed Bastien into the fray. He raised his cutlass as a figure stumbled out of the mist. At the last moment, he swerved away as he caught sight of the red sash around his waist. Jacob honed his eyes on the sashes to avoid an unfortunate accident.

He stood frozen in panic. Hysteria gripped his mind. He had not wrapped a sash around himself. Not around his arm, his waist, or even his leg. He stood sashless. After handing the last man a sash, he had thrown the canvas bag with the pile of unneeded clothing and equipment. He'd forgot to keep one for himself. He felt bare–a lone wolf cub lost between two packs of lions fighting over a kill.

He must find his crew. At least they would know him and protect him. To his left as the smoke thinned he found Klaude straddling a dead Spaniard. Klaude held his bloody cutlass in his left hand. His eyes looked closed and Jacob was sure he was chanting. He picked up a fist full of dirt and in a dramatic conclusion threw the full force into the dead mans face, before raising his cutlass high above his head and screamed into the jungle. Jacob followed.

From his right, a wild Spaniard charged. Jacob raised his cutlass in sheer panic, parrying the overhead blow. Another powerful strike parried, causing Jacob to retreat. The force sending a shudder of pain through his wounded left forearm. The third attack caused Jacob to trip over a tree root and land uncomfortably on the ground. Jacob's eyes widened as the Spaniard towered over him. Pure aggression stared back. The Spaniard raised his sword. It glinted in the sunlight. Jacob scurried backwards. His hands and feet churning up the dusty earth. The Spaniard fell to the ground with a violent thud. His right shoulder separated from his body.

Bakari grunted as he dislodged his axe from the Spaniard's Trapezius. The Spaniard gurgled. Bakari ended his misery by pummelling the haft through the man's skull with full force. Jacob sat watching the blood pulse from the victim. A tremble had taken hold of his entire body.

With no care for the young Englishman, Bakari turned and thumped back into the bush, looking for more food for his axe. Jacob found his feet and followed. Bakari was a brute, best avoided, but he was a brute who knew who he was.

Jacob ducked as Bakari's axe rotated three hundred and sixty degrees above his squat stature before landing in the neck of its next target. More delicious flesh for the axe. Jacob had heard about a wild beast in Africa called a rhinoceros. Skin as thick as a dugout canoe with more strength than three oxen pulling a chilcarroch plough. If this animal were a man, he stood in front of him now and he had found a use for an axe.

Bakari charged forward once again–and Jacob followed. This time keeping an axe length behind. Another rotation and another head rolled. If Bakari continued this momentum, there would be no need for Jacob or most other crewmen to kill any Spaniards. The hulk was a one-man army. Forward once more and yet another dead Spaniard.

The pair stepped through a layer of fog, but this time, nobody barred their path. Even the smoke had dissipated.

Bakari turned, wild. Jacob stared back at him, feeling as confused as Bakari looked. Had he carved his way through the entire Spanish line? Jacob turned to face the fog once more. Bakari growled an inaudible war cry that Jacob took as encouragement. He crept back into the chaos.

Bakari, exacerbated by Jacob's slow pace, shoved past. Still no sashless Spaniards to be found. Perhaps the fighting was over? The sounds of metal on metal and grunts and screams suggested it was not. The smoke drifted on the breeze, revealing the battle. With plenty of fighting left in the evening sun, Bakari had no passion to wait for this English boy to find his mettle. He charged again, into the rear of a pack of ten wild Spaniards fighting an equally sized pack of wild buccaneers.

It was carnage.

Montbars wrestled a tall Spaniard at the outer edge of the melee. Melchor held a knife at bay from a snarling soldier. Over all their heads Doyle grappled with two vicious looking beasts. Closest of all, Henri exchanged blows with a slender Spaniard, similar in age but not of equal swordsmanship. Henri had him on the back foot. The surprise rear attack from Bakari proved a worthy distraction. Henri caught his adversary in the left arm, causing him to retreat. As the Spaniards turned to find Bakari, they opened a crack to their front rank. The Frenchmen prised their way in.

Jacob stood rooted, watching the brave Spanish soldiers recover their position. They enveloped Bakari into their ranks. He was not having the same success, with less room to swing his axe.

The buccaneers matched the ferociousness of the Spanish, but it was costing them. Jacob gripped his hilt. The battle in front was gruesome. The demonic grunts and growls alone repelled his urges to join them. Each man was lost in his own battle. The buccaneers had them–he convinced himself. No-one noticed him trembling at the edge of the clearing.

The mist drifted through the battlefield, obscuring his vision. The sight of the skirmish faded, even if the sounds did not. These brave warriors did not need his feeble contributions. He heard

Henri's words in his mind. *"Don't be a hero."* He stood. If the mist cleared, he would help. He stepped backwards deeper into the fog. Shame replaced indecision as the jungle accepted him into its protective embrace.

Twenty-Six

The buccaneers slumped, exhausted. Half revelling in their victory, half moaning in agony. They had won the battle, but the cost was heavy. Anthony du Puis again had the unfortunate duty of ledger keeper. He did the rounds of each platoon, asking their leaders how many souls they had lost. The evidence clear to see. The Spaniards had fought hard. Many died, but most escaped through the bush back to the town with intelligence of the buccaneer's approach. The buccaneers may have survived the day, but at least twenty-five had lost their lives. Thirteen had sustained injuries sufficient to force them back to Puerto Cavallo. Another twenty-two joined them. Too sick from the fever to continue.

Jacob stood alone, wiping the mist from his blade.

"Jake, you made it," Bastien called. "I lost you. I thought you were a gonna."

Jacob could not look his friend in the eye.

"Henri had a near miss. He's well enough. A cutlass wound to his leg. He's all patched up, so he'll make it."

"Henri? Where is he?"

"Follow me. He's resting."

Bastien led Jacob a few yards back to where Henri sat with his back to a mahogany tree. His legs outstretched. As they approached, Henri opened his eyes and smiled.

"Jake, you're alive. That felt messy. All smoke and tree roots. I didn't know north from south. Not much time to think, but when I did, I worried you hadn't made it."

"I was fine. Bumped into Bakari." Jacob kept his gaze on the ground.

"That's great, Jake. Bakari, aye. You must have seen some action?" Henri stood with a grimace.

Bastien rushed to help.

"Be careful Hen." Jacob said. "I thought it was just a scratch."

"Yeah, I'll be fine. No worse than your arm. Got caught up with one too many Spanish pigs. One took a wild swing before I finished him off. No real damage done. I won't be running for a couple of days, I don't suppose."

The three ambled around for half an hour, searching bodies before Bastien and Jacob persuaded Henri to rest with the promise they would share their findings with him. They didn't return with much except for some powder and ammunition and some spicy Spanish sausages. L'Olonnais had ordered anything of value to be returned to the warehouses in Puerto Cavallo. The heavily wounded would follow. Henri brushed off the notion of returning to see the barber.

"My leg'll be fine in the morning." Henri snapped. "Just need Spanish gold and a tot of rum. I ain't come this far to have you pair have all the fun."

San Pedro was not far, but neither was sunset, so the buccaneers made camp. The trio settled in for another chilly night. They could see no value in the sausages so ate them huddled together. Jacob wasn't hungry, so Henri and Bastien accepted his half-eaten share before all three fell asleep.

The buccaneers woke before sunrise and formed into their platoons. The ever-present mist hung in the air. It could be the beginnings of rain, Piero grumbled as they hid their powder and pistols in their coats.

Jacob, Henri, and Bastien pushed their way to the front of their platoon, having struggled to keep up the pace due to Henri's injury. With the doctor remaining in Puerto Cavallo, Jacob had found Isaac, who cleaned the wound and tied strips of stolen Spanish shirt tightly around his thigh as a tourniquet. Jacob's arm still ached, but seeing Henri's bravery, he waved Isaac's concerns away.

The buccaneers halted at a river. They could smell the town on the breeze with the slightest hint of activity to their ear. It wasn't yet dawn, but there were the beginnings of bird call in the trees. The previous ambushes proved, if nothing else, San Pedro knew they were close. How many would be waiting for them? The buccaneers could not guess.

L'Olonnais passed his orders to his lieutenants, who passed those same orders to their platoons. He stepped to his own platoon, revealing his tactics. "I need my best marksmen. Each platoon is sending four partners. This platoon needs the same."

Three pairs stepped forward. Jacob had seen them on the march from Puerto Cavallo. These landsmen had proved their worth when counterattacking the ambushes.

"Very good." The captain nodded before searching the crowd. "Mr Bodine. I expect to see you and Mr Trivette amongst the skirmishers. The nerves got the better of you, lad?"

"No, sir. Not one bit. I got tickled yesterday in the skirmish and I ain't moving like I should be. I can shoot, but my running's hampered, sir."

"Nonsense. I saw you looting with the best of 'em yesterday. Get yourself loaded and ready to move out."

L'Olonnais turned his attention back to the bulk of the tactics. Henri stepped forward, followed by an apprehensive-looking Bastien.

"Henri?" Jacob intercepted him, placing a firm hand across his chest. "You're in no fit state to run the skirmish."

Henri stood, placing his weight on his right leg, glancing towards L'Olonnais. "Can't go against the admiral, Jake. I'll be alright."

Jacob lowered his arm and without warning flicked Henri's left thigh.

"Aaah. What you do that for?"

"How you gonna crawl and sprint if you can't even take a finger shank? You're far from useless, Hen, but you'll be no good in the field."

"What's the trouble?" L'Olonnais growled, turning on the trio.

Jacob turned to face L'Olonnais and in doing so caught sight of dozens of agitated eyes expecting the comeuppance of the mouthy pup.

"Ain't no trouble, sir." Jacob swallowed hard. "But Henri's in no fit state to skirmish." He looked at L'Olonnais, but found no acceptance of his words. "Figure he'd do more harm than good."

L'Olonnais gave an exacerbated sigh. "You know better than your admiral, do you, lad? Who you gonna suggest takes his place? You?"

Jacob looked to the crowd for an escape. No obvious answer came forward. "Well..."

"You ain't no marksman. Henri, get yourself ready."

"I can load." Jacob blurted. "I've been loading for Piero." Jacob searched the crowd again, finding his musket partner with pursed lips, shaking his head.

L'Olonnais found Piero and grinned. "Tis true. You're an excellent shot, Mr Galle. You happy to skirmish with the lad?"

Piero shuffled forward, not taking his eyes from Jacob. "Aye, sir. He's a good sort."

"It's no bother, Piero." Henri said. "I'm fine."

"The kids right, Henri. You're in no fit state. I'll skirmish with him."

"Very well. Now I've got my witnesses that'll testify it wasn't my idea to thrust young Mr Penjerrick into the firing line. We don't want Master Harvey sulking if anything should happen. Be ready in ten minutes." L'Olonnais turned back to the main platoon.

"Aye, sir."

"Mr Galle." L'Olonnais lowered his voice. "Left flank, if you please. Least dangerous."

"Aye, sir," Piero dragged Jacob by the shirt collar to the other skirmishers. "I hadn't planned on getting shot at today, young'un. These odds have crept uneven, even for my cravings. If we get out of this alive, I'll shoot you myself."

Jacob offered a rueful grin and crouched to one knee, loading the musket.

A quiet breeze unsettled the trees as he crouched with the other skirmishers, trying to control his breathing. He avoided Piero's scowls, instead turned his attention to the garrisoned town laying before them. It looked unremarkable. Just two stone turrets on either side of a large timber gate. Timber battlements fortifying the town. Four cannons protruded through the crenels, offering the only sizable defence. At this distance, Jacob could not denote their calibre. The town itself nestled at the foot of the westerly mountains that had shepherded their advance since Puerto Cavallo. A dense forest offered cover to the east. Between himself and the town, the ground had been cleared of trees–leaving nowhere to hide.

The companies of L'Olonnais, Lucas and Bequel would hug the trees to the east. Bastien supported Henri as he fidgeted with the bandage on his thigh. Henri nodded when Jacob caught his eye. Isaac stood not far over their shoulder with a serious expression. Jacob found Doyle, a head taller than his neighbours, scowling, in the closest of Lucas's ranks. The Irishman did not carry a musket or even a pistol, only his cutlass. His chosen weapons must be pure aggression and steel. Still, Jacob would bet good coin on Doyle making it through alive.

To his right, du Puis and Le Picard led companies that would attack from the west, hugging the foot of the mountains. Jacob lingered his gaze on Le Picard, wondering if the lieutenant was safe from L'Olonnais' vengeance. Once they were in possession of the silver and gold, all thought of mutiny would be forgotten.

The companies waited. For much of the journey since leaving *Marquise*, silence had been the primary order. For such thirsty cutthroats, always on the edge of life, they seemed comfortable in their own company. Jacob wondered where each man's mind disappeared to while they waited for the order to run and fire and kill. Did they dream of owning their own homesteads with wives and children? Did they ever pine for their native lands in France or Holland or England, wishing to be back amongst their familiarities? Or did their minds drift off to the ladies in Tortuga? Maybe they idly spent the Spanish gold not yet earned dreaming of warm beds and deep bosoms.

With this last thought, Jacob's mind drifted to Agnes—her lavender scent and her French-English accent. The brief time they'd spent naked in her bed. The small scar she tried to conceal beneath her left breast. The giggle she let out as he left. He hoped to see her again—to spend another night in her company.

Guilt gripped him as Lydia's sorrowful face filled his mind. She would be furious if she knew of his night of debauchery. The thought of him with another woman. A prostitute, no less. *"A whore,"* she would call her. *"A gentleman would not act in such a manner."*

Still, Henri was right. He would return home a changed man—a traveller, an adventurer, with experience of the world. And with riches enough to see them set up for life.

He picked at the grass at his feet, disturbing a grey green beetle, unaware it nestled in a giant battlefield. It was the size of a walnut with thick armour. It flew away, surprising Jacob, as he didn't expect the insect to have wings. He imagined the beetle witnessing the ensuing carnage from a branch in the middle distance. If he had the use of wings, would he opt for the easy route home, back across the Atlantic?

There were no great cries or screeched orders. Piero simply nudged Jacob, signalling the beginning of their game of cat and mouse. Piero scurried forward. After thirty yards, he crouched and took aim. Crack. His musket exploded, along with nineteen others peppering the silence. Dust puffed from the stone parapet. There would not be silence again for quite some time.

The cannons on the battlement each found targets and belched out chain and grape shot. But the targets fanning out across the battlefield. Jacob snatched up Piero's fallen musket and followed in his shadow. They flanked the left side of the skirmishers. Their directive, to zig zag to the main gates across the open plain.

Jacob thrust the loaded weapon into Piero's outstretched hand and went to work on the second firearm. Cartridge, bite, pour, close, frizzen, pour, push, twirl, ram, twirl, cock... Spit. Jacob was ready. His arm throbbed. Piero fired. They exchanged again and ran. This time west.

Jacob went to work once more. Piero delayed his shot, eyeing his target with care. His wizened, tanned face–devoid of emotion. Piero pursed his lips and exhaled his breath out of his lungs through his mouth and under the musket. Crack. A hint of a smile flickered his face before discarding the musket and stretching out his hand. The pair swapped weapons and ran. Forward–as always–east this time.

Adrenaline coursed through Jacob's entire body, inflicting an internal tremor only noticeable to him. The tremor did not impact his smooth actions as he loaded once more. From a separate and distant battle, Jacob heard the muffled shouts of his admiral.

"Run!" L'Olonnais bellowed. "Run, you butchers."

Over Jacob's left shoulder, the three platoons to the east stood as one and arched left, keeping within the tree line. Out of the corner of his eye, Jacob saw the two platoons to the west doing the same. He almost threw the musket to Piero and ran, collecting the discarded firearm as he swept past.

"Down." Piero's hand snatched at the back of Jacob's head, forcing him to the grassy earth. Jacob eased his head to face Piero on the ground. "Chain shot," Piero said. "Get up. Run."

They both ran again. Jacob's breathing was heavy now, and the tremors were becoming visible in his loading. Piero put a hand on the younger man's shoulder. "You're doing well."

Jacob nodded and finished with a spit. They had traversed half of the field and Piero's eye was finding its range. Jacob scanned the battlefield behind him. The pairing to his right was no longer a pair. The musketeer knelt, loading for himself. Twenty yards behind the motionless body of his loader lay face down in the dirt. Jacob averted his eyes, concentrating instead on the Spanish faces peering over the ramparts. Puffs of smoke plumed from their cannons. Boom.

He and Piero exchanged weapons before running another ten yards east once more. Jacob finished his loading, but Piero hadn't fired.

He glanced left to the parapet–ladders, made over night, using thick tree branches bound together with twine, arching towards the ramparts. The first of the men now scampering to the precipice, pausing as they attempted to outfox the blades thrashing down upon them. Cutlass met rapier with the Spaniards having the best of any individual joust. But for every failing buccaneer, another took his place until the ramparts overran with cutlasses.

More buccaneers scaled the timbers while others ran at the base of the wall to the main gates, screaming murder–rallying to make their attack.

Jacob's ears were alert to the sound of the cannon. The smoke cleared, revealing the muzzle, aiming directly at him and Piero. Hundreds of grape shot scaring the fortress backdrop.

"Run." Piero screamed, dragging Jacob by the collar. "Jacob, Run."

Jacob stumbled onto his hands, his musket tangling between his legs. He reached forward, his toes digging into the soil. Having got to his feet, Piero cursed as he fell, crushing them both to the earth. A shot struck the ground in front of Jacob and another in front of his right outstretched hand. Then it was over.

"Piero, we made it." Jacob wriggled from under Piero and raised to his knees. He padded his arms and thighs. He hadn't been hit. He picked up his musket and checked his cutlass. Everything felt in order. He got to his feet and checked the parapet. They had a few minutes while the cannon reloaded. He turned to Piero for guidance.

"East or west?" Piero did not answer. "Piero."

Piero was still lying face down, both arms outstretched, his musket in his right hand. He looked to be asleep. Jacob shook his comrade, noticing tiny holes in the back of his coat. He turned him over to find blood pooling into the grass. His eyes closed tight and his mouth in a grimace.

Jacob squatted, paralysed for a moment. He scanned the line to see the remaining skirmishers continuing their push for the main gate. He couldn't find the musketeer who had lost his loading partner.

On the parapet, the cannon must be halfway through loading–and they had his range. He had to move. He touched Piero's unscarred face and ran. Forward and west. At thirty yards, he raised his musket and fired. He had no care where it struck. He ran again–this time for the gates.

With a scraping of wood and chain, the two enormous gates creaked open, allowing the marauders to flood through. Jacob found himself towards the rear of the pack jostling for position, being sucked between the stone turrets.

Either the town had not been attacked for a long time, or its occupants did not think heavy defences were necessary. This felt too easy. Jacob came to a halt as the five companies converged on the road like two pythons down a rabbit burrow. In the town, screams and shouts could be heard as the first buccaneers squeezed through the opening, encountering more defenders.

A mix of earth and sweat tasted pungent as Jacob's face squashed into the back of the buccaneer ahead. His arms fixed tight to his chest with his muskets barrel aiming at the top of his right ear. He eased the barrel past his head, lessening the severity of the heat from the muzzle.

His mind could not hold on to a singular thought. Had Piero saved his life by smothering him, or had he simply become entangled in his fall? He should never have volunteered. But then, maybe Henri would have been killed instead.

Darkness descended, confirming they'd passed under the gatehouses. He stumbled forward, exploding out of the crush, almost falling to his knees. A hand grabbed the scruff of his coat and hoisted him to his feet. Le Picard grinned as he ran past.

"Come on, kid." Le Picard called.

Jacob checked his cutlass as he ran. It still fought with his knapsack. As the crowd thinned, he slowed his run. He caught sight of Henri and Bastien crouching at the end of a line of troops being formed by Le Picard.

Henri laughed as Jacob crashed next to him—a laugh only delirium could cause when you find yourself a whisper from death. You either laugh or cry. Jacob looked around. Nobody was in the mood to cry. He slung the musket from his shoulder and laughed himself—tears streaking his cheeks. Henri fired. All around, screams and shouts choked the air.

"Forward lads." L'Olonnais screamed, having made it through the gates. "We have them. Forward."

Bastien hooked his forearm under Henri's armpit. Jacob followed Bastien's lead and together they lifted Henri to his feet. Jacob unhooked himself, slung his musket over his shoulder, and unsheathed his cutlass. He allowed the aggression to grow in his mind, overpowering the nervousness that had lived there for so long. He looked back as men pulsated through the gates, screaming left and right. He stepped forward.

Bastien and Henri had found a contingent of buccaneers, forcing back a stubborn regiment of Spanish soldiers. Doyle, Montbars, and Andrieszoon led the attack, but the Spanish outnumbered them. Bakari and Klaude joined them, evening the odds causing the Spanish line to buckle.

Jacob ground his teeth; his knuckles white as he gripped his cutlass. The powder mist had evaporated. There was nowhere to hide. Piero's face came to his mind. Anger quashed fear within him. To Jacob's left, L'Olonnais stood–still, silent–staring at him. His cutlass drawn, his gait in battle stance. The slightest flick of his head encouraged Jacob to charge.

This was the moment.

He timed his attack to coincide with the Spaniards' stumble. His cutlass fizzed through the air, landing clumsily into the elbow of the soldier who'd been forced out of the right flank and had not seen him coming. The blow spun the confused Spaniard sideways into the path of Bakari. Startled himself, the rhino looked up to see the young pup. He raised his axe and with a saliva smile, turning to the next soldier in line for death–relinquishing this kill to the English firecracker.

Jacob raised his fighting arm. Locking eyes with the Spaniard. He looked a young man. Maybe twenty. A hint of stubble patched his jaw. He grimaced as he tried to raise his injured arm, but it refused to bend higher than his thigh. Jacob picked his spot. Then hesitated. All his training with Henri and Bastien forgotten.

Desperation flooded him. The Spaniard switched his rapier to his left hand and found the strength to lunge forward. Jacob thrashed his cutlass close to both Spanish and French limbs alike. The blow landed in the Spaniards' thigh, severing three flailing fingers. He slashed again, this time into the forearm and then again in the head. Each laceration was the result of an identical cutlass arch–the young Spaniard slumping after each blow, resulting in a different strike point.

The attack lacked skill, but it was brutal. The Spaniard succumbed to his wounds and crumpled to the ground. Jacob's wild hair hung damp over his face as snot, saliva, and tears dripped upon the corpse. His deafness melted away, his own roars filling his ears.

Doyle's voice surprised him—calm, almost gentle. "It's over now, lad. The fight's done. Ease off the sword, will ye?"

Jacob bucked as Doyle laid a hand on his shoulder. They locked eyes—man to man. "You did good, lad. Real good."

Jacob unclenched his jaw. He lowered his gaze. There could be no doubting it this time. He had killed a man. The bloody carcass at his feet was proof. The decisive difference to the skirmish. An exhausted Bastien nuzzled his head into Jacob's shoulder and Klaude gave him a heavy nudge.

"That's better, boy." Bakari grinned before stomping away.

Jacob let out a huge breath. He stood straight, composing himself. He scraped his hair back from his face in time to find L'Olonnais standing next to him–grinning.

"Ain't no going back, my soulless hell-hound." L'Olonnais said. "You're now a proper villain." He turned and began his prowl of the cobbles searching for victims to interrogate. Jacob found Henri gazing back at him–a serious expression marred his face.

Jacob stepped back to view the field beyond the gates. Piero's body lay in the grass. Jacob gritted his teeth–fighting back the tears.

Twenty-Seven

The smoke and dust settled. Victory hung in the air. The buccaneers would soon turn their attentions from killing to plunder. They had come for the silver and gold from the mines. The Spanish soldier captured in Puerto Cavallo had promised them it was here. They all wanted their share. Jacob wanted his share. The line he had crossed needed rewarding.

As the men quieted, surveying their surroundings, the pleading could be heard. The few remaining Spaniards huddled together with their backs to a brick building. They had relinquished their weapons. Their arms held high, showing their intent to surrender. L'Olonnais rewarded them for their bravery. He walked to the closest and ran his cutlass tip through the man's belly. A quick death. Jacob winced, shuffling away from his own victim. If they knew who stood in front of them, they would know it was the best they could hope for.

The others whimpered in unison. L'Olonnais sliced into a second, leaving only eight cowering with fear, praying for a miracle to strike down the devil standing before them. For two more of them, no miracle came as they followed their comrades to L'Olonnais' feet.

Above the dying, a pistol fired.

In front of a church fifty yards to the south, a Spanish officer stood, aiming his pistol to the sky. He wore a wide brimmed felt hat adorned with a clutch of red feathers. His hat looked small compared to his large square head. The red dye had long ago faded and signified the age of much of his clothing and armour. Yet the officer stood confident-defiant even-against his attackers. He was not alone. Twenty or more soldiers stood behind him, all with muskets aimed at the buccaneers. L'Olonnais turned to face the defiant enemy and raised his cutlass in mock surrender.

To Jacob's left and right, any attention drifting towards plunder abated. Over a hundred muskets or pistols, loaded or otherwise, were raised and aimed down the street. Jacob raised his own pistol, trying to suppress his tremors.

L'Olonnais stood with his back to his army, facing the remaining enemy. He walked casually into the middle of the cobbled street. His battle coat flapped in the breeze. The looming rain had not ripened, but moisture dampened the air. The buccaneer' numbers dwarfed the Spanish at least ten to one.

"You are outnumbered." L'Olonnais shouted in French to his opposite. "You think you can still defend this town?"

The Spanish officer stepped forward and responded in fluent French. "We would surely hope so. But there are civilians still in the town."

"Then they will die as you will. They should have fled when they had the chance."

"Some are old or sick. They could not leave quickly."

"Old and sick are close to death. We will release them from this world." L'Olonnais turned and chuckled to his crew. Some of the crew chuckled with him. Henri checked his pistol.

"I offer a bargain." The Spanish officer continued. "Give us leave for two hours. Allow the civilians to pack up some humble belongings and wait safely in the hills. After two hours, you may return to the town, and we will be most forthcoming. I will show you where our most wealthy goods lay."

"That is no bargain. We are already in your town, and I will walk over to the tiny remains of your army and make you tell me where your goods lay, or I will cut out your eyes and show you your own arseholes."

"You may do exactly that, François L'Olonnais." The Spaniard flashed a smile. "I know of your reputation. But there are twenty-two of us waiting for you and all of us would like to go down in our history as the man who killed the Bane of Spain. Maybe our powder has been kept dry waiting for you. I could order for you to be shot where you stand. Your men would seek revenge and we would surly die. But so would you."

L'Olonnais paused for a brief moment before raising his arms, laughing theatrically. "If you know my name, then you know I give no quarter to Spanish pigs."

"We ask for no quarter, only for two hours. To allow innocent people a chance. After that, we will surrender and hand over all the wealth the town has to offer. Nobody else need die."

L'Olonnais lowered his hands and bowed to the officer. "We have a deal. Two hours, Señor. Not a second longer."

"My name is Major Quadrado. I commend your intellect. Two hours and we will trade insults again."

The hourglass stood in the town's entrance between the open gates with two buccaneers keeping watch of the main street. Two hours were almost up. The dead buccaneers had been carried to the west of the town and a contingent of men had been assigned to dig their graves. Jacob had volunteered, and with a borrowed shovel, dug a grave for Piero. Henri and Bastien stood over him, but he'd refused their help. They had told him it was not his fault. They all knew the chances they took. Jacob did not speak. He simply dug. When he'd finished, Bastien returned from the woods with a rudimental cross. Jacob borrowed Henri's folding knife and scratched Piero's name into it before bowing his head and making a silent prayer.

The buccaneers strode back into the town. All weapons checked and loaded. The looting began. Bastien was one of the first back into the town and intercepted Jacob.

"Found this," he said, handing over a leather baldric. "It's for your cutlass."

Jacob accepted the baldric and secured it over his shoulder. "Thank you." He tried his cutlass, but it snagged. The frog was set for a thinner blade.

"You'll have to adjust the scabbard loop." Bastien stepped forward to help Jacob with the thong bindings.

Bastien stepped back admiring his friend but Jacob's mind was still a fog of emotions to care.

From across the street, Doyle stomped out of a house, a loaf of bread in his hand. "Bread," he grunted. "The grandest treasure I've found is bloody bread." He shouted over to Jacob, shaking the crust in outrage. "And not even good bread, mind ye — hard, bleedin' Spanish shite!" He tore the loaf in two with his huge hands. "Here, lad." He lobbed one half to Jacob. "Let's hope the captain's havin' better luck than us, eh?"

Other looters were smashing furniture into the streets. The town was devoid of wealth. Doyle stomped off to find the warehouse.

Jacob and Bastien followed, pulling lumps of crust free with their teeth.

The warehouse sat deeper into the town, to the east, near a secondary entrance concealed by cacti. The captured Spanish soldiers lined up against the church under the guard of Bakari and Melchor. A small crowd gathered in the street, intrigued by their admiral. Jacob circled to the side to see what held their attention. In front of the warehouse, he saw L'Olonnais standing with a smaller contingent of men. Le Picard stood with Lucas and Montbars, obscuring the contents in L'Olonnais' hand. Was it a sample from the warehouse? L'Olonnais looked to be preparing for a theatrical revelation of the treasure haul he had led them to. In a moment of frustration, Le Picard turned his back on the admiral, clenching his fists to the sky. Jacob caught sight of L'Olonnais' left hand. It did not hold gold or silver–not even silk or tobacco. It held the square head of Major Quadrado. His right hand held his bloody dagger he had moments earlier used to hack through the neck, leaving the body draining at his feet. Montbars marched over to the closest Spaniard, grabbed him by the collar, dragging him back to L'Olonnais.

"Damn that Major," Bastien said. "The town's empty. He knew there was nothing of value. He tricked us. He just wanted time for his people to escape."

Le Picard punched the air and kicked stones at the warehouse. He stomped back through an empty side street, out of sight. Jacob let his mind count the soldiers being guarded in front of the church. No more than seven. More than a dozen men must have left as protection for the civilians–probably with all the weapons and ammunition. Very clever. L'Olonnais could send a party to hunt them down, but more men would likely be lost with little or no reward. The bulk of the treasure would all be far away by now or scattered in hiding places all over the south–if it ever existed at all.

"Let's go back to Henri." Bastien said.
"You carry on. I'll follow." Jacob walked to the empty side street in pursuit of Le Picard.

Twenty-Eight

Jacob let out a deep sigh as he bunched it tightly in his fist. A fine mist of rain concealed his sadness as he stood in front of the warehouses at the dock in Puerto Cavallo. The smaller of the two stone buildings held a pitiful amount of treasure–a smattering of candle sticks, plate and silverware. The remains of the hidden spoils from the wealthier merchants and politicians. In the larger of the two stone buildings, soldiers and civilians lay in a bloody, twisted, sticky mess of arms and legs. It was impossible to discern which body part belonged to which corpse. This was the warehouse that saddened Jacob. In his hand, he held a bright yellow dress. He'd found it in a side alley, a pistol shot from where he now stood. He could not see her. Her olive skin and dark hair were just a memory.

A fly settled on his wrist, rubbing its front two legs like a miser might ring his hands. Jacob brushed it away, but a second fly escaped the warehouse to settle on his bandaged arm. He flailed his arm, retreating away from the taste of death to face the reality of the broken town. Anger lingered everywhere.

Lack of provisions had forced the captains to concede that the hunt for the townsfolk of San Pedro was futile. They had found little food in the garrisoned town and their own knapsacks were empty. They packed up the few items of worth hidden in barns and under floors onto stray mules found roaming free to the south of the town. They'd trudged back north to deposit them in the small warehouse at Puerto Cavallo.

There was no concealing it—the voyage was a disaster. He'd been away from home for eleven months. He was further away from England than he'd ever been, with no more wealth to show for his time.

Upon entering the town, they reunited with their comrades, who were busy questioning the last prisoners and entertaining the locals. The reticent drudgery was over. The hostility was about to begin.

Marquise lay in anchor in the harbour with only a skeleton crew. When they'd returned that first day, Jacob had found an excuse to be on the first barge back. Harvey had been alone in the navigation room. With nobody to intervene, Jacob had made his approach.

Harvey had glanced up from his growing stack of maps. He placed a weight on the current papers before turning to Jacob. Jacob could not confirm a flicker of a smile at the corner of the navigator's mouth, but he'd sensed a renewed warmth between them.

"You made it back then?" Harvey said. "I hear there was no loot." Jacob shook his head. "Got yourself a baldric now, I see."

Jacob did not answer. Instead, he stepped forward, arms wide, and embraced his cranky friend. Harvey's stubbornness melted, and he wrapped his brawny arms around his young apprentice.

"What happened to your arm?" Harvey asked, taking Jacob's wrist and unwrapping the bandage. The wound was healing but hadn't fully closed. The rim of the cut was a fiery red. "Does it hurt?"

"A little. It's getting better."

"You should let the doctor take a look."

"He'll cut it off."

Harvey laughed. "He does have that tendency. Don't let it get infected. Keep it clean."

With Harvey's help, Jacob re-bandaged his forearm. They'd sat on the bench together. Jacob had been happy to be back in the company of his friend. He'd wanted to ask why he'd ignored him, but didn't want to ruin the moment. He would wait a little longer. Instead, he asked about Harvey's time in Puerto Cavallo while he'd been away. Harvey had little to report, having spent most of his time helping Joseph with minor repairs. Both distancing themselves from the atrocities in the town.

Then it was Jacob's turn to tell his tale. He'd told of the native camp and the ambushes and finally of Piero's death. He'd winced when he'd reported his killing of the Spanish soldier. He'd toyed with omitting it, but knew it was pointless. Word of Jacob's bravery would have made it to Harvey soon enough. He'd wanted to impart his slant on the pain the death had imprinted on him. The death of the Spanish civilian in Puerto Cavallo felt almost insignificant. The brutality of his real first kill had sliced so deeply it had eradicated the small scar left by the maiming he'd caused. Reinhardt could claim that kill.

"Killing don't make you a man." Harvey had denounced.

"I know. I had no choice." Jacob said. "They were outnumbered. I made a difference."

"That may be, but there's always a choice. You'll live with his death 'til your dying days."

"But they killed Piero. Besides, I heard you've killed someone. Everyone's killed someone. It's the way of it out here."

"It is, lad. I've killed. And don't think it don't sit with me like a stone in my belly. That's why I need to get you free of it."

"I'm not a child, Harv. I can look out for myself. I don't need you protecting me."

Harvey rubbed his head, opened his mouth, then closed it again. After a moment, he stood, encouraging Jacob to the rail. He wrapped an arm around his shoulder.

"This world takes from you. The New World, I mean." Harvey pointed back to Puerto Cavallo. "The likes of us who grind its edges. We work the land and the sea. We must fight for scraps. This dream will leave you wanting. The longer you stay, the more of yourself will be lost. No amount of time at home will heal the wounds." Harvey had gestured to the scant crew busy getting *Marquise* ready for sail. "Can you imagine these men returning to a humble life? Ploughing a field or raising children in a quiet village back home?"

Jacob viewed the deck.

"Greed has them. Silver and gold are all they can imagine now. Their sleeps are filled with nightmares of death and wickedness. Most of these men can't return home. Their loved ones wouldn't recognise them. Imagine the shame that would cause. They're damned." Harvey trailed off. "Maybe I am too."

"I've spent time with them, Harv. They're good men. They look out for each other. They fight for each other. You're a good man."

"They fight for themselves, Jacob. There's no loyalty. Not from one of them. You need to see that."

Jacob shrugged Harvey's arm away. "That's not true. Henri and Bastien are loyal to each other. And me. And you if you'd let them. You're a stubborn old man, who'd rather take orders from the likes of Tardebigge. Your precious navy's no different. We fight for a king that would send us to certain death if it meant a few more inches of land or an extra ounce of silver. Everyone's in it for themselves. At least here they're honest about it."

"It's not about wealth, Jacob... it's about..."

Jacob had had enough. He'd spotted Isaac on the main deck, approaching the ladder to the barge. "If you want to leave, leave.

Don't worry about me." Jacob stomped to the steps and followed Isaac over the gunwale.

Now, two days later, standing at the warehouse, Harvey's words resonated in Jacob's mind. Greed was everywhere.

Jacob was brought back to the present as Le Picard strode only yards away from behind the south side of the warehouse towards the dock.

"We sail, Admiral. I don't care about your wishes. Your plans have yielded nothing."

"You have not the mettle to leave this crew, Pierre." L'Olonnais said, striding to catch Le Picard. "Who will you follow? You have been my bootlicker for so long you won't know the leadership of another." His words halting the lieutenant who turned and took strides back towards L'Olonnais.

"I will lead myself. There are men who'll follow. It should be no surprise this was your coupe de grace. Mutiny has been your shadow for many months now."

A crowd was gathering.

"True, it's no surprise Pierre. Mutiny is always a captain's shadow. You think you can lead this rabble and not cast the longest shadow of all? Where would you sail? Back to Tortuga, licking your wounds? These lands still hold vast fortunes. You know not where to seek. I have the maps and the resources." The captain paused. "In my head. The locations of the towns and ports all along the coast yielding high riches."

"Throw up your arms, François. Preach your sermons. But your flock ain't bleating." Le Picard pirouetted gesturing to the crowd. "The promise of riches. We have heard them all before. Too many men have been lost to your promises. We would need to lose another four hundred to make a fair share out of the latest spoils." He pointed past Jacob to the almost empty warehouse. "Or is that your plan? Kill the crew until only you return? Hide amongst the bodies of your friends and return home a rich hero?"

Jacob eased himself into the crowd and out of eyesight.

L'Olonnais drew his cutlass from his belt and stepped towards Le Picard. Le Picard drew his own cutlass and planted his feet with his back to the crowd.

"Pierre, François! Hold your steel." Moise stepped between them with his arms raised. "This mission has not bloated our purses. We can all agree. But each man deserves his say. There's no need for arms."

Murmurs spread through the growing crowd. Heads nodded. Jacob scanned the faces, finding Henri and Bastien at the statue. Doyle stood to their left with Lucas, Montbars, and Andrieszoon close by. From the dock, Jacob glimpsed Isaac approaching, fresh off a barge edging the outer circle of the crowd until he stood with Jacob by the warehouses.

"What's happening here?" Isaac asked before frowning at the contents of Jacob's hands.

"I think Le Picard's calling a mutiny," Jacob answered, stuffing the yellow dress into his knapsack.

"Le Picard's been threatening as much for months. Can't see this ending with a clash of tankards in the tavern." Isaac said.

"Nope."

"Le Picard might feel confident. I've heard many murmuring they would join him. Not I. The admiral gets my vote."

Jacob snapped a look to Isaac. "You would stay with L'Olonnais?"

"Aye. He's done me no wrong so far. Kept me fed and in plenty of coin. His plan's just as good today as it was in Bayaha. He's earned one last push south. His ways are a bit bloody at times, but so long as the Spaniards take the brunt and it don't foul the crew, I've no quarrel with it."

They fell silent–Isaac watching the scene unfold, Jacob side eying the unattended barge. Le Picard was calling out the other captains to state their allegiances.

"Anthony? How many men have you lost to this madness? The self-appointed admiral here has led you into trap after trap with no reward.

"And Philippe? Have you seen such a woeful hoard for so much pain and suffering? We all accept the fever could strike us down. We are hardy and dogged, but we hope for our suffering we will be rewarded. Will you be the man to tell your brethren–recovering from the sweats and the sickness, those that have not yet died–that San Pedro offered no rewards but L'Olonnais would insist we blindly follow his plan back into the jungle where there is little food and certainly no medicine.

"Jan and Daniel. You are new to these adventures. Are they to your liking? Months away, floating aimlessly in the doldrums, making land wherever God finds a fancy. Only to be cursed by the savages for pointlessly killing their women–for our admiral's own amusement.

"Whether you believe in Papa Nahualli and his curse, you cannot disagree–L'Olonnais is indeed ill-fated. I, for one, will not be following him into the jungle once again with the promise of treasures and riches. Maps that are only in his head."

"And how will you not follow me?" L'Olonnais lofted his cutlass and laughed. "You have no ship. You have no crew. *Marquise* is my ship, and its articles are to its allegiance. You are no captain. Not even in name."

"A ship I still seek, but men I have. No more hiding in the shadows. We seek no permission to un-sign the articles. Who has the claim on the ship taken in the harbour? Anthony, Jan. You captured it and have two ships between you. You have no need for a third. If there is ever a time, a fellow needs a ship, it is now. It will be used to free the masses from this tyrant. Which of you holds claim to the brig?"

Anthony du Puis stepped forward. "It is true that Lucas and I took the ship. But the admiral had already given orders the ship would be used for the fleet. For the plunder."

"Plunder." Le Picard scoffed. "What plunder. We could hold all the treasures of this voyage in that barge and still not knock our knees as we rowed. I stake a claim to her."

"She's already been divvied. You hold no claim." L'Olonnais waved Le Picard away.

"Who holds its claim? Who has it been promised to? Daniel? Have you laid claim?"

"Not I. But I would gladly take it. My crew would make great use of such a ship."

"Then who? Denis? Has the ship been offered to you? You would lead? Surely not ahead of me."

"Not I either, Pierre. I would play quartermaster, but I'm not fit for captaincy."

"Then who. That ship holds the route to riches and away from this madman."

L'Olonnais smiled and nodded to behind Le Picard, who turns to face the crowd.

Jacob craned his neck, intrigued to see the owner of the brig.

"The Brig is mine, Pierre. The admiral has bestowed it to me. I have served with him for many years and have earned its captaincy."

Le Picard signed, deflated by the answer. "You have earned its captaincy, Moise. I cannot deny you. To serve under such a pig's bladder is well deserving of a ship twice its wealth."

"So, you see, Pierre. These men are satisfied with their shares. From sixty-five, I have been earning them their riches, and we have lived like kings. Tomorrow's prizes will be no different from Maracaibo and Gibraltar. We set out as six ships and now we are seven. An extra ship with Captain Vauquelin promoted to join the fleet. We are fed and eager to continue to our original destination. You've said your piece, Pierre. You have waited for months to take your shot, and it has landed short. Your musket is empty, and you have not one loader amongst this crew. You will remain here when we leave, for you are no longer my lieutenant." L'Olonnais turned to the crowd and bellowed. "If anyone is found harbouring this traitor, you will find my wrath in your future."

"That was short-lived." Jacob said.

"Don't be so sure," Isaac replied. "Lucas and Montbars are shifting a bit uneasy. And Philippe's looking sheepish. This don't need a vote. Le Picard only needs one ship to not follow to make his escape, and L'Olonnais knows it. He'll be striking fear before the thoughts set in."

"Do you think they'll be ships heading back to Tortuga?"

"Maybe, or Port Royal. It's closer. If they feel the admiral, don't know the locations for his treasure, there'll be no allegiance's."

Jacob stood watching the crowd. Isaac was right. Lucas and Montbars huddled with their crew, and du Puis and Bequel looked questionably to their own men. Even Moise had not moved to L'Olonnais' side in solidarity.

"Where's Harvey? Still on *Marquise*?" Jacob asked.

"He is. Never seen a man so glum."

Jacob walked off in the direction of the barge.

"Where you going?" Isaac called after him.

"Going to see Harvey. See if I can cheer him up."

"Ain't you interested in how this'll decide itself?"

Jacob was very interested in how this would decide itself. And so would Harvey.

Twenty-Nine

"Jacob." Harvey didn't raise his head from his charts.

"I ain't sorry, Harv." Jacob stood with his hands on his hips. "I'm not a child."

"Hmm hmm. You're blocking my light."

"Just thought you'd want to know."

"What's that Captain Penjerrick?"

"There's talk at the dock of the fleet disbanding. The mutiny might be brewing."

Harvey rocked up on his heels. "Who?"

"Le Picard."

Harvey ran his fingers through his thickening beard, finally curling them around the coarse strands at his chin. "What's finally given him the courage, I wonder?"

Jacob raised his eyebrows but didn't respond.

"What is it, lad?" Harvey asked.

"I think he's acting on something I said."

"Is there more to your tale? What else happened on The Main? What's brewing, lad?"

Jacob winced, swishing a foot across the boards. "I told Le Picard L'Olonnais killed Reinhardt, and that Reinhardt had given his name as a mutineer."

"Is that what happened, lad? You saw him kill Reinhardt?"

"Yeah, with my own eyes."

"The man's worse than I thought. He's a monster. Just senseless killing. Someone needs to put an end to him."

Jacob's face tightened with worry as Harvey scratched his beard, lost in thought.

"Not us, lad," Harvey said with a reassuring smile. "Don't worry. I'm just saying there's too many hardened rogues in these waters. He'll cross the wrong man soon enough." Harvey edged to the quarterdeck rail and sneaked a look onto the main deck. "Why did you tell Le Picard? He can't be trusted. He might give your name over."

"He said he wouldn't. I couldn't stand by and wait for L'Olonnais to kill him as well."

Harvey sighed. "No, lad. I suppose not. We should've taken our leave when we had the chance." He ducked into the navigation room and rolled up the charts before huddling towards Jacob. "Who had the upper hand?"

"I thought L'Olonnais at first, but some of the other captains don't look convinced. Isaac said it's not about to go to a vote. Those wantin' to leave will just head their own way."

"What's Lucas and Montbars' mood?"

"Hard to say. They might be swayed to leave with Le Picard."

"Yeah, but I think Montbars' hatred for the Spanish will have him convince Lucas to continue to cruise The Main."

"Moise has the new Brig. He'll surely stay with L'Olonnais. Philippe and Anthony looked like they could go either way."

Harvey scratched his forehead and paced the boards. They were alone. Helario was in the hold, stock-taking the last of the supplies. Joseph hung in the rigging, repairing a broken spar. The rest of the skeleton crew were asleep or playing cards on the main deck. Nobody paid much attention to the two English conspirators nervously pacing the quarterdeck.

"What you thinking, Harv?"

"I don't know, lad. But surely you can see now. We must get away from this madman. If we follow him, we'll end up like Reinhardt."

Jacob paused for a breath and then nodded. "You're right."

"I can't deny these past few months haven't been exhilarating, but there's better captains than Tardebigge in the navy and there's still plenty to be had with this war. If one of those ships is heading for Port Royal, then I intend to be on it." Harvey stopped his pacing and stood in front of Jacob. "But you must come with me. I can't have your death on my conscience. Are you with me, lad?"

Jacob stood a moment, thinking. He was struggling to make sense of his thoughts. "I ain't joining the navy."

"Fair enough. But you need to get home. It's too dangerous here."

"Harvey, I ain't a child."

"No, but you're not a man either. You're sixteen. You should be at home helping your mother and winning the hand of that Lydia, fishing and enjoying a simple life."

"There's no way home without some riches."

"There aren't any riches. Not for the likes of us. Why can't you see that? L'Olonnais had you marching all over and you've come back with nothing but a black scar on your soul." Harvey pursed his lips. "Let's just get going. We make our way to Port Royal, then decide what to do next."

"What about Henri and Bastien? They're my friends, my brothers."

"They're not your brothers. They'd sell you for an eight. Trust me, lad, we just need to go."

"I ain't a lad. Stop treating me like a child. What ain't you telling me?"

"I'm sorry." Harvey placed a hand on Jacob's shoulder, composing them both. "I've been ignoring you. I had my reasons. I couldn't have you close to me. It was too dangerous. L'Olonnais will do anything to keep me on the crew. He knows he needs to deliver on his promise of gold and silver. Without me, he wouldn't have a chance."

"What you saying, Harv? Are you in trouble?"

"There's no time to explain now." Harvey locked eyes with Jacob. "Let's get back to the dock. We need to see if any of the captains are going to Port Royal. Once we have a plan, I'll tell you everything. Promise."

A call came from Joseph in the rigging. "L'Olonnais' approaching."

Jacob and Harvey jumped the steps to the forecastle to get a better view. A flotilla of barges had departed from the dock and were heading toward the various ships at anchor. Jacob could make out at least three barges heading towards *Marquise*. He could see L'Olonnais in the closest barge, but couldn't be sure who accompanied him.

"Damn it. The meeting's already over." Harvey said. "What outcome can that mean?" He scratched his head and paced the boards once more. "We can't row past him. He'll order us to turn about." He headed back to the quarterdeck. Jacob followed. "We'll have to play along. You head below. Make yourself useful to Helario. I'll mind my maps. Soon enough, the admiral–if that's what he still is–will be weighed down with strategies. I'll come and find you and we'll make our escape. We'll need to be quick as fleas when the time comes."

"If you get the chance, you can leave me here, Harv. I'll be safe enough. I've got Henri and Bastien."

"That's not an option. L'Olonnais can't be trusted if I'm not here to protect you."

"What does that mean? I can look out for myself."

Harvey craned his neck over the rail. "No time to explain. Get yourself below. Make haste."

Jacob's faced reddened, the phrase igniting memories from *Kestrel*. Over the bulwark, he heard L'Olonnais' voice. He scurried off, leaving Harvey deep in mock inspection of his maps.

"We're going to need much more grain than this. Much more."

Jacob almost trod on Tomilho as he thumped into the store. The dog jumped up with a start.

"Ah, Jovem." Helario looked up from his ledger. "Have you come from the dock? Did you see how much food we should expect?"

"I think this is all the food that's coming."

"This cannot be. We have barely enough to feed Tomilho. We'll need five times these numbers. What of the other ships? Do they have more?"

"I don't know. L'Olonnais' approaching. I think there's been a meeting at the dock. Seems like the fleet is parting ways."

"So, the mutiny has come?"

"Maybe. Le Picard's encouraging the other captains to leave the fleet."

From the deck above, fresh calls could be heard.

"That fool." Helario said, cocking his head to listen. "Sounds like the crew are heading back? I'll speak with Moise. We cannot leave with such a pitiful reserve." Helario picked up his ledger and headed out of the store. "With me Jacob. I must lock this door before the rabble devours its contents like the locusts they are."

Helario ushered Jacob to the orlop deck before hurrying up the companionway. Jacob was left alone. He could hear the stomping of boots from above as the crew boarded. He edged forward, listening to the grumbles leaching down the steps. Most of the voices he didn't recognise, but then he heard Isaac.

"This is madness," Isaac said.

"Is it true? Half the men gone?"

"What's Moise thinking? L'Olonnais' just given him a bloody ship, and this is the thanks."

Jacob stood in the darkness, listening. Shafts of light flickered as the men shuffled above, trying to make sense of the news. Jacob needed to think. Harvey's words lingered in his mind. Whoever had chosen the ship had stayed with L'Olonnais. He must not reveal their plan to escape to anyone.

"Isaac? Have you seen Jacob?"

It was Henri who had asked. Jacob's attention peeked at the sound of his friend, and he could not help climbing the steps to meet him.

"Henri." He said as he emerged from the hatch.

"Jake. Where you been? It was a shambles at the dock. Le Picard's mutinied and at least a third of the men have sided with him. Moise has joined the mutiny, made Le Picard his lieutenant. Lucas and du Puis have cut loose as well. L'Olonnais' in a foul mood and damned them all to hell. Said he'd rather sail with one ship than sail with treacherous snakes."

"Is L'Olonnais aboard?" Jacob asked.

"He is." Isaac replied. "He's with Harvey. He's asked for you."

"Me?"

"Yep. Not sure why? I'd head to the quarterdeck before his tempter has time to fester."

Jacob's heart raced. He needed to lay eyes on Harvey. He edged towards the stern of the ship through the chattering crowd. Harvey was in deep conversation with L'Olonnais and Denis. Denis and Harvey stood motionless, their palms flattening the edges of the charts as L'Olonnais danced around the boards. His arms flailing. Helario was shouting, but to no avail. The cook strode off to the steps with his hands raised to the heavens.

"Hey, boy. Admiral wants ya."

Jacob turned to find Bakari scowling back at him. "Yeah, Henri just told me."

"Well, why you hang around for? Get your bones to the quarterdeck."

Jacob trudged over to the steps, with Bakari close behind. He paused at the bottom, allowing Helario to pass.

"The voyage is doomed." Helario exclaimed. "With no food, this voyage is doomed."

Bakari's large leather hands palmed Jacob's back, encouraging him forward. "Found him, Admiral," Bakari said as they reached the navigation committee.

L'Olonnais turned in a flash to face Jacob. His scowl eased as he looked at the younger man. He flashed a smiled. "Ah, Mr Penjerrick, my friend."

Jacob shot a glance to Harvey but found no clues. "Yes, Sir."

"I have a special need for you in these difficult times." L'Olonnais inched over as he spoke and draped his arm around Jacob's shoulder. "As you've no doubt heard, we are parting company with some of the other ships. Their time on The Main has elapsed. They have more pressing matters to attend to." L'Olonnais shrugged. "So, there's been a reshuffle. Mr Touppin is our new quartermaster with the departure of Mr Vauquelin."

Jacob glanced to Denis standing proudly next to Harvey.

"As you can see, there are many fresh faces among the crew." L'Olonnais gestured to the seamen clambering over the gunwale swelling the ranks. "We need to account for their particulars. We have a lot to tend to before we embark on the next leg of our voyage and Mr Touppin will be very busy. So, Mr Varela will be assuming the role of ledger keeper."

Jacob nodded, waiting for L'Olonnais to continue.

"Mr Varela's writing skill is not as sharp as it could be, being Spanish, so we need you to hold his quill, so to speak." Jacob nodded again and glanced back at Harvey, who raised his eyebrows before hanging his head to the charts.

"Mr Obasi will set up a table on the main deck, and he and Mr Varela will usher the men—new and old—over to you to place their mark in the ledger, re-declaring their loyalty to the Articles." L'Olonnais grinned at Jacob. "I'm sorry for its laboriousness, my young friend, but any of the old crew who know their letters I cannot spare, and I do not trust any of the new just yet. And you are very fitting of the role having such an elegant writing style. I see you scribbling sometimes. I could not hope for a better ledger keeper."

Jacob stood straight and proud, forgetting himself for a moment, then caught sight of Bakari grinning at Harvey, who glared back.

"Oh, Mr Penjerrick. I never truly congratulated you on your bravery in San Pedro. I was right to put my trust in you. You may have the honour of adding your name first to the list."

"Thank you, sir."

"Master Harvey will be with you shortly to add his own loyalty." L'Olonnais held Harvey's eye. "Won't you Master Harvey?"

"Aye, sir." Harvey glowered at L'Olonnais before looking long and hard at Jacob.

"Follow me, firecracker." Bakari said, leading the way down the steps to find Melchor.

The other ships had already set sail and last seen heading east. The rumour was Montbars had convinced Lucas to continue cruising on the hunt for more Spanish revenge. Moise had indeed taken on Le Picard as his first lieutenant of the new brig. And with Philip Bequel on *Leopard* and Anthony du Puis on *Tigre*, the rest of the fleet had set sail for Jamaica.

"Good riddance," L'Olonnais had bellowed to his bolstered crew. "Let the English suffer them. It's no surprise they do not choose Tortuga to lick their wounds. They fear my wrath and the humiliation on our return."

After *Marquise* had weighed anchor and they were sailing into deep water, Bakari coerced Harvey to join the queue for the ledger.

"Looks like we're stuck here a little longer?" Jacob whispered as Harvey bent over to sign his name.

"It's like he knew we wanted to be gone and fettered your hand with that quill."

"Maybe Blauvelt will have a ship?"

"Blauvelt's worse than Tortuga. Just more rogues. We'd be lucky to find a ship heading anywhere other than another raid." Harvey placed the quill back in the well and stood from the ledger. "Keep your head low, lad. Stay out of the way of L'Olonnais. I'll find a way out of this."

Thirty

L'Olonnais had convinced many of the original crew to remain loyal, and his speech back at the dock was full of its usual inspiration and motivation. However, three quarters of the entire crew had shaken their heads and refused to fall for his theatrics. Many of the landsmen conscripted from Tortuga had not been convinced to stay with *Marquise*. A raucous laughter had erupted at the dock when one such landsmen had proclaimed "L'Olonnais, you scoundrel. You promised pieces of eight so readily available; they would be like pears from a tree. I have seen no pieces of eight since leaving Tortuga, or pears for that matter."

The men who remained were mostly able seamen–cutthroats who sought plunder and would rather starve than return home with nothing to show for their efforts. They saw no sense in regrouping in Port Royal or Tortuga. They would hold faith in the reputation of the ferocious captain a little longer. But, in total, only one hundred and fifty men were aboard *Marquise*.

"We're on a fool's errand." Helario fumed as he stomped over to the wall of wooden crates. He thrust his hand into the furthest crate and pulled out the last surviving chicken by its neck. He twisted his hands together, sealing the fate of the evening's supper. Jacob had not witnessed Helario in such a foul mood. The cook dropped the chicken head to the floor for the eager Tomilho, who snatched it up and scurried off to his corner to crunch his way through his meagre meal. "Even with these depleted numbers, we'll not make it past Gracias–let alone to Blauvelt. You know how far Blauvelt is, Jacob?"

Jacob shook his head.

"About two hundred and fifty miles. And we have one chicken. Christmas is only days away. One chicken's not enough to celebrate the lord, let alone get us to Blauvelt. If I had known the plan, I would have exercised my right to leave this galley and join with Captain du Puis."

Jacob no longer winced at the death of the chickens. He took the carcass from Helario and hung it over the trough–a pitiful sight, seeing only one bird where there could be dozens. He'd been helping Helario for these past few days and witnessed the cages, filled from Puerto Cavallo, emptied. It was hard to deny Helario's concerns. In the hurry to embark, no fair system of division had been implemented. Moise's ledger guided the careful division of the plunder from Puerto Cavallo and San Pedro, but provisions such as food had been skulked away with no records. Once onboard a ship, there had been no retrieving it.

The mood amongst the crew had darkened. The seriousness of their choice to stay with *Marquise* was becoming apparent. It was not only the crew that grumbled, but also many of the officers. The hierarchy seemed disjointed with the changes. Denis was likeable enough, but didn't command the respect of Moise or the fear of Le Picard. Many of the crew felt aggrieved, as they had little say in his promotion. L'Olonnais had nominated the former boatswain and before anyone could object or offer their own name for consideration, the proceedings were concluded and daily duties assigned. The crew stood firm when voting for the free role of boatswain, opting for Isaac to take the position. It at least eased some resentment from Isaac as he held the respect of the crew and would have been the obvious choice for quartermaster.

Jacob was no expert in the inner politics of a floating buccaneer community, but it was clear L'Olonnais could no longer claim the title of admiral—and that was a blow to his reputation. Even Henri and Bastien had made passing comments about his captaincy. All in hushed tones and to no one other than their huddle, which now only included Jacob and Isaac.

"A rousing speech is all well and good." Henri had whispered one evening. "But it must be backed with strategy. One hundred and fifty men isn't enough to attack these Spanish ports that are in the captain's head."

They had all been on quarter rations before and they would suffer them again now. The winds had returned, and they made fast time south, along the Moskito coast. There was a growing trepidation. Should they weigh anchor and risk the hostilities of the natives in an attempt to find food? Maybe attack one of the smaller ports? The captain had opted instead for Blauvelt. It had now become a race–would they reach the sanctuary of the pirate haven before the supplies ran short? Most wagered they would not. And as Jacob waited for the blood to drain from the chicken carcass, he couldn't help but agree.

Urgent thudding of feet stomping to an usual rhythm from the deck above disturbed the galley. The ship tilted sharply.

"Jacob, see about the commotion. I'll tend to this," Helario said, pointing to the weak broth in the cauldron.

Jacob climbed the steps to the main deck. Through the rain–which he'd been unaware of in the galley–he spied Harvey, more animated than he had been since leaving Puerto Cavallo. Bellowing instructions to the riggers while fighting the tiller. Jacob pushed through the crowd to Isaac at the gunwale to ask what had caused the excitement.

"Sand bar." Isaac said. "It looks like we're stuck, unless Harvey can perform a miracle."

"What's the problem, Master Harvey?" L'Olonnais barked, striding to the quarterdeck with Denis in tow.

"Sand bar, Cap'n. The sea's too shallow and the ship too heavy."

The captain stroked his goatee. "Did you not see its approach?" He came to stand in front of Harvey.

"No, sir. This rain found us just as we found the bar. No way of knowing until it was too late."

The captain puffed, examining Harvey. "Can we cut through?"

"I don't sense it, Cap'n. The bow is stuck tight." Harvey scratched his scalp.

"Add more sail then?"

"Let me think, Captain."

L'Olonnais fumed but suppressed his temper.

"The ship's too heavy. She's digging in. First thing, she'll need to be made lighter. Anything of use needs to go in the barges. Anything not needed goes overboard. Once I'm happy with the weight, we'll start with topsails only and backed. Furl all mainsails." These lasts remark was directed at the riggers.

The sailors shinnied through the rigging furling the mainsails on both masts.

"Hang the topgallants in the brails. Just in case."

"You wish me to give the order to throw valuable goods overboard?" The captain said.

"Only the unnecessary, sir."

The captain fixed a stare at his helmsman. "You best know your business, Master Harvey."

"It's unprecedented, *sir*. It's dark. The weather's against us and getting angrier. The bar is shifting beneath us. We're overweight. And I've never liked the rake of these masts. There's not a helmsman within a thousand miles that would know this business. Our odds are slim, but if everyone does as I say–we might just have a chance."

"I am the captain of this ship. It is I who gives the orders. You would do well to remember that, Master Harvey."

Harvey relinquished the tiller and took one step larboard. "Sorry, sir... I forget myself."

The wind and rain lashed down between them. The captain gripped the hilt of his cutlass, knuckles white. Swinging to face the main deck, he found the crew watching his every move. He turned back to Harvey and the man-less tiller. He spoke calmly.

"Mr Touppin." Denis scurried to his side. "Load the barges with everything heavy and useful."

Denis sprang into action. "All hands on deck." He called over the rail. He found the lieutenants and gave his orders.

Everyone not on duty or already curious was fetched from their bunks to help where needed.

"If she doesn't budge, Master Harvey–what then?"

"We passed a sizable island a league or two back." Harvey re-gripped the tiller, reigning in his dissent. "It'll be on a heading of north, northeast."

"What are you saying, Master Harvey? We should abandon the ship?"

"Aye, Sir."

The captain marched to the stern rail and, using his spy glass, scoured the horizon, looking for Harvey's island. A few moments later, he marched back to the tiller. "And what do you suggest we do with *my* ship?"

"I'm sorry, sir, but she's no good to any man stuck in the sand. I suggest we unladen her of as much weight as we can afford. If she doesn't release, we abandon her for the island. Guns, iron anything weighty that's not needed, will need to go overboard."

"Mr Touppin."

Denis scuttled back to the captain's side. "Yes, Sir"

"*Marquise* might need to be abandoned." He held up his hand to calm his quartermaster. "Not yet. I'm sure Master Harvey has more to say on the matter. But for now, ready the guns to be thrown overboard."

"Aye, sir" Denis eyed Harvey before turning to relay the captain's orders to Isaac. Jacob scurried back to the galley with the news.

The rain Jacob had turned his back on had intensified by the time he returned. Not a dry inch of clothing wrapped any man. Denis and Isaac had lowered a plumb line at various points around the hull, assessing the depth of the bar. The bow sat deep into the sand, but it was agreed it might be possible to free the stern, and in doing so dislodge the bow under sternway.

Jacob helped—as did all hands—to relinquish as much weight from *Marquise* as the captain was prepared to lose. The guns were unceremoniously thrown overboard. Weapons were loaded into the four barges and a dozen men rowed to a safe distance, knowing they might prove useful if the island became their only hope. The ocean around the ship was littered with empty wooden barrels, once used for salted meat and grain, and cages once holding hens. Helario had given an ironic chuckle when asked if he still needed them. Timber bulkheads were strapped together forming rafts stowing some of the less important items with a hope of reclaiming them once *Marquise* was free. The ship was at least a third of its original weight when the captain exited his cabin three hours later.

"The rudder feels looser, sir," Harvey said as he gripped the tiller.

Some hoped a gust might dislodge *Marquise* or shift the sand bar, but Harvey remained unconvinced

Jacob stood with Henri amongst the bulk of the crew, watching the wind tighten the sails. *Marquise* creaked.

Harvey listened and watched–and felt. "Topgallants." He called.

With topgallants unfurled, the crew waited. *Marquise* creaked some more. Harvey caressed the tiller.

"She's not budging, Cap'n." Harvey said.

"Add the mains?" The captain questioned.

"I don't see it. The strain will splinter the masts."

They waited. Everyone listening. Harvey watched as more crew wandered to larboard peeking over the gunwale for clues.

"Denis." He called, nodding to the main deck.

"All hands to the centre of the ship." Denis shouted. "We need to concentrate the weight."

Everyone retreated.

"She ain't budging." Harvey said.

The captain exhaled long and hard. He looked to Harvey and then to the crew huddled around the main mast. "Master Harvey?"

"She's not budging, Cap'n."

The captain made fists, suppressing his anger. "Ready the mainsails." He called to the riggers. "Maybe some good old-fashioned brute strength is what's needed."

"No, Cap'n. By backing the mains, there'll be too much strain on the masts."

The captain glowered at Harvey before turning to the riggers. "Do it. Start with the fore."

The ship creaked as the wind bellowed the sails. The foresail now unfurled and set. The foremast flexed as a gust caught the sail full on, intensified the creaking. A low murmuring infected the onlookers as they squinted through the rain. With mostly seasoned seamen among the crew, there was intelligent debate to whether this strategy would work.

At the tiller, Harvey cringed at the sounds. "She's not budging, Cap'n. The fore doesn't like the strain. It's taking the brunt."

The wind intensified, and *Marquise* lurched backwards. The crew steadied themselves. Some cheered.

Denis leaned over the gunwale, eyes scanning the shifting waterline for any sign of movement. "She's moving, Cap'n." Denis said, surprised.

Harvey hurried to Denis's side to confirm the observations. He looked to the fore mast. Then back to the sand bar. "She's moving, Cap'n–but not enough. The fore mast will give before she's free."

"Add the mainsail. Spread the strain." The captain shouted to the riggers.

"She'll not hold, Cap'n. We need to loosen the fore. It's gonna give."

The captain ignored his navigator and called up to the mainmast. "Do it. We need more."

The riggers did as their captain ordered.

"No, Cap'n. No more sails. The mains will add too much strain."

The captain snapped his head to face Harvey.

The topsails bellowed. The mainsails grasped everything the wind offered.

Harvey shook his head and looked back over the gunwale. "She's not gonna give," he said to Denis. "Tell him she's not gonna give."

Denis stared at Harvey open mouthed, then back to the sand bar–but said nothing.

Jacob stood with the gathered crew, fascinated by the fore mast. From over his shoulder, Gaetan hurried from the companionway.

"Captain." He shouted, fighting his voice over the wind. "The hull's springing leaks all over. Joseph says the strain's too much–she won't hold."

A crack from the foremast recaptured Jacob's attention. It flexed with the strain. A splinter snapped at the spar where the sail finished. The riggers on the yardarms could sense the foremast's distress.

Cautious shouts hurried back and forth. More than half ignored any intent to stay aloft and clambered down the rigging, trying to outrun the inevitable. For most, it was too late. The foremast splintered–then cracked. A deep, wrenching snap as the spar gave way. The sail whipped into the wind, hurtling the shattered mast overboard. The ship lurched–but still not enough. Riggers screamed. Some plunged cleanly into the sea. Others, not so lucky, bounced off ropes and timber before vanishing into the churning waves. Rigging snapped taut across the deck like crossbow strings at full draw. The wrecked mast dragged in the water, half-submerged to larboard. The captain, Harvey and Denis clenched, not moving until the danger of loose rigging was over.

Harvey glowered at the captain, then strode into the centre of the Quarterdeck amongst taut ropes and splintered wood. "Furl all sail. She's not budging. It's over."

The riggers looked to their captain, waiting for confirmation. The captain looked back over the gunwale then up to the riggers who, in that moment, had already started furling the sails. The captain nodded his agreement.

"Men overboard." Denis called. "Send over lines. Get men below to help Joseph."

Jacob found Bastien safe in the rigging, helping to tie in the mainsail. Jacob followed Isaac and Henri to heed the pleas of their fallen crewmates. In the distance, he caught sight of Harvey's island. It looked tiny on the horizon.

Thirty-One

Marquise lay on the horizon, her masts stripped clean, making her look like a skeleton ship. The violent gale had abated, and for two days the barges ferried the one hundred and fifty men and materials to Harvey's island.

The captain remained on the ship with Denis, instructing a contingent of the crew, led by Joseph, to strip her of all useful timber. The plan was to build a longboat to carry the men to the mainland.

A party of buccaneers searched the island for supplies. Within the hour, they sent news of fresh water–to the great relief of the rest of the crew. The island also had wild fruits and berries. Coconuts grew in abundance. Large palm trees lined the beach, reaching for the ocean at forty-five-degree angles. Bastien demonstrated his dexterity, racing up the trunks without the use of his hands, throwing the large nuts to his fellow marooned crew.

It was clear the construction of the longboat would take several weeks to complete, so the men wasted no time setting up a camp to sustain them in the meantime. All the rescued sails were used to create tents to house the one hundred and fifty men. Each tent became a rudimental mess-crew, with its own campfire and buccan awaiting the fish Klaude was confident he could teach the men to catch.

Harvey and Piero constructed a food store using timber from the palm trees and the foresail of *Marquise*. A makeshift infirmary was erected on the far side of the camp, where seven more men lay injured after the fracture of the foremast.

Dr Venette had been busy while the ship was evacuated, setting several bones. One unfortunate soul became the latest victim of the bone saw; he lay weeping most hours, contemplating his future.

The time away from their captain allowed the crew's minds the freedom for independent thought. By the second night, it was not only the infirmary where moaning could be heard. The seriousness of their situation had infected their loyalty. As more men landed, the grumbling grew more incessant.

"We should have followed du Puis," Alphonse said, as they sat around the campfire that evening. When not screaming orders to the gunners, he'd been a quiet, obedient supporter of the captain.

"Aye," came a quiet chorus.

Jacob sat hugging his knees under his coat, listening as the crew chastised their captain. He sat with Harvey, Isaac, Henri, and Bastien under the moonlight, finding himself agreeing with the comments being opined.

"Le Picard knew it. The captain's luck had run dry. He called it right back on the dock." Alphonse said. "God is punishing him for his butchery. Not all he tortured and killed were heathens or Spaniards. There's a fair share of good men and women in their number. I heard Le Picard say the captain himself had put the blade into Reinhardt's belly." Jacob coughed in smoke and shot a look at Harvey. "Says it was revenge for his talk of mutiny."

"Did Le Picard see it with his own eyes?" Harvey asked without looking up from the fire.

"He didn't say. I figured it was the spark to call out the captain. He didn't accuse him outright. Moise calmed his manner. I didn't believe it then, but I think it's the reason so many abandoned him."

"Aye," came the chorus again, louder this time.

"Papa Nahualli." Marin mumbled. Marin wasn't a well-educated man, few were, but Marin was particularly dull. He did as he's told, so his speaking up without rebuke was unusual.

"Aye, Papa Nahualli. The curse." Alphonse said. "His arrogance causes our suffering. The heathens knew it. They have cursed him. He's doomed until his cruelty is avenged."

"He'll be mad before the years through. We need to distance ourselves from him." Came a voice from outside the firelight.

"Aye." There had been no grog for many days, yet the crew mustered as if issued with potvaliancy. Resentment filled their voices.

"We must build this longboat the captain speaks of and make our way back to The Main." It was Alphonse who carried the bravery yet again. "Blauvelt can't be far. From there, we break from the captain and find passage back to Tortuga. Anyone who supports him need not join us."

Before the infection spread, a long shadow darkened the circle, blocking the moonlight.

"So, you mean to overthrow the captain?" Bakari said. He'd returned with Melchor and Klaude from the hunt, and they now loomed over the fire. "Let's see who speaks so openly tomorrow when he returns."

He stared at Jacob's huddle. Bakari dragged his gaze to Bastien, Henri, and Isaac before resting on Harvey. The others in the circle shuffled uneasily.

"The captain's put riches in your pocket for three years and now you turn when your belly gets empty? We should look to Mr Harvey, yes? Was it not he who ran our ship aground? Very clumsy for a man who claims to know these waters better than anyone. The ship lays trapped like an upturned turtle, yet you blame your captain. Strange, no? That the one man who would most like to leave this crew is the man who has found us stranded."

Harvey bucked his head but did not reply. Bakari walked out of the circle back to Melchor and Klaude. "For Buccan" He threw two carcasses onto the sand. "The island will feed us, you mutinous cowards. Let's see what Helario's herbs make of these."

The circle remained silent like scolded children. Their enthusiasm evaporating with the smoke. Jacob peered through the dancing flames to where a furry heap lay. Marin stood and walked over to their food supply for the foreseeable future.

"I don't know if I can eat this," he said.

Helario awoke early and surveyed his store. It was Christmas morning and the mood in the camp could be damned–it would not go uncelebrated.

"Well, we won't starve." He said as Jacob stumbled in behind him, rubbing his eyes.

It was true. The island offered a bounty of food. Coconuts were in abundance and once the nut was cracked, the water and flesh were quite delicious. Wild berries grew on the eastern slopes. They were not quite ripe, but Helario assured the men he could make use of them. Klaude had returned with fish he'd patiently caught using a pike from *Marquise's* armoury. Helario was most pleased when Bastien returned with a bunch of his beloved herbs. He hugged the young sailor, sending him back into the bush to pick more. Then, there was, of course, the meat. The hunters had found a method to trap and kill... monkeys.

"Are we doing this, then?" Jacob asked, staring at the six scrawny primates. They were the size of toddlers, but with long arms and a tail.

"It's Christmas, Jovem. It's a time to celebrate life, to make merry and pluck up the courage to butcher meat that looks like hairy babies."

Outside the store tent, the men stirred. From the sound of the chatter, all talk of mutiny had been silenced by the arrival of Christmas.

"Today we have to create a feast from what you see here." Helario picked up a monkey carcass and thrust it into Jacob's hands. "You can start by skinning this. My gutting blade's on the table outside."

Jacob ducked under the canvas and laid the monkey on the table.

"A merry Christmas, ye filthy dogs." The captain called across the camp. "We've had a poor show of it to date, but let's put those troubles behind us for one day. I say Advent's over—we've fasted for long enough. Let's skip to the feasting.

Any crew still asleep awoke with a start as a cheer erupted from those who were awake. Alphonse found Roland huddled under a blanket. "Play us a tune. Something with cheer."

Roland began with Noel, Noel. A little melancholic, Jacob thought, but within the hour the men were awake, and the camp was lively. Helario had spent that time preparing an assortment of *delicacies*. He'd recruited Henri and Bastien to crack open coconuts, scrape out their flesh while Isaac boiled it before pulping it into a porridge. Helario added squashed fruits.

"Breakfast's ready." He called to his waiting patrons with mock formality.

The crew laughed and joked as they ate their coconut broth. They swapped gifts which descended into a game. Who could find the most pathetic item for the most unlikely recipient? A large stone for Marin–a comment on his intelligence. A clump of seaweed for Harvey–to be fashioned into a wig. An unbreakable coconut for Bakari–the island's hardest nut. A monkey's foot for the sailor with the amputated leg. The most useless gift won a prize: a mug of sand.

"Who wants tidbits?" Helario called.

The crew groaned when they received sun-dried hardtack soaked in coconut water. They quietened when they tasted them, and many returned for more. They were proving quite addictive.

Jacob and Bastien waddled from the store tent, rolling a firkin towards the fire. "Grog's up." Helario called. The crew eyed it suspiciously, knowing it was not rum.

"What is it?" Marin asked.

"A delicate infusion of crystal-clear aqua, gently warmed, kissed by the lush richness of coconut milk. A dash of barrel aged brandy, and a graceful scattering of forest fruits. I call it Yuletide Palm Punch."

"Sounds like watered down grog to me," Melchor scoffed.

Roland changed the tempo, playing Il est né, le divin Enfant, about the divine Jesus Christ, which roused the crew as they helped Jacob and Bastien carry more firkins from the store. The crew drank the punch and ate fish, they'd cooked themselves over the fire trying to forget the predicament they found themselves in.

"Is it ready yet?" Bakari asked, skulking over to the buccan. "I need me some real meat."

"It is my friend," Helario replied. "Are *you* ready, though?"

Bakari grinned, taking a bite of monkey meat. "It's good. Like chicken." He pushed another hunk into his mouth. "I keep bringing them," he spat, "you keep cooking them." He slapped Helario's shoulder.

The crew descended on the buccan, intrigued to see how Helario could make monkey meat appetising.

"What's in the pot?" Isaac asked.

Jacob looked at Helario before answering. "Noel Noggin Broth."

"Noggin. I don't like the sound of that." Isaac prodded the water with a spoon.

"Monkey brains." Helario laughed. "It's good for the soul. The barbarians eat them on the dark continent."

"I ain't never had it." Bakari said.

Isaac dropped the spoon and stepped away. "I'll stick to the monkey meat. My soul's got enough to work through."

"Give here." Bakari pushed forward.

Henri passed Bakari a bowl and winced as he poured the contents down his throat."

"Gets my vote." Bakari wiped his chin. "Me soul feels cleansed already."

"Yeah, you look positively saintly," Henry said as he offered Harvey a bowl of monkey meat.

Bakari growled, throwing the bowl into the sand. "Cheeky maggot."

"Mr Dargate," the captain called, "time to bring out the rum you've been hiding."

"Aye, sir." Isaac trotted into the store tent to fetch a barrel of rum he'd stashed away with strict instruction to be untouched until this very day. A stream of helpers trailed behind, eager to lend a hand.

"Away with you, Jovem." Helario said, ruffling Jacob's hair. "Get some food and ale. The sun was setting and Jacob's time at the buccan was over. He cut himself some monkey meat and slumped down next to Harvey on the outskirts of the revelry.

"Seems like all is forgiven." He said, nodding to the crew happily wrestling in the surf or singing around the fire.

"It would seem that way," Harvey said.

"You not convinced?"

Harvey chuckled, shaking his head. "It'll take a long time to build this longboat they talk about. That's a long time for old wounds to open up." He was staring at the captain, who was sitting with Bakari and Melchor.

"You think the captain's plotting something?"

"He's always plotting something. There's too many people on this island. Something's bound to stir. My guess is they'll be more deaths at his hand." He turned to face Jacob. "Stay out of his way."

Jacob held his gaze. "What ain't you saying, Harv?"

"How do you mean?"

"Back on *Marquise*, you said it was too dangerous. You said you'd tell me what that meant. Why you've been different since Tortuga. What you hiding?"

Harvey scratched his thickening beard, placing his empty bowl on the ground. "You're right, lad. There's something I need to tell you. Come with me. Out of earshot."

The pair strolled out of the firelight, disappearing from the merriment into the shadows.

"I was never mad at you after Tortuga," Harvey began. "Well, I was at first. When you didn't turn up. But then Isaac told me how you had to hide in the hold, fearing Roche was out for you. The captain convinced you to stay on the ship."

"Not only Roche. He said the crew was after my blood. I didn't know what to do." A crunch of leaves under foot told the pair they had reached the edge of the beach and the beginning of the jungle. They had wondered far enough. "When I didn't turn up for what?"

"You don't remember, do you lad?"

"Remember what?"

There was a huge cheer from the camp. Jacob and Harvey could make out Bakari by the fire, pouring coconut milk into his mouth, having just cracked the unbreakable nut open with his head.

Harvey smiled, flashing the whites of his eyes against the dimming light. He turned back to Jacob. "Our conversation in the cove."

Jacob's face dropped. "I don't. I can't remember anything from that evening. I was sitting with you, but everything after... gone... Damn Roche."

"It's fine, lad." Harvey placed a hand on his shoulder. "I'd found a ship. Going to Bermuda and then back to England. I came to find you, but you'd disappeared. I spoke to Henri. He told me you were back on *Marquise*. Figured you'd changed your mind. Fancied a crack at finding riches. If truth be told, I thought you were enjoying the pirate life. You've got a greater ambition for adventure than me."

"You told me on the beach?" Jacob paused for a moment. "That's why you weren't talking to me? I messed up your plans. I'm such a fool."

Harvey shook his head.

"You should have gone." Jacob continued. "You hate this life. I would've been happy knowing you'd made it out safe."

"I couldn't."

"Why not?"

Harvey took a deep breath. "When I heard you'd re-joined the crew, I made my way to the bay and waited for Richards as planned."

"Who's Richards?"

"Richards was the navigator of *Griffin* going to Bermuda." Jacob tugged at his growing hair. "Yeah, from Hampshire. Why didn't you go with him? Didn't he turn up?"

"He turned up. He couldn't take me. There'd been a change of plan."

"What happened?"

Harvey stared at Jacob, who stared back with a childlike naivety. "The captain sent a message with Richards. If I didn't return to the ship... he would kill you."

Jacob did not move for a long moment. "Why would he kill me?"

"He knew I couldn't see you hurt."

"Why?"

"The captain has a way of getting you talking. I dropped my guard. We were talking about our past lives. I told him about my son."

"You have a son? I've never asked about your life before the navy. Do you have a wife?"

"I did. I had a wife and a son." Harvey locked eyes with Jacob. "They died."

Jacob lowered his head. "I shouldn't have asked."

"Don't fret. It was a long time ago. You weren't to know."

"What happened?"

"The plague."

"I'm sorry, Harv."

"My son would have been a couple of years older than you. I told the captain you reminded me of him. When he found out I'd made plans with Richards, he used that against me. He knew I wouldn't let you die as well."

"You came back because of me?"

"I had to keep you safe."

"But why did you need to ignore me?"

"I figured if I kept my distance from you, he'd forget about our bond. He'd leave you alone. And maybe you'd lose interest in learning about the Caribbean and wouldn't want to stay. Maybe you'd want to go home."

"The captain did leave me alone. If anything, I was one of his favourites."

"Yeah, but it was no coincidence that he wouldn't leave us alone together. Whenever there was a raid, you went with him, making sure I stayed with the ship. It became an unspoken pact. He keeps you safe, and I stay as his navigator. But if he hurts you, I have no reason to stay."

Jacob's face blushed with anger. "Why didn't you tell me any of this?"

"I wasn't sure how you'd react."

"You keep treating me like a child." Jacob snapped. "I can look after myself."

"Keep your voice down. You need to learn to control your tongue."

There was a crack from the camp. Isaac had whacked a coconut shell thrown by Bastien into the ocean, using a hefty piece of driftwood. Melchor stepped forward, wanting to try his hand.

Jacob returned his gaze to Harvey, eager for the conversation to continue.

"You might have challenged the captain." Harvey whispered. "You got a bit cock sure if truth be told. I heard you called him out in Puerto Cavallo." Harvey smiled.

"You know about that?"

"I wonder how much of that you've written in your journal. You've got a bit of a reputation, lad. Most of the crew can't work out why you haven't been keel hauled. I was also worried you'd tell Henri or Bastien or Isaac. They might have told the captain."

"Do they know?"

"That you've been held hostage. I don't think so. I wasn't sure at the time."

"Hostage?" Jacob's mind lingered on the word. "Am I *still* a hostage?" Am I in danger?"

"Well, we haven't got a ship. The captain's got bigger problems. So, if we keep our distance and you keep out of trouble, maybe we can slip away."

"Slip away where. There's nowhere to go."

"When the longboat's built, we'll have to make our escape once we make land on The Main. I figure there's others that might want to leave the crew if the chance presents itself."

"That'll be weeks away."

"It will, lad." Harvey shrugged. "A long time. Who knows, maybe the captain will upset someone before we set sail. I sense there's a few who are getting the itch to send him to his grave."

Jacob turned to the camp, wondering who amongst them might have it in them to kill their captain.

"Let's get back to the celebrations," Harvey said, "before we're missed.

Thirty-Two

The longboat's construction was well under way. With an abundance of timber from *Marquise*, the hull sat complete, cradled in a palm tree scaffold. The salvagers had rescued everything they deemed useful: both masts had been reclaimed, along with the sails, ropes, and even the belaying pins, nails, and rivets. All lay neatly organised at the southern tip of the island. If asked honestly–between the grumbling and tutting–Joseph and his carpenters, of which Harvey had attached himself, were enjoying their work. For five weeks, they toiled stubbornly. Many of these men had trained in the art of boat building back in Rochefort and they found pleasure in constructing something new rather than repairing the old.

These past two days, witnesses saw Joseph rubbing his forehead, striding out measurements, and huddling with his carpenters, who shook their heads. Something was wrong.

The captain left this morning's meeting and gazed over the sands. "Mr Penjerrick," he called, catching Jacob's eye.

Jacob shuffled over.

"Ah, Mr Penjerrick. How are you holding up? I trust this minor delay isn't causing too much distress. You'll soon be under way with your booty for your young lady back home."

Jacob fidgeted, furrowing the sand with his foot. "How long before we're back on the water, sir?"

"Not long now. Once we reach Blauvelt, we'll set about recruiting and strike out again." The captain turned Jacob away from the crowd and strolled along the beach towards the carpenters constructing the longboat in the distance. "We have a situation. The longboat ain't big enough for everyone." Jacob raised his eyebrows. "No need to panic, those who have to stay will not starve and we'll return with a new ship before they get used to monkey meat. But nonetheless, some will ultimately have to stay behind."

Jacob furrowed his brow but stayed quiet.

"You're a fine fellow and I wouldn't want to see your talents squandered waiting on this beach. You're young and would learn much by joining the longboat crew back to The Main. Would you like to leave this island, Mr Penjerrick?"

Jacob nodded shyly.

"That's good. Now some of the more senior crew are gathering and we'd like you and Master Harvey to join us when the final count is assigned."

Jacob offered a puzzled smile.

"I know me and Master Harvey haven't passed much pleasantries recently, but he's a talented man and much welcomed in the longboat. Mr Touppin will call a meeting tomorrow morning to discuss our options. We'd be delighted if you and Master Harvey would join our numbers. Some of the men will not understand the details and I'd hate for you to be left behind in the confusion. You are still tight with Master Harvey, yes?"

Jacob shrugged. He and Harvey hadn't spoken much, but their collusion had forged a bond as tight as any friendship.

"Do you think you could have a discreet word with him explaining, he with his nautical expertise and you with your potential, would be most welcome to join us when we set sail in a few days' time?"

Jacob nodded.

"Good lad. When it's a little quieter, why don't you have a little chat? Tell Master Harvey to make his way over when the meeting starts so we can account for the numbers."

With the men fed and the sun setting, Jacob huddled next to Harvey on his log seat at the edge of the camp.

"He's right, lad. There's not enough room on the longboat. Joseph figured it as soon as he set the keel. There's plenty of timber, but you can't just make a ship out of another ship."

"Why didn't Joseph say anything?"

"Would you want to tell this lot, half of them will have to stay behind?"

Jacob shook his head.

"We'll be drawing lots to see who stays and who goes."

Jacob lowered his voice. "The captain said we can go on the longboat with him."

"He's already heard my position on that matter. Now he's tasked you to try to convince me to join his deceitful splinter?"

Jacob lowered his head. "It's been six weeks. Don't you want to get off this island?"

"I do, son. But we can't leave innocent men without a fair chance with the straws."

"I thought you said they were damned. Not worth saving."

"Not exactly. I don't want to be a part of it no more, but that don't mean they deserve to be marooned and left for dead."

"The captain said he'll come back for them."

"The captain won't come back for them. He's only got his own ambition in mind. Those that get left behind will have to fend for themselves. I spoke to Helario this morning. He's found some haricot seed—French beans, I suppose, to go with his herbs. They'll grow quick. Whoever's left won't starve. It just might be a long wait."

"The captain wouldn't leave half his crew. Surely?"

"He's got no loyalty to any of us. Not even his longest serving mate. You told me how he dealt with Reinhardt."

"Yeah, but that was to prevent a mutiny."

Harvey gave Jacob a stern look.

"I ain't saying it was right."

"Le Picard knew he was next. And knowing that he made his escape. There's not a man here he wouldn't slit for his own gains... including you."

"Am I still in danger?"

"Well, I figured we might have had a chance to slip away unnoticed. But seems he still wants me in his crew."

"You're a good sailor, Harv. That move with the Stad Gauda was something most had never even heard of. But am I really worth killing to keep you at the helm?"

"It's not just my tiller work the captain wants." Harvey lowered his eyes. "The captain sees himself as a bold leader, commanding grand expeditions and returning with vast treasures of gold and silver. But the truth is, he doesn't even know where most of the Spanish towns and ports are. It was Le Basque who led him to Maracaibo, and Braziliano was supposed to accompany him on this voyage."

Jacob shifted in his seat. "What's this go to do with you?"

"My pride has let slip more than once my knowledge of these waters. He wants my maps."

"Then give him your maps."

"I've been working on them. Day and night. Since we set sail from Tortuga. I'm hoping, if I give them to him, he'll let us go. If he's to be on the longboat, we'll have to risk it on the island."

"But if we're pulling straws, what's to stop one of us ending up on the longboat?"

"That's the luck of the draw, son. But if he has the maps and you end up on the longboat, you just need to keep your head down. He won't need you no more, but neither will he need to hurt you. Stay out of trouble." Harvey tilted his head, scrutinising Jacob. "Do you think you can do that?"

Jacob nodded. "Did you sink the ship on purpose?"

"You think I'm that good I can find a sand bar in a storm?"

Sunlight flooded the beach, casting a long morning shadow. The crew had gathered, waiting for Denis to update them on timelines and strategies. Jacob sat in the shade, caressing his finger over his wounded arm. It had started to heal, and he hadn't worn his bandage for a long while, but it felt strange. He'd caught a faint whiff of sweetness and a mild sensation of throbbing that he hadn't felt for weeks. He hoped it was his imagination, or the lack of food and water had slowed the healing. He pulled the arm of his coat back down and followed Denis as he strode to meet his audience.

"As you all can see, the longboat is nearly finished." Denis pointed over his shoulder. "Joseph says it will take another week." Denis paused. "But there's a problem."

"Problems bigger than monkey brains? Spit it out, Denis."

"The longboat will only hold half of us."

The crowd fell silent. The realisation sharpening their loyalties. Each man eyeing his neighbour. The silence broke, and the bickering began. A thunder of noise swept the beach; no man aiming his tones at anyone of significance, merely shouting to his neighbour, who was not listening but instead offering his reasons to be included in the crew.

Jacob stood with Harvey. Both observing the verbal skirmishes. L'Olonnais' eyes taking in the scene, glanced in their direction. He twitched his head to Jacob indicating it was now the time for he and Harvey to join him. Jacob stood firm as did Harvey.

"There is a solution." Denis said, shushing the crowd. "There's a solution."

Nobody was listening. The fever had set in. Treachery and guile had replaced rationality. Nobody was in the mood for reason.

"Listen up, you toads. I have a solution." The captain stepped forward, raising his arms, demanding their attention. "Listen up. Quiet."

The noise lessened as the men turned to their captain, hoping for a miracle.

"What solution, Cap'n? We making another boat?"

"No." The captain snapped. "We're making one boat. We have enough materials for one longboat that'll hold seventy five of us. That much is true. Half of us will travel to The Main. We will find another boat and return here for the rest of you. Those that remain will not starve."

"We can't eat monkeys forever." Alphonse said.

"Monkey meat's not so bad when you get accustomed to it."

"I mean, the meat will run out. How many monkeys can there be on this island?"

"We will not be long. The longboat will be swift and nimble. We will reach The Main in two weeks. We'll strike for Blauvelt. There's plenty of ships that'll come to your rescue. If not, we'll take such a ship. We'll all be back on our way, cruising the coast for plunder in no time."

The men shuffled in the sand.

"How will we decide who goes and who stays?" Alphonse asked.

"When the time comes, you'll draw lots. Short straw stays here on the island. Long straws come with us on the longboat."

There were murmurs of approval, especially from the weaker members. "It gives everyone a fair stake." The captain concluded.

A chorus of "ayes" and "sounds fair" replaced the grumbling. Although not happy, many of the men melded back to their friendships.

"What about you, captain?"

Harvey's voice startled Jacob as it buzzed in his ear. The crowd parted and Harvey spoke again.

"You speak as if this longboat will be equipped with a captain's cabin. We all stand on this island with a single vote. Every man is equal. You hold no privilege. When the straws are drawn, I assume you'll be amongst the lottery... sir?"

The captain clenched his jaw and smiled. He eyeballed his inquisitor and then the crew. "Of course, Master Harvey. We are all equal men on this island. We suffer together. I have no entitlement over you or any other man. My name will be among those drawing straws. You can mark my word."

"Very good, sir. I knew you to be an honest man. I wish you luck."

"Thank you, Master Harvey. So glad you approve. In one week, we draw lots. Now, back to work."

A collective breath exhaled. Nervous chuckles were heard as the men sloped off to their tasks.

Jacob trotted to catch Harvey.

Harvey breathed a sigh of relief. "Your rashness seems to be rubbing off on me." He offered Jacob a wry smile. "At least that gives us some sort of chance to separate ourselves from him. Let's hope he accepts my maps with grace."

Thirty-Three

Joseph finished the longboat on the seventh day, as promised. It had taken six hours and every man working as one with rope and pulleys to launch her. A gentle slope was dug into the beach. Palm trees were cut to length and laid at angles to cradle the longboat as they heaved it to the shoreline. When the tide rose, so did the longboat. It now bobbed in the shallows offshore. She was a masterpiece–forty feet long, fifteen feet wide, and fitted with one main mast. Considering the constraints the shipwrights worked with, it couldn't have looked a finer sight.

It had one spare sail which, when not needed, was lashed to the stern, offering shelter from the elements. A simple boat: it had only one main deck and a small hold, barely tall enough to stand in. The men who crewed her would eat, sleep, and work as one. Four barrels of water had so far made it aboard, along with half a dozen monkey carcasses, fruits, berries, and coconuts. Additional supplies had been assigned to the longboat and lay in the shade, awaiting loading with the new crew–enough sustenance to last three weeks. More than enough time to find Blauvelt.

Jacob lowered his journal and watched Bastien return from the bush with twigs that would act as straws. Time for the crew to be divided.

Denis held thirty straws in his hand—fifteen long, fifteen short. Each man pulled a straw. Long straws determined you endured the journey in the longboat. Draw a short straw and you waited on the island. When the straws in Denis's hand depleted to ten, he would replenish to the original amount of thirty. When seventy-five souls were on the longboat or seventy-five on the beach, the draw would be over. Everyone would draw and there would be no exchanges. If you're on the longboat, you stay on the longboat. No man would be bullied into staying behind.

Immediately, Dr Venette refused to draw. And reminded the crew there were still five men who needed his assistance.

"I will not leave my patients. The rest of you pirates may do as you please, but a doctor will not abandon his post—no matter who he is treating."

With some deliberation, the doctor's stubbornness held firm, and the pulling of straws began. Denis pulled first and conducted proceedings, knowing he would be on the longboat.

Over half of the crew had drawn. A disgruntled party of marooned men slumped on the beach, indifferent to the proceedings.

Joseph drew a long straw. The crew gave him a subdued send-off when he hopped into the barge. He had worked hard on the longboats' construction, and nobody begrudged him the chance to flee the island. Gaetan playfully nudged Joseph, having also pulled a long straw. Marin followed, and the barge cast off back to the longboat. Klaude sloped past his disappointed captain as he made his way to the marooned party. Rolant picked up his fiddle and followed Klaude.

Jacob stood with Harvey, Henri, Bastien and Isaac waiting as Denis offered Melchor the twigs. The Spaniard pulled a long straw and sauntered off to the side to watch the proceedings.

"Who's next? Denis asked.

Henri pushed Bastien forward. He wrapped his arms behind his back and lowered his nose close to the twigs. Snuffling for a clue. Fifteen straws in Denis's hand and twisted in such a way it was impossible to tell one from another.

"This one." Bastien said as he plucking his favourite from the bunch. He closed his eyes and only opened them upon hearing the cheer from his friends. He placed the twig into his mouth and danced to the surf, making way for Henri, who limped over to make his choice. No child's play–he simply picked his target and pulled. A long straw.

"Whoop." Bastien cried.

Henri joined his friend in the wet sand and placed an arm over his shoulder.

"Twigs, gentlemen." Denis said to Henri and Bastien, who'd forgotten to place them back on the ledger table.

The pair retreated to the shoreline as Isaac stepped up. He studied the twigs. They all looked identical. No point delaying. He pinched the end of the closest one and pulled–a short straw. Bastien and Henri's shoulders slumped. Isaac made the walk back along the beach to the other marooned crew.

"We'll see you soon, Isaac." Bastien said. "Save us some monkey brains."

Isaac waved a despondent arm and sat in the sand some twenty yards away.

"You next, Harv?" Denis said, offering him his fist.

"S'pose so." Harvey pulled at a straw. He stood motionless–it was a short straw. Jacob watched on in disbelief. Harvey hadn't made the longboat. The gamble had let them down. He would be staying on the island.

Jacob had been watching the draw. By counting the twigs pulled, he'd discovered a ruse. There were eleven remaining in the bundle. Nineteen had been drawn since the last time Denis replenished his hand. Seven people had pulled long straws. Twelve had pulled short straws. Of the eleven left, eight must be long straws. The odds were most definitely in favour of joining the longboat crew. He looked back at Harvey, who nodded.

"Go on, lad," Harvey whispered.

"I'll go." Bakari pushed past Jacob and grabbed Denis's wrist. With his other hand, he pulled on a twig and smiled when it revealed its length. "See you in a month, land lubbers." Bakari threw his twig on the table and crouched into a fighting pose, and scuttled over to Melchor.

Denis picked up the twigs scattered on the table and fixed them into his hand. All the ends at various lengths. Jacob watched. Dumbfounded.

"Jacob?" Denis offered his fist.

He shuffled forward and looked at his options. Thirty twigs once more–fifteen long, fifteen short. Thirty people left to choose, and he had been relegated back to a fifty-fifty chance. He had most definitely drawn the short straw when drawing straws. He inspected his choices. All the straws looked the same–wooden twigs, the same diameter, neatly cut with Henri's–as always, sharpened knife. No frayed edges. No clues. As intended; a lottery. He raised his hand, and at the last moment, stopped. There was a difference. One twig looked damp. The twig Bastien had pulled and then delicately chewed in his mouth. The wet twig was a long straw. He could get on the longboat. He looked at Henri and Bastien in the surf, willing him to join them. Then back at Harvey, watching midway to the marooned men. To leave on the longboat would be to abandon Harvey. The captain hadn't yet drawn, so no way to know where he would happen. The captain was no fool—he would probably find his way onto the longboat. Jacob pulled a straw. He opened his hand and dropped it on the table. He turned his back on the surf and took a step towards the marooned crew. A short straw.

He heard Henri and Bastien groan from the shore. Alphonse and Helario stood together; the next to make their choice.

"Choose the wet one." Jacob whispered. "It's a long straw." He turned to face Denis, leaving the two men to talk over who would step up next.

Helario raised his arm, gesturing for Alphonse to step up. He chose wisely and walked over to the barge to take the last place at the stern. As it rowed away, to be replaced by the returning barge, Alphonse waved a thank you and condolence to Helario walking in the opposite direction. Jacob sat with the marooned party, watching as Denis's hand depleted of straws. Sixteen more people chose before the captain stepped up. Jacob shook his head.

"Shall we see where your captain will reside?" He strode over to Denis and pulled out a twig.

Jacob had been scrutinising the draw and knew the captain found himself in a similar position Bakari had stumbled into the previous round. The captain had played this game before. He held his closed hand aloft theatrically before turning to the huddle behind him and opening his palm, finger by finger.

"It's a short straw, Cap'n." Denis said. "I'm sorry. You'll be staying here."

The captain looked at his hand dumbfounded and then at Denis's hand in wonderment. "You've replenished your hand wrong." He cut his protest short and eyed Bakari and Melchor.

Denis opened his fist and revealed eight long straws and the two remaining short straws. "I'm sorry, sir. It's the luck of the draw. Everyone's had the same chance."

The longboat crew would soon hear the news, the marooned men already knew. L'Olonnais threw his twig to the floor and sidestepped to Bakari and Melchor to say his goodbyes. Jacob's heart sank. The captain would remain on the island until the longboat returned. It would be a long month. He hoped it would only be a month. He cast his eye around the marooned men. They were a good crew. He felt safe amongst them. He would stay out of trouble until the rescue returned.

He had no more investment in the final draws. When it was over, those not already on the longboat said their goodbyes.

Jacob strode over to Henri and Bastien.

"We'll be back, Jake." Henri said. "Blauvelt can't be far."

"Denis's a bit feckless, but he ain't cruel." Bastien said. "He'll come back for everyone. We'll make sure of it."

"Suppose he'll be Captain Touppin now." Henri said with the shake of his head. "Keep up the cutlass drills. Isaac's a good teacher."

"Don't get fat on monkey meat." Bastien chuckled.

"Don't forget to come back." Jacob said.

"Never. You're one of us now, Jake. We'll be back soon enough."

The three offered short nods of their head before Jacob turned and made his way back towards the marooned crew. He trudged past the captain, avoiding eye contact. His friends had been divided. He had Harvey and Isaac to keep him company and Helario could continue his culinary teachings. He would miss Henri and Bastien. There was always a hope a passing ship would see the remnants of *Marquise* and rescue them.

"I'm sorry to have to pull rank, my friends, but I must be on the longboat."

Jacob turned to find the captain hustling to the front of the awaiting barge crew.

"Captain. The straws have given their answer." Denis said, striding after him. "You pulled a short straw. You must wait on the island."

"I've been having a little ponder about that. My Christmas cheer has lapsed, and I feel my goodwill is all used up. I'm too valuable to be whiling away on a beach eating coconuts. The longboat must be equipped with a presence of mind to be able to negotiate a rescue."

"A rescue. Very good, sir," Melchor scoffed. "Step back Denis. Or it'll be you giving up your place for your captain."

Denis stood his ground, obstructing L'Olonnais as the barge landed at the beach's edge.

"Step aside, Denis." Melchor raised a pistol. "Be an obedient dog."

"Melchor, what are you doing?" Henri said, stepping forward.

Denis did not move, but nor did he step aside. Melchor pulled the trigger and with a crack and a thud, Denis fell backwards into the surf. Nobody moved. The water around Denis's head turned pink. Eyes flickered left and right. All trust washed away. Jacob could hear a commotion behind him, but he dared not take his eyes from the scene at the barge.

"Stay back, Master Harvey. Mr Dargate." L'Olonnais said. "You marooned men drew your straws and I'm sorry to say will be staying here. But you cannot expect me to waste my time when there's a fortune to be had."

"You treacherous bastard." Isaac snarled. "Did you ever intend to stick to the rules?"

"Of course." L'Olonnais laughed. "If I'd pulled a long straw."

Jacob could hear more bodies joining Harvey and Isaac behind him.

"Mr Dargate." L'Olonnais snapped. "Tell the men to stay back. We'll be boarding the barge now and nobody else need be hurt."

More groaning from behind Jacob. "Mr Dargate. I'm warning you. Mr Obasi–grab the pup."

Before Jacob could make sense of the words, a hand grappled across his chest and a knife pressed at his throat. He tried to wriggle free, but Bakari tightened his grip. He felt Bakari's breath in his ear.

"I did warn you." L'Olonnais said.

The marooned men edged forward, led by Harvey and Isaac, fire in their eyes. Searching for an opening.

"Stay back, Master Harvey, or Mr Obasi will be forced to open Mr Penjerrick's throat."

Harvey paused his pursuit, outstretching his arms to halt those behind. "Captain. It's me you want. I'll go in his stead."

"It *was* you I wanted Master Harvey; I would gladly have taken your seamanship, but you've been lacking in that of late." L'Olonnais gestured to where *Marquise* once occupied the horizon. "You've already *accidentally* stranded my ship. And when offered to join the leaving party, you threw it back at me and demanded my drawing of straws. You've handed over your maps. What else do you have to offer?"

Harvey stepped forward. The marooned men followed.

"Not one more step, Master Harvey, or Mr Penjerrick will be fileted like a fresh fish."

Harvey stopped and again, the marooned men quit their advance.

Bakari dragged Jacob away, forcing his upper body to arch backwards. Jacob rocked on his heels, his weight now resting on Bakari's chest, but the powerful man didn't seem to suffer under his weight. His knapsack strap tugged across his throat. Jacob thought of his quill that lay between the pages of his journal. He hoped it had not broken. His cutlass dragging in the sand. Bakari had his arms pinned by his side, making it impossible to grasp the hilt. Maybe if he leaned back further, his coat might snag under Bakari's feet, causing him to stumble—but his throat would be slit before they hit the sand. Jacob dared not struggle.

"I would rather not harm the lad," L'Olonnais said, walking backwards ahead of Bakari. "I've grown to like the cheeky rascal, but I fear without him, you will not allow me to make my escape. I promise, on my honour, when we reach Blauvelt, I will send back a ship."

"You have no honour." Isaac snapped.

From over his left shoulder, Jacob heard a scuffle.

"Let him go, Bakari." It was Henri who spoke.

Jacob had last seen him and Bastien by the surf, about to climb into the barge. He tried to inch his face to see, but Bakari's knife pressed deeper into his throat.

"I said let him go. You've gone too far, Cap'n. I ain't scared to show my allegiance no more. You should have left Jake out of this from the start."

Bakari rolled his hips, so he and Jacob faced the shore. Henri held his pocket folding knife to L'Olonnais' neck, much like Bakari held his dagger to Jacob's. Bastien stood by Henri's side, legs wide with his cutlass drawn. Jacob couldn't see him, but he sensed Melchor behind him in support of Bakari. To his right, he could see Harvey and Isaac braced to attack, but without a weapon between them. There was a moment's pause as each man assessed his situation. They had all acted rashly and maybe only Bakari cared little for the quandary they found themselves in.

"How's that leg, Mr Bodine?" Henri winced as L'Olonnais shifted his weight, forcing pressure onto Henri's left thigh. "Let's talk wisely. We seem to have found ourselves in a predicament."

"Of your making, Cap'n. You drew a short straw. And if I've heard rightly, you've got your maps, you've no more use for Jacob. Let him go."

"What are you saying, Mr Bodine? That I've been using our young friend here all along? How so?" L'Olonnais grinned.

"You know how. It was Harvey that you needed for all these months. The final piece of the crew."

Jacob's eyes sliced at Henri.

"I offered the boy an escape from his meagre existence. I cannot be responsible if Mr Penjerrick's ambition matched my own needs. I offered him a chance to better his prospects—the same chance I offered you some years ago. The same I offered all of you. To be rich. I do the same now. Join us Mr Bodine. We can leave together and continue our journey. There are still riches to be had. You have your place on the longboat. I see no reason to throw away your chance of escape. And as you say, I have Master Harvey's maps." L'Olonnais opened his jacket, patting his pocket.

Jacob stared back at L'Olonnais with venom in his eyes. He tried to struggle free, but Bakari tightened his grip once more.

The captain smiled back at Jacob. His rouse over.

"Let him go, Bakari." Henri spat, "or I swear I'll bury this knife so far into his neck it'll be back in my pocket." Henri waited. "Bakari. Captain says he has the maps. What use does he serve? Let him go."

L'Olonnais nodded. Jacob felt the tension ease from his shoulders. He shrugged himself free and as he did, Henri doubled over in pain, letting the captain loose. L'Olonnais turned and pulling his dagger from Henri's thigh. Henri swung his knife, but his wound restricted his reach. L'Olonnais stabbed again. Only this time into Henri's stomach. The force sending him to the ground at Jacob's feet.

"Henri!" Jacob fell to his knees, clasping his friend's wound. No blood. Jacob checked his friend. Where had he been stabbed? Relief. His friend was uninjured. Then, the shirt Henri was so proud of leached red.

"I'm sorry, Jake." Henri said. An absent gaze struggling to find Jacob's eyes.

"Harvey help." Jacob sobbed.

"Stay where you are, Master Harvey." L'Olonnais growled.

Henri grasped Jacob's coat, pulling him closer. "I should have let you go home."

Bastien crashed to Henri's side. Tears streaking his grubby cheeks.

"Henri. Stay with me," Bastien sobbed. "Don't go. I need you, brother. Dr Venette." He screamed. "Someone get the doctor."

"Grab him, Bakari." L'Olonnais said. "Stay back, Master Harvey, or he'll join Mr Bodine in hell."

Jacob felt the nape of his jacket tighten. Before he had the chance to fight, his legs were lifted from the ground, and he was bundled into the barge like a sack of coconuts.

"Klaude. With me." The captain snapped.

Klaude remained with the marooned men.

"Klaude. It's your last chance."

Klaude buried his feet in the sand defiantly. "You go too far, captain. The curse controls you."

"Suit yourself. Stay here and rot with the rest of 'em."

Jacob watched the marooned men flock to Henri's limp body. His vision interrupted by the swell of the crashing waves. Bastien held his friend's head as busy hands clasped his stomach, trying to stem the bleeding. Harvey left the melee and ran to the water's edge. Pressure on Jacob's head forced him below the gunwale. He lay confused, his vision now filled with the wooden planks of the barge. From somewhere above, a shot fired.

"To the longboat. Anyone wants to cross me will get a belly full of blade." The captain stood astride Jacob, glowering down at his prisoner. His cutlass drawn and at Jacob's throat. "You've lost your usefulness, pup. Don't give me a reason to run you through."

Thirty-Four

Jacob hit the deck of the longboat with a thud. He lay motionless, face down, staring at Joseph's handiwork.

A pair of feet slammed onto the boards next to his head.

"Mr Verela. Get a hold of the pup. Let's be sure he ain't got some use left before we set sail."

"Aye, sir," Melchor said.

"What's all the fuss?" Alphonse said with a hint of aggression.

"Can't have the captain laying on a beach for a month." Melchor answered, lifting Jacob by his coat collar. "Needs to be leading his men."

"From our viewpoint there looked to be more than a hint of foul play." Alphonse stepped forward. "I am right to think you pulled a short straw, captain?"

Marin and a mass of two dozen seamen flanked Alphonse. Some had unsheathed cutlasses.

"Let's not get carried away." The captain said. "There was some not happy with the pulling of the straws. Ain't it always the way? It turned into a mutinous mess. We only just escaped with our lives. Mr Touppin surprised us by joining their number. Luckily, Mr Obasi and Mr Verela had the sense to assist your captain to safety."

Bakari stood with L'Olonnais. His cutlass also unsheathed.

"What about the pup?" Alphonse asked. "Last I saw, he was sitting with the marooned men. How's he with the long straws? And not looking happy about it."

"Happen, he got mixed up in a swap. I'm afraid Mr Touppin and Mr Bodine will be staying on the island."

"Got permanent lodgings, I'd say." Melchor said with a grin.

Alphonse drew his cutlass and shot a glance at Melchor before returning his gaze back to L'Olonnais. "What straw did you pull, captain?"

"Mr Touppin was caught rigging the lots." L'Olonnais said.

"Don't sound like Denis."

"You're welcome to ask him." L'Olonnais said. "Only I don't think you'll get much of a response out of him."

Alphonse looked beyond the captain to the melee still gathered on the beach. "That don't explain the pup. I didn't see no cheating from him. How's he got mixed up here?"

Jacob's senses returned to him. He felt Melchor's grip. He'd heard every word being said, but his attention had become fixated on the alae already forming between the deck boards. His mind had found a new depth–one where vengeance ruled, and the world would be better off without L'Olonnais and his murderous intentions.

"I've no animosity with the pup. We just needed him to secure our lives. Mr Varela, let him go."

Melchor released his grip on Jacob's nape. Jacob stepped forward. Marin seized his wrist and pulled him to the gunwale.

"Stay there, kid."

Jacob did as he was told, turning to face the stern, noticing the mass of crew gathered aft behind L'Olonnais–at least twice that of Alphonse's faction.

"Is it as he says, kid?" Alphonse asked.

From Jacob's viewpoint, Alphonse and Marin's support was waning. The numbers did not favour the company at the bow of the longboat. Obviously, his life and the death of two crew members were not worth losing their own lives over. Cutlasses had lost their aggression, and some crew members even turned their attention to the bow anchor. Jacob nodded. "If he says so,"

"You're lucky to be with us, lad," L'Olonnais had said on the first evening aboard the longboat. He'd been sitting at the stern, flanked by Bakari and Melchor. "We'll have the better chance of survival. Mark my words." He'd waved the inch thick wad of maps drafted by Harvey. "And these maps show us every rich Spanish port between Blauvelt and Panama."

Jacob sighed, wrapping himself in his coat, turning away from L'Olonnais.

"Nice coat you got," L'Olonnais snipped. "Present, was it? Who do you think gave Mr Bodine the money for those new clothes of yours?"

Jacob raised his head.

"A nice little gift to make you happy. Make you feel like one of the crew. Just like that cutlass I gave you. The one I allow you to still wear. You may look like us, but you ain't one of us. If it weren't for Harvey, you'd be with that lieutenant on that hog island. You had one use. With you tucked up by my side, Harvey daren't not leave. Don't know why. You ain't that pretty."

L'Olonnais returned to the maps, leaving Jacob with his guardians.

"Did you know?" Jacob had asked.

Marin shook his head.

Alphonse sat for a while. "'Spose so. The captain made no voice of it, but it was obvious if you care to see. Harvey was the prize. An educated man of the sea. And the captain liked those maps he kept making. Your man made it clear he had no rum for a pirate's life, but 'spose the captain gave him no choice." He patted Jacob's shoulder. "Sorry, lad. We'll try to keep you safe, but keep your wits about you."

"Land ahoy."

Jacob awoke to see distant trees through the morning mist.

"It ain't Blauvelt." L'Olonnais declared, lowering his spyglass. "But we've got no choice. Head for the beach."

They had been aboard the longboat for eight days and in the rush to embark, not enough provisions had accompanied them. They'd started on quarter rations, but still water was low. Any anchorage would have to do. The mood was grim, with an almost physical divide between those happy to have their captain and those condemning his actions. Alphonse and Marin had become protective of Jacob and very much in the camp of condemnation.

Jacob glanced back at the mainland. Trees, a beach, and no sign of life. They could be anywhere. It had been just over a year since he'd woken up onboard *Kestrel*. He'd been scared, angry and alone. He slumped back against a barrel, staring at L'Olonnais. Nothing had changed in all that time. Well, almost nothing. His anger had most definitely grown.

Sixty-five crewmen landed on the beach. A small number stayed with the longboat. Jacob spent the afternoon with Marin collecting wood for a fire. Bakari and Melchor passed them as they entered the bush in search of fresh water and food.

"Stay close." L'Olonnais shouted after them. "I suspect we're in Indian territory."

Bakari raised his boarding axe, laughing as he disappeared. Jacob looked about the camp. There were some good men, but Jacob had forgotten who. He saw desperate survivors. Selfish pirates. They would trample what families they had to seize their fortunes. They could all be damned.

By nightfall, Bakari and Melchor had not returned, making the men restless. Some had tiptoed to the jungle's edge to make a tentative search.

Jacob sat at the fire, trying to hide under his coat. Henri's coat. Even though his friend had given it to him, he still thought of it as Henri's coat–a dead man's coat. Tainted with blood where Henri had reached out in desperation. Jacob had no inclination to clean it off. His reminder of the callous murder. His eyes remained on the blood-stained lapel. He had a sudden urge to check the secret pocket. He sat alone. He pulled out its contents. A piece of ham wrapped in a banana leaf given to him by Helario back in Puerto Cavallo. He sniffed it. Way past it's best. He threw it into the fire. He stuffed the purse of coins he'd found on the Spanish soldier back into the pocket. There was a third item. He recognised it immediately. Henri's folding knife. The same one held to L'Olonnais throat. How had it ended up in his pocket?

Bakari burst onto the beach with the search party in tow. Jacob palmed the knife and watched as Bakari rushed to the captain, panting and no longer holding his boarding axe. Or any weapon.

"Melchor. They have Melchor."

"Who? What's happened?" The captain clasped Bakari's huge shoulders, trying to calm the big man.

"Indians—Melchor. They take him." Bakari inhaled a huge breath, finding some composure. "I fight. They drag him into the bush. I think... he is gone."

The captain looked up at the sky. "Take a party and find him."

Bakari snatched a cutlass from a near crewman. "Aye, Cap'n. We'll avenge him."

"You will find him. I have sailed too many seas with that man to lose him now."

"Aye, Cap'n." Bakari raised his head to the sky, gulping in air before turning to assemble the search party.

Before the sun had set, the search party returned. Shoulders slumped and anguish in their eyes. Bakari approached the captain once more. Sullen this time. Marin split from the main crew and sat at the surf's edge, joining Jacob, who did not shift his gaze from the ocean.

"They think they've found Melchor." Marin said.

"They think? I hope he's missing his head." Jacob sneered.

"He's missing more than that. They only found a hand with a finger pointing back to the beach. They think he's been cooked and eaten."

Jacob looked at Marin, seeing the fear in his face. "Good." He spat, turning back to the horizon.

He did not leave his sandy seat for two hours. He could hear the arguments and discussions behind him. One of the two barges appropriated to make the escape was back at the longboat after ferrying the first of the men aboard readying their departure. The other surfed the waves back to the beach.

He pulled up his coat sleeve and rubbed the bandage that he'd taken to wearing again. He unravelled it to peek at his flesh. The skin around the wound was turning grey, and the smell had got worse. He hoped it was a whiff of seaweed, but he knew it wasn't. It had healed before—he was sure it would heal again. It hardly seemed to matter as he sat contemplating his predicament.

The setting yellow sun blinded his side eye as he ran golden sand through his fingers—noticing the tiny shell fragments. This beach was thousands of years old. Sulking, he scattered the grains into the wind. He had no control over his life. He had not made a decision for himself since being snatched in Falmouth. The English Navy had owned him, then briefly Lieutenant Craywick. Now Captain L'Olonnais held his life in his hands. He had lost the only friends he thought he had. Henri had died trying to protect him. Harvey, Bastien and Isaac were miles away—never to be seen again. Were any of them ever genuine friends? Who might be his closest ally now? Alphonse, Marin? Would they care if the captain became apathetic to the English pup and left him with his innards on the sand for the buzzards to feast on?

"I'm sorry, mother. I should have stayed at home and protected you. I let you down."

He stood, stretching his bones, turning to view the beach, and screamed into the wind. Tears streamed down his cheeks. He opened his eyes expecting a jeer, but nothing came. Though his vision was blurred, he sensed a commotion. He half expected a fist from the captain or Bakari. Nothing. Instead, he heard shouts of confusion washing back at him. He wiped his eyes to see men running in all directions—some towards the shore, some into the bush. Some west, some south. All panicking.

"Run." Marin screamed into Jacob's ear, grasping at his collar. "Run, lad."

Jacob did not run. He stood, shocked by the mayhem. A wave of natives crashed through the trees. Spears flying and buccaneers fell. Some of the crew stood their ground, but they'd been taken by surprise. A third of the crew had already boarded the longboat, leaving the beach party outnumbered. Pistols and muskets let off their only shots and some natives fell–but not enough. L'Olonnais was forcing some composure cajoling buccaneers to form line but there were too many natives.

Through the trees, white faces emerged. They wore the familiar brown jackets of Spanish infantry–more organised than their native collaborators and their weapons much superior. Word of pirates must have travelled the coast, and they sought revenge for Puerto Cavallo and San Pedro. Jacob could not blame them, but neither would he offer himself to their vengeance.

The barge lay north–to his left–towards the enemy. That way would be suicide. The Spanish would intercept him. As he watched, the barge pushed off and made haste over the waves. He ran south.

Heading for the blinding sun along the water's edge, his coat felt heavy, but he would not be discarding it. He pumped his arms high and long, encouraging his legs. He was swift. He passed slower men without care. The beach thinned, replaced with waves to his left and rocks in front. A smile caught his cheeks, and he laughed as he cut from the surf towards the tree line curving to meet him. Two minutes earlier, he'd not cared if he'd lived or died. Now, he was running for his life.

To his right, other pirates converged on his path. He could hear the dying behind him. He ran. He felt alive.

He dodged left and right through the trees, over rocks. The ground steadily rising. He scrambled up and up–higher and higher. His heart pounded. He paused and took a moment to gaze over his shoulder. There were musket shots in the middle distance over screams and shouts. He couldn't be sure if they were getting closer. Sweat trickled down his forehead. The taste of the salt reached the corner of his mouth. The trees below him rustled, encouraging him to turn and run.

Quieter now, more deliberate. He had put some distance between himself and the fighting, but he could not be certain if there were natives or Spanish following. For the moment, he needed stealth over speed. Each tree he passed covered the next few yards. Zig zagging until at last he was within striking distance of the summit. Stopping short, he doubled over behind a large tree, wheezing.

Wiping his brow on his coat sleeve a realisation struck him. Since *Kestrel* Island, he had not been alone. In fact, then and now might be the only times he'd been alone in his entire life. It felt exhilarating. A deep sense of freedom washed over him. A calmness.

He had almost nothing in his possession–no allies, no food, not even water–but he felt more energised than he had ever felt. He stood, surveying his surroundings. His hand on the hilt of his cutlass.

"Get down, you fool," came a voice from behind.

Jacob turned, scanning the trees, not finding the voice's owner. "Who's there?" He asked. The voice had been French, so Jacob guessed it must be a comrade, but no response came. "Stay hidden then. I've done my fair share of cowering." With that, he began the march to the summit.

A head popped up from a bush. "Wait. It's me."

"Alphonse."

Another head teased up with a grim expression.

"Marin."

"Get down." Alphonse said.

Jacob shook his head. "I'm sick of hiding. You can stay here waiting for the Spanish to muster the energy to make this ridge. I'm heading south."

"Wait." Alphonse pushed up to intercept him, but Jacob refused to be treated like a child.

"Jacob. Where you going to go? There's no escape."

Jacob turned on Alphonse. Marin had joined Alphonse's side. They both halted when the tall, angry young man glared down at them.

"There's no escape? No escape? Apparently, I've been held captive ever since I came aboard *Marquise*. No more than a hostage. This is the perfect time for me to make my escape. I'm sick of being tricked or told what to do. I don't know where I'll end up, but at least I'll be making my own decisions."

Alphonse looked down at the floor. "You've been treated badly, lad."

Jacob gritted his teeth, holding his clenched fists at his side.

"Sorry, Jacob. You're not a lad. But this is no time to be alone." Alphonse turned to look over the ridge. "We're deep in Indian territory, and they have the Spanish alongside. We need to stick together."

Jacob remained silent, seeing the honesty in Alphonse's eyes. Behind Alphonse's head and off the shore, movement caught Jacob's attention. He pushed the Frenchman aside and squinted through the sun's glare down at the ocean. "The longboat."

Alphonse and Marin turned and followed Jacob's gaze.

"The longboat." Marin agreed. "Where they going?"

Jacob scanned the bush below him. With no thought of a plan, he ran. He heard Alphonse and Marin following. He was younger and nimbler. They would not keep pace. Jacob dodged left and right–always heading down and south. A rock, a tree or a bush decided his next step. To his left, north along the beach, he could hear shouts. Musket shots still peppered the air. His stride developed its own style–a long step and a slide in the hill's scree. Not too long to lose balance before the next foot would overtake and continue the descent.

He jumped a large boulder and pushed off from a tree trunk. His muscles ached, and he breathed heavier than he'd ever done before. Without fear, he crashed out of the bush, onto the beach, running for the shore. The longboat sailed level with him, but at least one hundred yards out to sea. He had swum further but feared he would not out-swim the spears and muskets if the enemy saw him.

He considered his options. A spit of land jutted from the beach two hundred yards away. He ran south again, keeping pace with the longboat. He reached the outlier of land and raced to its end. At the water's edge, he stopped.

The beach where he sat sulking only minutes earlier was now in sight–carnage strewn from tree to surf. The fighting quietened as many of his crewmates lay dead in the sand. Others sat under guard by Spanish pikes. He hoped to see the captain amongst them, but he could not. In the middle-distance Marin burst from the bush followed by Alphonse.

Jacob knew his survival relied on swiftness. He kicked off his shoes and removed his coat. It would be a shame to toss it aside. These were not his old navy clothes. This was gifted to him by Henri. He couldn't believe it wasn't gifted through genuine friendship. Henri and Bastien had helped him. They had protected him and now Henri was dead.

No time to debate. He rolled the coat into as small a ball as possible and held it tight. A quick glance over his shoulder told him the natives had spotted the buccaneers and between them and him, more buccaneers made their escape. He needed no more encouragement.

He pushed through the surf into the waves. At waist height, he lurched forward and began his swim. With his free hand, he tugged at the pebbles until he'd escaped the shallows. He wished he'd unbuckled his cutlass. It dragged in the sand below. Hearing the shouts from the longboat incentivised each stroke. As he took a breath, he caught a glimpse of the barge heading towards him. He would not need it. The rowers paused as Jacob swam nearby.

"Go ahead. Rescue the others." He coughed.

"See you on board, Jacob." Joseph said, showing him a fist of encouragement.

He would make the longboat. He didn't care if he was the only one.

Thirty-Five

"The captain's making a run for it."

Jacob scraped back his drenched hair from his eyes in time to see L'Olonnais burst over the rocks close to the shoreline. His agility was still surprising.

"Bakari's following."

Behind the captain Bakari threw himself over the rocks, landing uncomfortably on the sand. He scrambled to his feet, his left leg dragging behind him. He harboured an injury—a broken spear protruding from his thigh. The captain outpaced the injured rhinoceros and there must already be thirty yards between them.

In the water, the barge had made the spit and men clambered in. The barge crew had brought muskets and now trained them on the pursuing natives and Spaniards.

The captain closed upon the spit. He threw his battle jacket into the sand to allow for a swifter arm movement. Bakari struggled behind. A dozen swift footed enemy thought they could catch him. The captain leapt for the barge, leaving only Bakari on the beach. Jacob slapped the rail with the palm of his hand.

"Full strokes," the captain growled, "to the longboat."

A landsman stood and grabbed a musket from a comrade. The barge rocked under foot and Alphonse and Marin steadied his legs as he took aim. A fast-paced Spaniard closed in on Bakari. The captain growled at the rowers, but they stayed poised. At least a dozen enemy chased the big man, but only one looked close enough to show any promise of catching him.

The landsman fired, and a second later, the Spaniard fell into the sand. Bakari did not flinch. The crew on the longboat erupted in whoops and cheers. Moments later Bakari leaped for the barge and the captain's calls to cast off were answered. Half a dozen spears arched in the air but fell short as the barge escaped over the waves.

Their exact location was unknown. After five days with favourable winds, the crew all agreed their first landing had overshot Blauvelt. They believed they were now in the Gulf of Darien. The crew could have said anywhere for all Jacob understood. His knowledge of these waters was near zero. He missed his cantankerous friend. Without Harvey to steer his understanding, he would never know where he would most likely die.

"You look rough." Alphonse said.

"I'm fine." Jacob replied. "Just need food. How much water do we have?"

"Not much. Bakari ain't shifted from the barrel all day. Thinks he's the purser. We'll make land soon. There'll be fresh water."

When Alphonse stepped away, Jacob rubbed his forearm before wrapping the blanket around his shoulders. Back home, this would be the depths of winter, but here it was sweltering hot–and still Jacob could not get warm.

L'Olonnais lay out one of Harvey's maps for inspection. "We're close to Panama."

"We need food, captain." Alphonse said. "We need to make land and hunt for bore or fowl."

L'Olonnais raised his head from the map. "'We strike for Panama. There, we will find food and water."

"We're in no state to strike anywhere." Alphonse said. "We're quarter manned and have even less firepower. We should return to the others on the island."

L'Olonnais turned on Alphonse. "You want to go back to that craven lot? Be my guest. But this crew is not for turning back. There are Spaniards to kill." He picked up the map in his fist. "And riches within our grasp. I will not return to Tortuga without them."

"We need food and water, captain." Bakari said from his seat at the bow of the longboat. He hadn't moved since the beach raid. It had taken thirty minutes and five men to remove the spear tip from his thigh. He grimaced and growled, but never once took his scowl from the captain.

L'Olonnais turned, and seeing the truth in Bakari's eyes, reluctantly agreed. "Panama can wait. First, we hunt."

"We go prepared." The captain instructed, once the only remaining barge returned to the longboat for the final time. "No camp on the beach. No search party. We all head into the bush and hunt."

The depleted crew sighed in agreement. Safety in numbers. After many months of belonging to an army of hundreds, twenty-two survivors fumbling in the jungle felt like dwindling odds. They were without their last remaining brute. Bakari had stayed with the longboat. He was defiant his injured leg would not be a problem, but convinced nobody. The allure of captaincy over the few remaining crew finally pacified him.

They appeared as vagabonds. Many had lost some portion of their clothing. The captain looked like any other crew member without his battle coat. And with diminished energy, nobody had thought it necessary to cut their hair or shave. They looked a desperate sight.

"What if we find Indians?" Alphonse asked.

"We kill them," the captain growled, "before they kill us."

"Maybe this time we trade or ask for help?"

"Trade with Indians." The captain scoffed. "They'd poison the food and slit our throats while we succumbed to their hallucinogens. We kill them."

They walked in solitude as they negotiated the estuaries snaking inland, promising fresh water. Mangroves grew in the shallows, making hard work of their progress from the beach.

The party halted and listened.

"Indians." Someone whispered.

Before any discussion, one of the crew scrambled the root ridden bank, causing a dozen of his comrades to follow. No cries of aggression, but a cautious sprint once they found hard ground. Jacob stayed with the stationary half of the men who crept up the bank and huddled together, waiting for their company to return.

"We wait, gentlemen." The captain said, aiming his musket towards the pursuing buccaneers. "Hopefully, they'll bring back a captive. I'll rip out his tongue if he does not show us where they keep their food."

Murmurs rose at the captain's words as the men aimed their muskets into the bush. Marin came to stand shoulder to shoulder with Jacob guarding him from the captain. Marin held his cutlass aloft. Jacob was struggling to even hold his at his side. He stared at the back of the captain's neck, so temptingly close. A flicker of a smile passed over his lips. In his left hand, he held Henri's folding knife. He swayed in the heat as he raised the knife inches from L'Olonnais.

Marin gently lay a hand on Jacob's fist, lowering his arm. Jacob turned to find Marin wide eyed staring back at him, shaking his head. Jacob glowered back.

"Ami, Ami." Came a call from the bush.

A moment later, the others returned—with them, five natives: four men and one woman. The sullen faces herded into the centre of the buccaneers and made to sit.

"There were more, but they knew the land and disappeared. We captured these five. They must have food we can share."

The captain took control and lifted the closest native to his feet, raising his cutlass to his throat.

"We need food." He snarled.

The native stared at the captain and the entire party held their breath. The captain growled, spittle crusted at the corners of his mouth. He paused—only for a heartbeat.

"Captain. Let him speak. It's not always time for violence." Alphonse stepped forward, sheathing his cutlass.

L'Olonnais swung to face Alphonse, but the gunner ignored him. Instead, placing himself between the captain and the native, smiling.

"Do you have any food?" He asked in French.

The native held a blank expression but relaxed his shoulders now he could no longer see L'Olonnais.

"Food?" Alphonse said again, raising his hand to his mouth, gesturing the motion of eating.

The native began to speak in his unfamiliar tongue. Alphonse sighed and raised his hands, halting his chatter.

"Parlez-vous français?" Alphonse asked.

The native shrugged and stayed silent.

"He's stalling." The captain pushed Alphonse aside, raising his cutlass back to the native's throat, who immediately stiffened. "He has food. Where's your food? Tell me or you will be the food."

Jacob stumbled forward, raising his open palms. "Let me try." He smiled at the native and spoke softly. "Do you speak English?"

The native shook his head, but before L'Olonnais could berate Jacob's attempt for peace, the native pointed to his fellow prisoner sitting behind him. Jacob side stepped and crouched, laying a hand on the ground to steady himself. He looked at a frightened younger native, suppressing his intrigue for the bone piercings through his ears, and asked again.

"Do you speak English?"

The younger native did not raise his eyes from his lap, but nodded. "A little." He said.

"Do you have any food we could share? We are very hungry."

The native nodded again. He looked into Jacob's eyes and then at his bandaged forearm. He paused, then offered Jacob his hand.

"It's a trap." The captain hissed. "He'll lead us to his tribe, who'll eat us. We're the food."

Jacob ignored the captain and willingly accepted the young man's hand. The buccaneers followed the native into the bush. Marin pressed in behind Jacob, thwarting L'Olonnais' agitation. The buccaneers allowed the remaining four natives to walk among them. Muskets and pistols at the ready, but lowered. For the next five minutes, not a word was spoken. Only the captain's grumblings were audible through the swishing leaves.

They came to a clearing and the young native sat, encouraging Jacob to join him. The other four natives sat with their compatriot and called into the trees. A few minutes passed before the bushes rustled and a sixth, slightly older native crept into the clearing and sat opposite Jacob. He offered a wooden bowl.

Jacob took the bowl and pulled out the folding knife and punctured a piece of meat. He teased it into his mouth. "Thank you," he said, offering the bowl to Marin. "It's chicken."

"How do you feel?" Alphonse asked.

Jacob shrugged. "Better for having food. You have more?" He asked the native.

The native nodded. "You trade?" He said.

"You see. A trap," the captain said. "They offer the food, but then they want our possessions." The captain spoke in French, but even so, the natives heard his disgust.

"Captain!" Alphonse pleaded. "They're helping us."

The captain grunted his displeasure but soon quietened.

Jacob turned to the circle and nodded. "We trade." Jacob tried to clear his head.

The young native eyed the folding knife.

"Knife," Jacob said, turning Henri's blade over in his hand. He swallowed hard, pulling it closer to his chest. After a short moment of contemplation, he accepted the knife's fate. He didn't need it to remember his friend. He wiped the blade on his sleeve, folded it closed, and offered it to the young native.

"Knife." The native took the knife into his own hands, feeling its weight and testing its pivot.

"Marin? Offer them your cutlass."

"Jacob. I'll need that."

"You need food more. Offer it and smile."

Marin sat in the circle and offered his cutlass to another of the natives, who passed the blade to his neighbour, feeling its sharpness. Smiles painted the once nervous faces.

"Thank you." The younger native said.

"Thank you." The other natives repeated.

Jacob opened his knapsack, exploring what else he might have. He ignored his journal, instead pulling, from the bottom, the forgotten yellow dress. Holding it from its shoulders, he dusted off the odd crumb clinging to the fibres, and let it display itself across his lap. He found the gaze of the native woman. With a smile, he stood and offered her the dress. Her eyes widened as she pressed the colourful garment to her half naked body. She turned and skipped into the bush.

Jacob smiled. "Food?" He said and held out his hands.

"Yes," said the younger native.

All the natives stood and walked into the bush.

"We'll not see them again, you fool," The captain said.

Before the captain had a chance to gloat the natives returned through the trees holding bowls of broth and two wild fowl. The buccaneers salivated at the sight of such a feast and encircled the natives, thanking them for their hospitality. The buccaneers offered more knives and cutlasses, and more food was bestowed. Spirits were raised, and all thoughts of hostility dissolved in the warmth of soup and meat. Buccaneers and natives sat together, sharing food, exchanging smiles and laughter. They used two felled saplings for the buccan's frame. The natives appeared with twine, happily helping to secure the horizontal spars. Together, the two tribes roasted the fowl and sat as one.

Jocob sat with the younger native, sharing his meat. His head felt lighter than it had for many days. They conversed fastidiously, the language barrier forcing them to weigh each word, careful not to cause offense. The natives had learned many English words and were eager to learn more.

"My name is Jacob." Jacob said, pointing a finger to his chest. "Jacob." He then pointed at the young native. "What's your name?"

The native stared at Jacob, then looked to his elder opposite.

"Mahma." The older native replied.

"Mahma?" Jacob repeated.

The young native nodded and smiled. "Friend?"

Jacob nodded. "Friend."

Mahma cradled Jacob's forearm, bringing it towards him. He unwrapped the bandage and poked the blackening flesh. Jacob could smell the faintest hint of sweetness mixed with egg.

"Wait." Mahma said.

Mahma disappeared into the bush, returning a few moments later with a handful of mixed leaves. He sat and began chewing the smaller leaves. He spat out a green paste into his palm and flattened it onto Jacob's open wound.

"Poison." L'Olonnais exclaimed. You'll be on your back any minute now."

"How can it be poison? The lad's just chewed it." Alphonse said.

The larger of the leaves Mahma wrapped around the forearm and secured with twine. "No more hurt," he said.

Jacob smiled. "Thank you."

"Jacob, friend."

Jacob sat for a moment, unsure what else to say. "My other name is Penjerrick." Jacob said. "It is the town where my mother was born."

"Town? Penjerrick town?"

"Yes."

"You are Captain Penjerrick?"

Many mouths stopped chewing, and all eyes glanced at L'Olonnais. L'Olonnais glared at Jacob.

"No, no." Jacob blushed. "This is the captain." He pointed to L'Olonnais and smiled. "Captain L'Olonnais."

The native cocked his head to the captain as he struggled with the pronunciation. Chuckles escaped the buccaneers' mouths. The captain stretched forward.

"Lol-On-Nay." He said with a sneer.

Mahma's expression became sullen. His eyes flickering to the members of his tribe. "Cap-Tin Lol-On-Nay?" He correctly pronounced, looking at the captain. "You Pirate?" He denounced.

"We're adventurers." Jacob said. "Travellers."

The captain sniffed at Jacob. "I'm a buccaneer, a filibuster, a privateer. The great François L'Olonnais. The Bane of Spain." L'Olonnais stood offering a theatrical bow. "Yes, Pirate."

Groans rumbled as the buccaneers glanced from face to shadowy face of their hosts. The crackle of the flames roasting the last of the chickens flecked the silence. Friendly smiles melted under deep set brows. Alphonse placed his bowl on the ground and nudged Marin next to him. Marin secreted a chicken leg into his pocket, then rested his greasy hand on his musket at his side. All the white men did similar actions, shifting uneasily while finding their weapons.

Jacob regained Mahma's attention and smiled. "We are friends. We eat. We laugh."

"Jacob, friend. Yes. But now you go. To water." He held up Henri's knife in the palms of his hands. "Thank you." He gestured back into the jungle where the ocean lay, and their escape could be found. He turned, and with his people, disappeared into the dense foliage.

The buccaneers eyed each other while scrambling the last of the meat into their knapsacks. The first spits of rain hissed into the fire.

"What now?" Marin asked.

"We kill them." The captain spat. "They dare disrespect the great François L'Olonnais."

"There could be hundreds of them." Alphonse retorted. "We're barely fed. We take the food and return to the longboat. The rest of the men need feeding."

"When did you become a dove?" The captain called after Alphonse. "You've turned craven now you're not behind your gun."

Alphonse turned on the captain and with no hint of fear stood defiantly blocking the captains escape from the camp. "Craven? Do you want to test how craven I am?"

"Marin, stop them." Jacob said, stuffing a hunk of chicken into his knapsack.

Marin stepped between the stand-off separating them until the aggression spell was broken. "We've no time to be brawling."

The others ignored the captain's berating's and Alphonse's mutterings as they collected their belongings.

Every musket and pistol were hurriedly checked. Their belly's now content and they held a new respect for the natives, but not one man among them would risk the thirty-minute walk back to the beach without a loaded weapon.

Thirty-Six

The hospitable buccan was a memory. The rain had worsened as the buccaneers trudged towards the beach. They had stuffed their firearms into knapsacks or under coats. Jacob felt healthier for the food and water. His arm itched, which he took to be a good sign. He could hear the waves swashing the shore and smell the salt in the air. He glanced over his shoulder, finding L'Olonnais towards the rear—with anger festering on his face.

Marin led the way. Jacob, a pace behind, spied the longboat through the trees, anchored just beyond the surf. The rain fell heavier now, obscuring his vision. He blinked droplets from his eyelashes, but still, he could not find the barge. Looking closer at the longboat, he noticed arms waving. Then the faint sound of a musket shot.

"What they raving about?" Marin asked nobody in particular. Jacob halted, as did the buccaneers behind him. They deployed their training—crouching and aiming their muskets with swiftness and precision. Jacob followed their lead. Marin had continued and sauntered out onto the beach. Before anyone could stop him, he stumbled backwards, spluttering into the long grass. Jacob dropped to his side, avoiding the spear pinning him to the ground. Marin's dirty shirt darkened with wetness. He stared at Jacob with frightened eyes–before relaxing into death. More spears whooshed through the air.

"Marin." Jacob stuttered.

A crescendo erupted and the familiar drifts of smoke wafted past Jacob. Moans could be heard on the sand beyond the trees. The rain had killed many of the sparks, but the bullets had inflicted some damage. More spears tore through the smoke, some finding homes in chests and heads. At least half of the buccaneers lay dead or injured. Perhaps only ten men were unscathed. Jacob turned to find a spear protruding from the ground, only inches away from his torso. He scrambled back into the trees, trying to suppress his rising panic. He found Alphonse crouched in the grass, holding the limp body of one of the crew.

"Do you have a musket?" Jacob asked.

"Aye." Alphonse raised his arm to show Jacob his musket, but in doing so, opened up the wound, turning his shirt a dirty red.

"Alphonse. You're hit."

Alphonse glanced down at his flank and with a rush of confusion and shock, he lay back, wheezing.

Jacob scanned the vicinity, but there was no spear. The puncture wound was close to Alphonse's armpit. "You've been shot." Jacob said, holding Alphonse's head. Alphonse spat blood. Dead.

No time for a prayer. Jacob fumbled with the musket–but it had already been fired. It was pointless trying to load it in the rain. The natives were closing in. The few remaining buccaneers regrouped and ran for the beach–away from Jacob. He stood, knowing if he followed, he would most likely be cut off by the natives' spears. The memory of the captain's tactic of hiding under the bodies came to mind. Surely, he would be discovered. He stared at the blood leaching from Alphonse. Could he bring himself to hide in such a manner?

Ten seconds later, he was scrambling through the jungle in the opposite direction, hugging the tree line, hoping to glance the longboat or the barge. His fever had eased after the food and the new bandage from Mahma was helping–but he felt tired. Up ahead, he could hear someone running. He was swift and Jacob couldn't keep pace, but he was able to track him through the disturbed foliage.

A shout called from the tree line attracted Jacob's attention. "Cap'n."

The figure ahead slowed, and Jacob slackened his stride. "Who speaks?" Jacob recognised L'Olonnais' voice.

"Joseph," came the reply.

Joseph and Gaetan emerged through the bush. "We came when we saw the natives. They got you good. How many are alive?"

L'Olonnais gasped. "I'm the only one who got away. Good thinking to come and rescue your captain." He scraped his saturated hair back from his face.

"Take this," Joseph said, offering L'Olonnais a musket.

"We had them." L'Olonnais said. "We could have killed them and taken their food. The pup wanted to trade. The others fell for his pleading. Then they turned on us. Fools. I should have left the pup on the island."

Jacob lay half submerged in estuary water. He thought about Marin and Alphonse. How did Alphonse get shot? They traded no muskets or pistols with the natives. And Alphonse was towards the back with L'Olonnais. He peered through the bush, listening to the familiar sound of muskets being loaded by the three men yards away. L'Olonnais must have shot Alphonse. The realisation fuelled Jacob's anger. He needed to escape.

Jacob crawled under the mangrove roots until he lay at the beach's edge. The barge was pulled up the shallow sand. It sat closer to him than the others. At least two hundred yards away from where they had been attacked. He couldn't see any natives. If he could make the barge, maybe he could get back to the longboat. They would finish loading their muskets soon. He Ran. It was a rash decision–but he didn't know what else to do.

He pumped his arms. The sand sapped his stride. He felt sluggish. He looked to his left, seeing the aftermath of the ambush creeping around the headland. The natives hadn't seen him. Most were in the trees. Killing. The barge was still one hundred yards away. He shot a glance over his shoulder. L'Olonnais stood at the beach's edge with his musket trained on him. Jacob zigged, but no shot fired. Eighty yards to go. He dared another glance. All three were sprinting across the beach. If he could hold L'Olonnais off long enough, maybe he could convince Joseph and Gaetan to abandon their captain. Surely they wouldn't stay with a man that might just as soon shoot them.

Bakari rose from the stern, where he'd been watching, guarding the barge. He levelled a pistol at Jacob.

"What's ya hurry, boy?"

"The natives attacked us?"

"I noticed that. Why you run from your captain?" Bakari eased himself to the bow of the barge. Wincing in pain with each step.

"The captain's a murderer."

Bakari laughed.

"He's just killed Alphonse. Shot him in the back."

Bakari glanced at his three comrades, fast approaching.

"He needs to be stopped, Bakari. He killed Reinhardt. I saw him do it. We all saw him kill Henri. He was willing to leave you running for the barge. The man's distracted. A lunatic. Anyone of us could be next."

"It looks like ya might be next."

Jacob turned. His heart sank.

THE PIRATE'S WAKE

Bakari threw his pistol into the barge and growled as he pushed from the bow.

Jacob gritted his teeth and unsheathed his cutlass. He felt its weight. Since San Pedro, it had only been used to open coconuts. He anchored his feet, watching the three pirates descend on him.

L'Olonnais stopped at the bow, eyeing Jacob. Joseph raced to the larboard side, gripping the gunwale. Gaetan joined Bakari, ignoring Jacob.

"Get in, lad," Joseph shouted over the noise of the waves.

Jacob stood, not taking his eyes from L'Olonnais. "You shot Alphonse."

Gaetan and Joseph shifted their gaze to Jacob–and then to their captain.

"Forget the pup," L'Olonnais snapped, searching for the natives along the coast. "He's Indian food. Get the barge launched."

Jacob circled larboard out of the surf. The four men heaved the barge from its sandy grasp until it fought with the incoming waves.

Jacob shimmied out of its way. L'Olonnais and Bakari pushed from the bow while Gaetan and Joseph jumped aboard.

"Jacob, get in!" Joseph shouted again. "He won't hurt you."

"Get in, lad," Gaetan concurred.

One more heave and they would be away.

"Murderer." Jacob screamed.

L'Olonnais stood from the barge and aimed the musket at Jacob, which up until now had hung over his shoulder.

"Captain. Don't shoot." Bakari said. "The Indians will hear."

"Grab him." L'Olonnais said. "We'll deal with him in the longboat."

Jacob edged away from Bakari into shallower waters. L'Olonnais' musket tracked him. The rain fell heavier now. Jacob wiped his eyes with his left hand while tightening his grip on his cutlass with his right. He ran at L'Olonnais, cutlass raised in a wild attack. The weapon felt heavy.

L'Olonnais pulled the trigger, but the powder was damp, as Jacob had hoped. L'Olonnais dodged the blade. just in time, almost falling into the spume. Jacob's sword shaved a splinter of timber from the bow, stumbling him into Bakari. L'Olonnais threw the musket into the barge and unsheathed his own cutlass, turning to face Jacob.

Bakari nudged Jacob away and gave one last heave, pushing the barge free from the beach. He bumbled aboard with the help of Gaetan. The barge crew each grabbed oars and pulled. Jacob and L'Olonnais stood as the barge cut through the surf. L'Olonnais reacted first and raced ankle deep after the barge. Jacob, deeper into the water, shot forward, intercepting L'Olonnais, offering him a long point.

"Move, pup. I ain't staying here to be food for the Indians." Jacob did not budge. "Mr Penjerrick. We can both escape. No harm will come of you. Ain't that right, Mr Obasi?"

Bakari pulled on an oar, wincing through his pain. "Sorry, boy," Bakari said, not glancing at L'Olonnais.

L'Olonnais snarled through gritted teeth and gripped his cutlass tight in a short guard. Jacob parried the first blow, stumbling back, knee-deep in the water. The sand sucked at his feet. He yanked himself free and lunged forward. His cutlass drove toward L'Olonnais, who parried with ease and countered with a thrust of his own. But surprisingly, the attack was weak.

L'Olonnais was not the swordsman Jacob had expected–or perhaps, like him, he was still weakened from the journey. Jacob parried, leaving L'Olonnais exposed to an empty fade. Jacob found some confidence hacking at L'Olonnais, causing him to stumble into an oncoming wave, knocking him off balance.

Jacob's attack lost its momentum, and his feet were taken from under him. Through his watery vision, he fumbled for his cutlass. Catching his breath, he opened his eyes to see the natives rushing ever closer. Were they his saviour–or his enemy?

He could hear L'Olonnais over his shoulder as a fresh wave crashed over his head. He spluttered before the tide rushed away and the sand became softer under his body. He opened his eyes to see L'Olonnais looming over him. His wet hair hanging loose over his confused face. His hand empty of a weapon.

"Good luck, pup." He snarled, gaining some composure, before kicking Jacob in the ribs and striding into the ocean.

In a moment of desperation, Jacob clasped L'Olonnais' trailing leg. The barge left the shallows and would be out of reach in a matter of seconds. Water washed over his body. His ribs burned. L'Olonnais' stopped his struggling. He had no more interest in his human anchor or his escaping crew. Backwash receded, sucking both L'Olonnais and Jacob into the wet sand. Jacob turned–and looking up he saw the spear tip six inches from L'Olonnais' nose.

J acob wheezed, catching his breath. He was no longer in the water. He'd been dragged to the dryer beach. Sand clung to him, making him itch. He could see the barge pitching over the waves, heading to the longboat one hundred yards out to sea. Bare feet churned the surrounding sand. He risked a glance upwards. The closest pair belonged to a native who he had recently shared food with. Jacob's head hit the sand–defeated. Sounds and sights faded, and his most prominent care became his dignity. His bowels must not betray him. He felt afraid–but he must not show it. He would die, that was for sure. The natives had made it clear—every white man must be eradicated. He had nothing left but his dignity. When the time came, he would die with pride. The native women in the village had shown him how.

He lay breathing heavily. He should never have wished to better himself. To have fallen for Mr Arundell's trap in the Seven Stars. To allow himself to be snatched by the press-gang. He'd left Seth to the mercy of the Dutch. He smiled as he remembered Moise's face when he emerged from the trees babbling French. What a fool. L'Olonnais had just used him. He had been a fool all along. And now he would die.

He raised his head to the sound of muffled moans—his moans. He lifted himself up on his elbows. If he were to make a run for it, this was his chance. He laughed at his optimism. He fixed his position. From the corner of his vision, he spied the tip of a spear, inches away, aimed above his head. He followed the spear from tip to owner. His heart skipped as he recognised the face. It was Mahma—but his face was not jovial and friendly. It was rigid and flinty. Jacob tested a smile. "Mahma, Friend." He said.

Mahma ignored Jacob. He was looking at something beyond. He spoke urgently in his own language. Jacob sat, not daring to move an inch. From behind, he heard a reply from a native, equally aggressive and urgent.

Mahma tensed as if about to thrust the spear into Jacob's neck—but then paused. They locked eyes and Mahma twitched the spear upwards, indicating Jacob must stand. Jacob did as ordered and after a nod from Mahma, he turned and walked towards the commotion not too far away.

L'Olonnais was the focus of a dozen natives circling him. He flicked his eyes to Jacob, not daring to move any other muscle. Three of the natives were armed with the gifted cutlasses. The chief native, who Jacob noted was the first to offer him food a mere hour earlier, snapped an order. The spears instructed L'Olonnais to follow their lead back into the dense jungle. The leader of the natives pointed at Jacob while barking an order at Mahma, who replied with matching curtness. The chief turned to follow the procession of guards and their captive into the jungle.

Jacob trudged after the natives, followed by Mahma and his spear. They walked for twenty minutes through the mangroves and thick shrubbery. Jacob's hair soaked at his shoulders. His neck was stiff through fear. He followed L'Olonnais into a clearing where a huge fire roared, winning the battle with the rain. Dozens of eyes watched as the white men were paraded around the flames. Screams and shouts erupted from the half-naked, brown-skinned women dancing and whooping, daring to touch the forbidden white skin.

Jacob's knapsack was snatched from his shoulder. He realised his cutlass must still be on the beach. He felt drunk–the delight of the atmosphere corrupting his fear. His head spinning. A yellow dress flashed before the fire, then disappearing behind the flames.

The natives quietened and the chief warrior raised a hand towards L'Olonnais.

"Lol-On-Nay. Pirate." The chief proclaimed. "Evil, bad spirit."

L'Olonnais offered a flicker of descent at the corner of his mouth. Not yet resigned to his fate. He snarled as the warriors stripped the shirt from his back, brandishing it into the fire.

The chief cast his finger to Jacob. "Pirate. Evil." He said. More whooping and cheering.

It would take all Jacob's effort to maintain his dignity. He stood–rigid–conjuring to mind the native women murdered by L'Olonnais. He stared straight ahead, feeling the tears streak his cheeks. He clasped his trembling fingers tight, trying to control his fear.

The chief stepped toward Jacob and exchanged words with Mahma, who stood just a spear's length away. Jacob couldn't follow the language, but he understood enough. The chief was asserting his authority, and Mahma was yielding.

Jacob lowered his head and closed his eyes. His lips fluttered as he prayed.

"Jacob, friend." He heard Mahma's voice.

Jacob opened his eyes. Huge tears cascaded over his eyelids. "Mahma, friend," he said.

Mahma glanced at the chief and then held Jacob's gaze. "Jacob, Pirate."

Jacob sobbed. All hope lost. "No. No pirate. Jacob, friend. Mahma, friend." He smiled. The crowd quietened.

"You, Pirate." Mahma waved Jacob's pleas away.

Jacob lowered himself to his knees, pleading for compassion—losing the battle to retain his dignity. "No pirate." He pointed to L'Olonnais. "Pirate. Evil." He thought of the final native women who sacrificed herself. Out of pure desperation, he exclaimed. "Papa Nahualli."

Silence flooded the camp. All eyes shifted from L'Olonnais to their chief and back again. L'Olonnais grinned hopefully.

Mahma approached Jacob. "Papa Nahualli?"

"Yes." Jacob sobbed. "Yucatan cursed him. Papa Nahualli searches for his soul."

The chief warrior circled the fire, taking care not to touch L'Olonnais, and spoke in his native tongue to Mahma. Mahma nodded to his chief. "L'Olonnais, cursed. Papa Nahualli?" He confirmed with Jacob.

"Yes." Jacob pleaded.

"That's it, lad." L'Olonnais sneered. "They're scared of the curse. They'll let us go."

"Jacob, cursed?" Mahma pointed.

"We're all cursed; aren't we pup?" L'Olonnais stood tall. "They dare not kill us for fear the curse will spread to them."

Jacob wiped away his rain filled tears and looked at L'Olonnais. "No."

L'Olonnais snarled. "Suit yourself. They won't mind eating you if you ain't poisoned."

The chief and Mahma spoke again. Mahma lowered his spear from Jacob's neck. "Jacob, Friend?" He said, offering his left hand. Jacob clasped his wrist, snuffling away more tears.

"Friend." Jacob said, raising to his feet.

The chief held Mahma's spear as the young native produced Henri's knife from his waist cord. "Jacob Penjerrick." He said, offering Jacob the knife. Jacob stared at it–puzzled. Mahma pointed to Captain François L'Olonnais. "You kill. Take away curse."

Jacob turned to L'Olonnais, who seethed silently. He could not see another way to escape. He must become the vessel the natives need him to be. He must eradicate the curse. He unfolded the knife, finding strength and courage in its weight. The edge looked sharp–as expected. Henri always kept his knife honed. Ready for both chicken or human flesh. Jacob inched towards his ex-captain, straightening his stature with every step. His head felt heavy. His senses numbed. Rain dripped from his saturated hair. The spears backed away but stayed pointed at the pirate as the younger white man stalked forward.

"You snivelling whelp. You traitor." L'Olonnais spat. "I told you I would make a fine pirate of you."

L'Olonnais looked older now. He stood at least a foot shorter than Jacob. His hatless head revealing his greying hair hanging loose over his thin shoulders. His pristine moustache lost to beard and grime. His shoulders marred with the unmistakable scars of the lash creeping from his back. Jacob felt compelled to touch them. He buried any sympathy creeping into his mind. "I just wanted to go home." Jacob sobbed.

"You're a fool. A lost pup. Washed up for my pleasure. You'll die trying to climb out of the shit. You'll never be rich. You'll never have your whore."

Jacob raised his knife, his knuckles white with rage.

"You won't kill me." L'Olonnais said. "You don't have the guts. The fear is tilted in your voice."

Jacob grinned, trying to mask his own doubts. He glanced at the spears inches from them – a reminder of what he must do. "I'm not killing you."

L'Olonnais' beady eyes shot left and right before leaning forward to hear Jacob's plan.

"I never wanted any of this. I understand the killing of your enemy—revenge for what the Spanish did to you." Jacob thought of Mr Arundell, and the revenge festering in his own mind. "But once that debt was settled, you became addicted to the power—to the fear. Killing became your way to rule, not for justice, but for control."

L'Olonnais smirked. "Men are weak. They grow obedient at the faintest whisper of a threat."

"You killed Reinhardt because he dared to speak his mind. You slit his throat to crush a mutiny you created. The native women—butchered like animals. They were defenceless. You *knew* they would not betray their menfolk. Their deaths were for your own pleasure." His voice cracked, but he pushed on. "And Henri... You killed Henri out of spite. He was only defending me. He was letting you go. Only an hour ago, you shot Alphonse in the back so you could make your escape. I've not seen you engage one man in a fair fight. Your tactics are torture and murder. You're a coward."

Jacob felt a demonic anger surge from within. He had never felt such rage. "No. I'm not killing you. You were fated to die months ago."

L'Olonnais' puzzled face recoiled in fear from the man standing inches away, armed with merely a knife–but a heart full of vengeance.

Jacob raised his voice so the tribe could hear. He summoned to mind the theatrics the man in front of him had delivered so many times. He raised his hands to the heavens. "I'm not killing you. Papa Nahualli works through me. The curse has caught you." Jacob pushed his face to meet Captain François L'Olonnais. Jean David Nau. The Bane of Spain. "Whichever face you use, I see only evil."

The Frenchman snarled and twisted. The native spears inched closer, reminding him of his fate. "You don't know evil. You're but a pup. You know nothing of this world. My name will live on. The great François L'Olonnais. I cannot die."

"You will die." Jacob answered with venom. "But I'll make sure your name lives on."

L'Olonnais grinned.

Jacob fixed Henri's folding knife inches from L'Olonnais' belly. "As a coward. A black-hearted craven coward. The world will know the real François L'Olonnais."

L'Olonnais' mouth twisted in anger, but before he could speak, his head jerked forward. He raised his hands to his face—and must have seen only blood. Jacob had driven the knife deep into L'Olonnais' flesh. He stepped forward. Their noses almost touching. He forced the knife deeper and angled it upwards until his entire hand had disappeared.

Jacob could feel the pulse through L'Olonnais' body as the old man's heart beat faster. Intestines wrapped around his wrist like a basket of warm eels. He eased the dagger back to his hip, shaking himself free from his delirium. He stood, shocked. The rain diluted the blood as it washed to the ground. He fell to his knees. Looking up through tearful eyes, he caught L'Olonnais in a moment of clarity. Bewilderment washed from captain's face as he focused on his blood-soaked hands. He caressed his fingers onto Jacob's head before forcing them into his mouth. Throwing his head back, he screamed with laughter.

"I cannot die." He gurgled. Blood trickling from his mouth. "I cannot die." He fell to the ground–half crumpling Jacob.

Whoops of delight bellowed from the crowd, as four warriors picked up the dead pirate and held him aloft. Chants pulsed in Jacob's ears as the natives paraded the body around the fire. Jacob witnessed the loudest whoops of all as François L'Olonnais was cast into the flames.

The screams of a hundred victims chased Jacob as he stumbled–on hands and knees–through the tall wet grass. His own whimpers muffled by the sounds in his head. He reached for the heavens, desperate to be free from the nightmare. Mahma stepped to his side, pointing his spear through the jungle, back towards the beach. "Go."

Yellow.

Through the foliage, he spied the dress. It disappeared, then found again.

Yellow.

For ten minutes the native women led him through the jungle, giggling just out of reach. Jacob stood disorientated as the yellow dress whispered back into the bush. The screams–a memory–forever engrained. He opened his trembling hand to cast off his crime, but the knife stayed stuck, crusted to his palm. He stumbled to the surf crawling the final yards like a turtle. Desperate to wash away the blood. The smell of charred flesh mixed with salt on the breeze. And as he tasted his freedom, he lost the battle to retain his dignity. The contents of his stomach emptied into the wash.

Thirty-Seven

"Told ya," Bart said. "The biggest pirate port in the Caribbean."

Jacob leaned on the gunwale, admiring the port. A huge round tower from the fort loomed over the town. "Yep, it's bigger than Tortuga. And full of pirates?"

"You won't find an honest man walking the cobbles. The scourge of the world it's called by some."

"Is it always this busy?"

"Maybe there's a gathering."

Jacob groaned.

When he'd stumbled through the bush, the smell of charred flesh burning his mind, Jacob had found only the empty expanse of the ocean. The barge and the longboat were gone. He had only rocks north and south–and the jungle to his back. He'd felt exposed. He feared the eyes in the bush and the tiniest rustle of shrubbery. Finally, he slept. He slept for two days. He startled awake with the taste of blood in his mouth–followed by the memory of

L'Olonnais' sneer and his innards wrapped around his forearm. A tremor pulsed through his entire body.

When he came to his senses, he noticed his first gifts–perhaps a reward for his bravery. A small fire, a skin of water, a freshly throttled chicken, accompanied by a handful of small leaves wrapped in three larger leaves tied with twine. Jacob had no choice but to trust their kindness. If it was poisoned, then so be it. He would die either way. He chewed the small leaves and re-wrapped his wounded arm. He cooked his chicken and drank his water.

Every second morning, he found the same tribute left on the isolated rock surrounded by jungle leaf litter. He never once saw it arrive. It seemed his neighbours would feed him and heal him–if he stuck to the rule: stay on the beach. If the curse was real, neither party wanted to risk its return. Jacob didn't believe in the curse, so he cleaned his knife and tracked his cutlass to where it had washed up on the beach. He ensured neither weapon left his side. But, throughout his time as a castaway, they were not needed in anger.

On the fourth morning his neighbours delivered his knapsack–empty of anything useful, except for his journal and quill.

As the days rolled on, Jacob's bravery grew. Although the jungle seemed out of bounds, he found the courage to walk the beach to where the buccaneers had been ambushed. At first the site was difficult to find, but eventually he discovered blood on leaves and a pistol half buried under earth and shrubs. He didn't expect to find anyone alive–or even their bodies–but he needed confirmation. He'd lost two more comrades in Alphonse and Marin. As he sat in the spot where they'd died, he whispered a prayer. When he returned to his camp–no more than a fire near the tribute rock–he couldn't help but wonder what cooked meat he'd smelled drifting from the jungle.

On the afternoon of the seventeenth day, he sat on his ponder spot, wrapped in his coat, feeding the fire. He felt rejuvenated. The chewed up leaves had worked their miracle and his fever had left his body. He placed his quill back in the book. He found charcoal from the fire a suitable substitute for ink and passed his days writing his account of the previous year. He'd tried to draw a sketch of Lydia, but he was losing his memory of her likeness.

A gull had taken to Jacob's patch of beach, and every day he would laugh his greeting. Jacob tossed him a hunk of chicken—it had become their ritual. He no longer had to fight the gull off; it waited to be fed, then vanished back around the headland.

While the gull wrestled with the meat, a sloop appeared from behind the cliffs, heading north. Spotting the fire and a young man waving, the crew brought her about and launched a barge to rescue him.

"What's ya business?" The leader of the landing party asked in a seafaring accent, with a hint of southern England.

Jacob looked the crew over and felt it wise to tell them the truth. "Buccaneer." He said.

"You'll fit right in." The Englishman said, slapping Jacob on the back. I'm lieutenant Wilson." He turned back to the barge. "Sharp." He beckoned a young man not much older than Jacob to join them. "What's your name, lad?" He asked, turning back to Jacob.

"Jacob, sir."

"This is Bartholomew."

"Call me Bart." Bart said.

"Bartholomew will look after you. Is there food and water in the bush, Jacob?"

"Nope."

Jacob told Lieutenant Wilson and Bartholomew about their attack and how he'd survived. The crew waited for Jacob to collect his scant belongings before hastily retreating to their ship.

On board the sloop, Jacob was quizzed by the captain. He told of his voyage and how *Marquise* had run aground on a sand bar. The captain, being a good Christian of sorts, and now knowing where to find water and dubious food, agreed to rescue the marooned crew.

The ocean had swallowed almost all evidence of *Marquise*. Jacob wandered the abandoned camp, leaving the landing party to forage for coconuts. He'd pointed them in the direction of Helario's bean patch and herb garden–both looked overgrown. The buccan remained where it had been erected two months earlier. Beneath the shadow of the palm trees, the stone seat circle wrapped around a tinged area of sand. The makeshift infirmary had gone replaced by three timber crosses. Jacob ambled to their site and slumped to the ground. Each cross had a name etched into the horizontal spar. The first read the name of a crew member who had fallen victim to the bone saw and must have succumbed to his injuries.

The second read *'Denis Touppin.'*
The third read *'Henri Bodine.'*

Jacob's legs became numb as he sat staring at the cross with his friend's name. His chin quivered, nestled into his fists. "This pirating life ain't what you promised. I ain't seen any riches and I'm no closer to home. Were you really my friend?" He pulled the folding knife from his pocket, nodding as he stared at it. "I avenged you though, mate. The bastard's dead." His eyes welled. He did not wipe away the tears. "I'm sorry." He sat quietly in prayer, ignorant of the barges being loaded behind him.

"You ready, pal?" came a voice from behind.

Jacob stood and secreted the knife. "Aye, Bart." He collected a sack of coconuts from the shoreline before clambering back into the barge to continue the journey north. He didn't look back at monkey island.

Three weeks later, Jacob stared at the island of Jamaica and the harbour of Port Royal–the biggest pirate port in the Caribbean.

"See you in a week." Bart said as Jacob climbed down the ladder. "If you ain't back onboard, the captain won't wait."

Falmouth felt like a lifetime ago, as Jacob strode up the jetty in Henri's coat–the folding knife in his pocket, a pistol in his knapsack, and his prized cutlass at his hip. He stepped from the jetty, disgusted by what squelched under his feet. This was definitely not Falmouth. Port Royal stank. Sewerage ran like murky streams between the cobbles. Flies and insects feasted at blockage points and dogs and cats had no fear of rolling or sitting in the sludge.

The streets of Port Royal overflowed with people–mainly sailors. Jacob could not find a sober man amongst them. The town was much larger than Tortuga, but similar in that every other building was either a tavern or a brothel. Doxies beckoned from windows to the drunks below. Who in turn shouted vile insults or over exuberant responses of love. Above it all, the most notable detail to Jacob's ear was the language. Although a mixture of tongues–and people spoke many in the same conversation–the overwhelming speech was English. As disorientated as Jacob felt, he relaxed his shoulders a great deal on hearing familiar words in the bustle of the streets. If he had his catch of the day and his mother's cottage over the hill, he could almost be back home.

In a tavern doorway ahead, between the sailors, prostitutes and mangy stray dogs, a malicious-looking man with rodent eyes sat on a stool with a large pipe of wine. His tone grated as he challenged every passer-by to drink from his bag. One man refused to partake and was apprehended with the flat end of the cutlass until he submitted. Jacob had no intent to confirm his suspicions, so dodged down a side alley to collect his thoughts.

In the quieter alley, he stood a moment, thinking. He missed Henri's lead and Bastien's investigatory prowess. If here, the remnants of the crew would have arrived with not much coin and an itch to relieve their taste buds of monkey meat. They would be looking for the cheapest ale and chicken they could find. Jacob pushed on to the end of the alley and found another high street. It might be days before he stumbled upon them. This town was much larger than Tortuga. And it was just as likely they were there instead of here.

There was nothing for it. It would be a swift stride to the edge of town and circle back to the centre trying every rundown, earth floored, flea pit until he found his comrades–or trouble found him.

Four hours later, Jacob had pushed open and peeked into almost every dog hole Port Royal had to offer. He thought he'd seen Michiel Andrieszoon through a window of a tavern. He did not investigate. Instead opted to come back if everywhere else proved futile. He'd even followed a terrier, he thought to be Tomilho, but lost him in a crowd. To the south, he found one last street to investigate, but it did not hold much promise. The mouth of the street looked uninviting, with no foot traffic heading its way. It was no more than an alley and, unsurprisingly, found it deserted. He could see a blacksmith's shop halfway on the left and a candle shop opposite. Then, a flicker of hope. At the end of the narrowing cobbles, a shaft of light shot the opposite wall, and a dog disappeared into the doorway. With no other options, Jacob sauntered up the alley to rule out another dead end.

A small, faded sign hung above the door, displaying the name of the tavern. Tomilho's Place. A sly grin flicked the corner of his mouth as he pushed open the door. The dim light from within illuminated the only table in the middle of the room. Sat around, nursing flagons of cheap ale, was the lost crew of *Marquise*. Rolant played a sober tune in the corner. Isaac sat half asleep and Bastien fussed Tomilho, who had just walked in. Harvey sat relaxing, with his pipe hanging from his mouth. His feet resting on an unoccupied chair.

"What a flea pit," Jacob jested. "Is this the cheapest place you could find?"

The table of lost souls looked up from their knuckles and almost spilled every drop of ale when they saw their young brethren—returned from certain death. Tomilho dodged feet and chairs as Jacob was almost tackled back through the open doorway.

A waterfall of questions fell from Bastien's mouth. "Where've you been? How'd you get back? Where's the captain? Who you with? Where are the others? Where have you been?"

"Hey, hey," Jacob said, freeing himself from the melee. "Can I at least quench my thirst? Where's the bar keep?"

Bastien flashed a glance at a door at the rear of the room. A stout lady with an apron tucked under her bosom poked her head from around the opening and beckoned to someone in the connecting room. A jovial barman entered, wiping an empty flagon. Upon seeing his new customer, he placed the flagon and towel on the bar. Jacob's eyes welled when he saw the bright smile.

"Helario." Jacob said. "You're here." He looked at the cook's attire, but still needed confirmation. "Is this your tavern?"

"Not exactly a tavern, Jovem. But yes. This cheap flee pit is mine and my wife's." He gestures to his wife. "Magdalena, this is Jacob. Jacob, my wife, Magdalena."

"Hello." Jacob stuttered towards Magdalena, unsure how to greet her.

Magdalena laughed heartily and wrapped two motherly arms around Jacob and kissed both his cheeks. "I am so happy you are here. Helario has been so worried."

Jacob blushed. Magdalena released her embrace, easing his embarrassment a little. He turned to Helario. "You never said you had a tavern."

Helario laughed. "At sea, with death following so closely, I forget I am a bar keep. When I return, I try to forget the sea."

Magdalena slapped a hand on her husband's belly. "You come home for some proper manjar."

Jacob laughed and embraced his friend.

"We need more ale, Magdalena." Isaac said. "We have too much to catch up on."

Jacob lowered the neck of his shirt and pulled out his pouch. "It ain't much, but it'll stretch to a round of cheap ale."

There was an ironic cheer.

"Your money's no good here, lad," Magdalena said. "You sit." She disappeared back through the doorway.

Helario hugged Jacob again and sat with his crew. Jacob sat next to Harvey, accepting an arm around his shoulder.

"I'm glad you're safe, my friend. I thought I'd lost you." Harvey wiped a smudge from his eye. "Now, tell the tale of how you found yourself back among us."

Magdalena bustled to the table with a clutch of ale tankards before returning with bowls of broth. For the next hour, they sat in good cheer. Jacob heard how they had buried Henri and sat waiting for two weeks eating monkey meat until a passing ship heading to Port Royal had rescued them. But they were more interested in Jacob and his tale. He told of Melchor's death and the Spanish attack. The desperate run for freedom. The meal with the natives. How the tribe had turned on them and set an ambush on the beach. His audience quietened, leaning in when Jacob revealed the circumstances of the death of the great François L'Olonnais–the screams he heard as he cooked to death. He omitted the stabbing, deciding the notoriety accompanying such a tale would beckon too much attention. For all his faults, the captain had many allies. And the Caribbean owned too many dark corners and too many deserted islands to leave the body of a traitorous boy. He merely told it was the gifts of Henri's knife–hidden in his coat pocket–and the yellow dress that welcomed sympathy from the natives. Saving his life.

When he'd finished, a melancholic quiet drifted over the table as each man cupped his tankards. Jacob looked at each in turn and smiled.

"I thought you'd have found a ship by now, Harv." He said after the long pause. "Get yourself back to the navy."

"War's over, my friend. No need for men like me anymore. I'm stuck here a while."

"So, they ain't looking for me? They won't get me back on their ship?"

Isaac laughed. "Did you really think they were looking for you? You died when you fell overboard. Or killed by pirates. Or by starvation. Or eaten by cannibals. In fact–how is it you're still alive?"

Jacob looked embarrassed and then smiled. "I cannot die."

The table laughed–except for Harvey, who shook his head. Jacob quietened himself. "What's your plan then, Harv? You tempted to stay."

Harvey folded his arms and sat back. "They ain't too bad when you get to know them, but I'm looking for a ship back to England. Maybe sign up with a merchant."

"Tomorrow, I'll introduce you to a friend of mine." Jacob said. "I've found a ship."

Harvey clinked cups and squeezed his friend's shoulder. They drank late into the night and slept where they fell. Helario and Magdalena made Jacob the same promise they'd made to the others. He could stay for as long as needed. Jacob slept peacefully for the first time in weeks.

"So, you found a ship?" Bastien asked the next morning as they walked on, avoiding the drunks and rivers of piss.

"Yeah. I think so. The ship that found me is resupplying and then heading back to England."

"You're not tempted to stay here with us. Helario will put you up. He needs a pot washer." Bastien laughed.

Jacob sidestepped Tomilho as he weaved between his legs. A doxie flashed her wares in a doorway and Bastien blew her a kiss.

"The other crews are here, you know."

"Which ones?" Jacob asked.

"*Leopard*, *Tigre*, *Stad Gouda*."

"How about *Moise*?"

"We haven't seen him yet, but Pierre's somehow here."

Jacob groaned at the mention of Pierre Le Picard. "If *Stad Gouda's* here, does that mean Doyle's here?"

Bastien laughed. "Yep. Lucas landed a catch after leaving Puerto Cavallo. Some fat Spanish merchant only half a day around the headland. Doyle's been swaggering through town with a pouch full of coins and two doxies on his arm. You ought to see the coat he nabbed himself. He's strolling around like the king of bloody Ireland."

They reached the harbour and looked out to sea. "I'm sorry about Henri." Jacob said.

"He made me promise not to blame you. The captain would do anything to save himself. We're pirates, Jake. One big happy family–'til we ain't."

"Not us, Bastien?"

"Not us, Jake. We're brothers. Not real brothers. Better."

Jacob pulled Henri's knife from his pocket. "He was your brother. You should have it."

Bastien took the knife and looked at it curiously. "I thought you gave this to the natives."

"They gave it back."

"I got my own. You keep it. He gave it to you. It's a shame it didn't avenge him, though. There would have been some justice to that."

Jacob pushed the knife deep into his knapsack and smiled.

"We didn't trick you, Jake." Bastien said. "The captain asked Hen to take you under our wing. You looked lost and scared. He'd have helped you, anyway. We saw no harm in it. We only found out the captain's motives for using you to keep Harvey and his maps after the mutiny. By then it didn't seem worth telling you."

"It's fine, Bastien. I figured as much. Henri gave his life to save me, and you were willing to do the same. No matter the reason, I couldn't blame you after that. And I know Harvey was just trying to protect me. Just wish everyone didn't treat me like a child."

"No more lies." Bastien said, pulling Jacob towards him."

Jacob slapped his shoulders and smiled. He turned to face the harbour. "So, what's all the fuss anyway? Why are there so many ships in anchorage?"

"Where have you been? Marooned on a beach?" Bastien laughed.

A huge smile lit up Jacob's entire face. "It can't be." He held his palms over his eyes to shield them from the sun. He could hardly control his emotions as he danced his way towards the jetty.

"Where you going?" Bastien called.

Jacob waved an arm over his shoulder, beckoning Bastien. "Follow me."

Jacob stood at the end of the jetty, jigging on the spot as a stream of soldiering sorts strode up the wooden boards. He held out his arms and snatched a skinny one from the procession.

The soldier looked up, startled. "Jacob. You're alive. You look like a pirate."

"I can't believe you made it," Jacob said, wrapping his arms around the soldier. "I thought you must be dead."

Bastien walked to the jetty and stood, waiting.

"Bastien." Jacob turned, not letting go of the soldier. "This is Seth. Seth, this is Bastien." The two shook hands. Jacob could not stop grinning. "Seth was my only friend on *Kestrel*. I was sure you must be dead."

"It was close." Seth replied, grinning and hugging his friend again. "We ended up on a deserted island. We had to stay in hiding as pirates looted the ship." Bastien glanced at Jacob. "When they left, we stayed there for four weeks until the fleet returned from Martinique and rescued us. I've had a hell of a time."

Jacob smiled.

"Guess who we found?" Seth said.

"Who?"

Seth grinned. "Craywick. The pirates had lashed him. Then left him to rot."

"Did he die?" Jacob asked.

"No. Nearly. We nursed him back to health. He wouldn't speak of it to anyone. Just said he would get his revenge. All I found out was it was some French pirate captain and some deserters. Said he won't stop 'til they're all dead."

Jacob's mouth gaped. "Where's Craywick now?"

Seth turned and pointed at the anchorage. "He'll be on the next barge."

"He's here? In Port Royal?" Jacob gasped.

"He heard of the gathering and he's chancing the pirate's here."

"The navy sanctioned this?" Jacob asked.

"No. By the time we got back to Nevis, the war was ending. Craywick commissioned his own ship. Been hunting pirates ever since. I had no choice. I couldn't find passage back to England without payment and I had no money to stay in Nevis, so I joined up."

"We need to warn Doyle."

"Doyle? What's that prick got to do with anything?"

Jacob smirked. "We're the deserters. Me, Harvey and Doyle."

"Fucking hell, Jacob." Seth said, doubling over in humorous shock. "The man's on the war path. Word got back to daddy, and he's got the family backing. If he finds you, you'll swing."

Jacob focused on the bay, looking for the Craywick's barge. With so many boats and ships, it was impossible to discern one from another. "Why are there so many ships?" He cried in frustration.

"The brethren, Jake." Bastien said. "That's what I was saying. The biggest fleet the Caribbean has ever seen." He flashed a fresh grin.

Jacob shook his head. "I suppose everyone's going to be rich?"

"It's going to be big. Since L'Olonnais disappeared, everyone's looking for a new leader. And he's called everyone to Port Royal."

"Who has?" Jacob asked.

"Captain Morgan."

"Who's that?"

"Henry Morgan." Bastien smiled. He'll be up with governor Modyford, plotting the next voyage."

Seth nudged him. "There he is." Pointing at the jetty. "Captain Craywick."

Jacob turned to Bastien with a face full of panic. "We need to warn Harvey and find Doyle." He found Craywick stepping off the barge. "You with us, Seth?"

"I ain't got no money for grub or digs."

Jacob didn't take his eyes from Craywick. "You can stay with us. Can't he Bastien."

"'Course."

"Shit." Jacob dodged behind a sailor carrying a sack of grain. "He's looking this way. Come on, let's go."

Bastien tugged Seth by the shirt. "Follow me." They ran through the crowd with Tomilho in tow.

Jacob ducked behind a horse-drawn cart. Through the sideboards he watched Captain Craywick stepping from the jetty, arrogantly sniffing the air. Beyond the jetty, the sloop rocked in the swell. On the horizon, dark, ominous clouds cast heavy shadows across the ocean.

"I didn't ask for any of this," Jacob muttered to himself. Turning on his heels, he raced to catch Bastien and Seth. "I just wanted to go home."

If you enjoyed this book, you could make a big difference.

Honest reviews are the most powerful tool in my arsenal and really help to bring my book to the attention of other readers.

I would be very grateful if you could spend a few minutes leaving a review on the book's Amazon page. (It can be as short as you like).

Thank you so much

Join the Crew

Sign up to my newsletter to receive news of my latest novels, exclusive content, and a peek inside the captain's cabin.
Discover the hidden research that shapes my tales of the high seas.
Sign up at:

www.martinblackshaw.com

Printed in Dunstable, United Kingdom